Down and Dirty Justice

Down and Dirty Justice

A Chilling Journey into the Dark World
of Crime and the Criminal Courts

by
Gary T. Lowenthal

New Horizon Press
Far Hills, New Jersey

Copyright © 2003 by Gary T. Lowenthal

Gary T. Lowenthal
    Down and Dirty Justice: A Chilling Journey into the Dark World of Crime and the Criminal Courts

Cover Design: Mike Stromberg
Interior Design: Susan M. Sanderson

Library of Congress Control Number: 2003105759

ISBN: 0-88282-235-7 New Horizon Press

Manufactured in the U.S.A.

2007   2006   2005   2004   2003   /   5   4   3   2   1

In loving memory of Jennifer Jessica Cohen

Table of Contents

Preface

Norval Morris, my mentor at the University of Chicago Law School, gave me some astute advice over three decades ago. "If you want to teach criminal law," he said, "you should understand how it is practiced. Work in the trenches. Practice in a prosecutor's office."

At that time I took only half his advice, accepting a position in a public defender's office in California. I viewed myself as a civil libertarian and felt more comfortable on the defendant's side of the courtroom. After a few years in practice, I joined the law faculty at Arizona State University, where for over two decades I have taught and written about criminal law and criminal procedure. Along the way I have also taught classes at Stanford, the University of California at Berkeley and the University of Virginia.

In my teaching career, I have found that some of my faculty colleagues never practiced law, believing that their primary role was not to train students to become practicing attorneys, but instead to explore and explain the theories and policies underlying the law. While I appreciate the importance of theory, I feel my scholarship and teaching have been informed and enriched by the years I spent as a criminal lawyer. I have attempted in my ongoing work to understand the law as it is practiced in court and as it affects the lives of the people who are touched by it and to pass this knowledge on to my students. But in the years since I left practice, I had long felt the need to understand criminal law "in the trenches," as Professor Morris had counseled long before.

With his words echoing in my mind, I wrote letters to the chiefs of the prosecution and public defender agencies in Maricopa County, Arizona, where I lived. I told them I wanted to work in each of their offices during a sabbatical leave from the university so that I could examine the processing of felony cases from both perspectives. Criminal lawyers depicted on television and in movies are always presented as brilliant trial attorneys who spend much of their time conducting scathing cross-examinations and delivering dramatic closing arguments to juries, almost always in murder cases. I wanted to scrutinize the actual work of prosecutors and public defenders, who—unlike their counterparts on television—had staggering caseloads and less-than-glamorous trials.

I knew that the Maricopa County courts, serving one of the largest urban centers in America, offered an excellent opportunity to see a real urban criminal court system. I indicated to the county attorney and public defender that I would be willing to take on a full case load while employed in each of their agencies, so that I could realistically experience the stress associated with the work. I requested no compensation, since my salary would be paid by Arizona State University during my leave. A free attorney for two agencies desperate for resources: an offer that should be attractive, I theorized.

Nevertheless, I had no idea how the county attorney, Rick Romley, would react. He had been a student in my criminal law class eighteen years earlier, but we had little contact since. I assumed that he viewed me as a liberal law professor. In addition to my criminal defense background before becoming an academician, I had participated more recently in prisoner litigation against the state and I represented a death row client on appeal. Romley had reason to be cautious.

But he surprised me. Two months after I sent him my letter, a friend in Romley's office informed me that Romley was seriously considering my offer. The catch was that he would want me to commit to a longer period than I had volunteered. According to my friend, Romley believed that I could not get a well-rounded view of the prosecutor's work life unless I went through an initial period of training and then handled all stages of criminal prosecution, from the filing of charges against a defendant, through the completion of sentencing proceedings.

Shortly thereafter, Romley's chief deputy, Paul Ahler, sent me a letter, suggesting that I come to his office to discuss my proposal. On the morning of the interview, I was not sure what to expect. Stepping from the elevator onto the eighth floor of the office building in central Phoenix that housed Romley's executive suite, I found a receptionist behind a plexiglass window, who pressed a button allowing me to enter the suite after I explained that I had an appointment with Ahler. As I waited on a sofa outside Ahler's office, I tried not to look nervous to the secretaries who were working just a few feet away. Fortunately, they appeared to be busy, paying no attention to me.

I sensed that Romley and Ahler were as unsure as I was of my appetite for sending people to prison and I wondered if they were taking my offer seriously. But as I talked to Ahler, he listened attentively. Finally, he announced that I was welcome at the County Attorney's Office after the school year was completed. They would assign me a full caseload and would treat me—as much as possible—like the other prosecutors in the office. It was an extremely attractive offer, even though it meant that I would not have sufficient time to serve a separate stint in the Public Defender's Office.

Ahler cautioned, however, that Romley had two non-negotiable requirements.

First, I had to begin my tenure by participating in the county attorney's training program, which was mandatory for all of the agency's new lawyers. I thought to myself that I could probably skip most, if not all, of the training, since I had been teaching criminal law for twenty years and before that had handled more than thirty jury trials, including two complex murder cases. Nevertheless, I realized that there was a huge difference between teaching and practicing law and that my courtroom experience was so ancient that I had lost touch with the practical craft of lawyering. Reacquainting myself might turn out to be highly beneficial personally and professionally.

Romley's second requirement was more puzzling: I had to pledge that I would never violate any of the county attorney's policies.

Although Ahler seemed to assume that I understood what this meant, I had no idea what the policies were or why they were so important that Romley needed to secure my promise of compliance eight months before my employment began. However, not wanting to ask questions that implied disloyalty, I agreed to the stipulations. Only later would I learn the importance of the policies.

I had heard that Rick Romley had almost unparalleled power. As the head of one of the largest prosecution agencies in the United States, his charging and plea bargaining decisions could either make or break the lives of criminal defendants. I was eager to see how he wielded that power and how much of it he would delegate to me, as one of his deputies.

When I was a child, I was enamored of superheroes battling the bad guys, fighting and punishing wrongdoers. Of course, many of my dreams had changed, but some of that little boy's awe and enthusiasm was still there. I wanted to be a trial lawyer, fighting evil and dispensing justice. Now I believed I would have my last chance. I felt exhilarated. I did not know the dark reality that awaited me.

When I was leaving my interview with Ahler, I noticed a large plaque in the corridor outside the prosecutor's office, prominently displayed for visitors. It pledged that the county attorney would vigorously prosecute criminals, while also maintaining the integrity of the court system and addressing the rights and emotional needs of victims and witnesses. It said nothing about fairness toward those who were prosecuted. Studying the plaque, I wondered if I was making a huge mistake.

In 1997 I began the sabbatical from my rewarding but sheltered existence in the ivory tower of academia. For the next nine months, I would serve as a prosecutor in Maricopa County, Arizona, assigned to a trial bureau that specialized in prosecuting members of street gangs and defendants in the prosecutor's repeat offender program.

My experiences there may not reflect the practices of other felony court systems or other prosecution agencies across the United States, because each local justice system has differences in some respects. Nevertheless, the Phoenix metropolitan area, with its ethnically diverse population of over three million people, is similar to many other urban centers in America and so, I believe, is its criminal justice system. Of course, as I began my training in my new prosecutorial role, I was unaware that my experiences as a prosecutor would culminate in the trial of *State v. Schilling*, a kidnapping and assault case, in which the victim and the defendant had spent more than three years on an odyssey winding through the criminal courts, touching virtually every component of the justice system.

The case would be my first major jury trial since I had been a public defender, a quarter of a century earlier. As my indoctrination in the role of novice prosecutor and the *Schilling* labyrinth converged, they would expose to me the profound changes that had occurred in the criminal system over the past three decades. The result would be a deeply disturbing revelation of American justice.

Acknowledgments

Thank you to the Arizona State University College of Law for providing invaluable support to make this book possible, and to the Maricopa County Attorney's Office for graciously opening its doors to me. The following persons made important contributions in guiding me along my path: Michella Abner, Sherry Bell, Gray Cavender, Ron Cope, Bob Dauber, Joan Dunphy, Donna Elm, Alison Ewing, Noel Fidel, Henry Florence, Vera Hamer-Sonn, Steve Lynch, Marty Lieberman, Jessica Lowenthal, Carrie Macias, Glenn McCormick, Suzanne Morris, Mike Morrison, George Mount, Cathy O'Grady, Laura Reckart, Ron Reinstein, Jodie Rhodes, Brad Ross, Paul Rubin, Jon Sands, Laura Sawicki, Barry Schneider, Deborah Schumacher, Ralph Spritzer, John Stookey, Steve Vance and Hugo Zettler. Most of all, a special thank you to Susan Cedar, my companion in life, whose insights improved every chapter of the book.

Gary T. Lowenthal

Introduction

To understand how the present criminal justice system came about, one must look to the major developments of the past four decades, which set the legal precedent for the current system. Beginning in the early 1960s, the United States Supreme Court, under the leadership of Chief Justice Earl Warren, undertook a major overhaul of law enforcement and criminal procedure in state courts, nationalizing the Bill of Rights' guarantees that defendants in federal courts historically enjoyed, and requiring that those guarantees applied with equal force in state courts. A series of Supreme Court decisions, mostly over a ten year period, extended an umbrella of constitutional protection over state court criminal defendants, including the right to counsel, freedom from unreasonable searches and seizures by police, trial by jury, confrontation and cross-examination of accusers, the right not to incriminate oneself, speedy trial, the availability of compulsory process for obtaining defense witnesses and the prohibition of cruel and unusual punishment. Equally important, the Warren court interpreted each of the Bill of Rights' provisions to include strict rules of enforcement. Some decisions placed limits on police discretion in conducting searches, arresting suspects and conducting interrogations. Others imposed restrictions on courtroom procedures.

The most significant Warren court rulings imposing sweeping constitutional limitations on the states' criminal procedures were *Mapp v. Ohio*, decided in 1961, and *Miranda v. Arizona*, handed down five years later. *Mapp* required state courts to follow the federal exclusionary rule, prohibiting prosecutors from introducing evidence against defendants if it was obtained by searches or seizures that violated the Fourth Amendment of the United States Constitution. The Court imposed the exclusionary rule for the explicit purpose of forcing state and local police to comply with Fourth Amendment restrictions. *Miranda* required police to warn suspects of their right to remain silent and right to counsel as a prerequisite for the admissibility of confessions obtained by custodial interrogation. It also precluded police from continuing interrogations when suspects invoked their rights.

These decisions, along with others creating uniform rules in every police station and state court, generated a backlash of major proportions. Widespread media attention increased public awareness of the Supreme Court's determination to expand the rights of criminal defendants. Billboards across America advocated the impeachment of Earl Warren and many politicians, at both local and national levels, built their careers by bashing the liberal federal judiciary. When Richard Nixon accepted the Republican Party's presidential nomination in 1968, he promised to appoint judges who would turn the tide on defendants' rights.

During the next quarter century, the composition of the Supreme Court became increasingly conservative, repeatedly narrowing the scope of almost all of the Warren court's ground-breaking criminal justice decisions, while restoring much discretion to the police and giving state courts the freedom to experiment with procedures that blunted the force of constitutional requirements. Defendants' rights remain in place today, but rarely is an arrest, an interrogation or a criminal prosecution sidetracked because of them.

In *Whren v. United States*, a 1996 Supreme Court decision, the effects of the restoration of broad police discretion can be clearly seen. Plain clothes vice squad officers in an unmarked car patrolling an inner city area became suspicious of the young occupants of a sport utility vehicle. After following the youths for a short distance, the officers pulled the SUV over for a minor traffic violation. When one of the officers looked through the driver's window, he observed two plastic bags containing what appeared to be crack cocaine in the passenger's lap. The officers ordered the occupants out of the SUV, arrested them and thoroughly searched the vehicle, finding other drugs. The United States Supreme Court affirmed the defendants' convictions, ruling that the officers' subjective intent (to look for drugs) was irrelevant when they pulled over the car, so long as they observed a minor traffic violation, even though internal police regulations barred plain clothes officers in unmarked cars from making traffic stops. Moreover, the vice squad's subsequent exploratory search of the SUV without a warrant or probable cause was lawful, according to another of the Court's decisions, as a search "incident to the defendants' arrest."

The legislative branch, not the court system, has produced the second major policy initiative to curb discretion in the criminal justice system. Beginning in the mid-1970s and continuing to this day, Congress and all fifty state legislatures have enacted laws that have substantially narrowed the range of sentences judges may impose on convicted defendants, while also dramatically increasing punishments. Punitive mandatory sentencing laws have proliferated, most frequently during election years. Some of these laws require judges to sentence defendants to severe mandatory minimum prison terms whenever the prosecution alleges and proves a single aggravating factor in the commission of an offense. Other enactments dramatically increase the maximum sentence for a crime if the government chooses to pursue a particular factual allegation. Variations of these laws affect both minimum *and* maximum sentences, as well as such matters as a defendant's eligibility for pre-trial release or parole.

The prison population in the United States tripled from 500,000 in 1980 to 1,500,000 in 1995, and then swelled to over two million by the year 2003. Even though crime rates decreased throughout the 1990s, more persons were locked up, for longer terms, every year. In taking sentencing discretion away from judges, mandatory punishment laws have placed that discretion squarely in the hands of the prosecutors who charge and plea bargain cases, profoundly altering the balance of power between judges and prosecutors.

When I was a public defender over two decades ago, the judge was easily the most important player in the courtroom, the one who determined the defendant's fate, with the power to pronounce a sentence from a wide spectrum of alternatives, sometimes ranging from probation to life in prison. Today, however, in most cases the prosecutor controls the extent of the judge's sentencing discretion.

Despite attempts to constrain them, American prosecutors have always enjoyed vast discretionary power. Over sixty years ago, Robert H. Jackson, the Attorney General of the United States (and later Associate Justice of the Supreme Court), commented:

> The prosecutor has more control over life, liberty, and reputation than any other person in America. His discretion is tremendous. He can have citizens investigated and, if he is that kind of person, he can have this done to the tune of public statements and veiled or unveiled intimations. Or the prosecutor may choose a more subtle course and simply have a citizen's friends interviewed. The prosecutor can order arrests, present cases to the grand jury, in secret session, and on the basis of his one-sided presentation of the facts, can cause the citizen to be indicted and held for trial. He may dismiss the case before trial, in which case the defense never has a chance to be heard. Or he may go on with a public trial. If he obtains a conviction, the prosecutor can still make recommendations as to sentence, as to whether the prisoner should get probation or a suspended sentence, and after he is put away, as to whether he is a fit subject for parole. While the prosecutor at his best is one of the most beneficent forces in our society, when he acts from malice, shameless ambition or other base motives, he is one of the worst.

Today, prosecutors are far more powerful than in Jackson's day. This book examines how I came face to face with the way many prosecutors exercise that discretion and how I came to feel that justice in America's criminal court system is sometimes twisted.

It should be said that there is often considerable tension

between the desire of many criminal court personnel to exercise discretion in individual cases and the constraints of institutional rules. The thoughtful practitioners I have known throughout the years, including trial judges, police officers, prosecutors, defense lawyers and probation officers, have all appreciated that each criminal case is unique. Aside from the ultimate question, guilt or innocence, infinite varieties exist in the factual nuances of crime, the culpability of offenders and the risk they pose for future criminality. Consequently, those who work in the justice system want as much freedom as possible in making decisions to achieve the outcome they feel is justified in each case. Probation officers, for example, resent rigid rules that require revoking an offender's probation whenever certain circumstances exist, even when the officers do not consider the circumstances important. On the other hand, they also feel constrained by other rules requiring the continuation of an offender's probation, despite violations that the probation officers do consider serious.

However, the ability of individuals who wield power to differentiate offenders basically guilty of similar crimes is also an ability to discriminate invidiously. For this and other reasons, policy makers have frequently sought consistency in the treatment of criminal cases. They have sought to impose stringent restrictions on individualized discretion. Sometimes this is appropriate and necessary, but in other instances, it results in untoward and unjust consequences.

Author's Note

This book is based on an exhaustive review of the records in *State v. Schilling* and other cases in which I participated during my time at the Maricopa County Attorney's Office, as well as interviews I conducted with the principal participants in those cases. I have endeavored to portray the events in question as accurately as possible. However, I have changed the names of the participants, other than those who are public figures and the defendants in *State v. Schilling*, in the interest of individual privacy.

Gary T. Lowenthal

Chapter 1

An Ugly Red Smear

July 4, 1994, 12:30 A.M.

Blood and perspiration had loosened the duct tape over Ray Hart's eyes, allowing him to see the men as they threw him into the trunk of a car backed into Steve Schilling's garage. Once they slammed shut the trunk over his head, it was pitch dark. He suspected he was in his own car, because the object underneath him felt like the extension cord he had placed in his trunk a few days earlier. Not that he could grasp it, as he lay on his side with his hands tied to his feet, behind his back. The roar of the Harley starting outside the garage unnerved Hart, but the motorcycle quickly squealed away from the driveway and faded into the distance. He listened intently, hearing nothing for several minutes, hoping that the last of his tormentors had departed.

The throbbing in Hart's head worsened as he tried to concentrate, fearing that someone was still in the house to prevent him from escaping. Even if he was alone, the men would surely come back soon. This time he believed they would kill him. He had lied when he told them that he had hidden Schilling's coin collection and jewelry inside a trailer behind an apartment complex a few miles away. They would probably take twenty minutes, twenty-five at most, to get to the trailer, discover the deception and then return. They had made it clear that if they did not find the property they claimed he had stolen, they would dump his body in a remote location in the desert—where it might not be found for months, if not years.

Even though it was after midnight, Phoenix was an unyielding furnace, with the temperature still hovering at one hundred degrees. Fires raged across the state. More than 80,000 acres of forest and desert had burned in the previous week and the governor had declared a state of emergency in all fifteen of Arizona's counties. Many popular Fourth of July getaways—from the Grand Canyon to the Mexican border—were closed because of their proximity to fires that had yet to be contained. Unable to flee the city for the holiday weekend, most Phoenicians remained indoors, watching television in air conditioned homes. One of the networks had shown *Dangerous Liaisons* that night, but many viewers chose the twenty-four hour news channels, fascinated by the unfolding developments in the saga of O.J. Simpson, who was accused of murdering his wife three weeks earlier.

The heat may have been relentless outside, but it was worse in the trunk. Hart longed for a sip of water as he tried to wiggle closer to the panel that separated him from the car's back seat. If he could some-how loosen the panel, he might be able to escape. His muscles ached as he kept rocking toward the panel, pushing his toes against the lid of the trunk for leverage. Maybe, he thought, if he could just get his teeth around the edge of the panel, he could pull it from the frame.

Suddenly the lid of the trunk popped open. It *was* his car. A year earlier, a couple of teenagers had pried the trunk open and stolen Hart's circular saw and power drill. He was now glad that he had neg-lected to repair the latch, but he could not afford to celebrate. If any of Schilling's friends were still in the house, they probably heard the sound of the trunk opening.

Hart held his breath for several seconds, but no one came into the garage. Satisfied that he had not been detected, he focused his attention on rolling out of the trunk, telling himself over and over to keep rocking his body. He had to get out of the garage before Schilling or his friends returned, especially the crazy one they called Pat, who had howled like a wolf earlier that night when he stuck a gun in Hart's mouth, pulling back the hammer.

Finally, Hart crashed to the garage floor. A jolt of pain shot through his battered torso, but he tried not to focus on his anguish. He remembered the toolbox he had left on the floor, no more than ten feet away. He had been using the tools to convert Steve Schilling's carport into a garage. Although it hurt to move, Hart rolled forward and tried to maneuver himself so that he could open the lid of the box behind his back. It seemed to take forever and he knew they would be back soon.

Slowly—too slowly, he was sure—he was able to lift the lid and fumble around inside, feeling for his wire cutters. Unable to find them, he grasped a pair of pliers, which he used with the little strength he had to clumsily unravel the duct tape that secured his ankles to his wrists, freeing his feet. He could now walk, despite the electrical cord that still bound his hands behind his back. But his sense of time was failing him. Although it had probably been no more than fifteen minutes since the last of the men had driven off on his motorcycle, it seemed much longer to Hart. He felt a desperate urge to get away from Schilling's house as soon as possible. With his back against the garage door, he was able to get his fingers on the handle, allowing him to slide the door partially up. Then he dropped to the ground, rolled out and struggled to his feet, able to look around once he was outside the garage. By now, however, his right eye was swollen shut.

He had to find someone, anyone, who could help him. Seeing a light in the window of the house next door, he began running. Maybe the owners were home—and awake. Once there he kicked at the front door of the neighbor's house and tried to ring the doorbell with his head. When there still was no answer, he began to pound his head on the door, shouting, loudly, even though the dryness in his mouth felt overwhelming. At the same time Hart listened for the sound of the Harley returning, deathly afraid that the terror would soon start again.

Merle Shuler had been a mechanic at an automotive repair shop in central Phoenix for over two decades. He owned his own home, a modest three-bedroom ranch-style house with a small yard on Dahlia Drive, no more than a half-hour commute from the car shop at rush hour. Like most houses in Arizona, Shuler's was less than twenty years old, in one of the many subdivisions that continually expand the boundaries of the Phoenix metropolitan area. Shuler chose this neighborhood because it was quiet, unlike the area surrounding the auto shop, where gangs and drug dealers were active and prostitutes paraded along the sidewalk in front of the mechanics. The only excitement in Shuler's neighborhood the previous year had occurred in December, when a kid on the next block had stolen his mother's car, bounced off a palm tree and smacked into a Dodge Ram parked down the street.

Shuler went out for dinner after work on July 3, not arriving home until 10:30 P.M. Although he went to bed early most evenings, he decided to watch a movie on television this night, because the shop was closed the next day for the holiday. When his son Rudy got home after midnight, Shuler prepared to turn in for the night. As he was about to switch off the kitchen light, he heard someone pounding on his front door, yelling wildly. A few seconds later the doorbell started ringing, over and over, while the banging continued. Puzzled and more than a little frightened, Shuler hurried to the door, looked through the peephole and saw a man kicking at the frame and banging his forehead against the doorbell.

The guy was tall and skinny, about 6' 3", no more than 160 - 165 pounds, and maybe in his late twenties. He had long stringy brown hair, but his head was bloody and he seemed to have both a towel and some kind of tape wrapped around his face and neck. Shuler did not think he recognized the man, who looked suspicious with his hands hidden behind his back, suggesting that he might be hiding something. When the man stepped away from the door momentarily, Shuler noticed that he was not wearing shoes. Also, there was something dangling behind him, probably rope. The man screamed: "Let me in! Let me in!"

Frightened, Shuler ran to his telephone to call 911. No way, he decided, was he going to open his door to a bloody lunatic at this hour of the morning.

Meanwhile, Shuler's son talked to the man through the door.

"What's the matter?" Rudy asked, looking at the man through the peephole, observing a line of blood trickling down the side of his face.

"They're trying to kill me!" the man bellowed. "God, you gotta let me in!"

Trying to be helpful, Rudy inquired: "Why don't you go next door?"

"I can't. They're the ones who want to kill me."

"Sorry," Rudy replied firmly, "we can't let you in." He added that his father was calling the police, hoping this would calm the man down.

But the man kept pleading. "At least untie me," he begged. "I'll leave and you won't have to let me in."

When Rudy would not open the door, the man turned and scurried away, turning to the right. Both of the Shulers watched him through the front window, noticing that his hands were tied behind his back, with a cord of some type swinging back and forth as he rushed out of sight.

A minute or so later, Merle Shuler opened the door and stepped outside, seeing two puddles of blood on the ground and an ugly red smear around the doorbell.

Running as fast as he could, Ray Hart was frantic, unable to understand why Schilling's neighbor had refused to let him in his house. "Asshole!" he screamed as he reached the sidewalk, certain that Schilling would be back any moment. Ignoring his increasing pain, Hart ran to the next house, two doors away from Schilling's. No lights were on, but he tried banging his head against the door anyway. When this brought no response and he could not reach the doorbell, Hart considered hiding in the bushes, but decided that his tormentors would see him if they came looking. As he ran toward yet another house, he listened to every sound in the distance, fearing the motorcycle was returning.

Mike Connor, a railroad technician who lived three doors away from Steve Schilling, was awakened by the sound of his doorbell ringing erratically and someone shouting outside his house. Connor noted the time, 12:42, on the digital clock next to his bed, swore and took his pistol from the top drawer of his night stand. The "ding-dong, ding-dong, ding-dong" of the doorbell reverberated through the house as Connor put on a pair of pants. "Call 911," he instructed his wife, shoving the gun into his back pocket.

When Connor peered through the peephole of his front door, he saw a man with his hands tied behind his back, standing two feet away, looking over his shoulder with his head turned toward the street. Connor put his hand on his gun and opened the door a crack. The man turned back.

"Help me! Help me! God, please help me!" the man yelled as

he looked back and forth between Connor and the street.

"What's going on?" Connor asked, horrified by the bloody wrapping around the man's head.

"The people down the street are trying to kill me," the man said, gesturing with his head. "They think I stole some of their stuff, but I didn't do it. I didn't do it! God, please help me. Let me in. They're going to kill me for sure if they catch me now."

Taking a chance, Connor let the man in, closed the door and locked it. Connor still held on to his gun, in case the man was not on the level.

A team of paramedics arrived a few minutes after Connor had untied the last of the knots in the electric cord behind the man's back. When his hands were free, the man began to cry quietly, then asked for a glass of water, gulping it down as the paramedics entered the house.

Ray Hart felt exhausted as he sat in Mike Connor's kitchen, tremendously relieved that he had finally reached safety. Five minutes later, he heard a motorcycle. He knew it had to be one of his tormentors headed for the house three doors away. This time the man would be moving in for the kill.

The voice of the Phoenix Police Department radio dispatcher crackled in Officer Carl Tate's patrol car. "A man covered with blood has been banging on doors in the 2200 block of West Dahlia, begging people to let him into their homes." The dispatcher instructed all patrol cars in the area to proceed to the location of the call, noting that the man's hands were tied behind his back and he appeared to have been severely beaten. Although West Dahlia was outside Tate's patrol area, the call had emergency status and he was close enough to respond, if only to serve as back-up for the officers at the scene.

A five-year veteran of the force, Tate liked working the graveyard shift in the Cactus Park precinct during the summer months. It usually was reasonably cool outside when he went home at 6:00 AM, allowing him to sleep through the mid-day heat. Additionally, he rarely felt endangered in this precinct, because the worst of the city's crimes occurred farther to the south and west. Most of Tate's nights were uneventful.

This one proved to be an exception.

Five minutes after the radio broadcast, Tate turned onto Dahlia Drive from 23rd Avenue and saw a couple of men on the sidewalk in the middle of the block. One of them was wearing a bathrobe, so Tate assumed that he lived nearby. A paramedic unit and two patrol cars with their lights off were parked two doors farther east.

Tate slowed as he approached the two men on the sidewalk, eyeing them closely. They were standing together, in front of 2201 West Dahlia. The man in the robe looked like he was about fifty, while the other individual was in his twenties. Tate exited from his car.

"What's going on?" he asked.

"Those other officers are talking to a guy who was covered with blood," the man in the robe replied.

"He wanted to get in our house, but we didn't let him," added the younger man, who identified himself as Rudy Shuler. "We didn't know what was going on."

"Did you see where he came from?"

"No, but he said he came from over there, " Rudy said, pointing toward the house one door to the west, at 2207 West Dahlia. The garage door was partially open.

Curious, Tate pressed for more information. "Is that door usually left like that?"

"Nah," replied Rudy. "I never seen it that way before. The guy who lives there usually closes it all the way."

Tate cautiously walked toward 2207 West Dahlia. If it was a crime scene, police protocol called for securing it as soon as possible, and the only other officers who had responded were attending to the apparent victim, a few houses away. He had no idea who might be present—alive or dead—in the house he was approaching.

He noticed a Nissan sedan parked alongside the house. He could hear his heart pounding as he searched for suspects hiding inside the car. It was empty.

He muttered under his breath, hoping that more back-up officers would arrive before he looked in the garage. Nevertheless, he wasted no time in creeping up to the partially open door. Shining his flashlight inside, he saw an older model Oldsmobile backed up against the rear of the garage, with its trunk lid open. He shined his light into the passenger compartment of the Olds and underneath it, but saw no one. Seconds later, he slipped under the garage door without touching it, still not knowing if this was the crime scene, if there were any other victims or if any suspects were lurking in the dark. He smelled the perspiration under his vest as he reached the back of the garage and peered into the trunk. Seeing a large red splotch on some papers, he decided to leave without touching anything.

Tate heard a motorcycle approaching as he crawled under the garage door and walked back out to the driveway. Rudy Shuler, standing on the sidewalk at the property line between the two houses, motioned toward Tate. "That looks like Steve, the guy who lives here," he said. "He's got a Harley." It was, in fact, a Harley, and the motorcycle stopped on the driveway a few feet from Tate, who was still trying to figure out what had happened that night.

Tate studied the man as he dismounted the cycle. He appeared to be in his late twenties, with a pockmarked face and a trim, five-foot, ten-inch, 180-pound frame. His dark curly hair was starting to recede and Tate thought he saw a slight trace of gray over his ears. A handgun protruded from his right rear pocket.

Walking up to him, Tate reached quickly into the pocket and removed the gun, a large black semi-automatic weapon, then stepped back and faced the man squarely, in case he reacted violently to being disarmed. However, the man remained calm, identifying himself as Steve Schilling, the owner of the house they stood before.

Tate asked if Schilling knew what was going on.

Schilling's face went taut as he launched into a monologue, telling Tate that "a guy stole some of my stuff and he told me it was at his house. I just came from his trailer, but there wasn't anything there."

Trying to understand the connection between Schilling's story and the 911 call, Tate asked, "What guy?"

"The guy that was doing some construction work for me inside the house. He took some jewelry and my coin collection."

Even more confused, Tate commented, "I don't know who you're talking about. What's his name?"

"Ray Hart."

Suspecting that Schilling was talking about the person who had been beaten up, Tate asked if Hart was still in the house.

"He was when I left," Schilling replied.

"How long were you gone?"

"Twenty to twenty-five minutes."

Tate remembered the blood in the trunk. Pointing toward the garage, he asked whose car was inside. Schilling replied that it was Hart's.

Trying to keep Schilling talking, Tate asked matter-of-factly if he had struck Hart that night. Schilling rambled again, upset that Hart had stolen his property, but eventually answered the question, admitting that he had hit Hart "a couple of times."

Tate called the dispatcher on his portable radio, asking for the name of the man who was being attended to a few houses away. Within seconds he learned what he had already assumed: the name of the man who had been wounded was Ray Hart.

Tate did not hesitate. "You're under arrest," he called out, grabbing Schilling's arm to turn him around and handcuff him.

Chapter 2

Searching for the Scales of Justice

My first four days in the County Attorney's training program were numbingly boring, but on the fifth, a potentially interesting assignment came my way. I was slated for a ride-along with a uniformed patrol officer in the Phoenix Police Department's South Mountain precinct, which included many of the city's toughest neighborhoods. Although I had taught a law school criminal procedure course for many years, frequently encouraging my students to ride along with the local police, I previously had never availed myself of this opportunity. I would now have that chance.

The night before, lying awake, I had imagined that the briefing session before the morning shift would resemble the beginning of each episode of *Hill Street Blues*, a popular television series of the 1980s, in which a burly sergeant talked about the dangerous felons currently on the loose and advised all the cops to be "careful out there" when they hit the street.

One of my classmates from the prosecutor's training program, Robert Romero, and I met in the parking lot at the precinct headquarters at 6:15 A.M. ready to participate in the briefing session. Robert chuckled when he saw me wearing my bulky bullet-proof vest, which felt uncomfortable in the Phoenix heat even at this early hour of the morning, but it did provide me with a sense of security. Nevertheless, I wondered how the police tolerated these vests in the midday sun on summer days, especially motorcycle cops and others who worked out-doors.

The precinct station was an imposing brick building located in the middle of one of the most blighted areas in Phoenix. Entering the front door, Robert and I found ourselves in a stark outer lobby separated from the remainder of the building by a locked metal door that failed to welcome visitors. The police clearly were not encouraging interactions with their neighbors. However, a man behind the door allowed us to penetrate the interior of the fortress when we identified ourselves as neo-phyte prosecutors who were scheduled to ride in patrol cars that day. Moments later, a uniformed officer ushered us into a spare, windowless room, where the briefing took place.

A few minutes after we arrived, a dozen officers strolled into the room. It was almost 6:30 A.M., but they sat around telling jokes. The only matter of substance during the "briefing" was the decision to assign Robert Romero and me to individual squad cars. Robert's partner for the day was the sole Latino officer in the room. Mine was the only one who appeared to be older than twenty-five.

I soon learned that Dick Farano, the officer to whom I was assigned, was anything but a typical cop. The manager of a supermar-ket for close to two decades, Dick had quit this work to seek "more excitement" in his life, hoping to find it in a squad car. His career change had been relatively easy to accomplish, he explained, because his wife was employed and his children were grown up. Some days he patrolled alone and others he rode with a fellow officer, but—to Dick—having a partner was not what was portrayed in the police buddy movies. The previous day, he mentioned, he had been paired with a cop who made racist remarks about Native Americans who failed to act like "conquered people."

After the briefing, Dick and I located our patrol car in the parking lot at the rear of the station. It was less well-kept than I had expected, a four-year old Chevy with 94,000 miles and a few dings on it, with a layer of grime on its exterior that added to its seedy appear-ance. Dick checked the oil before we left, found that it was more than a quart low, and complained that the officers who had driven the car the previous few days "didn't give a damn," neglecting to perform required maintenance. "The officers are assigned different cars each day," he explained. "They have to rely on one another to make sure they run properly." It bothered him that some of the cops were lazy.

"The only time an officer drives the same car each day," he continued, "is when he was found to be at fault in a collision." The department assigned the errant officer to the oldest, most run-down car in the precinct for at least three months, as punishment for his bad driving. Dick assured me that he had never suffered this fate, but when he turned the ignition key in our Chevy, its engine sputtered and groaned, causing me to wonder how much worse it could be to drive "the oldest, most run-down car in the precinct." Nevertheless, the Chevy sparkled after Dick drove it through a car wash on the police lot. I was also delighted to discover that its air conditioner was in excellent condition; the temperature was predicted to climb towards 110 degrees that day.

As we drove Dick explained, "I begin my shift each morning by driving past the vacant lots and isolated areas in the precinct where stolen cars might have been abandoned, almost always following the same route, waving to the early risers. On a typical week, I find two or three stolen cars, usually with their steering columns punched out and often stripped of everything that could be sold." We did not see any, but as we passed houses and apartment buildings along our route, Dick told me stories about some of the residents.

He pointed to one tiny, dilapidated house with a weedy front yard. "The thirteen-year-old prostitute who lives there is a nice kid," he said. Pulling over to the side of the road, he seemed preoccupied as he stared at the house, commenting after about thirty seconds that the girl was slightly retarded and had dropped out of school. "Her mother is her pimp," he added. The girl had confided to Dick that she was hiding some of her proceeds from her mother and he speculated that this could lead to serious trouble. He also worried about her eleven-year-old sister, who was not yet turning tricks, "but probably will be soon."

The diversity of the landscape in the precinct surprised me. In addition to its many inner-city neighborhoods, there were several agricultural fields and pockets of attractive homes on sizeable lots in the foothills of a huge mountain park that towered over the city. As we drove I also saw remarkable differences from one street to the next. On one block the homes had carefully maintained exteriors and immaculately manicured yards, while on an adjoining street the walls of buildings were filled with gang graffiti and the ground littered with broken glass and trash.

Our morning was going along pretty uneventfully, unlike the TV show, *Law and Order*, in which the police discover a corpse during the first two minutes of each episode. Most of the calls on the police radio were routine matters, almost all domestic disputes that appeared to have ended, according to the participants, by the time we responded. No one wanted police intervention.

One call, however, turned out to be more in keeping with my celluloid vision. The dispatcher reported that an eighteen-year-old woman, named Jennie, had called in a complaint that her boyfriend Carlos assaulted her the previous night and had taken their one-year-old son. Jennie had called the police from the apartment of a girlfriend, where she had spent the night after the altercation with Carlos. As we drove to the girlfriend's apartment, Dick typed the address on the computer in his car and instantly a wealth of information appeared on the monitor, describing the date and nature of each previous police call relating to that address.

The age of Dick's patrol car had not prepared me for the sophisticated technology within. The thoroughness of the information on his computer screen and the speed of its retrieval were remarkable, helpfully warning him of potential dangers he might encounter in responding to the call. Nevertheless, I found it unsettling. Whenever a police officer wanted to know the law enforcement history of a house, apartment or car, he merely punched in the identifying data and presto, it was laid out for him. What if the information on the screen related to an earlier report that had been unfounded? What if the prior occupants of a residence had moved? Wasn't there a substantial risk that the officer might make incorrect, prejudicial assumptions about the persons he encountered?

When we arrived at the girlfriend's apartment, another officer was already at the scene and Jennie was describing how her boyfriend had beaten her the previous night at their duplex apartment a mile away. Sure enough, we saw black and maroon bruises on both of her arms. Carlos would not let her leave their apartment with the child, Jennie explained to the officer, and she wanted the police to help her "get my baby back."

The officer asked if she would cooperate with a prosecution of Carlos for assault.

"All I want is my baby," Jennie asserted. If arresting Carlos would accomplish this goal, she was all for it, but she added, "I don't want a court case or anything like that."

The officer consulted with Dick, then informed Jennie that while they might be able to arrest Carlos for assault, they would not simply retrieve the baby on her behalf, effectively taking sides in a custody dispute between two parents.

We drove to Jennie and Carlos' apartment following Jennie, who rode in her girlfriend's car. The apartment was a duplex unit in a small, dirty building next to an apartment in which Carlos' grandmother, mother and brother lived. When we arrived, Carlos' grandmother and brother were standing in front of the duplex and claimed not to know where Carlos or the baby could be found. One of the officers walked through the house without first asking for permission—a textbook violation of the Fourth Amendment prohibition of warrantless searches—and confirmed that no one else was home.

Soon, however, Carlos and his mother arrived in his mother's car, with the baby seated on Carlos' lap. Seeing us Carlos handed the baby to his mother and hopped out of the car. He and Jennie glowered at each other in front of the small crowd of spectators that had quickly gathered on the sidewalk.

I tagged along when Dick walked Carlos around the side of the building to talk to him away from the onlookers. After informing Carlos of his rights, Dick began by recounting Jennie's allegations, then asked for Carlos' side of the story. Carlos' face reddened as he shouted, "It was self-defense! She threw a carton of milk at me!" His entire family had been present during the incident, he asserted, and they would confirm his account.

Carlos' brother and grandmother agreed that Jennie had started the fight, while his mother, clutching the baby, claimed not to have been present during the altercation. Nevertheless, she asserted, it was right for him to have taken the baby, because Jennie had earlier walked off with a stack of CDs belonging to Carlos' uncle. "Babies don't go away," she reasoned, "but you can't get your CDs back when someone rips them off."

Dick and the other officer conferred by the side of Dick's patrol car and agreed that they had probable cause to arrest Carlos—a reasonable factual basis for concluding that he had committed a crime—because of the welts on Jennie's arms and their perception that Carlos' self-defense story lacked credibility. Nevertheless, they decided against taking him into custody after his mother handed the baby to Jennie.

Police officers have traditionally enjoyed almost unlimited discretion in determining whether to arrest a person when they have probable cause. In recent years, however, there has been a growing movement in the United States to restrict that discretion in domestic violence cases, because of the frequent unwillingness of the police to "get involved" in family disputes, even when there has been evidence of severe physical abuse. With increasing awareness of widespread battering of women and children, almost half of the states and many cities—including Phoenix—have turned one hundred eighty degrees and have implemented policies *requiring* arrest whenever an officer has probable cause to believe that a person has committed a family violence offense.

According to the mandatory arrest policy, Carlos should have been taken into custody, because the officers had probable cause to arrest him for an offense involving domestic violence, but what I had just seen illustrated certain practical realities of criminal justice. Jennie seemed to care only about getting her baby back and she expressed an unwillingness to cooperate in any prosecution of her boyfriend. The officers doubted that she would appear in court if the case proceeded to trial and they believed, based on their experience, that even if the prosecution could force her to testify, it was highly likely that she would corroborate Carlos' claim of self-defense. Thus, despite the city's policy, the two officers chose not to arrest Carlos.

A mandatory arrest policy in domestic abuse cases addresses a serious problem, because roughly 25 percent of all couples living together experience episodes of physical aggression, while historically police have tended to look the other way. However, the effectiveness of mandatory arrest in reducing that violence is unclear. There is evidence from research studies that mandatory arrest has only a modest record of reducing the frequency of family violence during the first months after the incident triggering the arrest and no long-term impact.

I was only a few hours into my first day and already beginning to get a firsthand look at the inconsistencies between theory and practice.

It was getting close to noon when we left Jennie and Carlos to work out their own problems and returned to the precinct headquarters to eat lunch. The small, dreary lunchroom at the police station consisted of a handful of vending machines, three or four tables and a large potted plant. Nevertheless, a crowd of officers sat around the tables and when one of them discovered that I was temporarily working at the County Attorney's Office, the conversation became animated. It quickly became apparent that the cops in the room were unhappy with the treatment they received from prosecutors.

One officer, Sam Todd, complained "the County Attorney's Office cares only about its win-loss record, refusing to prosecute many cases in which the defendant is obviously guilty." Another commented that when prosecutors turned down cases the police had submitted for prosecution, they rarely gave adequate reasons, instead returning the officers' submittals with notations like "the case lacks jury appeal." Everyone in the room snickered in recognition. A third officer touched another raw nerve, complaining that most prosecutors did not seem to care about letting the police know what was transpiring in those cases that were being prosecuted. Several members of the lunch group simultaneously launched into stories about not learning that they were needed in court until the last minute and not being informed about the outcome of plea bargains, trials and sentencing proceedings.

The lunchroom free-for-all belied another common misconception fed by the television shows, which was that prosecutor and police officer fit together like hand and glove. My notions were already being demolished and my first day was only half over. But the atmosphere was calmer by the time we finished our meal, with the remaining cops trading jokes about a particularly notorious deputy county attorney.

The temperature outside had risen by several degrees when we hit the road again after lunch. The dispatcher spewed out a continual account of family quarrels, hostile confrontations on the streets, hit-and-run incidents and a wide assortment of other dangerous occurrences, including several reports of gunfire. Dick ignored all but one of the latter calls, explaining that gunshots had become so common that the police did not respond unless there was a report that someone had been hit or that property had been damaged. "Gunfire is just a routine part of life in the city," he explained.

The one call to which we responded consumed a major portion of the afternoon. The dispatcher reported that four people, two male and two female, had been seen driving back and forth in front of a house, displaying guns. By the time we arrived, three other patrol cars were already at the scene and the four Latino suspects were seated on the curb in the mid-afternoon sun. Three of them appeared to be in their mid-twenties, but one of the two women was much older. They were separated from one another by several feet and one of the two men was in handcuffs.

I listened while one of the officers briefed Dick. About a half hour earlier, a neighbor had observed the younger woman and one of the men carrying guns when they exited their car in front of the residence. They went inside the house, then re-emerged a few minutes later with two young men who lived there. Although all six drove away in the car, the four Latinos returned a short while later without the two men from the house. When the car again proceeded back and forth on the street, the neighbor called the police, who detained the four individuals. The first officers at the scene arrested the man in handcuffs for carrying a concealed weapon. A second gun was found in the car, but this did not constitute a crime, because possession of firearms is lawful in Arizona.

A detective arrived and began to interrogate each suspect, switching between English and Spanish. Although I could not understand portions of the dialogue, I learned that one of the men on the curb was from a small town in southern Arizona and the other was from Mexico. The detective speculated that the incident involved a drug rip-off in which a Mexican supplier had not been paid for a shipment. If so, it was possible that the two men taken from the house had been executed. The four detainees, of course, supplied a very different version of the facts. The younger woman explained in English that they had come to the neighborhood looking for a relative of one of the men. They were confused about where the relative lived and thus drove back and forth on the street while looking for him. As for the two men from the house, they had merely given them a ride to a local restaurant.

The police continued to detain the four suspects on the sizzling hot asphalt for almost two hours, even though there was no clear evidence that any crime—other than the concealed weapon offense—had occurred. Meanwhile, two officers were sent to the restaurant, reporting a half hour later that the two men from the house were not there and had not been seen by the restaurant staff. After further discussions, the detective directed the patrol officers to arrest the three younger persons, allowing the older woman (who was the younger woman's mother) to go home. The detective acknowledged to me that two of the three individuals would undoubtedly be released for insufficient evidence, but he nevertheless wanted them fingerprinted and photographed, in case two bodies were later found.

My head was spinning. Although the police had a legitimate basis for arresting the man with the concealed weapon, they had nothing more than a hunch that any other crime had been committed. The arrest of the other two suspects clearly did not meet the Fourth Amendment's requirement of probable cause, and—from the comments the detective had made—I was reasonably certain that he knew that the arrest was unconstitutional.

As I drove back home the incidents I had witnessed kept replaying in my mind. I had personally seen two instances that day in which police officers deliberately ignored the law: when they failed to arrest Carlos and when they took all three of the suspected drug dealers to jail. As a law professor, I was uncomfortable with both of these decisions, believing that police must adhere to consistent standards to assure that they enforce our laws even-handedly, especially those involving constitutional safeguards. However, I wasn't so sure that I wouldn't have made the same decision the police had made in each case.

I was quickly finding out that the stark reality these officers confronted each day was a lot different than my sequestered view from the ivory tower.

Chapter 3

Bending the Bill of Rights

July 4, 1994, 1:30 A.M.

Detective Rob Nicholson had been with the Phoenix Police Department for thirteen years and a detective since 1988. While most detectives worked day shifts in bureaus that investigated specific types of crime, such as homicide, sexual assault or drug trafficking, Nicholson was currently assigned to a detective squad that investigated all varieties of violent crime occurring at night. On any given night he might be called to a barroom shooting, a rape, a domestic quarrel that culminated in a stabbing, a suicide or a homicide without any suspects. His assigned hours were 6:00 P.M. until 2:00 A.M., but on busy nights he might work until daylight.

The night detectives conducted the initial crime-scene investigations before cases were assigned to other investigators, known as "case agents," for follow-up work. Their responsibilities included interviewing witnesses while they were still accessible and their memories were fresh; photographing and collecting physical evidence; directing technicians to examine items for fingerprints; interrogating suspects before they were represented by counsel and were no longer available for questioning; and sending evidence to the crime laboratory for testing. They were also required to prepare detailed police reports to document the work they had done in each investigation.

The success of many criminal prosecutions turned on the thoroughness and quality of initial crime-scene investigations and the willingness of detectives to memorialize the minutiae of cases in their reports. Prosecutors frequently refused to file charges in court when important evidence was not preserved and other cases were lost at trial for the same reason. As a practical matter, the night detectives did not have sufficient time or resources for careful investigations in many of their cases. Prosecutors at the County Attorney's Office complained to one another that some of the detectives also did not fully appreciate or care about the difficulty of proving defendants guilty in court beyond a reasonable doubt. Moreover, most of the detectives despised the tedious paperwork necessary to document their investigations and some did not bother to describe their observations in detail.

Rob Nicholson was atypical. Tall and thin, with an easy manner and a slow Southern drawl that belied a sharp analytical mind, Nicholson possessed a fondness for detail and a willingness to toil as long as necessary to complete an investigation competently. He recognized that the political and economic realities of urban police work meant that he was expected to wrap up a routine felony investigation as quickly as possible and move on to the next case. But he loathed sloppy and lazy detectives who cut corners more than necessary, and he hated having to deal with young prosecutors who bungled his cases by failing to understand the significance of small nuances in evidence.

This night, Nicholson received a call at 1:30 A.M. from his supervisor, Detective Sergeant Welty, who instructed him to go to 2207 West Dahlia Drive, the scene of an apparent kidnapping and aggravated assault. Welty and Nicholson met with fellow night detectives Sam Phillips and Bill Telgarden thirty minutes later on the sidewalk in front of that address, where they were briefed by one of the officers who had responded to the initial 911 call. A suspect named Steve Schilling had been arrested thirty minutes earlier for participating with others in beating and possibly attempting to murder a man named Ray Hart, who had been taken to the emergency room at John C. Lincoln Hospital.

Welty instructed Nicholson to go to the hospital to take a statement from Hart. Phillips was assigned to interview Schilling, who had been taken to the Cactus Park precinct station. Telgarden would remain at the scene to prepare an application for a search warrant, based on information gathered from the patrol officers who initially responded to the call and any further information that might be radioed in by detectives Nicholson and Phillips. Later that night, the detectives were all to return to 2207 West Dahlia, where they would serve the search warrant together.

When Nicholson arrived at John C. Lincoln Hospital, he was met by a uniformed patrol officer who had been stationed at the hospital since the paramedics arrived with Hart an hour earlier. Hart himself was unavailable for an interview, because he was having a CT scan performed on his head, as well as x-rays of his neck, chest and hand. After learning from the officer that Hart's wife and sister were in the waiting room, Nicholson met with them briefly, informing them, "I'll give you whatever information I can after I interview him." He then turned to Dr. Fred McBride, an emergency room physician. "How is Hart doing?" McBride replied that Hart had been beaten severely and was experiencing a considerable amount of pain, especially in his head and chest. The doctor said he might have a fractured skull, but he was alert and oriented and would soon be available to talk to the detective.

Twenty minutes later, Nicholson gasped when he saw Hart being wheeled into the emergency room.

Hart was lying on his back on a narrow stretcher, with a sheet pulled up so that only his head and neck were visible. Nicholson had seen thousands of crime victims, but none of them had been as badly beaten around the face and scalp. The pillow underneath Hart's head was soaked with blood. Both of his eyes were swollen shut and starting to blacken deeply. His nose was a deformed mixture of black and red, and the dried blood in both of his ears and his hair had already turned brown. Nurses hovered over him, cleaning his wounds and applying local anesthesia to prepare him for the sutures that would be sewn in several places in his scalp.

One of the nurses pulled down the sheet, exposing wounds all over Hart's lanky body. There were bruises and scratches on his neck, shoulders, chest, arms and legs and a welt near his right hip. Red marks on Hart's wrists and ankles appeared to have been made by some type of binding. When the nurses rolled Hart onto his side, Nicholson saw more bruises on his back. Hart had obviously been through a major ordeal.

While the emergency room nurses continued attending to him and the normal bustle of the emergency room swirled around them, Nicholson tried to question Hart. Although Hart was woozy, he was able to provide a coherent account of the events of the past several hours. Nicholson took thorough notes. Carmen Hall, a police technician, arrived during the interview and took a series of photographs of each major wound from several different angles. McBride poked his head into the room, reporting that Hart had a broken nose and hand, but no skull fracture. "More x-rays will be needed on other parts of Hart's body, but they can wait until you have finished talking with him." As Nicholson continued, Hart's sister appeared at his bedside, anxious about his condition and what was going to happen to him. Nicholson assured her that he'd talk with her as soon as he finished interviewing her brother.

Between the interruptions, he learned Hart's story.

Hart told Nicholson that Steve Schilling had hired him two months earlier to convert his carport into a garage and remodel his kitchen. He had known Schilling for about a year and a half and they sometimes went out together gambling at the casinos on nearby Indian reservations. Hart's voice was faint but understandable as he went on. "He paid me periodically for the remodeling, either with cash or with property, such as a radar detector, electronic equipment and rare coins." There was obviously something more. Nicholson prompted the injured man. Sometimes, Hart finally admitted, Schilling gave him methamphetamine in lieu of cash.

For the last ten days, Schilling had been extremely agitated, claiming that someone had stolen his coin collection and some jewelry, accusing everyone he knew. Hart was out of town for much of this period, working on another remodeling job in northern Arizona. Returning on July 3, he went to Schilling's house in the late afternoon to ask Schilling to pay him for remodeling he had completed. Schilling's girlfriend was present when Hart arrived, but she disappeared when the two men went into a back bedroom that Schilling used as an office. A few minutes later, she came into the room waving a black leather fanny pack in the air, claiming she had found it in Hart's car, which was parked outside.

When Schilling looked inside the fanny pack, he saw some watchbands he claimed were stolen from him. He began screaming obscenities at Hart and stuck a black handgun in his face, threatening to kill Hart if he did not return the remainder of the stolen property. Terrified, Hart tried to explain that he had nothing to do with the theft, but Schilling was completely out of control and would not listen. He made Hart sit on his living room sofa while he called some of his friends on the telephone. Each time Hart tried to rise, Schilling shoved him back, kicking him or pointing the gun at him, while continuing to yell in his face.

Hart recalled that Brenda Chase, Schilling's girlfriend, left the house to go to work in the early evening, about the time that three of Schilling's friends arrived, apparently separately. Schilling sent one of them outside to serve as a lookout, while the other two helped him tie Hart up on the living room floor with duct tape, extension cords and rope. They beat him for several hours, with a gun barrel and an aluminum bat, in addition to their fists and feet, trying to get him to confess to stealing Schilling's coins and jewelry. Hart had no idea how long the ordeal lasted, but believed that it went on for at least four hours after Schilling's girlfriend had left the house. He was not surprised to learn that it was close to 1:00 A.M. when he was rescued.

Nicholson pressed Hart for the names and descriptions of Schilling's friends. Hart paused for a moment, then recalled that their names were James, Cliff and Pat. James was the only one Hart recalled seeing at the house before July 3, but Hart either did not know or could not remember his last name. Schilling had referred to the other two men simply as "Cliff" and "Pat."

Nicholson asked Hart to close his eyes, try to visualize the three men and then describe them. Hart paused again, attempting to concentrate on their appearance. He remembered James as a short, husky individual in his late twenties, around 5' 6" and 175 pounds with a patch over his left eye. Pat was at least 6' 3", had long dark hair and a goatee, dressed like a biker, and had tattoos all over his body. Cliff was about 5'10" and skinny, with shoulder-length straight brown hair. Cliff might have been one of Schilling's neighbors, because he seemed to have arrived on foot.

According to Hart, Pat had frightened him the most. Although Schilling was angrier than the others and the most agitated throughout the incident, Pat struck the most blows and seemed to enjoy Hart's suffering. When Hart continued to deny the theft, Pat lost his patience, telling the others that they had to get rid of him. Not long after, they dumped Hart—blindfolded and hog-tied—into the trunk of a car that had been backed into Schilling's newly remodeled garage. "I knew that my time was short, so I concocted a story about where I had hidden Schilling's property," Hart said. This apparently worked. They all left the house a short while after they slammed the lid of the trunk over him.

About the same time that Nicholson interviewed Hart at the hospital, Detective Sam Phillips arrived at the Cactus Park police substation and met with Officer Carl Tate, who had arrested Steve Schilling outside his home a little more than an hour earlier. Tate was completing Schilling's booking information sheet, in preparation for taking him to the Madison Street Jail, the principal facility in Maricopa County for the pre-trial detention of persons charged with felonies. Phillips asked Tate to brief him on the events occurring after Schilling's arrest.

Tate told Phillips that he had advised Schilling of his rights, as required by *Miranda v. Arizona*, then began to interrogate him about the incident with Hart. Schilling was eager to discuss how he knew that Hart had stolen his coin collection, but when Tate probed for details of the events occurring that night, Schilling exercised his Fifth Amendment right to remain silent, stating that he did not want to answer any further questions. Tate immediately discontinued the interrogation, again following the guidelines set forth by the United States Supreme Court in *Miranda*.

Miranda was a watershed decision in 1966 that established a series of rules to govern the police in their interrogation of suspects in custody. The Supreme Court expressed concern about the inherent coerciveness of isolating suspects in the hostile environment of station house interrogation rooms, then wearing them down with questions or tricking them into incriminating themselves by the use of psychological ploys. The *Miranda* decision cautioned that if an individual in custody indicated "in any manner" that he did not wish to be interrogated further—even after he had already answered some questions—the police were required to cease all interrogation until after the suspect had consulted with counsel and consented to further questioning. If police failed to comply with this requirement, any incriminating statements made by a suspect in subsequent interrogation would not be admissible at trial.

At 2:40 A.M., Phillips instructed Tate to place Schilling in an interrogation room at the Cactus Park police substation. The detective then entered the room, sat across from Schilling and read him his rights again. Phillips acknowledged that Schilling had cut off Tate's earlier questioning and that he might not want to talk about the incident without an attorney present. Nevertheless, Phillips explained, he wanted to give Schilling another chance to tell his side of the story.

Schilling consented to answering Phillips's questions.

Phillips' resumption of the interrogation after Schilling had asserted his right to remain silent clearly violated one of the proscriptions set forth in *Miranda*. However, the Supreme Court in the post-*Miranda* era has permitted this type of tactic, so long as certain conditions are met. Tate's immediate cessation of questions after Schilling asserted his right to silence, the ninety minute interval before Phillips re-approached Schilling and Phillips' restatement of Schilling's Miranda rights before resuming the questioning would be sufficient to establish that the police had "scrupulously honored" Schilling's earlier assertion of his rights. Therefore, any incriminating statements Schilling might make to Phillips after the resumption of questioning would be admissible at trial.

Other Supreme Court decisions since the early 1970s have scaled back the protections *Miranda* afforded suspects during police interrogation. For example, if police find physical evidence or a witness by exploiting information obtained in violation of a suspect's Miranda rights, the derivative evidence—the physical evidence or the witness's testimony—is admissible against the suspect at trial, even though the suspect's statement itself cannot be used against him. *Miranda* has been so diluted that it provides little deterrence to detectives who see the prospect of securing a collateral benefit by ignoring its rules. The Supreme Court had an opportunity to overrule *Miranda* in 2000 but declined to do so, even though the Court had become more conservative in the thirty-five years since the ruling had been handed down. But the Court was not really reaffirming *Miranda*. Instead, it upheld a body of case law that bore little resemblance to the original *Miranda* decision.

Schilling loudly complained to Phillips that Hart was the one who had committed a crime; Hart had broken into his house ten days earlier and had ripped him off, stealing his collection of rare coins, which was worth between $12,000 and $15,000, as well as a Rolex watch, other items of jewelry and several personal belongings.

"What happened on July third and fourth?" Phillips asked.

Schilling began with Brenda Chase's discovery of some of the stolen jewelry in a black leather bag, allegedly hidden under the front seat of Hart's car. Hart made up a feeble story, saying he found the jewelry in a garbage dumpster down the street from Schilling's house. But he could not explain the presence of coin magazines in his car, the type of magazines one might use to determine the value of a collection.

Phillips was more interested in why Schilling and his friends had beaten Hart, tied him up and thrown him into the trunk of a car.

Schilling became angry, the pitch of his voice rising sharply and his eyes blinking rapidly as he denied the allegation. Hart was sitting in the living room, unharmed, when Schilling left the house, he swore to the detective. "If someone put Hart in a trunk, I certainly know nothing about it."

Shifting gears, Phillips asked for the names of the other people at the house that night. "I'd rather not answer that question," Schilling said tersely, then added, "As a matter of fact, I don't want to answer any more of your questions." Nevertheless, Phillips continued, despite Schilling's second invocation of his right to remain silent. He would not ask any "direct questions," he told Schilling, but if Schilling wanted to "volunteer" more information, it might help his case. Schilling mentioned only that the black leather bag found in Hart's car was a fanny pack. Then he just looked away blankly.

Phillips directed Officer Tate to book Schilling at the Madison Street Jail for kidnapping and aggravated assault.

The Fourth Amendment of the United States Constitution requires the police to obtain a warrant signed by a magistrate before entering a residence to search for and seize items relating to a crime, unless they have the prior consent of the occupants. A search warrant must be based on probable cause, which—according to Supreme Court case law—requires the police to present specific facts to the magistrate to support a rational conclusion that particular items associated with the crime will be found on the premises. Thus, for example, if police detectives believe that stolen television sets are inside a residence, they must set forth the facts supporting that belief in an affidavit under oath, to convince the magistrate that there is probable cause to conduct a search of the residence.

According to the law, the officer seeking the warrant must also describe the areas to be searched and the items to be seized with particularity, to ensure that the invasion of the occupants' privacy is no broader than necessary to further legitimate law enforcement needs. Thus, police officers executing a warrant to search a residence for stolen television sets may search only those areas of the residence in which a television can be hidden. They may not open a file cabinet and look through a person's private papers, because television sets cannot be hidden in file folders. However, if the police open a closet door looking for televisions and notice a cache of drugs in "plain view," they may seize the cache, because it was found within the legitimate scope of the search, even though drugs were not listed in the affidavit submitted to obtain the warrant.

By the time Detectives Nicholson and Phillips radioed to Bill Telgarden, Telgarden was already busy preparing a handwritten affidavit for a warrant to search 2207 West Dahlia. The three detectives would most likely be submitting felony charges against Schilling, probably kidnapping and aggravated assault, based on Hart's being tied with electrical cord and duct tape when he was found, his description of the events and the apparent seriousness of his injuries.

Since it was important to enter the house and collect all available evidence before someone acting at Schilling's urging got there first and destroyed it or carried it away, Telgarden began writing the affidavit at 2:50 A.M., sitting in his car in front of the house. He put down the facts he learned from the officers who had responded to the 911 call, then later added the information Nicholson had obtained from Hart. In this way, Telgarden would be able to establish probable cause to search for evidence related to the assault and kidnapping charges, based on Hart's injuries, the observations of the officers who had seen him and his statement to Nicholson.

Telgarden described the objects to be searched for in the house. He requested permission to seize any items that could be used as weapons, including guns, pipes, clubs, boots, shoes or bats. Knowing that there were likely to be blood stains in the living room, the study and the garage—the areas where Hart described the struggle to have taken place—Telgarden also sought authorization to seize any items bearing blood stains or evidence of other human tissue. He requested permission to look for fingerprints on objects in the house that the assailants may have touched. This would require a technician to dust those objects with a powder. Telgarden next sought authorization to seize items of clothing belonging to Hart or any of the suspects. Finally, he asked for an immediate night-time search, because biological evidence inside the house—such as blood, tissue or hair follicles from the victim or suspects—would deteriorate over time.

The detectives suspected that Schilling was selling methamphetamine, but they had no specific facts to support probable cause for a search for drugs in the house, other than Hart's assertion to Detective Nicholson that he had seen Schilling and his friends smoking meth that night and that Schilling had placed a small amount of the drug inside a compartment in his computer. Although this information would certainly support a search of the computer, it did not give the police sufficient grounds for a general search for drugs in areas and compartments in the house that were not within the permissible scope of the search for weapons and blood stained objects.

However, the Supreme Court's restrictions on the permissible scope of a search could be circumscribed by an authorization to seize very small items in connection with the assault and kidnapping investigation—especially items that could be found anywhere in the house. Thus, Telgarden also requested permission to search for any documents or papers that would show who lived in the house or might have been on the premises on the night of July 3-4, including canceled mail envelopes, utility and telephone bills, photographs, prescription bottles, vehicle registrations and similar items. While searching for such items, the officers executing the warrant would be able to seize any illegal drugs, drug paraphernalia, and items used for the sale, use or the making of illegal drugs that were seen in "plain view."

The Supreme Court has upheld such pretextual searches. It has instructed lower court judges not to second-guess the subjective motivations of the officers conducting a search, so long as there is an objectively reasonable basis for conducting it. In some instances, this judicial hands-off policy permits the very type of general search that caused the founders to include the Fourth Amendment in the Bill of Rights. The search of Steve Schilling's house was just such a case. The beating that Ray Hart was subjected to gave the Phoenix police the opportunity to explore the house for evidence of drug trafficking and other unrelated crimes, without probable cause.

Once he completed the warrant application, Telgarden called the home of a local justice of the peace from his car. Most magistrates do not meticulously examine the facts in affidavits, but instead rubber stamp the applications. The justice of the peace, of course, was not thrilled to be awakened at 4:00 A.M., but she nonetheless agreed to look at his affidavit, swear him in to avow that it was accurate and sign the warrant he had prepared. Twenty-five minutes later, Telgarden appeared at the magistrate's front door. She barely scanned the paperwork before signing the warrant. Telgarden quickly returned to Schilling's home, meeting the rest of the search party on the steps.

The team consisted of Bill Telgarden, Rob Nicholson, Sam Phillips and evidence technician Carmen Hall. Following standard protocol, one of the detectives—in this case Telgarden—served as the "finder" of evidence, the one who collected each item that was seized and stated for the record its location in the house. Nicholson was assigned the role of "recorder," taking notes on the layout of the house and each item that Telgarden identified. Phillips instructed the technician on which items to photograph and where to dust for latent fingerprints.

When they entered the front door of the three-bedroom house, the detectives found themselves in a small living room that opened to a kitchen and dining area under construction. The carpet and furnishings in the living room appeared to be inexpensive but new. A sofa faced toward the door, with a matching love seat against a side wall and a lacquered kidney-shaped coffee table in front. The walls were filled with framed posters, mostly of female models in stylish attire. A thirty-inch television stood on one side of the door and a small entertainment center on the other, surrounded by healthy potted plants. Schilling seemed to care more than most suspects about the appearance of his home. Except for one glaring sight, the front room appeared fairly pleasant and tidy, perhaps reflecting the touch of Brenda Chase.

On this night the view from the front door was dominated by a large, ugly crimson stain on the living room carpet roughly two feet in diameter, near the entry to the room. It was obviously blood. Looking more closely, the detectives saw that several blood spots dotted the carpet in other locations and a large reddish stain had soaked through the backrest of the sofa.

Telgarden cut swatches of the stained carpet and sofa for later laboratory analysis. Phillips recorded the location of the many smaller smudges and spots in the living room as Carmen Hall photographed them. The detectives seized a metal bar with blood on one end lying across the coffee table, the metal tip of a cowboy boot lying on the living room floor and a thirteen-gallon plastic garbage bag inside a trash can in the kitchen. The bag was filled with bloodstained newspaper and clothing, as well as a belt, a blood-soaked towel, chunks of duct tape and strands of electrical cord. At Phillips' request, Hall dusted the metal bar for latent fingerprints before Telgarden impounded it.

As Hart had described, one of the three small bedrooms was used as an office, with a small desk and computer table, a filing cabinet and three chairs. A number of items lay on the desk, including an electronic organizer that Hart claimed Schilling had taken from him that night and the black leather fanny-pack that both Schilling and Hart had described. Telgarden opened the CD-Rom compartment at the front of the computer, where he found a plastic Ziploc baggie containing a cream-colored powdery substance that he suspected was methamphetamine. Careful not to disturb any fingerprints on the bag, Telgarden removed it from the computer, initialed it and impounded it for laboratory analysis.

Moving through the house, the detectives walked into the garage through a door in the kitchen. They noted and photographed a large bloodstain on the rear wall next to the door. A 1983 Oldsmobile Cutlass was backed into the garage, its trunk lid open. A large, bloody stain spread across the bottom of the trunk. On the garage floor, they found a pair of black-gripped pliers, along with some bloody duct tape, which they seized. Phillips instructed Carmen Hall to dust the Oldsmobile for fingerprints, pointing to the trunk lid, the driver's door, the steering wheel and the gearshift lever.

Nicholson obviously took pride in the thoroughness of his work. His initial police report was nine single-spaced pages in length, and he also prepared three supplementary reports within the first twenty-four hours. Telgarden's supplemental report was six single-spaced pages long and Phillips' was another five. Altogether, the night detectives and uniformed officers at the scene generated fifteen separate supplemental police department reports and collected over thirty items of physical evidence. Carmen Hall took almost one hundred photographs. Nicholson sent more than a dozen blood-stained items to the crime lab, requesting blood typing for comparison with samples of Hart's blood, Schilling's blood and the blood of any other suspects that would be identified in follow-up investigations. He also requested an analysis of the powdery substance found in Schilling's computer.

The night detectives completed their reports and requests for laboratory analyses on the evening of July 4. The case would now be assigned to a "case agent," a detective from one of the regular investigation bureaus, who was to do the remaining work. Among the case agent's first tasks would be to submit a request to the County Attorney's Office to charge Schilling with kidnapping and aggravated assault.

Nicholson and his colleagues seemed to have laid a solid foundation for the prosecution of Schilling, but the case agent would need to conduct further investigations to identify and prosecute the other participants in the offense. Hart had given good descriptions of the three remaining suspects and would probably be able to identify them when he saw their photographs. At least one of them, Cliff, apparently lived within walking distance of Schilling. A follow-up investigation would certainly involve interviews with neighbors and associates of Schilling, in addition to Brenda Chase, who according to Hart had witnessed some of the events. Laboratory comparisons between the blood samples and latent fingerprints found at the house with those of Hart, Schilling and the accomplices, who would be identified later, would help to reconstruct what had occurred that night. The dark smears found on the tip of one of Schilling's boots—seized from him when he was booked at the jail—would likely be identified as Hart's blood, further solidifying the case.

Though they had not found any evidence to connect Schilling with drug trafficking, Nicholson's chances of initiating a successful prosecution on aggravated assault and kidnapping charges, once the case was developed, seemed extremely promising. If the case agent put any energy into the follow-up investigation, he probably would encounter little difficulty in finding James, Cliff and Pat. All of this, of course, depended on the willingness of the case agent to conduct the necessary investigations. Some detectives, like Nicholson, were conscientious and thorough. Others might not care.

Chapter 4

Teaching an Old Dog New Tricks

When I was hired in 1970 by a public defender agency in California, my formal training for that job lasted one day and consisted of tagging along with another public defender as he rushed from courtroom to courtroom handling misdemeanor cases at the Oakland Municipal Court. The lawyer I followed had recently graduated from law school and had been a public defender for barely three months. When I returned to the office that evening, a stack of fifteen case files lay on my desk. I was scheduled to represent the defendants in those cases in court the following morning.

Years later, I was to begin a more carefully orchestrated training program, a four week course for beginning prosecutors and paralegals at the Maricopa County Attorney's Office, led by two mid-career prosecutors. Four of my five classmates were recent law school graduates, while the other was a chain-smoking retired Air Force officer who was starting a new career as a paralegal. The month-long training promised to be a substantial improvement over the single day I had been given as a beginning public defender and, as a legal educator, I was keenly interested in what would be included in the course and how it would be taught.

The four attorneys starting with me were typical beginning prosecutors. None of the four had attended a prestigious law school, and three had grade-point averages that placed them in the lower half of their graduating class. Their job opportunities upon passing the bar examination were not comparable to graduates of top law schools, or even to those who had stronger academic records at their own institutions. The starting salary as a prosecutor was barely over $35,000, a third of what beginning associates earned at major law firms in many large cities, including Phoenix. Each of them, however, would handle a jury trial within the next two months, while many Harvard law graduates do not see the inside of a courtroom for years, except when they are clerking for an appellate court judge or carrying the briefcase of a senior partner from their law firm.

Randy, one of the four new lawyers, was a former student of mine at ASU and a reserve police officer. Shy by nature, Randy was very serious during the classes, trying to absorb every tidbit of information, terrified that he lacked the knowledge or ability necessary to handle the job competently. But another of my classmates, Will, was as cocky as Randy was afraid. Having worked as an intern in a prosecutor's office in the Midwest while attending law school, Will was sure that he understood all there was to know about trial advocacy and he sometimes made a point of contradicting our two instructors in front of the rest of the class. He was by far the most zealous of the trainees, firmly believing that all defendants deserved to go to prison for as long as possible and that he had the talent to put them there.

I found myself spending much of my free time with Robert and Tina, the other two novice lawyers in our class. Robert, the youngest of the group, had a charming smile and relished poking fun at the easiest target available, which in this case was a middle-aged law professor. Although he attended law school in Texas, Robert grew up in Arizona and was well connected in local Republican political circles. I knew little of this world and enjoyed his colorful anecdotes. Tina, the only woman among the trainees, had taught at a private boarding school before attending law school. The training regimen was more taxing for her than for the rest of us, because she was in the process of moving from Tucson to Phoenix, along with her husband and eight-year-old son, and was living with her in-laws while both house-hunting and beginning new employment. Remarkably, none of this seemed to overwhelm her, and—like Robert—she had a mischievous sense of humor.

I was the wild card in the class. Neither my classmates nor our two trainers, Angela and Jayne, understood why I was there. Angela had been notified only a few days before the class began that I would be among her new trainees and all she was told was that I was a law professor interning in the County Attorney's Office during my sabbatical. The thought of a professor scrutinizing her teaching for four weeks produced a great deal of anxiety. My fellow trainees were simply curious, assuming that I already knew everything there was to know about the subjects to be covered and that I could not possibly benefit from practice exercises in trial advocacy. But Robert and Tina, quickly sensing that I was as nervous as everyone else in the room, lightened the atmosphere by noticing aloud whenever I struggled.

No one suspected that I was Randy's true counterpart, afraid that I would not be up to the task. I had been away from the courtroom for over two decades and I secretly wondered if I was making a big mistake, fooling myself into believing that I could competently handle a high-stakes jury trial on my own. In my descent from the ivory tower, I worried that I would not be able to connect with a jury, or shake a wily defendant on cross-examination.

Nevertheless, after twenty-two years of teaching, it was illuminating to be on the other side of the podium.

Although our two trainers, Angela and Jayne, had partial control over the curriculum and taught several of our classes, most of the course content was determined in advance by the administration of the County Attorney's Office. This meant that we sat in a tiny classroom each day and listened to anywhere from four to eight hours of lectures presented by various members of the county attorney's senior staff. Almost all of these lectures were accompanied by lengthy hand-outs, but the speakers rarely referred to them. While the most effective of the lecturers attempted to engage the group in discussion, many of them simply droned on for as long as two hours at a time, without interruption, as the trainees took turns making new pots of coffee for the group to consume. Tina had the good sense to ask many questions, thus breaking up the long lectures and stimulating a bit of dialogue. But much of the time, we merely sat trying to take notes on the litany of information.

The array of topics covered in the lectures astounded me. At a relentless pace, our lecturers told us about procedures and personnel policies of the County Attorney's Office, victims' rights, substantive criminal law in Arizona, the stages of a felony prosecution, driving offenses, sexual harassment in the workplace, search and seizure law, effective case management, the Americans with Disabilities Act, the county's e-mail system, the law relating to confessions, Windows 97, the prosecution of drunk driving cases, filing and responding to motions in court, the rules covering the disclosure of information to and from defense counsel, the procedures relating to preliminary hearings in felony cases, the drafting of plea agreements, the state's system for keeping criminal records, the procedures related to guilty pleas in court, the rules of evidence governing the admission of exhibits, Arizona's drug laws and the effects of various forms of drug abuse. Most of the information thrown at us flew by harmlessly, with only Randy trying conscientiously to follow everything that was covered. Fortunately, there was no comprehensive examination at the end of the program. If there had been any sort of final test, all of us—including the law professor—would have failed miserably.

Much of this material was important for beginning prosecutors, but a barrage of unconnected lectures packed into a few weeks was not a successful way to communicate it and our physical setting only compounded the problem. Angela's and Jayne's tiny offices and our cluttered classroom were located in a dreary, windowless suite in the basement of an office building across the street from the courthouse, while the remainder of the county attorney's offices were "upstairs," on the fifth through eighth floors of the same building, with views of the city. Our trainers had to be keenly aware of their isolation from the other prosecutors in the agency, as well as the message this sent to the trainees about the relative importance of the program.

Nevertheless, certain subjects were covered thoroughly in the county attorney's training program. Several lecturers emphasized that we were employed by an elected official, repeatedly reminding us that the public's perception of that official could be influenced by our actions. If, for example, a defense lawyer filed a motion in court for the release of an incarcerated defendant, we were to make sure that it was the judge, and not the prosecutor, who agreed to the release, even if we had no objection. Also, whenever we made concessions in a plea bargain, we were to document in our case file that we had consulted with, or at least notified, the victim and the investigating officer, in case there were subsequent complaints about the leniency afforded to the defendant.

Indeed, a central purpose of the training program itself may have been to deflect political accountability. Although the seemingly endless stream of lectures we received on broad, unrelated subjects seemed to make little sense pedagogically, they might have served other ends of the County Attorney's Office. If, later, one of us were to mishandle a case in a potentially embarrassing way, the focus of the blame could more easily be placed on the individual prosecutor, rather than the agency or its leadership, when the mistake related to a subject that had been "covered" in training.

Speaker after speaker emphasized that working for the county attorney required unwavering loyalty and strict adherence to the agency's policies, especially when we offered plea bargains in our cases. We spent many hours going over the state's sentencing laws and poring through the county attorney's four-inch thick policy manual that instructed us in detail on how we were to interpret and enforce those laws. Three or four of the lecturers made jokes about the potential for being fired for failing to follow the policies, evoking uneasy laughter from the class while also sending an unequivocal message. The Maricopa County Attorney, Rick Romley, represented the state, and we were merely his deputies; if we disagreed with the agency's policies in the handling of a case, we nevertheless were to follow the rules and not our independent professional judgment.

The County Attorney's "deadly weapon policy" required a prison sentence for every defendant who displayed a gun or knife in the commission of a crime, regardless of the circumstances; if a gun was discharged, the defendant's prison sentence was to be lengthy, no matter what the facts were. Another policy prohibited plea bargains that reduced residential burglaries from felonies to misdemeanors. Our strict adherence to these policies, we were told, was necessary to carry out the county attorney's mandate.

I was beginning to understand the significance of the pledge I had made to County Attorney Rick Romley's chief deputy, in return for Romley's permission for me to work in the agency and write about my experience. One of his conditions was that I must agree to follow all office policies, *always*. This pledge, required of all new prosecutors in the agency, dominated our four week training program. While no one expected us to be polished trial lawyers, we were taught to appreciate the requirement of total fidelity to office policy. This way, our actions could be translated into useful re-election slogans, such as "Use a gun, go to prison" and "Your home is your castle."

The substance of the policies was unassailable. People who use guns to commit crimes *should* in general receive harsher punishments and the state *should* do what it can to help citizens feel secure in their homes. It also makes sense to seek consistency in the decision-making of almost three hundred individual prosecutors in charging and plea bargaining cases. Randy's views on appropriate prison sentences, for example, might have differed markedly from Robert's, Tina's or Will's. It would be unjust if the sentence a defendant received depended largely on the idiosyncratic whims of the person prosecuting him, especially when that person was relatively inexperienced in the criminal justice system.

Nevertheless, my instincts told me that it was wrong for every defendant using a gun or committing a residential burglary to receive the same harsh treatment. To me, the notion of "just desserts" required an assessment of the unique factual nuances of each case, as well as the culpability of the offender, while still taking into account the dangerousness of a gun and the sanctity of a home. In a case prosecuted by one of my colleagues, for example, a middle-aged man with steady employment, an intact family and no prior criminal record had fired a gun over the heads of his two teen-age sons to "get their attention" when they were fighting in front of their home. Although no one was hurt and the two sons were horrified that their father was being prosecuted, the most lenient plea bargain my colleague could offer required the father to serve at least five years in prison. This made no sense to me. The man had certainly exercised poor judgment in firing the gun, an especially dangerous act in a residential neighborhood, but his conduct also reflected an otherwise law-abiding parent's frustrated response to an emotionally charged situation. Although he may have committed the same crime as a gang leader shooting a gun in the direction of members of a rival gang, their punishments should not have been determined in a one-size-fits-all fashion. Nevertheless, the determinative decision in the middle-aged father's case was made by the agency's central administration and not by the individual prosecutor who was familiar with the facts.

Law schools teach their students that law is a profession and lawyers should exercise their independent professional judgment when representing clients. In reality, however, lawyers in large public agencies and associates in law firms are primarily employees who frequently must set aside their own sense of equity in order to follow their employer's rules.

Twenty years ago, a public defender with a huge case load working at the Legal Aid Society in New York City refused to take additional case assignments, because he believed that he would not be able to provide constitutionally adequate representation for his existing clients. When the Legal Aid Society fired the lawyer, he hired Ramsey Clark, the former Attorney General of the United States, to fight the discharge in an arbitration proceeding. Several of the nation's top experts on legal ethics lined up to testify for each side. The arbitrator ruled in favor of the Legal Aid Society, determining that the agency—not the individual lawyer—represented the clients and the public defender's discharge was upheld. If lawyers working in an organization disagree with the organization's rules, they must learn to subjugate their personal beliefs or find other employment.

One of our lecturers discussed the organization of the County Attorney's Office, explaining that while separate divisions handled such matters as juvenile delinquency proceedings and the county's civil litigation, most of the agency's lawyers were assigned to adult felony prosecutions in the downtown Phoenix superior court complex. These prosecutors worked in three divisions, known as pre-trial, trial and major felonies.

After beginning prosecutors completed the initial month-long training program, they were assigned to the pre-trial division, where they cut their teeth on misdemeanor jury trials and preliminary hearings in the less serious felony cases prosecuted by the agency. They then progressed to the trial division, which was responsible for the trial and sentencing stages of most routine felony cases. After a sufficient number of felony jury trials, the most skilled attorneys were elevated to the major felony division, where they were assigned to prosecute

either sex offenses, organized crime cases, family violence, major narcotics offenses, gang-related crimes or vehicular felonies. A few prosecutors reached the most prestigious level of the major felony division,
the homicide bureau.

In an ideal world, it would take a minimum of five years for a
lawyer to progress from the initial training program to the major
felony division, to assure that prosecutors assigned to the most serious
cases have sufficient maturity and seasoning. But when I went to lunch
with two more experienced prosecutors during my last week of training, they told me that lawyers with less than two years of experience
were being assigned to the major felony division. The turnover rate
among agency personnel had been stunning, with prosecutors resign-
ing almost every week during the previous year. Nearly a quarter of the
prosecutors in the agency had been employed there less than a year,
and over two-fifths had less than two years experience.

The two prosecutors offered differing opinions for the exodus.
One felt that the problem stemmed from the county's terrible compensation package, noting that the starting annual salary at city prosecution
agencies—which handled only misdemeanor offenses—was about
$12,000 higher than the pay offered to beginning prosecutors at the
County Attorney's Office. The other agreed that the pay was abysmal,
but cited additional reasons for the turnover in personnel, principally
the rigidity of office policies that restricted the ability of prosecutors to
do what they thought was right in each case. "No one likes to work the
assembly line in a sausage factory," he explained.

Despite their differences, my companions agreed on one point.
The most discouraging result of the high turnover was that prosecutors
were assuming responsibility for major felonies long before they were
ready. As we finished lunch, one lamented the situation in the sex crimes
bureau, which was responsible for prosecuting many of the most complex
and difficult cases, cases with extremely high stakes, vulnerable child victims, frequently uncooperative witnesses and defense counsel who were
usually highly experienced. The previous week, a prosecutor with fewer
than a handful of jury trials was assigned to this bureau.

There was, of course, more to the training than the lectures.
We went on tours of the court complex, the jail and various branches

of the prosecutor's office, periodically getting us out of the tiny classroom. We also participated in a few simulation exercises and courtroom proceedings in actual cases, with an opportunity for immediate feedback from Angela, Jayne and other prosecutors who assisted them. Unlike the lectures, these experiences were highly useful for developing professional skills and understanding legal institutions.

One afternoon, Angela, our lead trainer, gave us a series of case scenarios and instructed us to draft a formal plea bargain for each, to be discussed the following morning. Our proposed plea agreements had to be appropriate for the circumstances of each case, consistent with applicable office policies and legally binding contracts that could withstand judicial scrutiny. I took the assignment seriously when I went home, working on my plea agreements until midnight. Nevertheless, I was stunned the next morning when Angela walked me through the numerous ambiguities, inconsistencies and missing provisions in my proposed contracts. It was the most indelible moment of my training.

One lecture in the training program, relating to illegal drugs, would benefit me later. As I listened, however, it seemed very far from my sheltered life of the last two decades.

Arizona's voters had recently passed a ballot initiative that fundamentally changed the state's drug laws, over the opposition of most law enforcement and court personnel. The new laws, soon to be replicated in a number of other states in the next half-dozen years, shifted public policy in non-violent drug possession cases from punishment to treatment. Nationally, there had been a 400 percent increase in the incarceration of drug offenders during the decade preceding the voter initiative, and—as public spending on prisons increased dramatically—the percentage of violent prisoners decreased each year. Arizona's ballot proposition was designed to reverse this trend. Courts could no longer imprison persons convicted of possessing narcotics or dangerous drugs for personal use the first two times they were convicted of such offenses. Instead, first- and second-time offenders in drug possession cases had to be granted probation, with a requirement that they participate in counseling and rehabilitation programs.

Our lecturer believed that the new drug laws created by the voter initiative were terrible. Persons convicted of possession offenses

could now flaunt the justice system, ignoring their court-ordered treatment with the assurance that they could get away with it, because the
courts could not incarcerate them. Additionally, many first-time drug
offenders had long criminal records for *other* crimes, but prosecutors
could no longer use their drug possession convictions to send them to
prison as repeat offenders. The speaker asserted that the voters had
been duped, giving many hardened criminals a "get out of jail free"
card. Then she proceeded to talk about the harmful effects of the most
commonly abused narcotics and dangerous drugs, including heroin,
PCP, LSD and both powder and crack cocaine. She singled out one
substance in particular, which she described as the most widely abused
dangerous drug in Arizona and the fastest-growing illegal substance in
the United States: methamphetamine.

An easily produced synthetic drug, methamphetamine had
been popular among motorcycle gangs for several decades, but its use
did not become widespread until the mid-1980s, when increasing
numbers of drug users found it to be more powerful than cocaine and
far less expensive. Mexican drug lords quickly recognized that they
could make great profits by manufacturing the drug on a large scale
and marketing it in the United States, because the chemicals needed to
make it were cheap, legally obtainable and readily available. Known by
users as "meth," "speed," "crystal" or "crank," methamphetamine
increasingly became the drug of choice among less affluent segments
of the white community in many western states, around the same time
that crack cocaine found its way into inner-city neighborhoods on the
east coast. But while crack use decreased significantly during the
1990s, meth spread to all parts of the nation, across both racial and
socio-economic lines.

In addition to the supply of methamphetamine brought into
the country from Mexico, tens of thousands of underground laboratories in the United States began producing the substance in the mid-
1990s—in houses, apartments, motel rooms, trailers, vans and rural
barns. Our lecturer mentioned that the Phoenix police closed down a
meth laboratory about once every three days in 1997, ten times the
rate of only a few years earlier. The cost of cleaning the toxic waste
from these laboratories was enormous. Many of the underground lab-

oratories produced the drug by cooking a combination of poisonous substances, including Drano, Red Devil lye, muriatic acid for swimming pools, and—a particularly deadly chemical—phosphine. A typical kitchen laboratory produced ten pounds of toxicity for every pound of the drug.

According to our lecturer, meth users experienced intense feelings of energy, because the drug stimulated the central nervous system, inducing the brain to release massive amounts of dopamine and norepinephrine, two naturally produced chemicals. It was also a highly addictive substance, with users generally needing larger and larger doses as they developed a tolerance. Other symptoms, our lecturer told us, were loss of appetite, sleeplessness and sharp mood swings, characterized by irritability and deep depression. More troubling, from a law enforcement perspective, was the growing evidence of a positive relationship between meth use and violence. In one highly publicized case just a few weeks before the lecture, a meth addict was sentenced to life in prison for hacking off his fourteen year-old son's head and throwing it out the window of his van alongside a busy freeway.

By the last morning of our fourth week, the long, information crammed lectures had worn us down. Spending eight hours each day in close quarters with a small group had become increasingly difficult, especially because some of the personalities did not mesh. Will's pronouncements on "the way it was done" at the prosecutor's office in the Midwest were getting on everyone's nerves and the odor of smoke on the paralegal's clothing and breath was increasingly noxious. We were ready to move on.

Our morning seemed to be rescued when Jayne, the more laid-back of our two trainers, slipped the comedy *My Cousin Vinny* into the VCR in the tiny classroom. Joe Pesci played the role of Vinny, a lawyer with a thick New York accent who defended his young cousin and the cousin's best friend (also New Yorkers) when they were wrongfully charged with the murder of a grocery clerk in a rural Alabama town. We laughed uproariously until the scene in which Pesci conducted his initial lawyer-client interview of the two defendants, who were locked up in the local jail with hard-core criminals. At that point, the humor struck close to home. We watched intently as one of the defendants asked Pesci about his courtroom experience, hoping to be cheered by stories of Pesci's many victories. We watched the two young men slumping deeper into their chairs when Pesci first admitted that he had yet to try a murder case then conceded that he had never handled *any* criminal matters, and finally confessed that this case would be his "first foray into the trial process," after only six weeks as a lawyer.

A few minutes after his revelations we took our mid-morning break. My classmates were unusually sober, knowing that they too were about to handle their first court cases, making decisions that would profoundly affect the lives of others. Randy's anxiety had spread beyond me.

Chapter 5

Two Peas in a Pod

An Arizona native, Ray Hart was the youngest of four siblings and grew up in a rapidly vanishing rural area only twenty miles west of Phoenix. His family struggled financially, despite the fact that both of his parents worked. His father cut hair at the same barber shop for over thirty years, while his mother cleaned apartments for a local realtor, leaving Ray at home after school with his sister and two brothers. Ray raised pigeons and rabbits in his back yard, was an average student in school and never did anything worse as a teen than occasionally ditching classes and smoking pot. Encouraged by his father to learn a trade, he worked as a plasterer during the summers and easily obtained employment in Phoenix's booming construction industry when he graduated from high school. He married his teenage girlfriend two years later and—with help from his parents—purchased a small home in a new subdivision on the west side of Phoenix.

Although Ray thought his marriage was successful, his wife quickly lost interest, failed to come home one evening and called him at midnight to say that she was leaving him for good. Stunned, he asked a fellow construction worker to move into the second bedroom in his house, to help him make the mortgage payments. Until this point, he had drunk beer and smoked pot, but had not experimented with other drugs. This changed when his new roommate introduced Ray to cocaine, allowing him to dull the pain of his wife's rejection. At first Ray confined his cocaine use to the evening, after work, snorting thin lines of powder on a glass table top through a rolled-up five dollar bill. The pain, however, didn't leave and he found himself taking a hit or two before leaving the house in the morning and a few more during breaks at construction sites.

Cocaine was expensive on a plasterer's wages. Ray had never been very good at managing his finances and within a few months he found himself owing money to his parents, behind in his mortgage and maxed out on his only credit card. Even though it was usually easy to find construction jobs, his debt continued to mount and soon he was selling cocaine to other construction workers to pay for his growing addiction. A year after his wife had walked out, he lost the house for failing to make his mortgage payments. He had already lost everything else his parents bought for him.

Then Ray discovered methamphetamine, a drug he would be addicted to for the next ten years. A quarter gram of meth was good for six to eight recreational doses and usually sold for only twenty to twenty-five dollars on the street, an easily affordable price for a construction worker. In the early years, he usually bought a form of the drug known as "crystal rock," a pure, clear, glassy substance that smelled like ether. Later, however, most of the meth available on the street was called "crank," an off-white powder that drug dealers had cut with other substances to make a greater profit. Ray usually smoked it in a pipe, but sometimes he injected it, snorted it like cocaine or simply added it to his coffee.

He felt euphoric when he was on methamphetamine, his mind continually racing with grand plans to make money and a hyper-alertness to the details of objects around him. However, he frequently lost track of time, became obsessed with minutia while ignoring both his family and his employment responsibilities and went about with a false sense of self assurance, believing that he could do whatever he wanted, whenever he wanted. He was rude to his parents and he quarreled at construction sites with owners, general contractors and his fellow workers, sometimes getting into fist fights.

He smoked the drug in binges. His mood elevation after a hit usually lasted for at least six to twelve hours, depending on the dose. It then declined sharply and would turn into a deep depression—unless he took another dose, which he usually did. His binges sometimes lasted for a week at a time without his going to bed. But he inevitably crashed, like most other meth users, sleeping around the clock, depressed or irritable when he awakened. He tried to quit several times and once was clean for six months, but he kept coming back.

Convinced that he could be a great success as a stucco sub-contractor, Ray turned to his family for additional financial assistance. His father provided the money for him to start his own business, then continued to bail him out when his projects failed. Ray liked being self-employed, because it gave him the freedom to take days off with impunity, which he needed for his binges, and he always managed to employ a drug dealer among his workers. But his business failures steadily worsened and his company promptly went under when he lost $30,000 on a particularly disastrous job. He then worked for another contractor for several months, before being fired for unreliability. With his father's help, he opened a new business, but the cycle of drug abuse and failed projects repeated itself.

Ray met Ronnie, a petite, blond single mother, when she visited his house with friends who were buying methamphetamine from him. Ronnie was not willing to try the drug herself, because she had two young children at home and she would not jeopardize her new employment, selling real estate. She did not believe Ray's far-ranging stories about his shrewd business accomplishments, but he excited her with his enthusiasm. They became close friends, then lovers. When Ray was evicted from his house for failure to pay rent, she allowed him to move in with her and the children. Soon after, she began smoking meth too.

They were married within a few months, as much to the drug as to each other. Ronnie tried to continue selling real estate, even during her binges, but the marathon sleep-ins and inevitable depressions affected her productivity. Ray went to real estate school himself, but quit after a few weeks and went back to itinerant work as a drywall specialist. When Ronnie discovered that she was pregnant, she wanted to stop using meth and they tried to quit together. She was successful, but behind her back, Ray started smoking again a few months later.

Ronnie went back to work immediately after the baby—a girl—was born, but the downward spiral continued. The Internal Revenue Service and the Arizona Department of Revenue filed tax liens against them for failure to file returns for three consecutive years after they were married and a credit report from that period disclosed that Ray had an installment balance of over $13,000, as well as twenty-two past or current delinquent accounts. The Harts defaulted on their mortgage and were evicted from their home, then filed for bankruptcy. Ray realized that his methamphetamine use only exacerbated their problems, but he continued to smoke the drug anyway, becoming increasingly belligerent toward his wife and his two stepchildren and hardly noticing the baby.

He moved from job to job, at one point going to work for a company named Grayfield Plastering. One of his responsibilities for Grayfield was to order materials from local suppliers, including PARM Building Materials, an outfit in Glendale, Arizona. Two weeks after Grayfield fired him for excessive absences, Ray ordered more than $2,000 in materials from PARM, charging the purchase to Grayfield's account, but keeping the supplies himself. When Grayfield's general manager reviewed PARM's statement, he discovered the scam and filed a complaint with the police. PARM's sales clerk identified Ray as the person who had ordered the supplies and the Maricopa County Attorney charged him with fraud. However, the case was dismissed ten months later when it was scheduled to go to trial, because the prosecution could not locate the clerk, its only eye-witness.

Then, an odd incident occurred, giving Ray hope that his downward spiral might finally be coming to an end. Watching his stepdaughter play in a soccer game at a neighborhood park, he fell out of a lawn chair and injured his back seriously enough to take some time off from his construction work, which then consisted of remodeling a woman's kitchen. When he failed to appear at her home the next several days, the woman called him to inquire about his absence. He told her about the incident and mentioned that he had recently purchased the chair from a chain store. She speculated that he might have a good "products liability" case and referred him to a friend of hers, an attorney named Paul Kardan.

Ray retained Kardan to represent him in a lawsuit against both the store and the manufacturer of the chair. They agreed to a standard contingency fee arrangement for personal injury lawsuits, with Kardan to receive one-third of any sums Ray recovered from the defendants, after deducting for expenses. They discussed making a very large opening demand in negotiations with the store and the manufacturer, giving Ray confidence when he left the lawyer's office that there would be a substantial "six figure" settlement. But the two corporations refused to settle the case quickly, suspecting that the claim was fraudulent. Kardan told him that it still looked promising, but if the defendants continued to dig in their heels, Ray would probably have to take his case before a jury. It might take more than a year to prepare for trial, Kardan said, and they would likely need an expert witness to support the claim. Ray nevertheless remained confident that they would prevail.

One evening the following spring, Ray's car ran out of gas as he was driving home from a local hospital where Ronnie was spending the night after minor surgery. Seeing the car roll to a stop, a Phoenix police officer parked behind it to offer assistance. Ray seemed excessively edgy and talkative, appearing to the cop as if he was high on methamphetamine. Consequently, the officer ran a computer check on Ray's driver's license and learned that there was an outstanding warrant for his arrest, because he had failed to appear in court to answer a "dog at large" citation.

When he placed Ray under arrest, the cop could simply have locked the car and left it parked at the side of the road until Ray's release a few hours later. Instead, he chose to search the car thoroughly for drugs, even though the arrest was for a minor unrelated infraction. Such exploratory searches after arrests are lawful, according to the United States Supreme Court, because people do not have a "reasonable expectation of privacy" in their cars. In this case, it was a fruitful search: inside an eyeglass case on the front seat, the cop found a clear plastic bag containing 1.7 grams of methamphetamine, as well as a small glass pipe with traces of drug residue in its bowl.

Although Ray was released from custody that night, his problems worsened a month later when he took a compressor worth approximately $1,500 from a construction site without the permission of its owner, Todd Roberts. Roberts confronted Ray the next day when he showed up for work without the compressor. Frightened, Ray denied taking it and complained that Roberts owed him money for stucco work he had completed. Roberts grabbed Ray by the collar during the argument, shoving him to the ground and bruising him slightly. A deputy sheriff came to the scene, cited Roberts for assault and urged Ray to return the compressor.

Roberts and his wife complained several times to the Phoenix police when Ray failed to return the compressor during the next week. A detective went to Ray's house to speak to him about the dispute,and—from a block away—saw Ray in his driveway, loading a trailer hitched to his truck, apparently preparing to move from the house. When Ray drove away, the detective called on his radio for a patrol car to pull him over and arrest him for theft. Then—for the second time in six weeks—the police found methamphetamine when searching Ray's belongings.

Ray called Paul Kardan from the jail after each of his two arrests. Although Kardan normally did very little criminal defense work, he agreed to represent Ray on the two cases, with the understanding that his fee would come from the expected settlement of the lawsuit against the store and manufacturer. This was unusual, because criminal lawyers generally require their clients to pay a substantial retainer at the commencement of the representation. Kardan gambled, believing that the chain store would eventually settle the lawsuit. Many times during the next two years, Kardan second-guessed himself, wondering if he would ever be compensated for the hours he toiled on Hart's behalf.

Ray hit rock bottom when Ronnie kicked him out of their house. Hopelessly hooked on methamphetamine, homeless, having no steady employment and facing felony charges from two separate incidents, he sold meth on the street to survive, barely clearing enough money to support his own addiction. Sometimes he lived in his car, sometimes with friends. One of those friends was Steve Schilling.

Ray had met Steve in 1993, when Steve sold him a chrome grille for his pick-up truck, giving him such a great price that Ray assumed it was stolen. Steve invited him over to his house that day for some high quality meth and they spent the afternoon in Steve's back yard with a couple of his friends. Ray returned frequently, hoping to be offered a smoke and usually he was not disappointed. They went gambling together at the casinos on nearby Indian reservations, sometimes winning, sometimes losing as much as $500 to $1,000. Steve always seemed to carry a large amount of cash, which he used to pay for pre-owned merchandise that he later sold at local swap markets. He was generous in sharing his meth, but he also had an explosive temper, especially when he was coming down from a high and was arguing with his girlfriend, Brenda Chase.

Steve offered Ray work when no one else would take the chance, asking him to enclose his carport and remodel it into a garage. It promised to be a good arrangement for both men, because Ray was an excellent carpenter and Steve could pay him with a combination of cash, used merchandise and drugs. Then, a few weeks after Ray began working on the garage, they agreed that he would also remodel Steve's kitchen. High on methamphetamine, Ray frequently worked in the garage throughout the night, pounding his hammer, unable to sleep. Other times, he would disappear from the job site for days at a time, usually sleeping off a meth binge.

Like Ray Hart, Steve Schilling was born and raised in Arizona. Also like Ray, he was the youngest child in his family, the last of his parent's five children. Six years younger than his closest sibling, a sister, Steve grew up believing the family banter that he was an "accident." He never knew his father, who died when he was only a year old. But his mother wanted each of her five children to have a keepsake from her husband and she saved his father's coin collection for Steve, telling him years later that it had been his father's favorite hobby. Although it was a small collection, Steve held onto it as he grew up, adding coins of his own.

The family continued to live in the same residence, a cement-block house in Phoenix, even after his mother married her second husband when Steve was four years old. Steve never bonded with his stepfather, an alcoholic who could not seem to hold onto a job, instead relying on his wife to support them both. Then, when Steve was thirteen, his stepfather committed suicide. Adding to the family scars, one of Steve's brothers developed a serious drinking problem of his own, moved to California and died from an alcohol-related illness not long after their stepfather's death.

Steve was a highly emotional child with a low tolerance for

frustration and needed close adult supervision. Although his mother worked full time during much of his youth, his sisters seemed to be around whenever problems arose in elementary and middle school, finding time to take care of Steve when he most needed them. He grew up believing that he would always be able to count on his family; loyalty and trust were important tenets in the Schilling home.

The family member who most influenced Steve was his remaining older brother, Larry. Years older than Steve, he moved out of his mother's home before Steve was in kindergarten and was already married by Steve's tenth birthday, but he continued for several years to be a father figure for Steve, a role that their step-father could never play. He scolded Steve when he was disrespectful to his mother, but he also stood behind him when other kids from the neighborhood picked on him. After Larry got married, he and his wife took Steve on outings to the zoo and a local amusement park. Steve loved to spend nights and weekends at their home. Larry also shared his passion for motorcycles with his younger brother, giving him rides on his Harley Davidson and taking him to motorcycle races in the Phoenix area. When Larry became a bank guard and started his own security firm, Steve proudly went to his office. Steve worshiped his brother and wanted to be just like him when he grew up.

But his brother could not give Steve the same attention after he and his wife had their own children to raise and no one else was available to fill the void. His mother frequently was away on work assignments during Steve's high school years and his sisters had moved out on their own. Steve soon encountered disciplinary problems, being forced to transfer from his high school to another after a particularly ugly incident. He soon dropped out, never to return, instead getting a GED. He drank beer with his friends, undeterred by the devastation alcohol had already caused to his family, and then began smoking pot every day. He tried cocaine for a brief period, but discovered that he liked methamphetamine much more. By his early twenties, he was both hooked on meth and selling it.

Although Steve moved out of his mother's home before his twentieth birthday, living for a while in an apartment in Phoenix, he moved back within two years, because his mother was on the road much of the time and allowed him to rent the house from her. Not long after, his sister also experienced drug abuse problems. She asked Steve if she could move into their mother's house with him, not realizing the extent of Steven's own addiction.

It was a move that she would regret. Steve seemed to have an endless supply of methamphetamine available and her dependence on the drug only worsened. Moreover, while Steve was always generous toward her, he could be tense and unpredictable when he was high on meth. She also discovered that he was selling the drug, along with marijuana and an assortment of pills. He was using the house to conduct his business, telling her that it was safer there than on the street. Uneasily, she observed a stream of bikers and addicts come to their house, frequently congregating in the living room at night to smoke methamphetamine.

Unbeknownst to Steve and his sister, one of the visitors was an informer for the Phoenix police. Only a few months after his sister had moved in—on New Year's eve—a team of detectives from the Phoenix police's drug enforcement bureau raided the house with a search warrant, finding a small amount of methamphetamine and marijuana in his sister's bedroom, along with a pocket-sized scale and a drug straining device. She was immediately placed under arrest and spent New Year's Day in jail. A day later, she was charged with several felonies and was profoundly embarrassed, because her family had to spend money to help her retain a lawyer. She went to court four or five times in the ensuing months, frightened that she would eventually be ordered to return to jail. When she was offered a plea bargain that guaranteed her probation, she took it.

But the informer had observed Steve Schilling, not his sister, selling methamphetamine and Steve was the target of the police raid. Before they served the warrant, the detectives were not expecting to find very much, because the informer had seen only a small amount of meth and marijuana inside the residence. But they were surprised when they discovered a pound of methamphetamine in Steve's possession, worth between $5,000 and $10,000 on the street. They also found fifteen pounds of marijuana, a large cache of Valium tablets, two scales for weighing drugs, $39,350 in cash, six handguns, a shotgun and ten assorted rifles, including an Uzi.

Steve felt humiliated; he believed that he had ruined his sister's life, hurt his mother deeply and disappointed his big brother. Indeed, he had committed the worst sin of all, a betrayal of his family's trust. Within a few months, he too agreed to a plea bargain. Initially charged with drug trafficking, he pled guilty to a reduced charge of possession of dangerous drugs, with a stipulated sentence of five years in prison and the forfeiture of all the drugs, currency and weapons, as well as three automobiles and other property, including a house he and his sister co-owned. The government might also have taken his mother's residence, but on the family's assertion that she had no knowledge of the drug trafficking, her house was spared.

Steve's five year sentence did not mean, as a practical matter, that he would be locked up for nearly that long. Before the Arizona legislature revised its sentencing laws in the 1990s to establish what is generally called "truth in sentencing," few persons sentenced to prison served their full term. Parole boards determined the actual duration of incarceration, making release decisions based on predictions of likely recidivism. These predictions were highly subjective, regardless of the good intentions of correctional authorities. A major factor in the determination of whether to release a prisoner, for example, was an examination of his institutional behavior. Prisoners with an "attitude problem" lengthened their own incarceration by refusing to offer the platitudes sought by their keepers.

Steve Schilling, on the other hand, was a model prisoner. With no history of violence and a highly supportive family, he so impressed the parole board that it granted his release at the first opportunity, allowing him to return to the Phoenix community less than eighteen months after his conviction. He soon found, however, that the community had changed during the time he had been in prison; by now, methamphetamine use had reached epidemic proportions.

Steve tried to put his misfortune behind him, starting a new business, Anything Goes, which consisted of buying and selling used goods and appliances of all kinds. He rented a large storage locker to hold the merchandise he purchased at estate and garage sales, auctions and weekend swap markets. Later, when his business was going well, he bought his own house, a small three-bedroom residence just north of the neighborhood in which he had grown up. Sometimes people came to the house to sell him used items, and his back yard and one of his bedrooms were filled with building supplies, automobile parts, kitchen appliances, computer and stereo equipment, household furniture and goods, and even a pinball machine. His overhead was minimal and record-keeping was never a problem, since he paid for goods with trade, cash or even methamphetamine.

Many of his friends liked to visit him at the house, parking their motorcycles and pick-up trucks outside, appreciating that Steve was generous in sharing whatever meth he had on hand. He usually had enough to go around, even though he could smoke a half gram a day himself. It gave him the feeling that he could do nothing wrong. He loved to get high with his buddies, then drive his Harley across town to the casino on the Fort McDowell Indian Reservation and play the slot machines for over twenty-four hours at a time. He usually gambled with one or more of his friends, but sometimes he went alone. When he could get away for longer periods, he liked to take a four hour bike ride to Laughlin, Nevada, where he played at the casinos along the Colorado River, as addicted to gambling as he was to methamphetamine.

One of his best friends was Brenda Chase, an attractive woman with auburn hair, who was a registered nurse working for a local home health care agency. Before Brenda became his lover, Steve sometimes jokingly referred to her as his "big sister," since she was about the same age as his own sister. Although Brenda and Steve spent many nights together, they maintained separate residences, which served them well because their relationship was stormy and their arguments sometimes erupted violently. Brenda was less interested in a romantic relationship than Steve was and she resented his jealousy over her innocent flirtations with other men. Steve, on the other hand, felt threatened by Brenda's red-haired beauty and irritated that she was becoming increasingly dependent on methamphetamine.

Ray Hart, who was remodeling Steve's garage and kitchen, also irritated him. Ray was a competent handyman when he chose to work, but he frequently failed to show up, causing the project to take far longer than Steve had anticipated. Moreover, whenever a group of Steve's friends came to socialize in Steve's living room, Ray was always hanging around, regardless of whether he had been invited. Like Steve, Ray loved to gamble and they frequently went to the casinos together, but Steve grew tired of Ray's constant bragging about his many scams, about his plan to sue the chain store that sold him a defective lawn chair.

Despite these irritations, Steve was reasonably happy with the progress he had made after his release from prison, until the day the one thing he had to remind him of the parent he had never known was stolen.

Chapter 6

Trial and Tribulation

The late Irving Younger, a renowned prosecutor, law professor and expert on the law of evidence, spent the last two decades of his life giving lectures to trial lawyers around the United States on the art and science of cross examination. Younger asserted that an attorney needed a minimum of twenty-five jury trials to become competent at cross-examination and that true brilliance in the courtroom could only be achieved with much more substantial experience. I had handled several hundred felony cases as a criminal defense lawyer, including over thirty jury trials, and I considered myself to be rather good at my craft, obtaining eight consecutive "not guilty" jury verdicts at one point. But my courtroom experience was ancient history when I became a prosecutor, more than two decades after I had last appeared before a jury.

Like most other prosecution agencies, the Maricopa County Attorney's Office recognized that new lawyers needed to hone their courtroom skills in simple, low-stakes proceedings before graduating to felony trials. Thus, after their initial four-week classroom training, beginning prosecutors usually spent the next six months handling preliminary hearings and misdemeanor jury trials before justices of the peace. Most had at least four or five misdemeanor jury trials before they moved on to a felony caseload. However, this grooming period was cut to one month in my case, allowing me as much time as possible for

felony trial work. My supervisors tried diligently to assign me misdemeanor cases that were scheduled for jury trial, hoping to make my brief
transitional period as useful as possible, but—as luck would have it—
each of these cases resulted in a guilty plea.

Then, only a week before I was to leave the "baby prosecutor"
office to take over a felony trial caseload, one of my colleagues asked if
I would be interested in a one-day jury trial on a driving while intoxicated charge, to begin the following morning. The prosecutor handling the case had a conflict in her schedule and the trial would have
to be either postponed or re-assigned to a new prosecutor at the last
moment. "It promises to be a very simple trial," my colleague said,
"since the defendant refused to take a breathalyzer test when he was
taken into custody and only one witness, the arresting officer, will testify for the state." The file indicated that the defense lawyer might also
call one witness at the trial. Excited, I jumped at the opportunity.

The defendant was Jose Hernandez, a farm worker who had
been arrested in a rural area sixty miles west of Phoenix. According to
the report of the arresting officer, deputy sheriff Bob Weston, Hernandez had almost struck a telephone pole after starting his car at night in
a parking lot outside a bar, then failed to turn on his lights before driving onto the road. The deputy wrote in his report that he pulled Hernandez over and administered a field sobriety test, which consisted of
a series of coordination exercises. The deputy arrested Hernandez
when he performed poorly on the exercises, declined to answer any
questions relating to how much alcohol he had consumed and refused
to submit to a breath test. Deputy Weston then transported him to
downtown Phoenix and booked him into the Madison Street Jail,
along with everyone else arrested in the county that night.

I called Deputy Weston the night before the trial to go over
his testimony. To my dismay, he told me that he had conducted relatively few traffic stops and had never testified in court on a driving
while intoxicated charge. Although he had been employed by the sheriff's office for seven years, he spent most of this time as a guard at the
county jail. He admitted that he had limited training on DWI investigations and was not certified to conduct any of the sophisticated tests
police sometimes used to detect intoxication, expressing the hope that

I would bail him out if he ran into trouble as a witness. I decided not to inform him that it would be my first prosecution too.

I stayed up well past midnight preparing my opening statement and closing argument to the jury, direct-examination of the deputy and cross-examination of the defendant, in the event that he testified. Although the defense lawyer had listed another potential witness, Teresa Smythe, Deputy Weston's report did not mention anyone by that name and he could not remember any witnesses being present when he arrested the defendant. I did not know what to expect from Smythe, since no one from the prosecutor's office had made any effort to conduct a pre-trial interview. Hence, there was not much I could do to prepare my cross-examination.

The trial took place in the justice court in a small town an hour's drive from Phoenix, the last third of which transversed country roads through cotton fields and dairy farms. As I parked alongside a long row of neatly stacked bales of hay outside the courthouse, I realized that the six jurors I was to select that morning probably lived in the same community as the defendant and I wondered how they would respond to a prosecutor whose accent betrayed that he had grown up in the suburbs of New York City. However, I told myself that even if the jury turned out to be hostile, I assumed that the judge would at least be impartial, since he was a former police officer, like many other justices of the peace.

The courtroom was the oddest one I had ever seen. Designed as a meeting hall for the town council, it had a large gallery for the audience, but virtually no space for the lawyers to use when addressing the jurors, who sat in a box that was separated from the rest of the room by a brick barrier. The witness stand was as far from the jury box as possible, partially screened from the jurors' view by the corner of the judge's bench. The jurors at one end of the box could only see the top of a witness's head, and the others could not see much more, unless the witness leaned forward when testifying. I was certain that at least three of the jurors had no view at all of Teresa Smythe, an attractive gray-haired woman, when she testified that day for the defense.

The jury selection was completed in a little over an hour. I had an uneasy feeling when the judge asked if any of the prospective jurors were familiar with Ms. Smythe, who, it turned out, was born and lived there. Several persons raised their hand, asserting in follow-up questioning that they could be fair to both sides, even though "Teresa" was "quite a gal," according to at least one member of the panel. Nevertheless, the four women and two men who remained after we exercised our peremptory challenges looked reasonably fair-minded to me.

Deputy Weston looked tired when he arrived in court, having worked the graveyard shift. He never smiled at the jury and was obviously uncomfortable as a witness, but he came across as very conscientious and thorough when questioned on direct examination. Following the narrative he had scripted in his police report, he testified that he first observed Mr. Hernandez while seated in his patrol car across the road from the only business establishment in town, a combination bar and general store. The deputy described how Hernandez almost hit a telephone pole when he backed his car out of the parking lot in front of the bar, then failed to switch on his headlights until several seconds after he had entered the roadway. The deputy followed the defendant for a short distance before pulling him over and administering the field sobriety test. Although Hernandez refused to answer any of the deputy's questions about how much he had drunk that night, he had a strong odor of alcohol on his breath and performed poorly on the coordination tests.

Frank Lawrence, the defense lawyer, a public defender, shocked me when he began his cross-examination, asking the deputy if he had participated in a tape-recorded pre-trial interview with an investigator from the public defender's office. Weston had forgotten to mention to me that he had given a statement to the defense. I learned later that the prosecutor initially assigned to the case had known about the statement, but had nevertheless failed to obtain a copy of the tape or even to note in the state's file that it existed. Apparently, the deputy had not reviewed his police report before his pre-trial interview with the defense, because he told the investigator that the only reason he had pulled Hernandez over was the absence of a light over Hernandez's rear license plate. The inconsistency between his direct and cross examination was glaring.

Hernandez never testified, but Lawrence called Teresa Smythe, who told the jury that Hernandez had been conversing with her at the general store for close to an hour before his arrest and she insisted that he had been both coherent and clear-headed, with no odor of alcohol on his person. She contradicted herself in several key details and it was apparent to me that she was offended that a cop had been hiding for the specific purpose of catching a drunk driver. But she was very likable and I tried not to seem too boorish when cross examining her.

Lawrence and I presented our closing arguments to the jury in mid-afternoon. Normally I like to move about when addressing an audience, but I was trapped that day in a cramped space, talking to six faces as expressionless as the brick wall that separated us. Although Teresa Smythe was the more colorful of the two witnesses, I felt that I could rely on the seemingly objective field sobriety test, which, according to the deputy, the defendant had failed miserably. I would describe how Hernandez had been unable to count aloud, "one, two, three, four, four, three, two, one," three consecutive times, while simultaneously touching his thumb to his fingers. However, when I began to argue this fact to the jury, I blurted out: "He was so impaired that he couldn't say four, two, three, one." I tried to cover my error, but I knew at that point the state's case was in trouble. If the prosecutor himself could not successfully perform the field sobriety test, how could a poor farm worker do it in the middle of the night, under stress?

The jury began deliberation shortly before 4:00 and debated the facts for about two hours before informing the judge that they were deadlocked 3 - 3, with no desire to fritter away more of their evening. My first trial as a prosecutor ended abruptly with a tie.

It was a humbling experience. I drove home with the realization that courtroom advocacy is different from riding a bicycle. When not practiced regularly, it can easily be forgotten. Having been at the university for a long, long time, I had felt uncomfortable trying to connect on a personal level with six citizens from a world different from my own. When I had been a criminal defense lawyer in the 1970s, I usually had a single goal at trial: to find reasonable doubt and bring it to the jury's attention. I did this most of the time by conducting a cross-examination that damaged the credibility of a key prosecution witness, breaking just one link in the state's chain of evidence, just as Frank Lawrence had done with Deputy Weston.

Now, as a prosecutor, my challenge was different: to build a case, not tear it down. If there was a gap in my evidence, it mattered little whether I could successfully question the credibility of a defense witness, such as Teresa Smythe. I would have to prepare my own witnesses thoroughly, not only to present a coherent, believable account of the facts in question, but also to withstand an assault from any direction on cross-examination. All of my evidence would have to fit together like the pieces of a jigsaw puzzle, explaining how and why a crime occurred and leaving no room in the jury's mind for reasonable doubt.

However, I knew now that if these were the skills I needed for a prosecution to prevail, the Hernandez case had demonstrated that I had a long way to go.

Chapter 7

Jail Time

July 4, 1994, 7:50 A.M.

Steve Schilling stared intently at the bearded man seated directly across from him on a bare steel cot in a crowded holding cell in the Madison Street Jail. The man was obviously mentally ill; disheveled, he seemed totally unaware of the other people in the cell as he sat with his legs crossed, mumbling to himself, his odor disgusting Schilling. A few feet away, two men took turns vomiting into the single seatless toilet in a corner of the dingy cell. Schilling thought that one might be an Hispanic farm worker, while the other appeared to be twice Schilling's age. A young black kid urinated in another corner, unable to wait for the toilet.

Schilling had spent several hours earlier that morning at the precinct substation in which he had been interrogated. Then, after the arresting officer had completed the initial booking forms, he placed Schilling in the back seat of his patrol car, drove the ten miles to downtown Phoenix and parked on a ramp outside a back door of the Madison Street Jail. Schilling entered the jail at 5:00 A.M., while his family and most of his friends and neighbors were still fast asleep. After the arresting officer signed the papers necessary to transfer his custody from the Phoenix Police Department to the Maricopa County Sheriff's Office, a deputy sheriff placed him in a holding cell on the ground floor of the jail, in an area known as the "horseshoe." A short while later, he was moved to his present location, another cell in the horseshoe.

Schilling counted twenty-nine men in the eleven by sixteen-foot cell, but it felt more like one hundred fifty, and most of them seemed to be either drunk or under the influence of some other substance. Schilling himself felt agitated as he came down from the methamphetamine he had taken the previous night. A few of his cell-mates were standing, but most sat or slept on the concrete floor or on one of the two steel cots in the cell. When they were later herded into court, he learned why each was there. One had been arrested for shooting his son in an argument a few hours earlier. Several others were being held for driving while intoxicated. One had been picked up on a warrant for failing to pay child support. Another, with a tattoo depicting the Virgin Mary, was charged with a gang-related drive-by shooting. The shoplifter who stood next to him appeared to Schilling to be addicted to cocaine. Most of the men were unkempt, but one wore a tie and jacket.

The Madison Street Jail was a dreary six-story brick fortress that occupied a full city block in downtown Phoenix. In the early morning, a lucky inmate on the fifth or sixth floor might have been able to see the sun peeking over the roof of America West Arena three blocks away—that is, if he looked carefully through the iron grating over the narrow plexiglass slit of a window high on the wall of his cell. A few weeks before Steve Schilling arrived at the jail, Charles Barkley and the other members of the Phoenix Suns had filled the arena while going through their annual elimination from the N.B.A. playoffs. Prisoners in the jail were tantalizingly close to the hubbub of city life, only a few hundred yards from Patriot's Square park, two massive luxury hotels, Phoenix's stunning Symphony Hall and the glass office towers that housed many of Arizona's most prestigious law firms.

But the inmates were separated from the energy and splendor of central Phoenix by the Maricopa County Superior Court, conveniently located across the street from the jail. A tunnel connected the courthouse and the jail, so that prisoners could be shepherded quickly to and from their court appearances without troubling the Phoenix residents, tourists and suburbanites enjoying the many attractions of the downtown area. The occupants of the Madison Street Jail were invisible to the world outside.

Constructed nine years earlier with only 960 beds, the Madison Street Jail housed approximately 1,500 prisoners on its upper floors, in addition to those crammed into the holding cells in the horseshoe area of the ground level. Another 1000 inmates were located in "Tent City," an outdoor facility removed from downtown Phoenix. With no air conditioning, the temperatures at Tent City frequently rose to well over one hundred degrees. Maricopa County's sheriff, a budding media star, Joe Arpaio, described it as a place where he "entertain[ed] drug dealers and sex offenders and murderers, too, with no more than two or three detention officers guarding them at any one time."

Most inmates of the upper floors of the Madison Street Jail were defendants awaiting trial in felony cases, unable to post bail. Their food was intentionally dreadful. Arpaio bragged that he spent more to feed his dogs than it cost to sustain the inmates, who paid a dollar a day for the privilege of eating green baloney. The prisoners wore pink underwear beneath their pajama-like outer garments that came with garish red, white and black stripes, compliments of the sheriff, who claimed that the humiliation of being forced to wear such clown-like apparel was an effective deterrent to crime. Whether or not this colorful theory of punishment actually worked, it was immensely popular with voters, a fact keenly appreciated by Arpaio.

However, the aspect of the Madison Street Jail most hated by its residents had nothing to do with the food, the pink underwear or the striped jump suits. Instead, it was the horseshoe, a U-shaped configuration of cells that functioned as a human conveyer belt to serve law enforcement's need to collect as much information as possible, as quickly as possible, on the 110,000 to 120,000 new inmates entering the jail each year. Schilling and his fellow arrestees moved from one packed cell to another, around the horseshoe, while detention officers completed the arduous process of memorializing their arrests, identifying them in several different ways and entering their personal information into state and national data banks. Conditions in the horseshoe were far worse than those encountered on the upper floors of the jail or across town in Tent City.

An intake officer filled out the jail's initial paperwork while

Schilling waited in his first cell, near the entrance at the rear of the jail. Although there were only a handful of men in this cell, about twenty women were packed into the next cell, most of them prostitutes who had been arrested a few hours earlier in a sweep of East Van Buren Avenue, the red light district in Phoenix. When the booking paperwork was completed, another detention officer transferred Schilling to a cell farther along the horseshoe, where he was held before being photographed. He waited in another cell before being fingerprinted and yet another before being interviewed by a court employee gathering information to be used in determining his eligibility for bail. The largest of the holding cells was only twenty by twenty feet, but some were considerably smaller, and almost all were over-crowded on the holiday weekend.

Both federal and state laws require the fingerprinting of every arrested person. Most jurisdictions also routinely photograph arrestees during the booking process and an increasing number of law enforcement agencies are collecting DNA samples as well. The police are supposed to forward each arrested person's fingerprint and arrest information to state and national data processing centers, where the information can be quickly accessed by law enforcement agencies in other parts of the country. Nevertheless, local practices vary substantially throughout the United States. Many people are arrested each weekend in major metropolitan areas and intake systems can get hopelessly congested and backed up. Data are sometimes not collected and, once collected, they are easily lost.

An efficient assembly line can facilitate this process, making life far easier for law enforcement personnel. But administrative efficiency does not translate to creature comfort. The horseshoe was a nightmare for Steve Schilling and the others jammed into each holding cell, waiting their turn to be fingerprinted and photographed.

Schilling was growing increasingly claustrophobic. Unable to watch the bearded man any longer, he closed his eyes. The question that must have been on his mind was how this mess could possibly have occurred.

Only two weeks before, he had seemed to be pulling his life together. His business, Anything Goes, had become profitable and he had built a substantial inventory of pre-owned merchandise, allowing him to purchase a house that spring, making the down payment with his own money, not his family's. While he knew that he could never measure up to his older brother, he believed that both his mother and brother were pleased with the successful turn his life had taken. He had many friends and he enjoyed the way they prized his Harley Davidson, which he maintained in excellent condition. He also had a steady girlfriend, Brenda Chase, whom he adored, even though they argued a great deal.

But things began to unravel on a Saturday morning in late June, ten days before his arrest. The previous evening, after the last of his friends had left his house, he had smoked some methamphetamine and had ridden his Harley to his favorite haunt, the casino on the Fort McDowell Indian Reservation. He had planned to play the slot machines for at least twenty-four hours, certain that he'd be a winner. However, he was not enjoying himself at the casino that night; the meth was apparently of inferior quality and he quickly began to come down from the high without an additional supply on hand. Characteristically, his mood was terrible and became worse when he began to lose consistently.

His head ached, his mouth was parched and he began dry-heaving as he rode his cycle home that Saturday morning. Even at 9:00 A.M., the Phoenix sun in late June was merciless. Dehydrated when he reached his house, he went directly to his kitchen, where he immediately noticed that the security bar from the sliding-glass door leading to his back yard was lying on the floor in the middle of the room. Curious, he checked the door itself and discovered that it had been unlocked during the night, after he had departed. Then he walked through the house to ascertain what, if anything, had been disturbed. The only missing item appeared to be the gun he normally left on his desk. He was relieved to find that his file cabinet was locked, since he kept most of his valuables in the bottom drawer.

Later that morning, however, Steve unlocked the file cabinet to retrieve some papers and was horrified to discover that his bottom drawer had indeed been emptied. Its contents had included a currency collection, numerous items of jewelry, a Rolex watch, and—most important—the collection of rare coins he had inherited from his father. He sat in disbelief for several minutes before the realization hit him: the house was not in disarray; the file cabinet had not been pried open. The person who stole his property had known exactly where it was hidden.

A guard tapped Schilling on the shoulder, interrupting his stream of consciousness, to usher him from the holding cell into a courtroom, a few yards away.

This was no ordinary courtroom. A long, narrow, spare, windowless room in the heart of the jail—right at the center of the horseshoe—the courtroom served as Maricopa County's cost-saving response to the constitutional mandate that arrested persons must appear promptly before a magistrate. The United States Supreme Court has interpreted the Fourth Amendment to require that when police arrest a suspect without a warrant, the arrested person may not be held in custody for longer than forty-eight hours without a judicial determination that there is probable cause to believe that he has committed a crime. Additionally, the magistrate must inform the arrested person of the charges against him and his right to counsel. The judge also typically determines the conditions of pre-trial release, such as the amount of bail necessary to assure that the defendant will show up at each of his scheduled court appearances.

Assuring a prompt judicial hearing for all persons arrested each day in urban America is a major challenge for local government. Maricopa County's solution to this problem was not to transport newly arrested individuals to the courthouse, but instead to bring the court to them. The always busy "jail court" at the center of the horseshoe was in session twenty-four hours each day, seven days each week. There were no holidays in this court. Indeed, Steve Schilling entered the jail court at 1:00 P.M. on Independence Day, when most Americans were preparing for their afternoon picnics or were watching television in air-conditioned rooms.

Schilling was seated on one of the benches in the rear of the room as the clerk called out the names of several persons to appear before the magistrate. The men lined up wearily along the side of the room, looking as if they were purchasing cigarettes from the only cashier at a busy, late-night convenience market in a run-down part of town. One by one, the magistrate called each case and advised each man of the charges for which he had been arrested and his right to be represented by counsel if the prosecutor proceeded with a court complaint against him. The judge then scheduled a date for a preliminary hearing in another court and determined the person's eligibility for release, based on the recommendations of the arresting officer and the court staff member who had interviewed the person in the jail. There was a rubber stamped probable cause finding in every case, with no defense attorneys in sight.

The magistrate set a bond of $35,000 in Schilling's case and scheduled a preliminary hearing in the Northwest Phoenix Justice Court eight days later. Schilling indicated to the judge that he thought he'd be able to pay the ten percent needed to post the bond and that he planned to retain his own lawyer. For the first time in this brief encounter, the magistrate looked up from the papers on his desk, taking measure of the man standing before him. Then, just as quickly, he looked down again, scratching a note on the form on his desk, indicating that—unlike most cases—a public defender was not to be appointed. Schilling's initial appearance in the jail court was over in roughly forty-five seconds. The magistrate moved on to the next case while Schilling was led away to yet another holding cell.

Schilling continued around the horseshoe after his moment in court, moving from cell to cell with other persons who had already been before the magistrate. Those inmates who were able to post bail, as well as those not charged by the county attorney within two days after their initial appearance at the jail court, were released from the Madison Street Jail. The remainder were interviewed by jail classification personnel to determine where in the jail system they were to be housed pending the disposition of their cases.

When a detention officer gave Schilling an opportunity to make a phone call, he reached Brenda Chase. "Will you retrieve the documents in my study that prove I own the house on Dahlia?" When she agreed to do as he asked, he directed her to put the house up as collateral at the bail bond agency recommended to him by one of his cellmates. For the next several hours, Schilling waited, not knowing if he would be one of the lucky ones to be released on bond.

Chapter 8

Cash and Computer Up Front

July 4, 1994, 7:00 P.M.

Steve Schilling waited exhaustedly in the Madison Street Jail, hoping that Brenda Chase would bail him out. Although less than twenty-four hours had passed since Ray Hart had arrived at his house, it seemed like more than a week. Schilling worried about the charges he faced and what his brother Larry would say when he learned that Steve had screwed up again.

He was relieved when Brenda came through for him, arranging the bond and picking him up at the jail. He chose to spend the night at Chase's, hoping to avoid his family for a while. He was sure that they would stand behind him, regardless of how long it took to resolve the problem, but it pained him to think about their disappointment. Chase's home was also a convenient refuge from his own. He knew that the police had searched his place the previous night and he feared that its condition would upset him.

It did. Schilling was shocked when he walked through the front door the following morning. The living room carpet, sofa and love seat were ruined, first by the ugly blood stains that had dried on them, then by the large swatches the police had cut out for evidence. The detectives had turned off the air conditioning, leaving a stale odor in the house that nauseated him. The police had also ransacked the house, going through all his drawers and personal belongings and he saw dark powder everywhere, a memento left by the technician who had done the fingerprinting. Schilling felt violated.

73

His anger toward Ray Hart rose as he began the unpleasant business of cleaning the house. None of this would have happened, Schilling felt, if Hart had not stolen his coin collection. The confrontation had escalated only because Hart continued to lie about the theft after Schilling confronted him. Adding insult to injury, the kitchen was in shambles because Hart had abruptly abandoned the remodeling after the burglary ten days earlier. Schilling reasoned that Hart, not he, should be facing felony charges.

His thoughts danced. He really *did* have a good case. He knew Hart was a meth addict, and he was sure Hart also was a liar and a compulsive thief. Any reasonable person looking at the case would see that Schilling was the true victim, not Hart. All he was doing when he confronted Hart was trying to get his property back, without getting Hart in trouble with the police. Besides, his brother had told him, a citizen had a right to make an arrest. A few years earlier, when Schilling had been arrested for selling drugs, he rolled over, pleading guilty within a few months. This time he was determined to fight the charges.

He would need a really good lawyer to defend him in court, even though it was going to be expensive. Schilling had very little cash on hand and few other resources, since he had already used his house as collateral for the bail bond and there was no way he would part with his Harley Davidson. His mother and brother might be able to help a little with the lawyer's fee, but neither of his sisters had any money. Even Brenda Chase was tapped out. It was not going to be easy.

In fact, it turned out to be even more difficult than he anticipated. The first lawyer Schilling contacted was Ryan Brent, who had negotiated the plea bargain in Schilling's drug trafficking case. Even though Schilling later filed a claim against Brent from his prison cell, alleging that Brent had provided constitutionally inadequate representation by lying to him about the consequences of his plea, he knew all along that it had been a reasonably good bargain. Now he wanted Brent to represent him again, but Brent declined the case, saying that he was not taking new criminal clients and instead was specializing in personal injury law. Brent sounded sympathetic as he listened on the telephone to Schilling's story, but though Schilling kept pressing, he could not convince the lawyer to take the case.

Schilling next tried Todd Dailey, a lawyer recommended by one of his friends. The receptionist who answered the phone said that Dailey was "with a client." Schilling left his number, along with a message for the lawyer to call him back as soon as possible, stating that he needed help on an urgent matter. But the lawyer did not call that morning and failed to respond to the three additional messages Schilling left in the afternoon. The next day, he finally reached one of Dailey's associates on his second call, but the associate, Ben Feldman, informed him that Dailey was in trial and would likely be unavailable the remainder of the week. Feldman agreed to discuss the case with Schilling on the phone, asking a few questions about the charges. After learning some of the details, Feldman offered encouragement, commenting that the case sounded interesting and might be a winner at trial.

However, when Schilling asked about the fee, Feldman said he couldn't provide a definite answer, stating that it would depend on such matters as the amount of investigation necessary to prepare the case, the number and complexity of pre-trial motions he would have to file, whether a jury trial would be necessary and—if so—the length of the trial. It would not be fair to either of them, Feldman said, if he quoted a fee before he had an opportunity to review the police reports. Nevertheless, Feldman told Schilling that he would probably need a $20,000-$25,000 retainer at the outset. Schilling groaned, "That's more than I can afford." The lawyer recommended the public defender.

There had to be an alternative. Schilling had always believed that you get what you pay for and the public defender came free. He started calling acquaintances who had recently had criminal cases. One was unable to recommend a lawyer, but another told him that he had been pleased with his attorney, Frank Mahoney, who really knew the system, inside and out. This was especially good news, because one of his brother's friends had also recommended Mahoney, saying that he had an excellent reputation. Schilling immediately called Mahoney's office and was excited to get an appointment with the lawyer later that day. At last, things were looking better.

Frank Mahoney's office suite was located in an ornate stucco building near the superior court. The building had housed many of the movers and shakers in the early stages of Arizona's development boom, including some of the state's most influential law firms. But the major law firms and developers eventually moved to the sleek new glass structures that dwarfed the once majestic building, leaving it to budget-conscious criminal defense lawyers, such as Frank Mahoney, who appreciated its proximity to the courthouse.

Sitting across from Steve Schilling in his spacious office, Mahoney had ample time to study his potential client, who had arrived fifteen minutes early and was highly agitated when asked about his case, his darting eyes and nervous energy bespeaking drugs. The color in Schilling's face darkened each time he mentioned Ray Hart, whom he described as a con artist and a liar. He had tolerated Hart, he claimed, only because Hart was good with a hammer and saw. He should have known better than to trust him, especially after Hart had bragged to him about stealing from previous employers.

Schilling then launched into a monologue on the remodeling scenario, which had not gone as he expected. Hart sometimes disturbed Schilling's neighbors with the buzz of his drill when he worked at night. Two full months after Hart had begun, both the kitchen and the garage were still in disarray. Whenever Schilling's friends visited him at the house, Hart would stop working to join in the banter, regardless of whether he had been invited. Sometimes he irritated Schilling by disappearing for days at a time, just when he was in the middle of an important phase of the remodeling. It appeared that the work would never be done.

Mahoney directed him to the facts of the case, asking when his property had been stolen and how he knew that Hart was responsible.

Schilling looked at a calendar briefly, then stated with certainty that it was Friday night, June 24. Hart's brother and cousin had come over that afternoon to help Hart install a new dishwasher that Schilling had acquired through his business. But they were not making much progress and instead were drinking beer from Schilling's refrigerator and watching a baseball game on the television in the living room. When the game was over, Hart told Schilling that he was going to spend the weekend with his brother, who was building a pond in a woman's back yard in northern Arizona. An hour later, Schilling locked the house and took off for the night.

Schilling's voice became scratchy when he described his discovery of the theft the following morning. "The coin collection," he told Mahoney, "was my only remaining possession from my father, who died when I was a year old. You don't know what losing it means to me." Although he would never have sold it, he was sure that it was worth at least fifteen thousand dollars, maybe even twenty. The Rolex watch and other stolen items also were costly; the face value of the rare bills was over five hundred dollars, putting aside their worth as part of a collection.

"Not many people knew," Schilling said, "that I kept my valuables in the bottom drawer of the file cabinet and only a handful of my friends were aware that the key was in my desk drawer." His first thought had been his girlfriend, but he doubted that she would take his jewelry and coins. He also thought about a couple of friends who had been smoking methamphetamine in his study the last time he had taken the coins out, but his mind turned to Hart, who quickly became the prime suspect. He liked to hang around the study when he should have been working on the remodeling and Schilling was fairly certain that he knew where everything was hidden. Hart also knew that Schilling would be away that Friday night.

"My suspicions of Hart were confirmed," he explained to the lawyer, "when my girlfriend Brenda Chase came over to my house on the afternoon of Saturday, June 25. Together, we retraced the burglar's steps. We exited the house through the sliding glass door, then crossed the yard to get to the alley, where Brenda spotted the key to my file cabinet." On the way back to the house, Schilling noticed footprints on the dirt outside the door. Looking closely, he realized that they were not regular shoe prints, but instead were made by someone wearing flip-flops. Ray Hart wore flip-flops.

Mahoney interrupted to ask if he had called the police to report the burglary. No, Schilling admitted, he had not considered that until later. Mahoney took note of this.

Schilling continued. A couple of days after the break-in, he decided to confront Hart, hoping to persuade him to return the coin collection. Hart denied the theft and Schilling could not find any of the stolen property when he searched through Hart's belongings and his brother's apartment. However, Hart failed to return to Phoenix the next week to continue working on the garage and kitchen, solidifying

Schilling's suspicion.

Schilling uttered an obscenity, then vented for a couple of minutes as Mahoney sat quietly. Hart was a crook, a thief, a loser. Schilling said what had hurt him the most was the feeling that Hart had betrayed his trust.

Hart finally returned nine days after the break-in, paging Schilling in the afternoon to discuss the remodeling that had yet to be completed. They agreed to meet at Schilling's house that evening.

Brenda Chase was at the house when Hart arrived, around eight o'clock. Both Schilling and Chase said they noticed that Hart was unusually nervous, acting as if he were hiding something.

After Schilling and Hart retired to the study to discuss the remodeling, Chase went outside to Hart's car, where she found a black leather fanny pack she had purchased for Schilling a few months earlier at a fancy shopping mall. Schilling said he had not realized that the pouch had been taken in the burglary, but when Chase dumped its contents on the desk, he saw a few items of his stolen jewelry, along with a bag of Hart's methamphetamine. Schilling added that Hart tried to talk his way out of the situation, saying that he had found the pouch at a thrift shop a few blocks from Schilling's house, but Schilling said he was sure Hart was lying.

"Suddenly," Schilling told the lawyer, "Hart sprang from his chair and grabbed a pistol that I kept in my office." Schilling froze momentarily, but recovered in time to reach Hart's hand just as he was about to point the gun at him. They struggled for several seconds before Schilling was able to gain control, shoving Hart back into his chair.

According to Schilling, he held the gun at his side, shaking, taking deep breaths as he tried to figure out what he should do. Hart pleaded with him not to call the police, saying he was afraid he would be sent to prison if Schilling turned him in. Schilling said he didn't want to get Hart in trouble, so he agreed, instructing Hart to sit on the living room sofa. He asked what Hart had done with the rest of the stolen property. However, Hart continued to insist that he hadn't taken it, despite the evidence.

Schilling's girlfriend left the house an hour or so later, about the same time that three of Schilling's friends arrived. One, named Pat, was upset that Hart had stolen Schilling's property and wanted to work him over, but Schilling said he was able to restrain him. Then Hart aggravated the situation by bolting for the front door, getting into a tussle with Pat and James, Schilling's friends. It looked to Schilling to be a fair fight, with Hart throwing as many punches as he received. Nevertheless, according to Schilling, Pat and James finally subdued Hart, tying his hands together to prevent further violence.

Hart continued to beg Schilling not to call the police, eventually saying that he had hidden the coin collection and the other property in a shed behind his wife's apartment on the other side of town. Schilling left on his cycle to check it out, not returning until ninety minutes later, when he was arrested. According to Schilling, Hart was still in the living room when he had left and Schilling had no knowledge of what the others might have done when he was away.

Mahoney and Schilling then discussed the lawyer's fee.

The fee arrangements between criminal defense lawyers and their clients are different from those in other areas of the law. For example, the legal profession's ethics rules prohibit criminal attorneys from setting fees that are contingent on the outcome of a prosecution, thus differentiating them from plaintiffs' counsel in many areas of civil practice. And unlike attorneys who represent business entities or other clients who can afford to pay ongoing legal bills on a monthly basis, criminal lawyers rarely, if ever, bill their clients by the hour, after services have already been rendered. Instead, most criminal lawyers in private practice determine their fees in advance, based on two important considerations.

The first factor is that criminal defendants—as a group—are generally less reliable than others in paying their bills. As a result, it is customary for a criminal attorney to ask for a substantial retainer at the beginning of a defendant's representation, to assure that the lawyer will in fact be compensated adequately. The size of the retainer usually reflects such matters as the lawyer's experience and reputation for obtaining good results in similar cases, the seriousness of the charges and the lawyer's prediction of the amount of time it will take to represent the defendant.

Second, most criminal cases result in guilty pleas. With this in mind, criminal lawyers typically determine their initial fees by estimating the time and resources they will spend representing clients through plea bargains and subsequent sentencing proceedings. The retainer generally reflects what the lawyer and client negotiate for this service and the lawyer usually asks for all of this fee to be paid in advance, rather than in installments. The initial agreement usually includes a further understanding that an additional fee will be assessed later if the case proceeds to trial.

Although most criminal lawyers follow these practices, the amounts they charge their clients vary tremendously. The elite criminal attorneys in cities, experienced practitioners representing white collar defendants or drug traffickers in federal court, typically have relatively small case loads and may receive six-figure retainers from some of their clients. Others, such as lawyers representing "street crime" defendants in state court, charge far less for their work. Even among these lawyers, there may be substantial differences in the fees they charge.

Frank Mahoney generally represented "street crime" defendants in state court and he could afford to charge smaller fees than other lawyers with a similar practice, because he and his two associates worked economically. They limited their pre-trial interviews of the state's witnesses to those cases in which they thought there was a reasonable chance of proceeding to trial. Even then, they tended to conduct the witness interviews themselves, rather than hire an investigator, and they kept them short. They retained expert witnesses less frequently than some of the other lawyers in town and they chose not to file pre-trial motions unless they thought they would have a significant bearing on the outcome of a case.

On those occasions in which Mahoney was unable to arrange a plea bargain for a client, he usually sought an additional fee to prepare and try the case, just as most other criminal defense attorneys would do. Unlike some other lawyers, however, Mahoney did not often withdraw from representing a client who was unable to pay the additional fee for taking a case to trial. He was loath to abandon a client. Hence, when he entered a case, he usually committed himself to seeing it through to its conclusion. This meant that his hourly compensation for cases resulting in jury trials could be abysmally low, which he accepted as an inevitable risk of practice, one that was offset by the higher return he received when clients pled guilty.

Mahoney also understood that the State could prove most of his clients guilty and that indeed a majority of them were in fact guilty. When a client insisted on going to trial, he acceded to the client's wishes. However, if he viewed a plea bargain offered by the state as more favorable than the likely outcome of a trial—a prevalent circumstance—he could be highly persuasive in explaining the realities of a client's options. Mahoney felt that he always acted in his clients' best interests, even when he pushed them toward accepting plea bargains they did not like. Although Mahoney was less likely than some other lawyers to engage in exhaustive investigations before entering a plea agreement, he was confident that he had a good eye for the strengths and weaknesses of a case and that he knew how to get generous offers from prosecutors.

After his initial interview of Steve Schilling, Mahoney believed that the case against Schilling would probably not go to trial.

Schilling's version of the events suggested two threads of defense: that he had legal justification for his use of force and that Hart's injuries were sustained after he had left the house. If Hart was the initial aggressor in the struggle for the gun, Schilling had a right to defend himself during the scuffle. Additionally, an argument could be made that Schilling would be justified in holding Hart at gunpoint, at least briefly, either to prevent a felony from occurring or to detain a dangerous felon until the police arrived. If the state had no evidence that Schilling was present during the beating, aside from Hart's testimony, it would come down to a credibility contest. Schilling assured Mahoney that he had witnesses to corroborate his account. Brenda Chase was present during the initial events and one of the three men who showed up later—Schilling's friend James—would be available to testify about the events that occurred after Chase left the house.

Nevertheless, there were good reasons to make the lawyer skeptical that a jury would be sympathetic toward Schilling. Hart apparently had been severely beaten, tied up and thrown into a trunk, indicating that his assailants intended to kill him. Additionally, certain aspects of Schilling's story did not add up.

Why hadn't Schilling called the police when he discovered the theft on June 25? Mahoney assumed that Schilling's home actually had been burglarized, but he suspected that Schilling's true reasons for not reporting it were less than exemplary, possibly because the principal item taken had been drugs. Even if the theft involved a valuable coin collection, Mahoney speculated that the coins might already have been stolen. Schilling called his business Anything Goes and he described it to Mahoney as buying and selling "pre-owned merchandise." He operated the business from his house and kept most of his inventory in a storage locker three miles away. He said that he kept no business records, preferring to pay for goods either with cash or other used merchandise and he frequently kept $1000 to $1500 in currency on hand to buy things that people brought to his house. It was possible that Schilling was dealing in stolen property.

If Mahoney was skeptical, a jury might be too, and Schilling probably would not come across as a credible witness. When Schilling testified, the prosecutor would be allowed to inform the jury that he had a prior felony conviction. Even if he wore a tie and jacket during the trial, it would be difficult to prevent jurors from stereotyping him as a "biker," an image that would not sit well with a group of conservative citizens. Moreover, Schilling's protestation of self defense sounded hollow. If Hart was the initial aggressor in the confrontation, why did Schilling have a loaded gun sitting on top of his desk?

On the other hand, this man was entitled to counsel and there were reasons to believe that the prosecution would be highly anxious to settle the case and might offer a sweet plea bargain to make it disappear. From Schilling's account, it appeared that Hart, like Schilling, had a felony record, a fact that could be brought to the jury's attention. Prosecutors frequently found witnesses with Hart's apparent lifestyle to be highly uncooperative, and he might not even show up for trial. Even if he did, the jury would probably not like Hart any more than Schilling. It would likely be a credibility contest with neither side's star witness looking good.

Regardless of the strength of the state's case at trial, Mahoney believed that the prosecutor might be persuaded to cut a reasonably good deal for Schilling. Although Hart didn't "deserve" to be roughed up by Schilling's friends, his egregious conduct had likely provoked the beating and this might lessen the prosecutor's desire to hammer Schilling.

Schilling and Mahoney negotiated a fee. According to Mahoney's notes, they settled on $6,000, which included a desktop computer for Mahoney's office. The bar's code of ethics permitted lawyers to accept property as payment for services, but cautioned against this practice because of potential disputes over the value of the property. Indeed, Schilling insisted that he had paid a $10,000 fee to his lawyer. Although the code of ethics recommended written fee agreements, they were not mandatory. Mahoney did not ask Schilling to sign a formal agreement as to the fee. This would prove to be a mistake.

Chapter 9

Wheeling and Dealing

I would spend much of my first month as a prosecutor at one or another of the county's twenty-three justice courts. Most days, my assignment would be to conduct preliminary hearings in felony cases, usually during the afternoon, allowing me to spend the morning in the office preparing. When I was lucky, I would be responsible for only five or six cases a day, but sometimes I would be given as many as ten to handle and on a few days I had twelve. Each case file included charging documents, one or more police reports (sometimes with as many as thirty single-spaced pages), hand-written notes from other prosecutors and the defendant's criminal history records. I never felt ready when I went to court.

Some of the defendants faced lengthy prison sentences. A competent and experienced lawyer at a private law firm representing business clients would never participate in a significant courtroom hearing without carefully scrutinizing each document in advance. These attorneys would probably take weeks to prepare for evidentiary hearings in five separate cases and the notion of taking on ten to twelve in one afternoon would be completely absurd.

Moreover, sometimes I was assigned to an afternoon calendar one day and a morning calendar the next. This meant that I had to work late into the night to prepare before going to court. Some of my colleagues refused to do this, as government lawyers who were paid far less than most attorneys in private practice; they did not feel compelled to remain in the office past 5:00. Instead, they tried to "wing it" at the preliminary hearings, no more prepared than the indigent defendants' lawyers, public defenders who had to read the police reports and introduce themselves to their clients minutes before entering the courtroom.

Preliminary hearings took place in justice courts, which, along with city magistrate courts, were the lowest rung on the state's judicial ladder. Each justice court was headed by an elected justice of the peace. The courts of many justices of the peace, known informally as JPs, were like fiefdoms. In addition to felony preliminary hearings, the justices of the peace were processing traffic citations, small civil cases and misdemeanor prosecutions on an assembly-line basis. Several hundred litigants were herded through a typical justice court each week, allowing little time for careful consideration of individual cases. Many JPs were not lawyers and some had little or no familiarity with the rules of evidence that governed court trials, instead following their own informal practices.

The justice courts were also plagued by mismanagement, ineptitude, inexperience and even corruption.

Some of the JPs worked only part-time, despite receiving full-time salaries, improperly delegating their judicial responsibilities to court clerks. Others ignored regular court business to conduct mid-day wedding ceremonies for which they were compensated privately, in violation of the code of judicial conduct. One justice of the peace resigned after the state's commission on judicial conduct found that he had made racist remarks in court and was intolerant, sarcastic and patronizing toward defendants. Another pled guilty to federal charges of fraud and conspiracy, receiving a sentence of thirty months in prison. The state's supreme court removed a third JP from office for habitual tardiness, circulating racist and obscene materials and engaging in improper communications with litigants and attorneys. Yet another JP routinely brought one or two large dogs to work. The animals urinated and defecated in the courthouse.

This would be the world in which I would prosecute my first preliminary hearings.

In most states, the preliminary hearing, often called the "prelim," is the first major step in a felony prosecution after the defendant has been charged. The official purpose of this hearing is for a supposedly neutral fact-finder, usually a lower court magistrate or justice of the peace, to screen the prosecution's charges to determine if there is sufficient evidence—probable cause—to bring the case to trial. Historically, this was a role played by grand juries, to protect citizens accused of crime from having to defend themselves against unfounded allegations. Grand juries are still used in many locales, either as an alternative to preliminary hearings or as an additional stage for screening prosecutions, but prelims have become the most common way to screen cases today.

On the surface, a preliminary hearing resembles a mini-trial. The defendant has a constitutional right to be represented by a lawyer, who can cross-examine the prosecution's witnesses and present defense evidence. In reality, however, there is little scrutiny of the state's case, primarily because hearsay evidence is admissible, allowing witnesses to testify even if they have no first-hand knowledge of the facts of an alleged crime. At my prelims, the victim never testified. The sole witness would be a police officer, who would read the police reports before the hearing, then would testify to what the other witnesses would say if they were present, allowing me to "hearsay in" all the evidence necessary to send each case to the superior court for trial.

A similar use of hearsay evidence at preliminary hearings is common in most states. It is a highly economical approach to testing the sufficiency of the prosecution's evidence, since most of the state's witnesses do not need to take the time to come to court. Prosecutors can shield crime victims and eyewitnesses from having to submit to cross-examination, thereby minimizing defense counsel's ability to use the proceeding to ferret out potential weaknesses in the state's case and to uncover evidence that may be favorable to the accused. However, this wholesale use of hearsay evidence also minimizes the important screening function that grand juries historically served and preliminary hearings are supposed to serve today. Cases are rarely thrown out at this stage.

Prosecutors in Arizona can choose between a grand jury and a preliminary hearing in each case. During my tenure, the County Attorney's Office submitted most major felonies—such as homicides, sex crimes, gang-related offenses and white collar crimes—to grand juries. However, routine felony prosecutions, roughly seventy percent of the agency's cases, were normally sent to the justice courts for preliminary hearings. The defendants in these cases were charged with such crimes as burglary, car theft, possession of small amounts of illegal drugs, possession of a firearm by a felon, driving under the influence of alcohol at a time when the defendant's license was suspended and credit card fraud. The chief advantage of the preliminary hearing in these cases, from the prosecution's perspective, was that it brought a defense lawyer into the case at the first possible juncture. This provided an early opportunity to negotiate plea bargains, weeding cases out of the criminal justice system at the outset.

Thirty-five preliminary hearings were scheduled on the afternoon calendar at the East Phoenix No. 1 Justice Court on the first day I went to that court. I took a deep breath and let it out slowly when I learned that nine of the cases were to be mine. The files showed that most of the defendants in my cases were unemployed, with transient lifestyles and drug or alcohol addictions. For some, this would be their only brush with the criminal justice system and they wanted to get it over with as quickly as possible. Others went through the system on a revolving door basis, getting probation for a first conviction, a term in the county jail on the second, and finally, state prison for a third offense.

I arrived at the office at 6:30 that morning, armed with a thermos of coffee and two glazed donuts, determined to be ready to present my evidence in all nine of the cases, making sure that an officer had been subpoenaed in each instance and that I could prove every element of each charge through the officer's testimony. I soon learned that in one case the arresting officer was on vacation and I had to scramble to find another witness to testify in his place. I struggled to decipher the computer-generated reports of the defendants' criminal history records, known as "rap sheets." In several of my cases, the rap sheets included incomplete information and ambiguously coded entries and I needed other prosecutors to help me determine if prior convictions could be used in court to lengthen the defendant's sentence. I called the crime laboratory in connection with three of my cases to ascertain if tests had been conducted on physical evidence. I also determined the plea bargaining offers I would make in each case, discussed my proposed plea bargains with the crime victims on the telephone and drafted plea agreements that public defenders could sell to their clients.

Although I spent much of the morning readying myself to present evidence in the nine cases, my preparation of plea agreements was far more important to the agency. Indeed, my primary role that afternoon was to strike deals in as many of my cases as possible to get them out of the system at the earliest possible stage, thereby preserving limited prosecutorial resources for more pressing cases, particularly those that were more likely to go to trial. I thought it rather satirical that the success of the four prosecutors assigned to the East Phoenix No. 1 Justice Court that afternoon would be defined largely by the number of cases we could get rid of. One of my mentors at the County Attorney's Office called it "down and dirty justice." It was a phrase that stuck in my mind.

Our supervisors had instructed us on how to make "bargain basement" offers. These induced defendants to waive all their trial rights and plead guilty to felony charges. In each case, the sentence called for in the plea bargain was to be substantially less severe than the sentence the defendant would receive if convicted at trial. This required us to stipulate in many of our cases that the defendant would be placed on probation. When a prison sentence was required under the County Attorney's policies, we would offer a plea bargain that shortened the term the defendant would have to serve. Many of the high pressure sales tactics used were reminiscent of those employed by automobile dealers to move cars off their lots as quickly as possible. For example, we would communicate to the defense that the offer would be available for only one day and we would make clear to the defendant that the prosecution would never give him a better deal in later stages of the case.

That afternoon, a bit nervous but determined, I passed through the metal detector at the entry to the East Phoenix No. 1 Justice Court at 12:50 P.M., ten minutes before the court's calendar was to begin. The building appeared to be almost empty and when one of the two security guards at the front door called to a friend passing by on the sidewalk, his words echoed through the cavernous lobby. East Phoenix No. 1, along with the Central Phoenix Justice Court, was housed in an old brick building on the fringe of the downtown area, two blocks from the Madison Street Jail. The justice court complex consisted of three unadorned courtrooms with modest judicial chambers, two tiny offices for prosecutors and public defenders to use, a large open room for each court's administrative personnel, and a spacious central corridor.

In addition to the thirty-five felony preliminary hearings scheduled that afternoon at East Phoenix No. 1, a jury trial was in progress across the hall. Minutes after my arrival, participants in all of these proceedings began to fill the central corridor. By 1:15 the front half of the building took on the appearance of a three-ring circus, since the doors to the individual courtrooms remained locked. Prosecutors and defense lawyers for the thirty-six cases mingled with the defendants and their accompanying family and friends, as well as a small army of police officers subpoenaed to appear at the preliminary hearings, crime victims from many of the cases, volunteers who were present to assist the victims, jurors and witnesses participating in the trial across the corridor, English interpreters for some of the defendants and witnesses and other court personnel. It was a sea of humanity.

The four prosecutors assigned that afternoon to handle the preliminary hearings shared an eight by ten foot room that opened directly onto the central corridor, near the metal detector at the front of the building. Three of us had completed the county attorney's training program a few weeks earlier, while the fourth had barely two months experience. Our supervisor had an appointment that afternoon and would not be able to join us until after 3:00. It was just as well, since a fifth person in the tiny room would have made our game of musical chairs that much more difficult. Only one small desk and three chairs could fit in the room and the four of us had to share the sole telephone on the desk, along with several of the police officers subpoenaed to testify in our preliminary hearings.

When the clock on our wall indicated that it was 1:30 P.M.—thirty minutes past the scheduled start of the afternoon calendar—the bailiffs for the two justice courts had still not opened their respective courtroom doors. Waves of people flowed into our office. Many of the first arrivals were police officers and it became increasingly confusing as we tried to ascertain which officers were subpoenaed for which of the thirty-five cases. Those officers summoned to testify about incidents occurring within the previous few weeks were generally familiar with the facts of their cases, but others had been subpoenaed for cases involving crimes that had occurred twelve to eighteen months earlier. Most of these overworked officers remembered little or nothing about the long past cases we were now prosecuting until we refreshed their memories with the reports they had written at the time of the incidents.

I tried to meet with the officers in my cases, but it was difficult to communicate since my three colleagues were talking at the same time with their own witnesses and attempting to use the telephone. Several bewildered crime victims and criminal defendants wandered by, asking where they were supposed to go and what they were to do when they arrived there. The public defenders assigned to handle the afternoon's cases also came by, asking for copies of the police reports and inquiring about the plea offers we were making in their cases. Chaos reigned.

In court that afternoon, I met Juan Pacos and Maria Gomez, who were charged in one of my cases with automobile burglary and theft, both relatively minor felony offenses. The victims in the case were two fifteen-year-old girls and a sixteen-year-old boy who had parked their car by an irrigation canal in Phoenix on a steamy July evening to go swimming after consuming a few cans from a twelve pack of beer. The teenagers made the foolish mistake of throwing off their clothes and diving into the canal without locking their car. A few minutes later, Mr. Pacos and Ms. Gomez parked their pick-up truck nearby, noticed the unlocked car, and found the remainder of the beer inside a cooler on the back seat. Ms. Gomez took the boom box next to the cooler and the two defendants made off with the teenagers' backpacks, CDs, cash, camera and clothing. Twenty minutes later they were arrested, when a witness saw Ms. Gomez perform a strip tease on the hood of the truck while Mr. Pacos sat on the front seat, drinking the victims' beer, with the stolen property on the floor by his feet.

Mr. Pacos had a prior felony conviction and was in custody on the day of the preliminary hearing, represented by an attorney from the public defender's office. Ms. Gomez, who had no prior record, had been released on her own recognizance and had a court appointed lawyer with her in court.

The County Attorney's standard plea agreement at the preliminary hearing of a run-of-the-mill case like this called for a different offer to be made to each defendant. We told Ms. Gomez if she pled guilty to the theft charge, she would be guaranteed probation, with the opportunity for the crime to be reduced to a misdemeanor if she successfully completed her

probation. Some defendants who accepted such an offer did in fact successfully complete probation and had their offense reduced to a misdemeanor
at that time. Many others—especially those addicted to drugs—committed new crimes while on probation, and instead of their first conviction
being reduced to a misdemeanor, it served as a prior felony conviction
when they were charged with a new offense. As a result, they received less
advantageous plea offers when they re-entered the court system.

That is exactly what happened to Mr. Pacos, who had been
through the system once before. As we had to Ms. Gomez, we offered
probation if he pled guilty at the preliminary hearing, but his plea had
to be to the burglary offense, the more serious allegation, and he was
not given an opportunity for his charge to be reduced to a misdemeanor if he successfully completed probation. Although this restriction meant that Mr. Pacos would now have two felony convictions on
his record, his alternative to accepting the deal was far worse. If he
refused the prosecution's offer and went to trial, his prospect for an
acquittal was very slim. Moreover, if he was found guilty at trial, the
court would be required to sentence him as a repeat offender. He
would not be eligible for probation and instead would face a mandatory prison sentence with a presumptive term of four and a half years.

As a result, both Ms. Gomez and Mr. Pacos had strong incen-
tives to accept the plea bargains that were offered to them. I dutifully
informed their respective attorneys "The terms I am offering will only
be available this afternoon; a better deal will never be on the table."

Juan Pacos had never met his public defender, Barbara Hanley,
before that afternoon. Hanley represented four of the defendants on the
court's calendar and she'd had no opportunity to read the police reports
until I handed them to her at 1:20 P.M. Although it had taken me two
hours that morning to analyze the facts and legal issues in her four cases,
Hanley had to quickly scan all the reports, introduce herself to each of
her clients (three of whom were in custody, in a small holding cell behind
the courtroom), discuss the state's evidence in each of their respective
cases, ask them for a brief account of their version of the facts, explain the
plea offers and convince them that accepting the state's deal was in their
best interest, because the offers would be withdrawn at the end of the
afternoon and better ones would not be forthcoming.

Mr. Pacos balked at his plea agreement, telling Hanley, "It's not as good as Maria's, and the theft was her idea." I sensed that he was highly suspicious of Hanley, who was: (1) a woman; (2) not Latino; (3) employed by the county ("just like the prosecutor"); and (4) seemingly anxious to persuade him and the other two defendants in the holding cell to plead guilty. The three men talked together in Spanish and did not believe that their public defender was looking after their interests. Mr. Pacos was particularly upset when Hanley informed him that the judge was likely to sentence him to several months in the county jail as a condition of probation and it rankled him that he would now have a second felony conviction on his record, while Ms. Gomez could end up with none.

Nevertheless, after several rounds of negotiation with his lawyer, Juan Pacos begrudgingly accepted the deal.

The prosecution's strategy of making its best offer available for only one day presented a serious dilemma for the defendant in another of my cases, Teddy Baker, who was charged with being a felon in possession of a gun. Baker and his girlfriend had been driving on a major artery in Phoenix, when two police gang squad detectives pulled them over for having no mud flaps on their car. According to the police report, a second reason for the stop was that Baker had made a "wide right turn" a few minutes earlier. Although the detectives' interest in stopping the car was to look for evidence relating to street gangs and their normal responsibilities did not include traffic code enforcement, they had the authority as police officers to stop cars for such violations.

When the detectives questioned Baker and his girlfriend, they found no basis to connect them with any street gangs, but they saw a holstered pistol in "plain view" in the car. One of the detectives then ran a record check on Baker and discovered that he had been convicted of theft, a relatively minor felony, a few years earlier. Carrying a holstered gun is lawful in Arizona, but not if the possessor has a felony record. The detectives arrested Baker for this offense even though he claimed that someone else owned the gun. The county attorney's charging bureau decided to file the charge in court, since "possession" is a much broader legal term than "ownership." Regardless of who owned the gun, the prosecutor charging the case had determined that there was a substantial amount of circumstantial evidence to show who *possessed* it. As the driver, Baker was in control of the car and he had ready access to both the holster and the pistol.

The county attorney's plea bargaining policy relating to guns limited my discretion in this case. It precluded me from offering a plea bargain that reduced the charge against Baker to a lesser offense and it required a stipulation that Baker had to be sentenced to state prison. The presumptive prison term for a felon in possession of a gun was two and a half years, a stiff penalty for a crime that consisted of driving with a holstered gun in one's car, especially in a state that normally allowed its citizens to go about freely with loaded firearms, even concealed ones.

Sam Roberts, Baker's lawyer, was livid, angered by both the detectives' conduct and my offer. He castigated the cops for pulling his client over, as well as their assertion that the gun was in plain view, and he expressed confidence that the superior court would grant his pre-trial motion to suppress the gun from evidence, on the ground that the police had violated his client's rights under the Fourth Amendment. He also argued that the case "reeked of reasonable doubt," since the jury would not be convinced either that Baker knew the gun was present in the car or that it was within his personal control. He scolded me, saying, "It's an outrageous offer. You ought to review the case with your supervisor."

However, I had already done that in the morning and had been instructed that the plea bargaining policy was strictly enforced, with exceptions permitted only in "extraordinary circumstances." According to my supervisor, there was nothing extraordinary about Teddy Baker's case. If anything, it was routine. The best deal I could offer was an agreement that allowed the court to impose a mitigated prison sentence, with the possibility of Baker serving only a year in custody.

I reminded Roberts that the deal had to be accepted or declined that day. Baker would have to choose between accepting the prosecution's best offer for a plea bargain or gambling later in superior court. His motion to suppress evidence involved questions of federal constitutional law and it could not be made at the preliminary hearing before a justice of the peace. The police report was written in such a way that the detectives' conduct appeared, on its face, to be acceptable under the case law. The seizure of the gun might not hold up at a full evidentiary hearing in superior court, but the courts usually ruled that an officer's hidden agenda for pulling a car over was irrelevant if he spotted a violation of the state's traffic laws, no matter how minor. The reasonable doubt issues were also highly speculative. "A jury might not believe Baker, a convicted felon, if he testifies that he did not know there was a gun in the car or that it was not under his control," I pointed out. "Additionally, Baker will be exposed to a possible sentence of seven and a half years in prison if he is found guilty at trial and the absolute minimum the court could impose will be four and a half years."

Just as Juan Pacos had done a short while earlier, Teddy Baker decided to plead guilty. Despite Roberts' belief in the weakness of the state's case, his motion to test the unconstitutionality of the search and seizure would never be litigated and there would be no jury trial. It left me with a hollow feeling.

By 5:00 P.M., my colleagues and I had managed to work our way through all but two of the thirty-five cases we'd been assigned. We negotiated guilty pleas in almost half and in several others the defendants waived their right to a preliminary hearing, agreeing instead to send their cases directly to the superior court without formal findings of probable cause. A few cases were dismissed because of the unavailability of prosecution witnesses and two preliminary hearings were postponed with the defendant's consent to enable prosecution witnesses to be present. Four of the defendants failed to appear in court, causing the justice of the peace to issue warrants for their arrest. The defense requested probable cause hearings in only two cases and these were the two that remained on the court's calendar. One of them was mine.

In this case, the defendant, John Kinsey, was charged with driving under the influence of alcohol. Although DWI was normally considered a misdemeanor, the County Attorney's Office had filed this case as a felony because Mr. Kinsey's privilege to drive had already been suspended for a previous DWI conviction. In fact, Mr. Kinsey had three prior DWI convictions.

I didn't know Kinsey's privately retained counsel, Brian Perkins, who was not in court at 1:00, the scheduled time for Kinsey's preliminary hearing. Both Mr. Kinsey and Bob Johnson, the arresting officer, had arrived on time, and Johnson was anxious to get the hearing concluded as soon as possible, because he was off duty and needed to go home to babysit his children at 2:30. When Perkins had not arrived by 2:00, I asked Johnson for his home telephone number and sent him on his way, with the understanding that he would have to return if we needed him to testify later in the afternoon. I was more than perturbed when Perkins appeared in court almost two hours late, but the justice of the peace said nothing to the lawyer about his tardiness.

Perkins asked for a plea agreement reducing his client's charge to a misdemeanor, contending that the state had never notified Mr. Kinsey before the current offense that his driving privileges had been revoked. I would not agree to this reduction, because Kinsey had a poor driving history and the motor vehicle department's records indicated that the revocation notice had been sent to him by certified mail. I offered the standard plea bargain in felony DWI cases: four months incarceration in state prison as a condition of supervised probation. My supervisors had told me that many defendants in this situation turned this offer down, since they were likely to get the same sentence if convicted at trial. Felony DWI was one of the few offenses for which we did not have substantial leverage to induce guilty pleas at the preliminary hearing stage.

So I wasn't surprised when Mr. Kinsey rejected my offer. His lawyer asked to proceed with the preliminary hearing when he learned that my witness had gone home. At 3:45 P.M., I called Officer Johnson, who reluctantly agreed to return to court to testify.

Although the preliminary hearing went smoothly, it was not completed until 6:15 P.M., because Perkins cross-examined Johnson at length on each of the field sobriety tests the officer had administered to Kinsey at the scene of the traffic stop. The cross-examination clearly was not intended to demonstrate that the state lacked probable cause to send the case to superior court, but instead to obtain an in-depth discovery of the prosecution's case and to pin Johnson down on a specific version of the facts, looking for inconsistencies that could be seized upon if the case proceeded to trial. It was a thorough and well conducted cross-examination, but it was long. Eventually, however, the testimony concluded and the justice of the peace found probable cause, sending the case to superior court.

Wearily I trudged to my car. It was 6:30 P.M. and I was happy to be heading home. I still had to complete the necessary paperwork on my nine cases, but that could wait until the morning.

Chapter 10

Hidden Power

July 6, 1994

Two days after Steve Schilling's arrest, the police submitted his case to the Maricopa County Attorney's charging bureau. A prosecutor with extensive experience in civil practice, Pat Harlin, who worked at the charging bureau, was given the case. Although filing charges to initiate prosecutions could not match the excitement of jury trials, Harlin enjoyed the respite from the pressure and hectic pace of his previous assignment in the agency's homicide bureau. Harlin now spent one day each week presenting cases to the grand jury. However, most days, like this one, he sat quietly at his desk, sipping coffee and reading police reports in preparation for making charging decisions.

Determining whether to file charges can be challenging and is more cerebral than almost all other prosecutorial responsibilities, reminding Harlin of his law school classes, when professors would spin out fine-tuned hypothetical questions that always seemed to fall between the cracks in the law. In the same fashion, Harlin and the other attorneys in the charging bureau had to analyze the fact scenarios presented in police reports to determine which crime definitions, if any, they fit. This could not be done without a thorough knowledge of both substantive criminal law and the rules governing the admissibility of evidence in court. Equally important, charging cases required a sound practical understanding of how juries react to different types of witnesses and evidence. Most people felt Harlin, a seasoned prosecutor, had a good eye for the strengths and weaknesses of a case.

Although few people outside the agency were familiar with the county attorney's charging bureau, Harlin and his colleagues had enormous power. When initiating a felony prosecution, they threatened or took away a defendant's liberty, frequently draining his or her family's emotional and financial resources. The costs of defending a felony charge could be devastating, even if a defendant was later acquitted or the case dismissed. On the other hand, when Harlin decided not to proceed with a case, his decision could crush or anger the victim of the crime.

Despite this discretionary power, charging decisions were rarely, if ever, subjected to meaningful review outside the prosecution agency. When Harlin or one of his colleagues charged a person with a crime, the law required very little evidence to support the decision; the courts would sustain the charge if there was a mere probable cause to believe that the defendant had committed the offense. While not a precisely defined term, probable cause obviously required far less certainty of the defendant's guilt than proof beyond a reasonable doubt, the requirement for a conviction at trial. As a practical matter, the courts interpreted the probable cause standard liberally, not wanting to interfere with prosecutors' decisions, except in the most extraordinary circumstances. If the County Attorney's Office filed a charge, the defendant had to answer it.

Similarly, when the charging bureau declined to prosecute a case submitted by the police, neither the crime victim nor the officer who referred the case had legal recourse to reverse the decision. Courts in the United States, unlike those in many other countries, have always refused to second-guess prosecutorial discretion in turning down cases, regardless of the strength of the evidence against the accused. Under the constitutional separation-of-powers doctrine, only prosecutors can initiate the criminal process. And while the Maricopa County Attorney's Office policy manual allowed disgruntled police officers to pursue informal appeals within the prosecutor's office when a case was turned down, this rarely resulted in a reversal of the decision.

Harlin's charging decisions sometimes resulted in tension between the County Attorney's Office and the many law enforcement agencies that submitted cases to it for prosecution. Although prosecutors in the county attorney's major felony division worked closely with the police in investigating and prosecuting such crimes as homicides and sex offenses, these represented a very small percentage of the county attorney's caseload. The vast majority of prosecutions were routine criminal cases in which the police and prosecution agencies served independent and sometimes conflicting functions. And because of these differences, the attorneys in the charging bureau often were caught in the crossfire between police investigators who were eager for their cases to be prosecuted and the county attorney's trial lawyers and administrators, who wanted to avoid messy trials.

The conflict reflected a fundamental difference between the goals of police and prosecutors. Law enforcement agencies normally considered their work on a case to be complete when it was "cleared." This occurred when the police investigator assigned to the case identified the offender, typically submitting the police reports to the prosecutor's office with a request for charges to be filed in court. Police agencies defined their success by the percentage of cases they could clear; a crime cleared was a crime solved. From a law enforcement perspective, it was important to clear cases as quickly as possible, to free up limited resources for other matters. Lengthy investigations in routine felony cases were costly and unusual. As a result, police investigators cringed whenever prosecutors returned already cleared cases to them with a request for further investigations to be conducted before formal charges were filed.

On the other hand, the County Attorney's Office had to meet the rigorous legal standard of proving guilt beyond a reasonable doubt in order to convict a defendant, a requirement that profoundly impacted the processing of cases. The stronger the evidence the state could muster in a case, the more likely it would be resolved expeditiously by a guilty plea. Conversely, the more doubt that existed regarding a defendant's guilt, the greater the probability that the defense would vigorously contest the case, with more time and money spent on pre-trial witness interviews, motions to suppress evidence, expert witnesses and jury trials. Prosecutors in the agency's trial division could more easily manage large caseloads with small percentages of seriously contested cases than they could handle small caseloads filled with cases that proceeded to trial. Even just a few hotly contested cases were likely to cause scheduling nightmares for a trial prosecutor. Thus, the county attorney's policy manual cautioned the charging bureau to turn down risky cases, to "assure an efficient use of our limited resources."

The policy manual set forth detailed rules for charging cases, to minimize the chance that Harlin and his colleagues would make bad decisions. The most important of these was a strict prohibition against initiating a prosecution in the absence of a "reasonable likelihood of conviction." Although the courts permitted prosecutors to file charges based on the lesser standard of probable cause, the County Attorney's Office, like most other prosecution agencies, adhered to a far more restrictive test. The "reasonable likelihood of conviction" standard permitted prosecutors like Harlin to initiate a case only if the available evidence provided assurance that the state could prove the defendant's guilt at trial, beyond a reasonable doubt.

The policy manual also required Harlin to take several steps to implement the "reasonable likelihood of conviction" rule. First, it instructed him to examine the police reports on a purely technical level to determine if sufficient evidence could be produced in court to establish each essential fact. Second, he had to assess each witness's credibility, availability and willingness to testify if the case were to proceed to trial. If doubts on these questions could not be resolved satisfactorily, the manual instructed him to reject the case, even when the police reports seemed on their face to support a conviction. Finally, it told him to determine if the case had sufficient "jury appeal" to justify going forward, boldly cautioning: "DO NOT BE AFRAID TO TURN DOWN A CASE WHEN IT IS APPROPRIATE."

The County Attorney's Office's policy of turning down high-risk prosecutions reflected two considerations. The first was a concern for efficiency, avoiding the costs and administrative headaches associated with contested cases. The other, according to some courthouse observers, was political. Since the county attorney was a locally elected official, high conviction rates would demonstrate to the voters every four years that he was doing his job well. The county attorney, Rick Romley, had a website that boasted that his agency's percentage of convictions exceeded the national average for several consecutive years. It made no political sense to charge cases that did not ultimately result in convictions. The county attorney could not afford to lose too many cases.

Other than homicides, some sex offenses, major drug busts and crimes in which the victim or defendant was a celebrity, individual cases generally were not reported in the news media. As a result, there was rarely any negative publicity when the County Attorney's Office refused to file charges in connection with routine, low-profile street crimes, even those involving serious injury. What could be politically troublesome for the county attorney in routine cases was not a refusal to file charges, but instead the risk that a significant percentage resulted in either an acquittal or a dismissal. The need to drive up aggregate conviction rates translated into a policy of rejecting prosecutions when the evidence was a little shaky—or the facts lacked "jury appeal."

Thus, a combination of economic and political forces caused the charging bureau to decline prosecution in many of the cases the police submitted and to send others back for further investigation. Filing charges in cases unlikely to result in conviction was a path to professional oblivion in the County Attorney's Office. Most years, the county attorney had not proceeded with felony charges in 50 percent of police submittals. Although the police believed they had sufficient evidence of a crime to support a felony prosecution, the prosecutor's office disagreed. Not surprisingly, within the ranks of law enforcement agencies there was a great deal of resentment.

Like most other Americans, Pat Harlin grew up embracing the theory that a criminal defendant's guilt or innocence was to be determined in court by a jury of his peers. Harlin's law school instructors taught him that defense lawyers and "not guilty" verdicts were the citizenry's principal protections against over-zealous prosecutors. But he discovered that, sitting alone in his office searching police reports for reasonable doubt, he absolved more accused persons than all the juries in the county. He stopped dozens and dozens of cases from going forward when he questioned a confession or a search and seizure, many more cases than the most heralded of defense lawyers. Still, almost no one knew his name.

On a typical day, Harlin had at least ten case submittals to review and usually many more after a long holiday weekend. The submittals were placed in two piles. One consisted of "in-custody" cases, those requiring immediate attention, because the persons accused by the police were detained in jail awaiting his charging decision. If he did not file a felony complaint within two days after a defendant's initial appearance in jail court, the defendant was to be released from custody immediately. The second group consisted of "basket" cases, or cases in which the accused person was not incarcerated. There was no deadline for making charging decisions in these cases. They sat in baskets in the charging bureau until prosecutors had sufficient time to attend to them. Some of the prosecutors reviewed their basket cases whenever they had lulls in their schedule, but others allowed them to collect dust on their desks.

Harlin could quickly dispose of the in-custody submittals when they included only a short police report prepared by the arresting officer. However, on July 6, the Phoenix Police Department submitted an in-custody case with more than sixty pages of police reports to digest. The case agent in the Schilling matter had requested the county attorney to charge Schilling with kidnapping, aggravated assault and drug trafficking, all major felonies. The submittal did not inform Harlin that Schilling had posted bond, obtaining his freedom a few hours after his initial appearance at the jail court. Thus, although Schilling's file appeared in Harlin's in-custody pile, there really was no urgency in charging the case.

This oversight would prove to be significant, because a substantial amount of investigation needed to be completed in Schilling's case. Once the county attorney charged a defendant, the trial prosecutor often found it difficult to light a fire under the police department's case agent to conduct the investigations necessary to bring the case to trial successfully. As a result, the County Attorney's Office sometimes completed these investigations at its own expense and on other occasions they were simply not undertaken. However, if a suspect was not in custody, Harlin was more likely to send a case back to the police agency that had submitted it, requesting further investigation by the police before the County Attorney's Office would charge it.

In the Schilling matter, no one had interviewed a key eye-witness, Schilling's girlfriend, Brenda Chase, to learn if she corroborated the victim's version of the events or if she could and would identify the three persons who participated in the crimes with Schilling. Latent fingerprints lifted at the crime scene had not been compared to the known prints of the victim, the defendant and other possible suspects in the case. Blood samples were yet to be analyzed at the crime lab and compared with the victim's and defendant's blood types. Nor had the drugs found in the computer in Schilling's study been examined at the crime laboratory.

Harlin decided to file felony charges against Schilling on the kidnapping and aggravated assault allegations. The submittal met the reasonable likelihood of conviction test for several reasons. First, Hart had obviously been tied up and beaten severely. Unlike some crime victims, he was willing to cooperate with the prosecution and there appeared to be substantial physical evidence to corroborate his version of the facts. A self defense claim seemed unlikely to succeed, since Hart had wounds all over his body, while the police reports did not indicate that Schilling had been injured at all. Sending an in-custody case back to the police for further investigation normally meant that the suspect would be released from custody. Unaware that Schilling had already posted bond, Harlin went ahead with the charges.

However, Harlin did not file the requested drug trafficking charge, despite the fact that the police had found what appeared to be an illicit substance in the computer in Schilling's house. Although the detectives conducting the search assumed the substance was methamphetamine, the crime laboratory had yet to determine whether this was true. The quantity of the substance was insufficient to raise a strong inference that it had been possessed for sale, rather than personal use, and the police did not find scales, packaging materials or other items indicative of a drug trafficking operation. Moreover, without fingerprints or other evidence connecting Schilling himself to the plastic bag found in the computer, there was a fair possibility that a jury might acquit him of even a simple drug possession charge. In any event, the allegations that Schilling had participated in the assault on Hart were far more serious than a drug charge.

Harlin also had to determine the seriousness of the specific charges to file against Schilling. According to Hart, Schilling had pointed a gun at him, threatening to shoot him if he did not return Schilling's property. Hart also claimed that Schilling had kicked him, hit him with the butt of his gun and participated with others in hog-tying him with duct tape and electrical cord. Each of these acts—pointing a gun at Hart, striking him and binding him—could form the basis for alternative criminal charges with differing penalties upon conviction.

At a minimum, threatening a person with a gun constituted the crime of "assault," a misdemeanor with a maximum sentence of four months in jail. It also fit the definition of several more serious crimes, such as "threatening or intimidating," "endangerment," "disorderly conduct with a deadly weapon," and most importantly, "aggravated assault," a major felony with a maximum punishment of eight years and nine months in prison. Yet another law rendered a defendant ineligible for probation, requiring a prison sentence and enhancing both the minimum and maximum terms that could be imposed, if a felony was "dangerous." For example, a person convicted of a dangerous aggravated assault would face a mandatory prison sentence, with a minimum punishment of five years in prison, and a maximum of fifteen years.

The statutory definitions of all of these crimes, as well as the mandatory prison sentence provision, substantially overlapped. Under the circumstances of Schilling's case, the prosecution's evidence to prove the crime of simple assault would be identical to the evidence necessary to establish a dangerous aggravated assault: merely that Schilling pointed a gun at Hart, intentionally causing Hart to fear for his safety. This overlap would have a substantial impact both on Harlin's initial selection of charges and on subsequent plea bargaining in the case.

Overlapping crime definitions also existed in connection with Hart's assertion that Schilling bound him with duct tape and electrical cord, intending him harm. This conduct could be characterized as "unlawful imprisonment," a felony with a maximum punishment of two years in prison. It also fit the definition of "kidnapping," a major felony with a maximum sentence of twelve and a half years. If the county attorney chose to charge it, a kidnapping allegation could also qualify as a dangerous offense, because Hart claimed that Schilling used a gun to facilitate the crime. This would make a prison sentence mandatory, with a possible range of seven to twenty-one years.

This array of alternatives was not unusual. In most cases that Pat Harlin charged, the suspect's conduct fit more than one statutory crime definition, giving the prosecution the option to choose among several levels of crime, many with mandatory prison sentences, when selecting charges to file in court. In some instances, the County Attorney's Office policies gave Harlin the discretion to make this decision. But Harlin's options were sharply restricted in Schilling's case by a policy that applied to all instances in which a gun was used in the commission of a crime. In such cases, policy required prosecutors to charge the defendant with the most serious crime applicable to the conduct in question and to allege that it was dangerous.

Following the policy, Harlin charged Schilling with three crimes. The first count alleged kidnapping, designated as a dangerous offense, based on Schilling's participation in binding Hart with duct tape and electrical cord. The second count alleged aggravated assault, also designated as a dangerous felony, based on Schilling's pointing a gun at Hart. The third count alleged aggravated assault for breaking two of Hart's bones. It did not include a dangerousness allegation because there was no evidence that Schilling used a gun to cause the fractures.

The county attorney restricted Harlin's charging discretion in gun cases for distinctly pragmatic purposes. By filing dangerousness allegations along with the most serious felony charges applicable to the facts of each case, the county attorney was able to maximize the pressure on defendants to enter plea bargains, rather than take the risk of proceeding to trial. For example, if Steve Schilling was found guilty at trial, the judge would be required to sentence him to at least seven years in prison and could also stack his sentences to over forty years. By offering Schilling a plea bargain that would dismiss counts two and three, as well as the dangerousness allegation in connection with the kidnapping charge, the prosecution could substantially discount his sentence, to as little as three years.

Thus, a defendant in Schilling's circumstances had a strong disincentive to take his chances at trial, even if he believed that he had a reasonable prospect of acquittal. In this way, the county attorney's charging policy used the legislature's mandatory sentencing laws to maximize the state's plea bargaining leverage. Similar approaches were used in conjunction with other mandatory sentencing provisions, such as those requiring enhanced prison sentences for repeat offenders, for crimes committed when an offender was on probation or parole and for crimes committed against children. The strategy was simple: always charge the mandatory sentencing provision when it was available, then offer a plea bargain that substantially discounted (or in rare cases eliminated) the time the defendant had to serve in prison.

Only three to four percent of all felony prosecutions in Maricopa County proceeded to trial most years. This was not unusual for an urban state court system. Nationally, more than ninety percent of all defendants in American criminal courts have pled guilty in the past two decades, usually as a result of plea bargains.

Chapter 11

Rancor's Seeds

Popular culture often shows the prosecutor/defense lawyer relationship as ferociously competitive in the adversarial arena but capable of profound intimacy at the end of the day. In an episode of *The Practice,* a television series that attempts to present the true-to-life concerns and ethical dilemmas of lawyers, Lindsey, a defense attorney, successfully defends a man accused of a grisly murder in which the victim is decapitated. Helen, the prosecutor in the case, is appalled by the defense lawyer's apparent lack of concern about freeing a monster. Nevertheless, in their private celluloid lives, Helen and Lindsey are not only best friends, but also roommates.

This message is not consistent with my real life experience.

When I was a public defender in California, prosecutors and criminal defense attorneys never displayed anything resembling warmth or affection for one another in their private lives. Ours was a different culture, filled with distrust and disdain. It was an article of faith among defense lawyers that assistant district attorneys either would not or could not appreciate the humanity of our clients, their possible innocence and/or the unfortunate circumstances of their lives. Our adversaries disliked us just as much as we did them, frequently complaining of sleazy tactics and cheap tricks. I respected some prosecutors—and admired a few—but I never dreamed of forming friendships with them after work. There was a strong taboo against socializing with the enemy.

Since becoming a prosecutor, I now see that the relationship between prosecutors and defense lawyers has grown much worse, especially among the younger lawyers.

I walked into the office of attractive, dark-haired Lynn Michaels, one of my colleagues at the County Attorney's Office, as she slammed her telephone onto its receiver, abruptly ending a conversation. Rising from her desk, Michaels threw a book onto the top of her file cabinet, screaming, "Harry Barnes is a damn bastard!" "Should I come back later to discuss my case?" I asked quietly, but she insisted that I remain in her office while she vented her frustration. Barnes, a public defender, had filed a motion asking the court to impose sanctions against Michaels. According to the motion, Michaels had accompanied a detective, Evan Klein, to the county jail, where she allowed Klein to question one of Barnes' current clients without his consent.

Michaels was livid, telling me that Barnes' client, a man named Terry Ames, had sent a note to Klein asking for a private meeting with the detective to provide information about a homicide that was totally unrelated to the charges against him. When Klein discussed the note with Michaels, she instructed him not to meet with Ames until she called Barnes, as a professional courtesy, offering him the opportunity to talk with his client before the interview. She tried to reach Barnes, leaving a message on his answering machine, asking him to return her call. However, he either missed or ignored the message. "Now he's making my professional integrity a public issue."

Barnes was a former student of mine who had been popular with his classmates. Though I had not seen much of him since his graduation, we had maintained a cordial friendship and I both liked and respected him. It jarred me to hear him described with epithets such as "asshole," "jerk" and "liar," especially when they were uttered by another person I admired.

Thus far, I had been enjoying my interactions with fellow prosecutors at the County Attorney's Office. At lunch most days we discussed politics, sports, family crises, judges' personalities and upcoming trials. Office banter was clever and contagious. Almost all of my colleagues were interested in my work at the university and legal education in general.

Although my views on politics were generally less conservative than those of most other prosecutors, I respected their opinions and felt comfortable in this environment.

Except when they discussed criminal defense lawyers.

Almost every young prosecutor I encountered had strong enmity for the entire defense bar, deeper and more bitter in connection with private attorneys than public defenders, but applicable to all. Most of the prosecutors expressed that it was a rare defense lawyer who would not bend—and often break—the bar's ethical rules. It did not occur to Michaels that Barnes had merely been doing his job protecting his client, even if it meant misjudging the purpose of the jail interview with detective Klein. In her view, he had deliberately distorted the facts in a devious attempt to get his client off on a technicality, not caring that he smeared her in the process.

And Michaels' tirade was not the only expression of enmity toward adversaries I came across when I re-entered law practice.

One norm at the Maricopa County courthouse was that prosecutors and defense lawyers went to lunch with their own. Even though they frequented the same restaurants in downtown Phoenix and stood behind or in front of one another while waiting to be seated, it was extremely rare for criminal court adversaries to be seen at the same table. As I settled into my job I generally tried to conform to this de facto segregation, but occasionally I could not resist the temptation to dine with friends from the defense bar, hoping my fellow prosecutors understood that I was only temporarily part of their world, with a parallel life in another universe.

Thus, only an hour after listening to Michaels' discourse on her unhappy colloquy with Barnes, I was scheduled for an outing with two defense lawyers, Alan Rogers and Kyle Periffin, one a public defender and the other in private practice. We were to meet at Tom's Tavern, a popular midday venue separated from the court complex by a pretty patch of grass known as Patriot's Square Park. I mulled over the incident I had witnessed in Michaels' office as I walked through the park, but decided not to bring it up during lunch, since Michaels had asked me to represent her at the upcoming hearing on Barnes' allegations. Instead, I wanted to solicit the defense lawyers' advice on another unrelated matter on which I needed some insight.

I considered both of my friends to be excellent attorneys. Each had been a guest lecturer in my classes at the university and we had served together on more than one bar association committee. I assumed they had many professional contacts with the lawyers in the County Attorney's Office and had some good and some bad associations. However, I was surprised when they began a dialogue with an unmistakably dark undertone, asking how I enjoyed being part of the "evil empire." To my surprise, they asserted that no one in the prosecutor's office could be unbiased.

In the opinions of my two companions, the county attorney acted in a tyrannical and heartless manner and forged a climate where his deputies doled out harsh punishment. His rigid plea bargaining policies mandated severe prison sentences without regard to the presence of factors mitigating the defendants' culpability. Anyone with compassion or "balls," they believed, wasn't going to be heard or move ahead in the prosecutor's office. Individualized justice was not to be and those who felt differently either left the County Attorney's Office or kept their discontent to themselves.

I was quickly finding out that in the criminal justice system today even the best of the new breed of prosecutors and criminal defense lawyers appear to have a serious professional flaw, a blind spot for the human decency of their adversaries. Trial advocacy requires a keen sensitivity to the values of the other participants in the justice system. Appreciating the motivation and beliefs of opposing counsel is just as important as understanding judges, juries, witnesses, clients and crime victims. Even though my lunch companions at Tom's Tavern had always been courteous in their public relations with prosecutors, they were brutally contemptuous of them in private, failing to see that their view of the world could be equally rational. Similarly, I had seen that morning that Lynn Michaels, who I thought intelligent and principled, seemed unable to accept that Harry Barnes, who was equally intelligent and principled, was genuinely upset, honestly but mistakenly believing that she had interfered with his lawyer-client relationship and had violated his client's rights. Sadly, both these lawyers were among the most professional I'd met during my time at the prosecutor's office. Many others, both prosecutors and defense lawyers, were less able to control their disdain in public.

The root of the problem was—and continues to be—antagonism between the two sides about their roles, a fact of life in the legal profession. All lawyers like to believe that they serve the public good and both prosecutors and criminal defense lawyers are convinced of the virtue of their own work. Nevertheless, the ethos of each side is dramatically different.

Prosecutors are at the center of a culture that abhors defendants and those around them. Every day, they interact with police officers who see themselves to be at war with criminals and who loathe the lawyers who try to keep them on the streets. Crime victims, another important constituency, often have wrenching personal stories and cannot fathom why the courts allow their tormenters to get off lightly. Exposed to these views, prosecutors often develop a black and white view of the world. They feel putting law breakers away, thereby protecting the good people in the community, is one of society's most worthwhile pursuits. When defense lawyers interfere with this mission, prosecutors see them as siding with the "bad guys," taking morally inferior professional roles.

On the other hand, the criminal defense ideal is one of due process and protection of the underprivileged. Defense lawyers revere the Bill of Rights as the centerpiece of American justice, the most sacred protection against governmental tyranny. They view themselves as the sole champions of liberty and believe prosecutors enjoy far greater resources and that judges are unsympathetic to their clients. Many of their clients come from poor, dysfunctional families, with few opportunities for the education, training and employment offered to others. In a world of inequality, frustrating the criminal process is both a necessary and an honorable role. The best strategies to prevent crime would be to eliminate poverty and discrimination, not to punish the wretched individuals who violate the laws.

This discord in values was just as real years before when I had been a public defender. However, I could now see that the face of criminal justice had changed dramatically in the last quarter century, with a proliferation of harsh mandatory sentencing laws that greatly augmented the ability of prosecutors to take firm stands on stiff prison sentences. Defense lawyers have reacted to these changes by becoming increasingly bitter. They resent what they commonly describe as the "tilt of the playing field." In many cases, their role has been reduced to persuading clients to accept unattractive take-it-or-leave-it plea bargains. Rancor has grown accordingly between the two sides. Even those most respected often cannot see the virtues of their adversaries.

Chapter 12

Disdain and Deception

August 15, 1994

The tensions underlying the prosecutor/defense attorney relationship would prove to be glaring in the Schilling case. The County Attorney's Office assigned it to Adam Fields, a prosecutor in the agency's trial division. Unlike most of his peers, Fields had attended a prestigious law school on the east coast and had numerous professional options upon graduation, initially accepting a position with a large Arizona firm. He left this lucrative practice to seek professional fulfillment, believing he would find it as a prosecutor, taking criminals off the streets. With several years experience in both the civil and criminal arenas, he hoped that he would eventually become an attractive candidate for a judgeship.

Fields began reading the Schilling file early Friday morning and did not move from his desk until he had digested all sixty-three single-spaced pages of police reports, as well as the notes of Pat Harlin, the prosecutor who had charged and presented the case to the grand jury. The facts fascinated Fields. He wondered why Schilling and his friends had beaten Hart to a pulp and dumped him into the trunk of a car. Was it a drug deal that had gone sour? Were they planning to kill him? He was aware that the drug culture could be nasty, but he had not encountered a case as hideous as this.

Pat Harlin's notes indicated that the grand jury hearing had not gone smoothly. Harlin had instructed the state's sole witness, Detective Ben Reynolds, not to testify about the drugs found in

Schilling's computer. Reynolds instead offered his opinion that
Schilling had possessed drugs for the purpose of sale. Things were getting more and more messy. The grand jury then voted to indict
Schilling on a drug trafficking count, in addition to the kidnapping
and aggravated assault charges Harlin had requested. Fields groaned.
There was no chance of proving at trial that Schilling had intended to
sell the small amount of methamphetamine found in his computer.

Fields was mildly irritated that he had not received the file
until the previous Monday, seventeen days after Schilling's initial court
appearance in Superior Court, called an arraignment. Arizona's court
rules required the prosecution to notify the defense of all evidence it
intended to present at trial, including the name and address of each
witness, no later than ten days after the arraignment. It typically took
close to ten days to route a case to a trial group in the County Attorney's Office, assign it to a prosecutor in the group and physically
deliver the file to the designated attorney. This left little room for the
prosecutor to provide the necessary disclosures to the defense in a
timely fashion. A seventeen day delay meant that Fields was already
late.

The file was also incomplete, lacking the photographs of the
victim and crime scene that had been taken on the night of the
offense. The only laboratory report in the folder was the criminalist's
determination that the substance removed from Schilling's computer
was methamphetamine. The crime scene detectives had requested
numerous other analyses of evidence from the police laboratory, but
none of these appeared to have been undertaken. There were no notations from Detective Reynolds after Schilling was charged. Fields did
see in the file that Schilling had retained Frank Mahoney, an experienced criminal lawyer who was less likely than most others to raise a
fuss over the missing material or the delay.

Fields immediately called Reynolds to request all photographs,
lab results and supplemental police reports that had been generated in
the case. He then gave his secretary the information needed to prepare
the required disclosures to Mahoney, relying on the same boiler-plate
word processing forms he used in all his other cases. There was not
much to disclose. Fields' "Notice of Discovery" simply informed the

defense lawyer that he would provide him with the photos, lab results and physical exhibits when they became available.

Since he hadn't made a final decision as to which witnesses the prosecution would call at trial, Fields sent Mahoney a list of every officer, technician and civilian identified in the police reports, a total of fifty-three individuals, regardless of how tangential they were to the case against Schilling. It was safer to list persons he would not call at trial than to guess now and discover later that he had not included an essential witness. Occasionally, a judge would not allow witnesses to testify if their identities were not disclosed to the other party before trial. There was also tactical value in sending a long list of "intended" witnesses, because Mahoney might have difficulty determining which ones he should interview. He might overlook a key witness, wasting his time with others who would be of little use to either side.

Defense lawyers often used similar tactics to obscure their intended trial strategy. Although court rules required them to provide prompt written notification of the theory of defense they would present at trial, the typical "Notice of Defense" used by defense attorneys listed every conceivable defense, including patently inconsistent theories. Mahoney's disclosure statement, for example, listed both self-defense and Schilling's lack of presence at the scene of the offense, among several other defenses. Obviously, Schilling could not have acted in self-defense if he was absent from the scene of the crime. Although the discovery rules were designed to provide each party with a fair opportunity to rebut the other's side's evidence, the lawyers did what they could to subvert this purpose.

Along with his Notice of Discovery, Fields sent Mahoney the terms of a proposed plea agreement, cognizant that the county attorney's "deadly weapon" plea bargaining policy limited the settlement options in this case. The indictment charged Schilling with using a gun in the commission of the crimes and this required Fields to insist on a guilty plea to the most serious of the charges, kidnapping, with a stipulation that Schilling was ineligible for probation. A prison sentence was mandatory under the policy and the minimum term was three years.

Many defense lawyers complained bitterly about the county attorney's rigid "deadly weapon" policy, but Fields nevertheless remained hopeful of getting a quick deal. Mahoney had a reputation among prosecutors as a defense lawyer who liked to dispose of his cases by guilty pleas and Fields had substantial plea bargaining leverage against Schilling. The state charged in the indictment that Schilling's kidnapping and aggravated assault crimes were "dangerous." If Schilling was convicted at trial of the kidnapping charge, the dangerousness allegation meant that he faced a mandatory minimum sentence of seven years, with a maximum sentence of twenty-one years. Schilling could receive an even longer sentence if he was convicted of one or both of the aggravated assault charges, in addition to kidnapping. Therefore, even though agency policy required a prison sentence in Schilling's plea agreement, Fields could still offer a substantial reduction in time by dropping the dangerousness charge.

Fields took certain factors into account when determining the specific terms of his offer. First, he knew that Mahoney liked to barter with prosecutors. Additionally, Schilling had retained Mahoney as his counsel and would likely want the lawyer to demonstrate that he had earned his fee by negotiating a good deal. Thus Fields offered a stipulated six year prison sentence, clearly on the high side for settling this type of case. Mahoney would probably make a counter-offer. If they eventually agreed to a lesser prison sentence, Mahoney would be able to show his client that he was working diligently on his behalf. Fields had the authority to agree to three years in prison, but he did not believe that Mahoney would push him that far. As is customary, Fields let Mahoney know through the disclosure statements only the first superficial layer of his strategy. The defense lawyer gave an equally veiled statement.

Two weeks later the plea negotiations came to a screeching halt. Ray Hart called Fields, excitedly exclaiming that Schilling and a bunch of guys had been to his apartment a few minutes earlier. "Schilling threatened me with a gun!" Hart shouted into the telephone. Fields instructed Hart to call 911, then prepared a motion to revoke Schilling's release from custody, asking the court for an expedited hearing. The first available time was the following Tuesday, the morning after the Labor Day weekend. Fields made sure that Hart could come to court that morning, then notified Mahoney, requesting Schilling's presence at the hearing.

A half hour before the hearing, Fields met with Hart at the County Attorney's Office to review the details of Schilling's threat. In most respects, Hart appeared to have recovered from the pummeling he had taken at Schilling's house two months earlier, with only a few scars on his face, but he still had a plaster cast that extended from his right elbow to the tips of his fingers. He was very unhappy when he learned that he would have to testify that morning, telling Fields, "My wife is afraid for my safety." He had hidden in a motel room for several days after his discharge from the hospital, then had moved in with his brother-in-law until it appeared to be okay to return home. However, not long after he went home, he had been looking out the window and saw a group of men driving by his apartment on motorcycles, one of them carrying a gun, gesturing toward his third-floor apartment. Hart said he knew it was Schilling because he recognized Schilling's Harley-Davidson.

The hatred the defendant and victim felt for each other was clearly visible. Hart and Schilling glared at one another when Schilling entered the courtroom for the bail revocation hearing. Alongside him were Gayle Rogers and Dick Tanner, two associates of Frank Mahoney. After the lawyers discussed a few preliminary matters, Hart testified to the same story he had related to Fields a half hour earlier. Schilling took the stand to deny Hart's allegation, adding that his cycle had been at a repair shop when the incident was alleged to have occurred. The judge took Hart's word over Schilling's, ordering the defendant into custody.

But Schilling's lawyers did not quit. Two weeks later, Gayle Rogers filed a motion that requested reconsideration of Schilling's custodial status, citing new evidence. The judge granted them another hearing, which took place a few days later. Frank Mahoney called only one witness, the owner of a motorcycle business, who testified that Schilling's Harley had been in his repair shop on the day that Hart claimed he had seen the defendant. When the state offered no rebuttal evidence, the judge gave the benefit of doubt to Schilling, ordering his release.

Plea negotiations began again two days later, when Dick Tanner,

Mahoney's associate, called Fields. Tanner reported that Schilling was not interested in Fields' offer of six years in prison, suggesting politely that the state might want to re-evaluate its case. He asked if Fields was aware that Hart had recently been placed on probation for a theft offense and whether Fields knew Hart had a second felony prosecution, a drug charge, pending against him. Schilling's lawyers had also located a woman who told them that Hart had burglarized her home within days of stealing Schilling's coin collection. She'd be a great witness, Tanner opined, at Schilling's trial.

Tanner requested that Fields consider asking for a deviation from the county attorney's deadly weapon policy, allowing Schilling to be eligible for probation, if Schilling gave testimony on the other three men who had participated in the incident. He assured Fields that Mahoney's firm had not had any contact with these individuals, but he thought that Schilling might be willing to identify them if the state provided sufficient incentive. Fields didn't give him an answer, since a deviation could be granted only with the assent of the chief of the trial division and the chief deputy county attorney.

Fields considered Tanner's suggestion throughout the day. It had been apparent at the bail revocation hearing that Hart and Schilling loathed each other. One of them had lied in his testimony, but Fields had no idea if it was the victim or the defendant, a bad omen for the trial that lay ahead.

By the time he went home that evening, Fields had decided not to seek a deviation from the county attorney's plea bargaining restrictions. A few weeks earlier, he had requested a promotion from his current trial group to the major felony division in the prosecutor's office and had been told that one of the next available positions would be his. While he could take a few of his cases with him when he transferred, most would be re-assigned to other lawyers. The Schilling case looked very messy. When he changed assignments someone else would have to figure out what to do.

Chapter 13

Selective Prosecution

The County Attorney's Office allowed me to work in the felony trial group of my choice, now that I had spent a month handling preliminary hearings in the justice of the peace courts, managing to wobble through two misdemeanor jury trials during this stint. I was eager to move on and wanted to join a trial bureau in the major felony division. Major felonies were generally the sexiest prosecutions, with the highest stakes, and I was hoping for an interesting case to take to trial. Moreover, lawyers in this division worked with police detectives in ongoing investigations and charged their own cases. Working here, I would be able to see and do as much as possible as a prosecutor.

It was unusual for a lawyer to advance to the major felony division this quickly. Like most other prosecution or defender agencies, the County Attorney's Office wanted only seasoned lawyers handling important cases. Beginning prosecutors normally spent about six months in the preliminary hearing courts before they advanced to the agency's trial division, where they managed a caseload of routine felony cases. They typically remained in the trial division for three to five years before their promotion to major felonies and some never made it this far. The agency made an exception for me.

I chose to join the Gang/ROP bureau, a trial group that specialized in prosecuting two categories of offenders: members of street gangs and defendants who had been targeted by the police as future recidivists. It seemed odd to me that there was no similarity between the two types of cases, which the agency paired in one trial group for reasons of expediency. However, the combination offered a richer diversity of cases than was possible in the other trial groups in the major felony division. A typical Gang/ROP caseload included a number of violent crimes, such as attempted murders, armed robberies and aggravated assaults, as well as most types of property offenses, drug trafficking crimes and weapons charges. Working in Gang/ROP would also gave me an opportunity to experience the pressure associated with a large caseload. The trial group was under-staffed and had only eleven prosecutors in its downtown bureau.

One of the other lawyers soon took a four month leave-of-absence from the prosecutor's office, dumping a stack of thirty-eight case files on my desk the day before he departed. I quickly acquired additional cases from other Gang/ROP prosecutors who were eager to accommodate my desire for trial experience, thereby reducing their own workloads. Most days, I charged new cases submitted by the police, filling whatever space remained in my file cabinet. Still, my circumstances could have been worse. My next-door office neighbor had sixty-five active cases, including homicides and rapes, and she spent countless hours advising a law enforcement task force investigating prison violence.

The defendants in my gang cases, roughly half my workload, were dangerous. Some were charged with drive-by shootings or similar crimes and many of the victims and prosecution witnesses were members of rival gangs who had little interest in cooperating with the state. One weekend night each month, I patrolled the streets on the south and west sides of Phoenix with rough-and-tumble detectives who specialized in gathering intelligence on street gangs and their members. Most of the prosecutors in Gang/ROP looked forward to their ride-alongs with the gang-squad detectives, but a few declined to go because of the hazards. For me the rides were eye openers, because I knew little about gangs, the culture surrounding them and the organized efforts of law enforcement to control them.

The other half of my file cabinet consisted of "ROP" cases, the acronym for the county's repeat offender program, which was based on a study conducted by the RAND Corporation in the 1980s. The RAND researchers had interviewed and collected data on a few thousand felons in California, Michigan and Texas, examining the patterns in their criminal behavior. The study resulted in an astounding finding: while most felons committed only a handful of crimes each year, a few committed as many as two hundred and fifty. Thus, a relatively small number of persons accounted for a large percentage of the serious crimes committed in America each year. Subsequent researchers in other states replicated this finding.

The RAND study identified several criteria that could be used to predict a particular offender's risk level for high-frequency recidivism. Based on this assessment, the principal researcher recommended a policy of "selective incapacitation," arguing that criminal justice resources could be used most efficiently by directing efforts at catching those offenders most likely to be high rate recidivists and locking them up for as long as possible. Assuming, for example, that one of ten convicted burglars is predicted to be a high risk for recidivism, imprisoning that offender for fifteen years and granting probation to the other nine would be considerably less expensive and far more likely to reduce the over-all crime rate than incarcerating all ten offenders for three years apiece.

Following the RAND study, numerous cities and counties in the United States created programs, such as ROP, to catch and lock up offenders who appeared to present a high risk for recidivism. In Phoenix, a committee of police detectives met every two weeks to screen crime suspects for inclusion in the program, using a variation of the criteria suggested by the RAND researchers. If the committee "ROPed" an individual, he or she was assigned to a detective from the program. These detectives monitored the activities of several suspects in the ROP system, making sure that the crimes they committed were fully investigated, charged and prosecuted. The detectives located and interviewed witnesses who otherwise might not be found, assisted Gang/ROP prosecutors in assembling evidence for trial and made stiff sentencing recommendations to the court. Additionally, the County

Attorney's Office implemented special plea bargaining policies for ROP defendants, so that they would receive longer sentences than those given to others who committed similar crimes.

In theory, at least, the ROP program made great sense. The streets and taxpayers would be much safer when the criminals most likely to commit more crimes were successfully removed from the community for as long as possible. However, a sound idea on paper does not necessarily result in a well-advised program in practice.

Six months earlier, on a fall afternoon while I had been adjusting to my prosecutorial duties, two uniformed police officers who were parked on a side street in downtown Phoenix, observed a tall, skinny man with long hair and a beard standing in front of the cash box at an unattended commercial parking lot. The man had the distinct unkempt appearance of the many homeless people who roamed the streets each day. The two officers watched him pull a dollar bill from one of the slots in the box by manipulating a small wire he had taken from his pocket. When the officers approached him, the man told them his name was Cal Stewart. The wire turned out to be a bent paper clip with a hook on its end. Stewart, who had three dollars in his pocket when arrested, readily admitted that he supported himself by fishing currency from parking lot cash boxes. It was an open-and-shut case, with two cops as eye-witnesses and Stewart's own confession as evidence.

Normally, swiping a dollar bill from an unattended cash box was considered to be a minor transgression, charged as a misdemeanor. Persons convicted of this crime would usually be placed on probation, sometimes with a few days in jail. Those with a substantial prior record might spend a few months behind bars. Stewart, however, was "ROPed," landing him in the county's repeat offender program. This meant that the state prosecuted his crime as a major felony, deserving special attention, with a senior police detective and a deputy county attorney working together to make sure that he received as long a sentence as possible.

When I inherited Cal Stewart's case several months after his arrest, I began to question the wisdom of the ROP approach. It appeared that the detectives in the program found it much easier to identify and keep track of relatively minor property offenders than to build cases against those repeat criminals who were truly dangerous. Although a few of the defendants in my ROP cases had committed violent crimes, the great majority, I found, were charged with such offenses as car theft, credit card forgery and stealing scrap metal from industrial yards or personal belongings from unlocked cars or, in Cal Stewart' case, filching a dollar bill from a parking lot cash box.

A second problem I soon saw was the subjectivity of the screening process, which appeared to result in the disparate treatment of offenders. Prosecutors at the County Attorney's Office were sometimes puzzled by the detectives' inclusion of some defendants in the ROP system and their omission of others. Frequently, defendants with as many as five or six prior felony convictions were not prosecuted by the Gang/ROP bureau, but instead by the county attorney's regular trial division. On the other hand, defendants without any prior felonies were sometimes "ROPed." In part, this anomaly may have been related to the criteria the detectives used when screening candidates.

Cal Stewart, I was to learn, was an example of how the system failed. Stewart, a drifter with a drug habit, had moved from city to city for years. He had three prior felony convictions for minor, non-violent property crimes before he arrived in Phoenix. When Stewart was apprehended for the parking lot theft, the arresting officers nominated him for ROP. The screening committee considered his history of felony convictions and his failure to complete probation successfully in the past. Both were objectively ascertainable facts that traditionally had been taken into account in prosecuting and punishing offenders. Likewise, the detectives weighed Stewart's drug addiction, which was readily verifiable and logically could be correlated with ongoing criminal activity.

However, the detectives considered additional factors in their decision to include Stewart in the repeat offender program. Some of these, such as his "lifestyle" and "family background," were inherently subjective and potentially capricious. Other criteria, including Stewart's current employment status and the age at which he was first reported to juvenile authorities, were based on socio-economic factors that might have been beyond his control or upon idiosyncrasies of the justice system itself.

Once the screening committee voted to include Stewart in ROP, they assigned a detective to work with the County Attorney's Office to build as strong a case as possible on as serious a charge as possible. The ROP detective reviewed the accuracy of the arresting officers' report; took photographs and measurements of the parking lot cash box; and contacted law enforcement agencies in other states to obtain certified records of Stewart's prior convictions, to be used in court to enhance his sentence. On the detective's recommendation, the County Attorney's Office charged Stewart not with simple theft, but instead with third-degree burglary, which was a felony. Given Stewart's prior convictions, he faced a mandatory prison sentence if he was convicted at trial, with a presumptive term of ten years. The minimum sentence the judge could impose was imprisonment for six years.

By the time I inherited Stewart's case, he had already spent six months in pre-trial custody, unable to post bail. His lawyer, a public defender named Robin Parker, whom I once taught at the university, was angry, unable to comprehend why the prosecutor's office would treat such a petty offense so severely. Parker assumed that the problem stemmed from my predecessor's warped sense of justice, hoping that I might make a more lenient plea bargaining offer. However, the county attorney's plea bargaining policies relating to ROP defendants limited my options. The best deal I could offer would require Stewart to serve at least four-and-a-half years in prison.

Parker filed a motion in court, asking the judge to dismiss the burglary charge. According to the statute, one committed third-degree burglary by entering "a non-residential structure" with the intent to commit a theft. Parker acknowledged that Stewart intended to steal money from the parking lot cash box, but she questioned whether the box—six inches deep and a foot wide—was substantial enough to qualify as a "non-residential structure." She filed an exhaustive brief on the legal definition of "structure," and I filed one in response, with oral argument scheduled a week later.

I saw Stewart for the first time when I entered the courtroom. Although handcuffed, Stewart looked healthier than the man described in the police report, probably a reflection of the starchy food served in jail. However, he looked at me with terror in his eyes, causing me to turn away quickly.

When the judge called the case, I began my oral argument in

legalese that only a law professor could offer, pointing out that the state legislature had defined the word structure as "any building...or place with sides and a floor," which the cash box definitely had. Technically and legally, I asserted, the defendant's conduct came within the language of the statute. But the judge did not appear convinced, asking if any part of Stewart's body had physically penetrated the cash box. No, I acknowledged, he had entered the box solely by inserting his paper clip through a slot in the front.

Parker was low-keyed but persuasive in her argument, asserting that burglary was a more serious crime than theft because it involved a threat to human safety. As support, she noted that the statute referred to both "residential" and "non-residential" structures, implying that the legislature meant the crime to apply only to buildings large enough for humans to occupy. Otherwise, a person could commit burglary by entering an area as small as a fruit basket or even a tiny jewelry box. That defied common sense, she argued, as the judge nodded approval.

The court's decision arrived in the mail a few days later. The judge dismissed the felony charge against Stewart, ruling that one could not commit burglary by prying a dollar bill from a cash box. But when I called Parker to congratulate her on the excellent job she had done for her client, she was still rankled by the hard line the prosecutor's office had taken in plea negotiations, asking if I had ethical concerns about offering a four-and-a-half year prison sentence for a one dollar theft. She reminded me of the many times I had stated in my lectures to first-year law students that courts in a free society impose punishment only for a defendant's past transgressions and not on guesses of what he might do in the future. I could not disagree. I suggested that she advise her client to leave Arizona when he was released from jail. If he chose to stay, an unhappy ROP detective probably would carefully monitor Stewart's activities, day and night.

I felt weary and dissatisfied as I reviewed all the substantial energy and public resources that had gone into apprehending, prosecuting and punishing a man who had committed a petty theft.

It would not be the only time I was deeply troubled by the ROP program. Each criminal trial judge at the Maricopa County Superior Court conducted a morning calendar beginning at 8:30 A.M. to hear such matters as guilty pleas, sentencing hearings, pre-trial motions, probation revocation proceedings, case status conferences and postponements of trial dates. The average morning calendar in each courtroom included anywhere from a half dozen to thirty separate proceedings. Prosecutors and public defenders scurried from courtroom to courtroom, with as many as six matters scheduled to begin in different locations at the same time. The judges tried to get through their calendars as expeditiously as possible to reserve most of the day for conducting jury trials, but often this was impossible because lawyers were occupied in other courtrooms. Most of the judges took recesses when attorneys were delayed, allowing court personnel to attend to administrative duties or chatter idly with other lawyers who were awaiting the arrival of their adversaries. The judges responsible for the overall administration of the superior court hated long mornings and every few years they instituted reforms to minimize them. After a while, however, the delays began again.

Both the prosecutor and public defender agencies assigned a "warm body" to cover the morning calendar in each courtroom, serving as substitute counsel on routine proceedings when colleagues were detained in other courts or were otherwise unavailable. Each trial group in the prosecutor's office was responsible for providing these warm bodies on a more-or-less rotational basis. One morning every two weeks I was assigned this duty and soon it was my turn in Judge Boynton's courtroom.

Judge Boynton's morning calendar included twenty-three matters. Most were either sentencing hearings or proceedings in which the defendant was to change his plea to guilty as part of a previously arranged plea bargain with the prosecution. In eight of the cases, the assigned prosecutor appeared in person to handle his or her own case. I had the County Attorney's case file for the remaining fifteen cases, with instructions to serve as substitute counsel. The first time I had seen these files was 8:15 A.M., roughly twenty minutes before the judge took the bench.

The instructions from the assigned prosecutors in a few of the fifteen cases were thorough and clear, making my job easy. In most of the others, however, the prosecutor had provided little or no guidance, either because of insufficient time or laziness. Now as I stood before the judge, I knew he expected me to be familiar with the content of the files on all the cases. He wanted the prosecutor to present the factual basis for each guilty plea correctly and to argue the state's position on each sentence he was to impose. During the frequent recesses in the morning calendar, I tried to rifle through the files of the cases where there were few instructions. I knew that I could not represent the state competently in some of the cases. The victims deserved more.

One of my own cases, a ROP prosecution, was scheduled for a status conference this same morning in Judge Carol White's courtroom in an adjacent building. I dashed off to White's court during one of the recesses in Boynton's calendar, promising Boynton's judicial assistant, "I'll return in thirty minutes." Another prosecutor agreed to fill in for me—one warm body for another—if Boynton took the bench before I returned. It took ten minutes to rush from one building to the other, not leaving me much time to conduct my business.

When I arrived at White's court, a prosecutor and a defense lawyer stood at their respective counsel tables, addressing the judge on a contested motion. Several other lawyers sat inside the railing that separated the area of the courtroom where legal business was conducted from the spectator's gallery. A handful of defendants and a few other persons watched the proceedings from the back of the room, while eight defendants in custody sat quietly in the jury box, chained together to prevent an escape. One of the defendants on the chain was Tyler Roberts, the man I came to see. Charged with two counts of shoplifting, Roberts represented himself.

The United States Supreme Court had ruled in 1975 that a criminal defendant has a constitutional right to self-representation. Not many defendants avail themselves of this opportunity, but when they do it is usually because they do not trust public defenders or other defense lawyers who are paid by the state. Trial judges generally loathe cases in which the defendant represents himself, because the presence of a defense attorney usually makes the proceedings flow smoothly. Nevertheless, as long as a defendant is mentally competent, the court cannot refuse his request to represent himself, even if he is uneducated and ignorant of court procedures and evidence rules. But the trial judge usually appoints a stand-by lawyer to advise the defendant during the proceedings and to step in if the defendant later changes his mind about the need for representation.

Tyler Roberts chose to represent himself two months earlier, because he did not like the advice he received from his public defender, who had recommended that he accept the plea bargain offered by the state. Although the prosecutor's office usually considered shoplifting to be a minor offense, it occasionally charged it as a felony when the accused had previous convictions for similar crimes. With seven prior shoplifting convictions, Roberts faced felony charges for his two latest arrests. The Phoenix police had ROPed him and the county attorney was trying to put him in prison for a long time.

The prosecutor who had the case before me had offered a plea agreement in which Roberts would receive a stiff prison sentence on one of the shoplifting charges, followed by a period of probation on the other. The offer represented a substantial reduction of the time Roberts faced if convicted at trial under the applicable mandatory sentencing laws, but he nevertheless believed it was unfair, blaming his public defender for not getting a better deal. Roberts was sure that he could negotiate more favorable terms if he represented himself, despite his prior record, the lack of a viable defense to the charges, the mandatory sentencing laws and the County Attorney's strict ROP policies.

I wanted to talk with Roberts, person-to-person. Prosecutors normally negotiate with defense lawyers, rarely getting the opportunity to speak privately with defendants themselves. This could be my only chance to do so while I was in the County Attorney's Office. I felt comfortable in this role because I had been a defense attorney for many years, and I believed that I could see the world through Tyler Roberts' lens.

Roberts' story was a familiar one in the justice system. A biracial baby born to an unmarried teenager, severely abused by his mother's boyfriend, he was a ward of the state by his third birthday, with several foster home placements during the next two years. A family in Denver had adopted Roberts when he was five, but they were ill-equipped to deal with his emotional problems. He had a learning disability that went undiagnosed for several years, fell behind in elementary school and was held back twice. He also suffered from an eating disorder and weighed over two hundred pounds by the time he was fourteen.

Teased constantly by his classmates, he smoked at least three joints of pot each day and dropped out of school on his sixteenth birthday. He was addicted to crack cocaine by age nineteen and was arrested three years later for selling a small amount of the drug to an undercover federal agent.

Remarkably, Roberts managed to stop using cocaine during the two years in which his federal case was pending, even though he did not qualify for a publicly funded drug treatment program. He submitted to random drug testing as a condition of his pre-trial release and each of his urine samples was clean. He also maintained steady employment during this period, married a college-educated woman and became a parent. The federal court rewarded Roberts for his success, placing him on probation for four years, with continuing mandatory drug testing. He successfully completed this probation and remained drug-free for another year.

However, he eventually succumbed to his cocaine addiction, stealing liquor from supermarkets and selling it to local bars to support his need for crack. In a period of ten months, he incurred six misdemeanor shoplifting convictions. The police ROPed him on his seventh arrest, persuading the court to send him to prison for two years. After his release, he immediately began to steal baby formula from markets, selling it on the street. This resulted in his current charges, two felony shoplifting allegations. In fact, he picked up the second case while on pre-trial release for the first. It appeared that he could no longer escape his addiction; if released to the streets again, he would almost certainly begin to steal immediately.

I met with Roberts and his stand-by counsel to discuss a plea bargain when Judge White took a recess. We had no privacy, as Roberts was still chained to the other prisoners in the jury box. Some of the men pretended to focus their attention elsewhere, but they all listened closely to our negotiation, as Roberts begged for an opportunity to succeed in a residential drug treatment program, acknowledging his long history of cocaine abuse and chronic shoplifting, "But I believe I can still beat my addiction," he implored. He reminded me that he had gone seven full years without drugs, saying that he tried to get into a secure rehabilitation program shortly after he relapsed, but no facility would accept him. He was not on probation at the time and thus could not take advantage of a court-ordered treatment program. Now he pleaded for that chance.

Roberts' stand-by lawyer had not checked with any community drug rehabilitation programs to ascertain if they would take his client. But even if he had, the county attorney's plea bargaining policies would not have permitted such a deal. I was able to reach an agreement with Roberts that knocked a few months off the sentence previously offered to him, but no more than that, even though my instincts told me that the ROP detectives might have been shortsighted in their certainty of his future criminality. If placed in a treatment program, Roberts—in his late thirties—might not pose much of a risk when he was later released. Regardless, he was a shoplifter, not a rapist.

The success of the repeat offenders program depends on the detectives' ability to accurately predict whether Roberts and persons like him will continue to commit crimes at a high rate over an extended period of time. Unfortunately, predicting future crime is an imperfect science. Persons with identical profiles nevertheless commit crimes at different rates and most offenders' crime patterns change over time. Although researchers have refined prediction models since the original RAND study, even the best techniques have disturbing rates of inaccuracy, with both false positives and false negatives. Some future recidivists are not identified, while other persons are falsely labeled as such.

I saw firsthand how the justice system fails whenever a sentencing decision is based on such inaccuracies.

Chapter 14

Where's the Evidence?

Fall/Winter/Spring 1994-1995

Gayle Rogers was unhappy with the direction the Schilling case was heading. The previous July, she had agreed with her law partner, Frank Mahoney, that she and Dick Tanner, another lawyer at the firm who'd been at Schilling's bail hearing, would have joint responsibility for handling pre-trial preparation, court appearances and meetings with the client. At first it had appeared to be a case that would likely be resolved expeditiously with a guilty plea to a lesser charge. However, Schilling adamantly insisted on his innocence and the prosecution was standing behind its deadly weapon plea bargaining policy. To make matters worse, they soon found out that Schilling was a high maintenance client, calling or just showing up at the office. Sometimes he had new information on Hart, but usually he just wanted to know what the lawyers were doing on his behalf. The case was requiring much more attention than the law firm had anticipated.

Moreover, Schilling was becoming increasingly difficult to deal with. In November, Brenda Chase's sister had called the office to report that Schilling had threatened to harm Chase. Rogers immediately called her client, warning him to chill out and not to do anything to hurt his case; they would need Chase to corroborate his version of the events if a trial became necessary. Schilling assured Rogers that he had the situation under control, but his relationship with Chase continued to deteriorate over the next several months. Brenda began claiming that he was stalking her.

Complaining about the slow pace, Schilling sometimes berated the lawyers, unable to understand why they were hesitant to go to trial, explaining that his brother had told him that he had a strong defense. One afternoon in December he came to the office without prior notice, accompanied by a man named James Thornton, who told Rogers that he was one of the three men who had aided Schilling in the incident with Ray Hart. Thornton volunteered to be a witness at Schilling's trial, but as he told his version it became apparent that his account of the facts was as favorable to the prosecution as the defense. Schilling did not seem to understand this, insisting that both Chase and Thornton would be excellent defense witnesses.

Schilling, Chase and Thornton did agree that Hart was a liar and a crook, and Rogers could assume that the jury would not like him, but she wondered if it would make any difference in the outcome of Schilling's trial. Even if Schilling had acted in self defense when he disarmed Hart, it bothered Rogers that he failed to call the police that night. The prosecution had gruesome photographs of Hart taken in the hospital and Schilling had yet to plausibly explain what he was doing during the four hours between Chase's departure from the house and Hart's escape from the trunk. While the law provided that the burden of proof never shifted to the defense, it would be difficult for Schilling's lawyers to convince the jury that he did not participate in the mayhem. Regardless of the prosecutor's problems with Hart, Schilling's prospects for an acquittal did not look good.

Preparing for trial was proving to be difficult, as Rogers was now dealing with her third prosecutor on the case. The first, Adam Fields, had transferred to the major felony division of the County Attorney's Office in September. The case was next assigned to Barbara Powers. Powers twice requested a postponement of the trial, in October and November, explaining that she was busy with other cases and did not have sufficient time to prepare the Schilling prosecution. When Powers left the County Attorney's Office for other employment in early December, yet another prosecutor, Gerry Baylor, inherited Schilling's case and he too requested a thirty day continuance to get up to speed.

Rogers was slowly being worn down. She could not get far in her pre-trial preparation without the assistance of a prosecutor. Whenever one of her cases did not result in a quick guilty plea, she normally conducted informal tape-recorded interviews with the prosecution's likely witnesses, including the police officers who participated in the investigation and arrest of her client, to discover if they had information favorable to the defense that was not included in the police reports. The prosecutor handling the case frequently insisted on being present, arranging for the interviews to take place at the County Attorney's Office, to protect the witnesses. In Schilling's case, Rogers wanted to interview most of the five police officers and three detectives who participated in the crime scene investigation, as well as the victim, Ray Hart. She could not begin to conduct these interviews until Baylor, the new prosecutor, was familiar with the case.

Refreshingly, Baylor proved to be less controlling than other prosecutors in the County Attorney's Office, suggesting to Rogers in early January that she arrange and conduct the interviews on her own, so long as she sent him a copy of each tape. However, some of the officers, including Detective Reynolds, failed to return her calls for several weeks, either because her messages were not forwarded, they were too busy, or they were simply not eager to cooperate with a defense lawyer. At the end of January, she filed a motion requesting court-ordered depositions of Reynolds and four other officers. The judge granted her request a few days later, but by mid-February, Rogers, who'd been busy on other matters, had yet to conduct most of the interviews. Now she, not the prosecutor, sought a postponement each month.

Although the judge had now continued Rogers' client's trial a seventh time, Rogers was still making little progress. In April, she sent Gerry Baylor a letter requesting the state to compare the fingerprints found at the crime scene with those of Schilling and Hart, but a month later she still awaited his response. Carl Tate, the officer who arrested Schilling, had yet to return her call to schedule an interview and Baylor had failed to send her a copy of Hart's felony conviction records. Nevertheless, she saw no point in complaining, since Mahoney did not appear eager to try the case.

In a significant development, Baylor extended a new plea bargaining proposal: if Schilling pled guilty to kidnapping, the prosecution was willing to dismiss all other charges and stipulate to a sentence of three and a half years in prison. Rogers discussed it with Mahoney and his other associate, agreeing that it was a reasonable deal under the circumstances, a substantial reduction from the prosecution's original offer of six years and probably as far as Baylor could go under the county attorney's deadly weapon policy. Mahoney called in his secretary. "Call Schilling to schedule a meeting to discuss the proposed agreement," he instructed. She related later that Schilling had asked if members of his family could accompany him. Mahoney readily agreed, recognizing that his client would probably balk at Baylor's offer.

Mahoney and Rogers could be highly persuasive in selling a plea bargain to a recalcitrant client if they believed he was not assessing his situation realistically. At such times their discussion of the evidence sometimes resembled a prosecutor's closing argument to a jury, emphasizing all the strengths of the state's case against the client. Occasionally, Mahoney and Rogers used family members or close friends of the defendant to help the client appreciate how a neutral juror might view the evidence. It could be difficult for a client to resist when people he trusted joined his lawyers in urging him against going to trial. Mahoney knew from experience that family members appreciated being brought into the decision-making process and usually deferred to the lawyers' assessment of the prosecution's case.

Steve Schilling's family proved to be an exception.

Schilling arrived at the appointed time with his mother and brother Larry. He appeared to be tense when he shook Mahoney's hand and turned off the lawyer's attempt to engage in small talk to set a less formal atmosphere. His family sat close together in Mahoney's office, with his brother Larry immediately to his right. Rogers sensed that the meeting would not go well when she saw Larry's arms folded firmly in front of him.

Schilling began by complaining that Mahoney had handed the case off to his two associates without his approval. "I hired you," he exclaimed. "I expect to see you at the defense table during the trial."

Mahoney assured him that he would try the case if it went to trial. However, he added, the police interviews were not going well; the prosecution's case was looking stronger than they had anticipated.

Schilling's brother interrupted, asserting that Steve had a *right* to defend his property. A successful private detective, Larry spoke with authority, atypical for a client's relative. Mahoney tried to correct him, explaining that the law did not permit the use of deadly force to recover personal property, but Larry glared at the lawyer and again insisted that his brother was within his rights. The meeting was becoming more and more tense.

Mahoney's voice rose sharply above Larry's. Steve had *no chance* at trial, he shouted, adding that Hart had stolen the coins more than a week before the incident. This could not justify beating Hart up and throwing him in a trunk.

Steve entered the fray, protesting his innocence, telling Mahoney that *he* hadn't beaten anyone up and *he* hadn't thrown anyone in a trunk. He asked the lawyers angrily if they had checked to see whose fingerprints were on the trunk. He was sure they weren't his.

But Mahoney persisted in his strongly worded advice, telling Schilling he would be a "damn fool" if he went to trial.

By this time Rogers knew it would be pointless discussing Baylor's offer. Schilling was determined to go to trial, regardless of what the prosecution would give him in a plea bargain and his family stood firmly behind him. She was not surprised a month later when Schilling fired Mahoney and hired a new lawyer, one who promised to take his case before a jury.

As the new defense attorney began assembling Schilling's case, Gerry Baylor, the prosecutor, stared at the front page of the newspaper on his desk. The article grabbing his attention recapped the latest development in the O.J. Simpson case. A Los Angeles crime laboratory analyst had admitted in his testimony that blood samples were sometimes contaminated from unknown sources. Baylor pondered how this could occur.

Suddenly Baylor's telephone rang. Ben Reynolds, the case agent on the Schilling case, was returning his latest call. Two months earlier, Baylor had asked the detective to submit a request to the Phoenix crime laboratory for an analysis of the fingerprint impressions found in Schilling's house. Baylor later discovered that the case file also lacked laboratory reports on blood typing, necessitating another call to Reynolds. Normally unflappable, Baylor was perturbed, believing that these loose ends should have been tied up long before.

The detectives participating in the initial crime scene investigation almost a year earlier had collected between thirty and forty items that appeared to have blood on them. Rob Nicholson, one of the detectives, sent over twenty of these to the crime laboratory the next day with a request for serological analysis—a determination of whether the substance on each item was human blood, and if so, a determination of the blood type, for comparison with blood samples taken from Hart, Schilling and any other suspects arrested in the case. Nicholson wanted the lab to analyze swatches from the carpet and sofa in Schilling's living room; a metal bar found on the coffee table; rags and towels from a plastic garbage bag in Schilling's kitchen; the tip of one of Schilling's boots; his pants; a leather belt found on the living room floor; and pieces of duct tape found in Schilling's garage.

To Nicholson, the most important item was the gun that Officer Tate had seized when he placed Schilling under arrest. Serological analysis of the gun promised to be significant because Tate noticed a dark red stain on the end of the barrel and Hart told Nicholson in the hospital that Schilling had struck him with the barrel of a gun. The analysis would corroborate Hart's testimony if the substance on Schilling's gun matched Hart's blood. Similarly, if the stains on his pants and boot tip matched Hart's blood, but not Schilling's, the evidence would support the prosecution's case and cast doubt on Schilling's claim of self defense.

Although Nicholson submitted the evidence for serological testing, the crime laboratory could not proceed with the requested analysis until it received samples of the victim's and defendant's blood, for purposes of comparison. Eight weeks later, one of the laboratory technicians requested Hart's and Schilling's samples, but Detective Reynolds, the case agent assigned to the Schilling prosecution, did not secure them. Reynolds' active caseload included several serious offenses that had not yet been cleared, a higher priority than getting blood comparison samples to the lab in a case that was two months old, especially when a suspect had already been arrested and charged with the offense.

The responsibility for getting the serological comparisons completed also rested with the prosecutor. Once Schilling had already been charged in court and was represented by counsel, the only way to obtain a blood sample from him was for the prosecutor to file a motion requesting that his blood be drawn for analysis. Although the courts routinely granted this type of motion, none was filed in Schilling's case. The first two prosecutors handling the case were mere caretakers and quickly moved on to other work. The third prosecutor, not assigned to the case until almost a half-year after the offense, apparently had not recognized that the pending serological comparisons awaited his motion in court.

The twenty items of evidence Nicholson had sent for blood testing remained in a freezer at the crime laboratory for nine months. The following April, the laboratory returned them to the police property room without any serological analysis.

The saga relating to fingerprint examinations was similar. Hours after the search of Schilling's house, Detective Nicholson requested the crime laboratory to examine several pieces of evidence for the presence of fingerprints. The items included duct tape found in Steve Schilling's kitchen and garage, as well as the metal bar the police seized from Schilling's living room and the magazine inside Schilling's semi-automatic handgun. The examination for fingerprints on the duct tape and metal bar was especially important, because it might establish the identity of one or more of the persons who struck and hog-tied Hart.

The crime laboratory's protocol in a case like this required fingerprint technicians to wait until after the items were examined for the presence of human blood. An examination for fingerprints could be conducted only after all blood samples to be analyzed were scraped off the items in question, because fingerprint examination required treating the items with chemicals, which could easily compromise a later serological analysis. Thus, when the serological analysis was stalled by the lack of comparison blood samples from the victim and the defendant, the fingerprint examination also went unperformed.

Similarly, Nicholson's request for an analysis of possible fingerprints on the bag of drugs found in Schilling's computer went unfulfilled because the identification of the drugs as methamphetamine had a higher priority. After the drug testing was completed, neither the police investigator nor any of the three prosecutors assigned to the case sent a follow-up request to conduct the fingerprint comparison.

The crime laboratory did have an opportunity to examine other fingerprints lifted from the crime scene. Carmen Hall, the police evidence technician on the case, had dusted the Oldsmobile found in Schilling's garage on July 4 with a powder designed to expose latent fingerprint impressions, successfully finding fingerprints on the exterior and interior of the trunk, as well as the driver's door handle and the gear shift. Within days of the offense, a fingerprint examiner at the crime lab studied the latent fingerprints lifted from the car and determined that several of them were sufficiently detailed and clear to permit a comparison with the fingerprints of the victim and any known suspects. However, no comparison was made until two years after the offense.

The failure to complete routine laboratory analyses in Steve Schilling's case reflected a broad problem that has plagued police-prosecution relations in the United States. Once a criminal investigation has been "cleared" by the identification of a suspect and his arrest, police agencies consider it important to focus their resources on other investigations, since new crimes are committed every day. After a prosecution agency has charged a case, it is often difficult to get the police to conduct further investigations because their priorities are elsewhere. For this reason, prosecutors with the responsibility for charging cases return case files to the police instead of filing charges whenever possible if there are further investigations to be completed, even when strong evidence against the accused already exists.

Nevertheless, formal charges are sometimes filed and assigned to trial prosecutors with important investigations needing to be completed. Trial prosecutors frequently have caseloads with as many as sixty or more active cases and most of these are eventually resolved by plea agreements that obviate the necessity for fully completed investigations. In the small percentage of cases that do proceed to trial, prosecutors sometimes do not discover unfinished investigations until shortly before the trial begins, when they focus their attention on the details of the case for the first time. At that late date, the unresolved investigation will not be completed unless the prosecutor makes a concerted effort either to prod the police department's case agent or to spend the prosecution agency's own limited resources to finish the investigation.

In some cases, it never gets done.

It was July, 1995, when Joyce Carter, a criminalist at the Phoenix Police Department's crime laboratory, studied the request on top of the stack of papers on her desk. After Gerry Baylor's third call, Detective Reynolds had submitted a vial of blood and five items of evidence to the crime lab, requesting a determination of whether the sample of blood in the vial matched any human blood found on the five items of evidence. According to Reynolds' request, a local clinic had drawn the blood from a crime victim named Ray Hart a few days earlier. The five items of evidence were a swatch of carpet, a section of fabric taken from a sofa, a pair of man's pants, a cowboy boot, and a gun.

It was a routine assignment for Carter, who had long experience at the crime laboratory and currently was assigned to the serology section, where she spent most days attempting to identify the characteristics of body fluids—usually blood, but also semen, saliva or urine—and compare them to samples from known individuals. Carter had a bachelor of science degree in chemistry, and had taken courses on serology at the FBI academy in Virginia. She occasionally testified in court as an expert witness on serology for the prosecution in criminal cases, most often involving homicide or sexual assault.

Carter immediately noticed from the case number on the police report submitted by Reynolds that the investigation was a year old. Any blood on the items submitted to the laboratory was not fresh. She winced. Even when blood-stained items were carefully packaged and stored in freezers, the blood was subject to degradation by moisture, heat and light. Carter scanned the earlier police reports in the case trying to determine the reasons for the delay, but could not find any, other than a lack of blood samples from the victim and the defendant to compare with the blood found on the items of evidence. There still was no sample from the defendant, which seemed odd. She also did not understand why the prosecutor or case agent had submitted only five items for testing. The original request submitted twelve months earlier had included approximately twenty other items not included in the present request.

There was a sufficient amount of dried stain on all five items for Carter to determine that each item was spotted with human blood.

Her next task was to compare the blood stains with Hart's blood, to see if it matched. There are many genetic markers, or inherited characteristics, in blood that can be used to differentiate between persons. If the genetic markers of a blood stain do not match the markers of a person whose blood is being compared to the stain, the person is excluded from the population of individuals who could have been the source of the stain. On the other hand, if there is a match between the genetic markers in the stain and those in the person's blood, the serologist cannot conclude with absolute certainty that the stain was made by the person's blood. Instead, the match between genetic markers only permits a conclusion that the person is within a portion of the general population that shares the same genetic markers.

When there is a match between genetic markers, the percentage of the general population that cannot be excluded as a source of the stain is critically important. The smaller the percentage that cannot be excluded, the more confident one can be that a particular person with matching genetic markers is the source of the stain. DNA profiling is by far the most precise method to compare genetic markers in blood (or other tissue) samples, but DNA analysis is also more expensive and time consuming than other, more conventional, methods of comparison. In Maricopa County in the mid-nineties, DNA analysis was permitted only when approved by a special committee in the prosecutor's office, after a written request was made by a trial attorney, usually in homicide or sex offense prosecutions, and virtually never in routine felony cases. Baylor made no such request in the Schilling case.

Carter compared the stains with Hart's blood sample by using the conventional ABO blood group system, as well as by comparing seven proteins or "iso-enzymes" in blood that could be used to differentiate between individual persons. The blood on the carpet, the sofa and Schilling's pants matched Hart's group O blood, and the enzymes were also consistent with Hart's, allowing her to conclude that Hart was within the four percent of the general population who could have been the source of these stains. But the blood on the tip of Schilling's boot had deteriorated substantially in the previous twelve months, making a comparison of some of the enzymes impossible. Although the remaining enzymes did match Hart's blood, Carter was only able to conclude that Hart was within the fourteen percent of the population who could not be excluded as the source. The blood on the gun had deteriorated so much that a comparison with Hart's blood would only be possible with DNA testing, which Carter was not trained or authorized to do.

Neither Reynolds nor Baylor asked Carter to test the metal bar, the duct tape or the other bloody items seized at the crime scene by the police. These items remained in the police property room and were never again submitted to the crime laboratory for either serology analysis or fingerprint examination. Carter also formed no conclusion concerning the probability that Steve Schilling was the source of any of the blood stains on the five items she tested. No one ever asked her to do so.

Although Schilling's new lawyer was not yet aware of these problems in the state's evidence, there appeared to be plenty of reasonable doubt in Schilling's case.

Chapter 15

Gang Warfare

I was now involved in gang-related cases, many of which involved routine crimes that were similar to those prosecuted by other trial groups, with the only difference being the defendant's alleged affiliation with a street gang. Others, however, reflected the violence associated with some street gangs. Among these were an attempted murder of a police officer, three drive-by shootings, a brutal home invasion in which two persons were stabbed, a shoot-out at a social club, another at an inner-city church and several armed robberies. I acquired a number of these cases from colleagues at the Gang/ROP bureau who knew that I wanted to prosecute more challenging crimes.

In one of these cases the defendant, Paul Croft, was charged with attempting to murder his cousin, a former member of his street gang, who survived the shooting with a bullet lodged in his brain. Two neighbors of Croft's cousin saw a man creep toward the cousin's house, hide in the bushes next door and shoot the cousin at close range while he was sitting on his front porch. Croft admitted before trial that he was the shooter, but claimed that he had acted in self defense; his lawyer planned to offer evidence of the cousin's lengthy history of violence, as well as prior threats he had made against Croft. Although the physical evidence did not support a self defense claim, the cousin refused to cooperate with the police, while the neighbors were afraid to testify against Croft, belatedly saying that the cousin might have been armed at the time of the incident. The trial would probably boil down to a question of which cousin looked more ornery to the jury, but both sides blinked as we were about to select the panel. The case settled with Croft agreeing to a seven year sentence.

I learned that the problems I encountered in *Croft* were typical for Gang/ROP prosecutions, with many of the state's witnesses disliking and distrusting police and prosecutors more than the defendants, while others were intimidated by the defendants and their friends. Witnesses sometimes disappeared on the eve of trial. Those who begrudgingly came to court under subpoena frequently alienated juries, appearing either bored or angry, dressing sloppily and recanting earlier statements. The Gang/ROP prosecutors leaned on these witnesses, sometimes resorting to heavy-handed threats of incarceration, to get their cooperation. But witnesses still refused to testify, in some cases because they had received death threats. One of the prosecutors was also the target of death threats during my time in the group.

Not long after *Croft* settled, Lynn Michaels, my fellow Gang/ROP prosecutor, handed me another file that she thought I might find interesting. The defendant, Garry Espinoza, was charged with possessing cocaine and marijuana for sale, possessing prohibited firearms and committing each of these crimes with the intent to assist a criminal street gang. Michaels expressed confidence that the case would proceed to trial because Espinoza had refused a plea agreement, insisting on his innocence. The trial was to take place in two months (unless the court postponed it to a later date), about the time of my scheduled departure from the County Attorney's Office. We agreed that if I wanted the case, I would extend my tenure at the agency until the completion of the trial.

Espinoza's prosecution was based on evidence obtained the previous April when the Phoenix police served a search warrant at an inner-city home owned by a woman named Juanita Sanchez. In a rear bedroom, they found Espinoza's birth certificate and social security card not far from a cache of narcotics, an assault rifle and a sawed-off shotgun. Espinoza himself was outside the house, in the front yard, with $1450 in his pocket. A gang-squad detective participating in the search questioned a twelve-year-old girl on the front porch. The girl, who lived in the house with several members of her family, told the detective that Espinoza and another man, Tony Montoya, lived in the rear bedroom.

At first, I did not see how we could possibly convict Espinoza. The circumstantial evidence tying him to the drugs and weapons would probably get us past a directed verdict for the defense, but other circumstances hurt the prosecution's case. At least twelve persons were on the premises at the time of the police raid, most of them inside the house, physically closer to the drugs than Espinoza. The rear bedroom was littered with papers, linking many people to the room in addition to Espinoza, and the state had not found any fingerprints on the drugs or the guns. Tony Montoya had already pled guilty to possessing the cocaine and had been placed on probation, with a six month jail term. Espinoza's defense lawyer planned to call Montoya as a witness, to testify that he was the only person residing in the bedroom, that he alone possessed the drugs and weapons and that Espinoza knew nothing about the illegal activity. Juanita Sanchez was going to testify that although Espinoza had lived in her home in the past, he was only an occasional visitor at the time of the police raid. To corroborate Sanchez's testimony, the defense lawyer had produced a lease, showing that Espinoza lived at another address. The case reeked of reasonable doubt; I was reasonably sure I did not want to try it.

However, a week later, Tom Kelly, the gang-squad detective assigned to the case, visited me in my office, urging me to reconsider. Tall, stocky and full of exuberance, Kelly towered over my desk, insisting that I had misread the file. Espinoza's prosecution was not a mere drug possession case, he argued. Instead, the trial would tell the story of a gang, Espinoza's gang, the Southside Gangsters. "I *guarantee* you won't lose this case," he told me fervently.

Kelly returned the next day with a large stack of material relating to Espinoza, the Southside Gangsters, frequently called the "SSG," and Juanita Sanchez's house, an address I would soon know well. The pile included over twenty police reports covering a period of more than eight years, dozens of photographs, a thick scrapbook filled with letters, another with gang-related drawings and a four-page dossier the gang-squad detectives had compiled on Espinoza. He invited me join him and his partner when they patrolled south Phoenix the following Friday night, to learn more about the gang. It was an invitation I could not refuse.

Many officers in the patrol division of the Phoenix police aspired to join the elite Gang Squad, a group of detectives who generally worked night shifts and traveled around the inner-city in older model, unmarked cars. The cocky detectives wore distinctive black T-shirts emblazoned with the words "Gang Squad," viewing themselves as modern incarnations of Elliott Ness, engaged in an all-out war on street gangs. By 1997, roughly eighty percent of the police agencies in urban America had such a unit. In Phoenix, their principal role was to gather intelligence relating to gang activities and affiliations, maintaining a database of all street gangs known to have engaged in criminal acts. When they saw young men in areas frequented by gangs, which also happened to be predominantly Hispanic and African-American neighborhoods, they struck up conversations with them to learn whatever they could. They detained possible gang members for "field interrogations" and they pulled over cars with suspicious looking occupants, using their authority to enforce the traffic laws, even though they rarely, if ever, wrote citations.

Whenever gang-squad detectives acquired information connecting a person with a street gang, they entered it in the database. The information came in many forms, such as statements the person made relating to his gang associations during a field interrogation, the color or style of clothing he wore, the persons he was seen with, any gang-related tattoos he had, his name appearing in gang-style graffiti, his flashing of gang signs with his hands and the like. As soon as a person acquired two separate entries in the gang database, the Gang Squad identified him officially as a street gang member and shared this information with every law enforcement agency in the county. Thereafter, whenever the police arrested the person, they contacted a Gang Squad detective, who submitted the case to the Gang/ROP bureau in the County Attorney's Office, where the prosecutors applied special charging and plea bargaining policies designed to break up gangs.

Savvy gang leaders, aware of the Gang Squad's elaborate intelligence gathering operation, did whatever they could to hide their affiliations. However, less sophisticated kids who were marginally connected to gangs but hoped to look important, the so-called gang "wannabes," sometimes entered the database unwittingly. In this way, police records on gang membership could be misleading or wrong, leading to erroneous decisions in the handling of criminal prosecutions.

Tom Kelly had been a patrol officer working the streets of south Phoenix for a number of years before his promotion to the Gang Squad. On several occasions, he had responded to incidents at the same house, sometimes involving Garry Espinoza, whom he arrested more than once. Kelly had been assembling information on the Southside Gangsters for years and he was probably more familiar with the gang than anyone else, aside from the SSG members themselves. When he joined the Gang Squad, he asked to be assigned to the area he had patrolled, rather than the west side of town, where many of the city's largest and most violent street gangs operated. His request was granted.

Kelly spent much of our ride-along recounting the history of the Southside Gangsters.

Under the leadership of Jose Chavez, the Southside Gangsters had split off from Hayden Park, a larger street gang in south Phoenix, in the early 1990s. Most SSG members lived in the four square blocks in south central Phoenix that surrounded East Jones and East Southgate Streets, and the gang claimed this neighborhood as its turf. The focal point for the gang's activities seemed to be Juanita's house, where she lived with her son. Sometimes Juanita's sister also lived there.

The police had been there countless times, responding to reports of fights, loud noise from late night parties and gunshots fired on the premises. On one occasion, a neighbor called 911, saying that she saw a woman being dragged by her hair into the house, screaming. On another, police officers found a man with eight stab wounds lying in a pool of blood on the sidewalk in front of the house. The man refused to say who had stabbed him, apparently frightened of the repercussions. A group of young men and teenagers assembled in front of the house most nights, drinking beer and directing rude, derisive comments at passers-by, often flashing a distinctive SSG hand sign. Most of them wore belt buckles adorned with the letters SSG and some had SSG tattoos. There was no mistaking the membership of this particular street gang.

A few years earlier, members of a rival gang had driven by the home of an SSG gang member, a block away from Juanita Sanchez's house. One of the passengers in the car shouted "brown pride" and "Westside," while another stuck a gun out of his window and fired several shots in the direction of the group standing in front of the house. A bullet went through the shoulder of Juanita Sanchez's son, an SSG member. A few months later, when another car passed through the neighborhood, a group of SSG members chose not to wait to see if it was a rival gang, firing a barrage of shots at the car while shouting "Southside Gangsters!" The car's startled occupants, who had no apparent gang affiliations and just happened to be passing by, called the police.

Garry Espinoza had been a central figure in the Southside Gangsters, frequently in the middle of the group in front of Juanita's house. Espinoza had gang tattoos, admitted his SSG affiliation to Gang Squad detectives on at least two occasions and appeared in many of the photos in Kelly's collection, wearing clothing and jewelry with SSG insignia. When the gang's leader served time in prison, he wrote several letters to Espinoza, stating in more than one that Espinoza was in charge of SSG business during his absence. He instructed Espinoza on who was to be jumped into the gang, who was to be watched carefully and how they were to deal with rival gangs.

Kelly had assembled police reports relating to at least eleven incidents in which the police had encountered Espinoza with a loaded gun in his possession. Sometimes he carried a 9 mm Ruger semi-automatic. On other occasions it was a Glock 9 mm with a laser sight, a Smith & Wesson .38 caliber, or a .45-caliber semi-automatic. Once, when a man had driven his car by Juanita's house to drop off a friend several doors away and then drove back in the direction from which he had come, Espinoza pointed a long, menacing gun at him, seemingly taking aim. Espinoza was not prosecuted, because the man left the state shortly after the incident.

All this occurred before the police raid at Juanita Sanchez's house.

That night, Garry Espinoza and Roberto Senna had barely popped open their beer cans, not yet settling into the lawn chairs in Juanita's back yard, when they heard the rumble of cars in the alley behind them, still a few houses away, but coming toward them. Espinoza had no reason to expect trouble from the Westside Phoeniquera or other rival gangs, but trouble usually came when he was not ready. His first instinct was to retrieve the gun he had left in his car, parked on the street in front of Juanita Sanchez's house. The cars in the alley stopped abruptly as Espinoza turned the corner of the house and suddenly five or six plain clothes police officers appeared at the rear of the property. Espinoza kept running, reaching the front yard when two unmarked police cars pulled up on the street. One of the cops pointed a gun and shouted at Espinoza to lie down with his hands behind his head. The police were everywhere.

Within seconds, they rushed through the front door of Sanchez's house, at least half of them from the Gang Squad, some of the same ones Espinoza said had been picking on him for years. He knew most of them by name and they all knew him. He could not understand why they had singled him out, constantly hassling him, saying that his friends from the neighborhood, his homeboys, were criminals. They had stopped him on the street at least once a week for the previous three years, always frisking and questioning him, not caring if he had important business to take care of at the time. Almost every hour, patrol cars drove slowly past Juanita's house, looking for trouble. If they saw Espinoza and his neighborhood friends in front of the house, they would park nearby and watch them, shining a spotlight on them if it was dark outside. Whenever they saw Espinoza in a car, they'd pull him over for no reason at all, sometimes detaining, searching and questioning him for a half hour or longer before they let him go. Espinoza was sure that none of this would have happened if he were white.

He recalled the time when two officers in a patrol car followed him as he drove away from Juanita Sanchez's house with Tony Montoya and Roberto Senna in his car. He immediately saw them in his rear-view mirror, so he was extra careful to come to a full stop at the corner before turning onto the next street. They pulled him over anyway, searched the car and arrested Senna for possession of marijuana and Montoya for giving them a false name. They didn't come up with a charge against Espinoza, but they handed him a citation for failing to signal before making his turn at the stop sign.

Espinoza insisted they had tried to pin charges on him on other occasions. One night, a couple of years earlier, when he was living at Juanita's, he came home around midnight and noticed an unmarked police car drive by the house. It was always easy to spot the police. As he walked up to the front door, the cops—from the Gang Squad—parked in front of the house next door told him to freeze. They searched him, took the gun he was carrying in a holster and arrested him for carrying a concealed weapon. He protested that it was legal to carry a gun in Arizona, but it was to no avail. He spent the next twenty-four hours in jail, then was released when the prosecutor declined to file charges against him.

A few hours after his release, he sat outside the front door of Sanchez's house drinking a beer with a few of his friends. But then Tom Kelly, whom Espinoza called the worst of his tormentors, drove by the house with another Gang Squad detective, first in one direction and then the other, staring at him. When Espinoza yelled at them to go away, Kelly arrested him for disorderly conduct, saying that Espinoza's words were offensive and that little children from the neighborhood might hear him. Once again, Espinoza spent the night in jail and once again he was released without formal charges.

Now twenty-four years old, Espinoza had never been convicted of a crime, aside from a case in juvenile court when he was sixteen years old. Moreover, despite all the attention he had received from the police during the previous few years, with countless detentions on the street and at least seven or eight arrests, he had faced only one adult prosecution, when Tom Kelly arrested him a few months before the April drug raid.

Kelly and two other Gang Squad cops had followed Espinoza and Roberto Senna when they left a party at Juanita's one night. Senna was driving on this occasion and Espinoza told him to be careful, because Kelly would try to find some reason to bust them. Espinoza made sure that the gun he was carrying was in plain view, on the dash board, to avoid another bogus arrest for carrying a concealed weapon. Nevertheless, after they had gone about three blocks, Kelly signaled them to pull over, claiming later that Senna had rolled through a stop sign.

Kelly grabbed the gun from the dash board, a .45 caliber semi-automatic that Espinoza had purchased at a gun show. Handing the gun to his partner, Kelly said that Espinoza was not permitted to carry it, because the juvenile court had found him guilty of robbery seven years earlier. Espinoza said he had no idea what Kelly was talking about. The Phoenix police had probably seen him with a gun at least thirty or forty times before this; while they sometimes accused him of conceal-ing it, not once had they mentioned anything about his juvenile record. Nevertheless, the county attorney charged him a few weeks later with being a "prohibited possessor" of a firearm and the case was pending in court.

Espinoza had always carried a gun for self-protection, feeling vulnerable because of his ties to the Southside Gangsters. He said every young Hispanic he knew was associated with a gang, an important and necessary part of life in this area of the city. The SSG had rivalries with other gangs, including Westside Phoeniquera, Southside Blood, Southside Posse, and—on and off—Hayden Park. Members of those gangs had shot at him six times and he had shot back twice, defending both himself and his neighborhood. Now, with Kelly telling him that he was not allowed to have a gun, he felt damned if he did and damned if he didn't. Constantly followed by the police and a target of rival gangs, he was sure that he would be dead in a year or two.

The SSG was the only family that Espinoza had. Juanita's son and Tony Montoya were like brothers to him, he said, and he referred to their mothers as his "aunts." According to Espinoza, his own parents abused him as a child and he moved in with Juanita when he was twelve years old. As a teenager, he sometimes stayed at Juanita's home, and he occasionally resided with Tony's mother. Other times, he lived on his own, never seeing his parents.

Espinoza had been arrested for robbery and sent to a juvenile correctional facility during his freshman year of high school. After his release, he decided not to return to school and he saw no reason to obtain a GED. He sometimes mowed lawns for a friend, who had started a landscaping business, but most days Espinoza just hung around (or "kicked back," in his words) with a close-knit group of friends from the neighborhood. They drank beer and smoked pot together and were proud of both their Mexican heritage and the neighborhood, which they referred to as their "barrio." Espinoza liked to say that he was "down for the hood," meaning that he would do anything to protect it from outsiders. He and his closest friends were intensely loyal to one another and each had special nicknames like "Gee Gee," "Wino" and "Froggy." Espinoza himself was the "Joker."

On the day of the drug raid, a police officer stood over Espinoza in the front yard of Juanita's house, while nine detectives, including Kelly, entered the house with a search warrant. The warrant was based on a marijuana sale made to an undercover officer working for the Phoenix Police Department's drug enforcement bureau two days earlier. The undercover agent had purchased a small quantity of pot through a rear window of the house while standing outside, with the seller remaining out of view during the transaction. The seller told the agent through the window that he could deliver another fifty to seventy-five pounds within the next two days.

Both the drug enforcement bureau and the Gang Squad participated in the search of the house, finding at least eight or nine persons inside and another four or five in the yard. Everyone cooperated with the police, lying face down, including the three children who were in the front room when the detectives burst through the door with their guns out. The police went through the house quickly, finding most of what they were looking for in a rear bedroom, apparently the same room from which the sale had been made two days earlier. No one was inside the room when the police arrived, but they found substantial evidence of drug trafficking, including seventeen grams of crack cocaine and twenty-eight grams of powder cocaine, a small amount of marijuana, five cell phones, a police scanner, a two-way radio, $350 in currency on one shelf, $575 on another and $175 on top of a dresser.

The room was also filled with weapons and memorabilia of the Southside Gangsters. A sawed-off shotgun lay on one of the two beds, next to an assault rifle. Strewn about the room, the detectives saw dozens of photographs of SSG members, including Garry Espinoza, and in several of the pictures, Espinoza and his friends pointed guns and flashed SSG signs with their fingers. Kelly and his partner collected these, as well as numerous drawings with references to the gang and correspondence discussing gang activities. They also took a three-foot by four-foot poster from one of the walls. The poster displayed a blown-up photograph of four individuals standing beside a car. Initially, the detectives could not identify one of the four men, but they identified the others: Roberto Senna, Tony Montoya and Garry Espinoza. Senna had a rifle in his hand, Montoya carried a sawed-off shotgun and Espinoza was wearing a baseball cap with the word "Southside" across the front.

Tom Kelly was sure that the drug raid finally had given him the evidence to nail Garry Espinoza. Several months earlier, the County Attorney's Office had used an obscure statute to charge Espinoza after Kelly had arrested him for unlawfully possessing a firearm, but the prosecutor handling the case believed it would be difficult to convict Espinoza for this crime. At most, he said, Espinoza would get three years of probation. A drug trafficking conviction would be far more serious; the amounts of both crack and powder cocaine found in the rear bedroom were well over the threshold for mandatory prison sentences.

Kelly understood that the circumstantial evidence connecting Espinoza to the drugs was shaky, but he also believed that the gang-related material found in the bedroom would strengthen the state's case immeasurably. When he submitted the case to the County Attorney's Office for charging, he requested prosecution of Espinoza and Montoya not only for possessing the drugs and weapons found in the room, but also for committing the crime to "assist a criminal street gang." The gang charge was central to the case, in Kelly's view, because it demonstrated the defendants' motive for committing the crimes, while also allowing the jury to learn about their violent lifestyle.

However, the prosecutor charging the case rejected the gang motivation allegation, explaining that such a charge was limited to situations in which criminal conduct was explicitly intended to further a gang's interest. As an example, he hypothesized a case in which a gang member shouted his gang's name while shooting from a car at members of a rival gang, contrasting it with the present case, in which persons arrested for drug trafficking also happened to be gang members. Although the circumstantial evidence linking the defendants to the drugs was not overwhelming, the case would have to stand on that evidence alone.

Kelly was incensed by this decision, repeatedly lobbying the Gang/ROP bureau to re-staff the case, at least against Espinoza. He argued that in rejecting the gang motivation charge, the prosecutor's office had failed to consider the substantial evidence linking Espinoza and the SSG to Juanita Sanchez's, especially to the rear bedroom of the house. A strong case could be made, Kelly urged, that the *gang* was selling drugs from the rear bedroom and that Espinoza was at the center of the gang. When the jury learned the nature and extent of Espinoza's gang involvement, it would certainly convict him, even if the evidence that he personally had possessed the drugs was less than perfect.

After six months of Kelly's complaints, the Gang/ROP prosecutors relented. Tony Montoya had already pled guilty to his role in possessing the narcotics, but Espinoza's case was still pending, so the prosecutors charged him in a separate indictment with committing the drug trafficking and firearms crimes for the purpose of assisting a criminal street gang. This charge guaranteed that the jury would know about Espinoza's gang involvement when it weighed the evidence on the other charges. It also upped the ante, precluding a probationary sentence on any of the charges and adding two years to the prison term the court would impose on each count.

"All you need is twelve good citizens" Kelly urged me, confident that a jury would decide Espinoza's guilt as soon as it heard about his gang activities.

The plan was to bury Espinoza in gang-related evidence. At Kelly's insistence, I filed a pre-trial motion seeking permission to offer evidence demonstrating Espinoza's involvement in the gang, to establish his motive for selling the drugs and possessing the weapons. The motion listed a large number of items including: photographs of SSG graffiti on neighborhood walls that featured Espinoza's gang name, "Joker"; photographs of Espinoza in SSG attire, posing with automatic weapons, similar to the notorious photos of Bonnie and Clyde; letters from the gang's incarcerated leader; Espinoza's own prior admissions of gang ties, made to the police; and fourteen incidents of gang-motivated crimes associated with Juanita Sanchez's house, Espinoza or both. I was unsure of how much of this evidence to use at trial. Kelly, who had painstakingly assembled it over a period of years, wanted the jury to see it all, but there was a danger of a backlash from the jury if we went full tilt. The prosecution might resemble a persecution.

In the end, Lynn Michaels made this decision, because the defense requested and received a postponement of the trial, which would occur after my departure from the County Attorney's Office.

When it occurred I promised to watch closely from the sidelines. And I did. The trial was over in a matter of days. The defense lawyer was so confident of a not guilty verdict that he accepted the first twelve prospective jurors. Michaels, in turn, pared her case to its essentials, cutting back substantially on the potentially inflammatory gang-related evidence that Kelly had assembled. What remained, however, undoubtedly left its mark on the jury.

The judge permitted Kelly to testify as an expert witness, on the ground that most jurors lacked familiarity with the ways of street gangs. Kelly offered his interpretations of the few photographs and letters that Michaels had placed into evidence and rendered his opinions on Espinoza's gang-related motivations. Kelly told the jury that Hispanic street gangs such as the Southside Gangsters frequently trafficked in narcotics to finance the purchase of sophisticated weapons. They needed the weapons, Kelly testified, to use against rival gangs and others they perceived as threatening.

Michaels also introduced into evidence the large poster of Garry Espinoza and his friends posing with assault weapons, as well as a group of color photographs of Espinoza's tattoos. On his stomach was a large picture of a gun, with the inscription "Lado Sur," the Spanish words for Southside. A tattoo on one of his shoulders depicted a gangster pointing a gun, and on his other shoulder was a picture of a man going to prison in handcuffs, with the letters "SSG."

There were no surprises in the defense case. Tony Montoya testified that he alone stayed in the rear bedroom of Juanita Sanchez's house and that all the narcotics were his. Sanchez told the jury that Garry Espinoza had not lived in her house for more than a year before the police raid. The twelve-year-old girl recanted the statement she had made to the police. The defense witnesses testified that the graffiti, photos and correspondence referred to by Kelly in his testimony were at least two years old. Espinoza also testified, denying participation in or knowledge of any drug sales at Sanchez's house. He admitted his former association with the Southside Gangsters, but asserted that he ceased being an active member of the gang months before the police searched the house.

After all the evidence had come in, the judge dismissed the charge that Espinoza had committed the crime of assisting a criminal street gang, based on a technical reading of the statute. The judge also remarked to Michaels that she was surprised the prosecutor's office would charge a drug possession case with such weak evidence.

The jury began its deliberations at 3:10 P.M. on a Tuesday afternoon. After recessing overnight, it returned a unanimous verdict at noon on the following day, finding Espinoza guilty of all remaining charges, overlooking the weakness of the possession charges.

Cases like this rarely went to trial because of the threat of the inflammatory trial evidence, coupled with the mandatory prison sentence. Most defendants would plead guilty to the underlying drug traf-ficking charges. This time, as Kelly had predicted, twelve good citizens had not questioned Espinoza's guilt.

Chapter 16

Damned Luck

August 3, 1995

James Thornton slowly walked across the asphalt parking lot in 113 degree heat, approaching the Lawton Corporate Center, a modern high-rise complex in uptown Phoenix. Two weeks earlier, he had received a subpoena, directing him to appear this day at the law offices of Masters & Associates, where the defense lawyer in Ray Hart's products liability lawsuit would depose him. Thornton's face looked apprehensive; he had never testified in court or even appeared at a deposition.

The trial in Hart's lawsuit against Budget Stores, Inc. was scheduled to begin in mid-August. A few months earlier, the lawyer for the defense, Oran Hasting, came across a news article in the *Arizona Republic* that described the circumstances of Steve Schilling's arrest for kidnapping and assaulting Hart. The article referred to Hart, tantalizingly, as the "bad penny who pilfered [Schilling's] coin collection." Intrigued, Hasting left a message on Schilling's answering machine, explaining that he represented a store Hart was suing and wanted to learn what he could about the man.

Schilling returned to his house a few hours later, accompanied by James Thornton, and replayed his messages. Stirred by Hasting's message, he called the lawyer immediately, eager to describe how Hart had burglarized his home, adding—to Hasting's satisfaction—that Hart had bragged to him several times about his phony claim against Budget. Recognizing that Schilling's credibility as a witness would be tainted by the pending criminal case against him and his possible vendetta against Hart, Hasting asked if anyone else had overheard Hart boasting. Schilling handed the telephone to Thornton, who echoed Schilling's version, saying Hart had boasted about swindling Budget. Hasting added Thornton to Budget's witness list for the upcoming trial and, to be safe, decided to take his pre-trial deposition.

When he was notified of the deposition, Hart's lawyer, Paul Kardan, called Hart to ask what he knew about James Thornton. At first, Hart had no idea who Thornton was or why Budget would want him as a witness at the trial, but the name James Thornton sounded vaguely familiar. Hart tried in vain for several days to remember when and where he had heard the name or previously run across the man. Then, shortly before the deposition, he remembered that James—he believed—was one of the men who had assaulted him at Steve Schilling's house a year earlier, the short man who had hit him with a baseball bat. On the night of the incident, they had referred to the man only by his first name, but Hart had seen him on other occasions at Schilling's house and had heard his last name in passing. Now he made the connection.

Excited by the possibility of catching one of his assailants, Hart called Detective Reynolds, who grumbled that he did not have time to investigate every remote possibility, but he nevertheless punched Thornton's name in his computer, finding out that the Phoenix resident fit the description of one of the assailants Hart had described a year earlier. Realizing that Hart might be correct, Reynolds located a booking photograph of Thornton from a March 1995 arrest for drug possession, then asked Hart to come to the police station to see a photo lineup. When Hart got there and Reynolds showed him five pictures, Hart immediately chose Thornton's image from the group.

Thornton was relieved to escape the heat when he entered the air-conditioned lobby of the Lawton Corporate Center, paying little attention to the expensive modern art on the wall and the small group of men in Hawaiian shirts who sat reading newspapers in the middle of the room. Thinking he heard his name, he looked up, noticing two men in dress shirts and ties—apparently lawyers—peering at him from behind a mahogany railing on the balcony above. Unknown to Thornton, Ray

Hart now watched him walk across the lobby toward the elevator. Hart nodded to the men in Hawaiian shirts, undercover police officers, who sprang from their chairs and tackled Thornton, just as he was about to enter the elevator. Thornton never did learn what occurs at a deposition.

Oran Hasting was furious that no one had cared to inform him of the impending arrest until moments before, when Paul Kardan excitedly broke the news on the balcony. He felt the police had created a tawdry spectacle in the lobby of the law firm's building. Now he had one less witness for his upcoming trial. Kardan, on the other hand, had reason to be thrilled.

Thornton had no idea why he was being arrested. He had discussed the Schilling/Hart incident with several attorneys, including Hasting, and none of them had warned him that he risked arrest if he testified against Hart. They had all seemed friendly towards Thornton, especially the lawyers representing Steve Schilling. This had lulled him into the naive belief that they were all on the same side of the case, pitted against Hart and the state. No one informed him that the interests of Schilling— or even Budget Stores—might well conflict with his own.

Thornton had agreed to help because he considered Schilling to be his best friend, almost an older brother. But Schilling's first lawyers, Mahoney and Associates, had sought to get Schilling a better plea bargain from the state by offering to turn Thornton in. The lawyers had not acted improperly, according to the ethics rules of the legal profession, because they had a fiduciary duty to Schilling, but not Thornton. Later, Thornton met at a restaurant with Ted Carter, an investigator Schilling retained to assist his new lawyer, Bill Warren. Carter surreptitiously tape recorded the interview, although Thornton had told him he didn't want to have his statement recorded. Like the lawyers, Carter had violated no laws, since it is legal in Arizona for a person to secretly record a conversation without the consent of another participant.

Nevertheless, Thornton felt betrayed when he eventually learned what had occurred. It was a feeling Thornton knew well.

A Phoenix native, James Thornton had been raised solely by his mother, not learning until adulthood that his father had run off with another woman shortly after James was conceived, whom he ultimately married. When he was a little boy, his mother had a series of relationships with alcoholic boyfriends, men with little tolerance for the antics of

young children. One of her male companions believed that the best way
to discipline James was to lock him in a closet. The abuse ended by his
eighth birthday when his mother found steady employment and married
a decent man, but Thornton never managed to pull his life together. He
dropped out of high school in the eleventh grade, gravitated towards
drugs, had difficulty holding jobs and got his girlfriend pregnant. By his
early twenties, James had two sons, each with a different mother. He also
had a minor criminal record, with numerous arrests for driving offenses,
domestic violence and property damage, in addition to at least one misdemeanor conviction for assault.

    Finally, Thornton met his birth father, who was still married to
the same woman and by this time had four other children. The reconcil-
iation between the two men was successful, with his father and step-
mother providing the structure Thornton sorely needed. They gave him
a job, repairing tires at a shop they owned, as well as a mobile home at
their trailer park and a weekly allowance for his expenses. Thornton
responded well, bonding with his half-siblings and trying his best to be a
good influence on his own two sons. However, he could not escape his
affinity for drugs, which, by the mid 1990s, had become a serious addiction. He smoked methamphetamine almost every day.

    Five months before his arrest in Hasting's lobby, a police officer
had observed Thornton running a red light, then discovered that his
license plate was stolen. A few minutes later, when Thornton stopped at
a gas station to fill his tank, the officer pulled up behind him, informed
Thornton that he was under arrest and instructed him to step away from
the gas pump. Thornton suddenly lunged backward, causing the officer
to trip over the hose, breaking his eyeglasses. When Thornton attempted
to flee, the officer grabbed his jacket and the two men fell to the pave-
ment, wrestling furiously. An alert customer at the station jumped on the
two of them and assisted the officer in subduing Thornton. Moments
later, police cars filled the lot, responding to the back-up call. Two officers searched Thornton, finding a bag of methamphetamine and a pipe
in his jacket pocket.

    Although the County Attorney's Office prepared felony charges
against him for resisting arrest and drug possession, the prosecutor
assigned to Thornton's case offered him the opportunity to enter a pre-
trial diversion program. If Thornton attended a six-hour drug abuse class,

submitted to random testing for one year and paid a fine, the state would dismiss the criminal case, allowing him to avoid a felony record. However, Thornton failed to enroll in the program during the next six months, despite several letters from an administrator at the drug treatment center. The prosecutor finally reinstated the charges.

Although the methamphetamine and resisting arrest charges against him were both felonies, they paled in comparison to the allegation that Thornton had participated in the assault and kidnapping of Ray Hart. After the police arrested him at Hasting's office building and took him to the Madison Street Jail, he wanted to retain a lawyer to fight the new charge, but when he called his parents from the jail, they were either unable or unwilling to help. His mother claimed that she could not even afford the $1,600 needed to obtain a bail bond. Thornton remained in jail, without counsel, for the next thirty days, until his mother won enough money at a slot machine on a nearby Indian reservation to bail him out. That same day, the superior court appointed the Maricopa County Public Defender's Office to represent him.

Two weeks after Thornton's arrest, a large crowd filled the gallery of a courtroom in downtown Phoenix, excitedly watching Richard Djerf waive his constitutional right to an attorney and instead represent himself. The case had generated substantial media attention, because Djerf was charged with four counts of first degree murder, the victims being his neighbors, four members of a family on the west side of town. Djerf stunned the packed courtroom, including relatives of the deceased, by insisting on pleading guilty, admitting that he had committed the crimes. The judge repeatedly interrupted, trying to determine if he understood the consequences of his plea, admonishing him that each admission could result in a death sentence. Djerf nevertheless continued his grisly confession.

There were no spectators in a second courtroom a few doors away, where Bill Warren presented oral argument on a motion to dismiss Steve Schilling's case and send it back to the grand jury. The only ones present were Warren and Schilling, prosecutor Gerry Baylor, the judge and his clerk, bailiff and a court reporter. Warren, who had been representing Schilling for two months, urged the court to dismiss the indictment on the grounds that the prosecutor had given incorrect legal instructions to the grand jury and that Detective Reynolds had not presented the facts objectively in his testimony. Warren argued that the detective had given his own subjective opinions. In response, Baylor argued that the motion had been filed a year too late. The judge informed the lawyers that he would take the matter under advisement, but he nevertheless set aside Schilling's trial date.

Schilling was angry. He felt that his former lawyer, Frank Mahoney, had tried to bully him into accepting a plea bargain a few months earlier. Although Mahoney was congenial, there was something about him that had made Schilling uneasy, possibly his frumpy attire and attitude. He suspected that Mahoney had done little to prepare his case for trial, secretly wanting him to plead guilty. Schilling's suspicion increased when his new lawyer informed him that Mahoney and his associates had never requested a transcription of the grand jury proceedings that took place a year earlier.

When Warren read the transcript, he felt that Detective Reynolds hadn't given an accurate accounting of either Schilling's or Hart's statements to the police. Schilling felt satisfied that he had made a good decision in firing Mahoney, but it gnawed at him that he had paid Mahoney so much money. He soon filed a complaint against Mahoney with the state bar, requesting a return of part of the fee he had paid to his former lawyer and he felt even more confidence in his new attorney when Warren agreed to assist in the bar's investigation.

Warren had initially asked for a retainer of $10,000 to take over the case, but was willing to settle for $7,500 if Schilling hired Ted Carter, a private investigator who worked on a number of Warren's cases. The way to win the trial, Warren urged, was to bury Hart in his own dirt and Carter was an expert at digging. However, Schilling soon learned that Carter did not come cheaply, wanting his own retainer, a sum of $3,500. Schilling was forced to sell his most beloved possession, his Harley-Davidson, to hire both the lawyer and the investigator. By this time, he hadn't made a mortgage payment on his house for several months.

In a third courtroom that same morning, Ray Hart and Paul Kardan stood at the counsel table watching the jury retire to begin its deliberations in Hart's case against Budget Stores. The usually good-looking attorney had deep pockets under his eyes that betrayed a lack of sleep.

Once the jurors had filed out of the room, Kardan's shoulders slumped as he talked quietly with Hart, explaining that the jury would probably need a few hours to decide the case, but that Hart should nonetheless remain nearby, in case they returned with a quick verdict. Exhausted, Kardan informed the bailiff that he was going to the cafeteria on the first floor for a cup of coffee. Leaving his briefcase in the courtroom, he quickly headed for the elevator, not lingering for the usual chat with Oran Hasting, the Budget lawyer or the courtroom staff.

Kardan sat listlessly for several minutes in a corner of the cafeteria. He looked as if every ounce of energy had been sapped from his body and he was happy to escape from the courtroom and his client. After a while, however, the jury's verdict occupied his thoughts. How large would the verdict be? Kardan was entitled to a third of the damages awarded to Hart, his contingency fee for the case. The first $15,000 from Hart's share also would go to Kardan, compensating him for fronting all the pre-trial litigation costs and for representing Hart in two criminal cases. There was good reason for Kardan to be cautiously optimistic: even a verdict as small as $60,000—resulting in a $35,000 return for Kardan—would makes the case worthwhile. But if the jury's award was less than $15,000, the meager sum Budget had offered before trial, Kardan would be a big loser, both in the civil action and in the two criminal prosecutions.

Kardan had devoted substantial time and attention to Hart's legal matters. Not long after the beginning of the Budget lawsuit, his client had been charged with felonies in two separate criminal prosecutions, one for stealing construction equipment and the other for possessing methamphetamine. Despite Kardan's limited criminal law experience, he had managed to negotiate decent plea bargains, with Hart avoiding jail in each case and the state promising to reduce the two convictions to misdemeanors if Hart successfully completed probation. Kardan had also filed a lawsuit against Schilling, seeking $300,000 for Hart's injuries. However, he had yet to collect a penny in fees, despite all this work.

Kardan had done as good a job as possible in the Budget case. Although he could not afford the experts Hart needed for a six figure damage award, he had still presented strong evidence that Hart had been seriously injured by a defective lawn chair he purchased from the chain store. Additionally, he had persuaded the judge to deny Oran Hasting's pre-trial motion to introduce evidence of Hart's drug addiction, theft of the construction equipment, theft of a woman's property and the alleged theft of Schilling's coin collection. This ruling was a major victory.

Nevertheless, the trial itself did not go as well as expected for Kardan. Oran Hasting's cross examination of Hart was deft. He forced Hart to admit that he had filed two worker's compensation claims for lower-back injuries during the three years preceding his fall from the lawn chair, raising the inference that Hart's herniated disc was a pre-existing condition. Hasting called an expert witness, who offered the opinion that someone had tampered with the lawn chair before it collapsed under Hart. One of Steve Schilling's friends also testified for the defense, claiming that Hart had boasted of defrauding Budget.

Kardan's pager buzzed, alerting him that he was needed in the courtroom. He straightened his tie and returned immediately, surprised to find that the jury had completed its deliberation after only one hour. A few minutes later, the foreman read aloud in open court the verdict. It was a total victory for the defense. Unanimous. There would be no damage award. It got even worse. The following month, the judge ruled that Hart was to pay Budget's costs in preparing for trial, a sum of $17,562.69. It was, as a practical matter, a meaningless ruling, because Hart had no assets.

The case had turned into a terrible mistake for Kardan, who had at first expected a favorable outcome. Even worse, he had not insisted on a retainer before he undertook Hart's representation in his two criminal prosecutions, with the result that he received nothing for the many hours he had devoted to Hart. It would not be until 1998, three years after the disastrous Budget verdict, that Kardan would receive his first legal fee in a matter involving Ray Hart. But the money did not come from Hart himself. Instead, it was paid by Hart's wife Ronnie when she retained Kardan to sue Hart for divorce.

The kidnapping case was winding through its second year when Steve Schilling arrived promptly for a 9:00 hearing on July 10, 1996. Although the judge was not on the bench when Schilling entered through the rear door, a half dozen lawyers buzzed about the counsel tables discussing cases, while ten prisoners sat chained together in the jury box, wearing the black and white striped uniforms that advertised their current living arrangements. Not surprisingly, James Thornton was not among the fifteen persons in the gallery; Thornton almost never made it to court on time. Schilling took a seat in the back row.

His agitated look told of emotions raw from the many ups and downs of the previous year. That was understandable. It had begun melodramatically when Ted Carter sent Bill Warren a confidential report on Ray Hart's checkered past. Page after page detailed Hart's criminal convictions, dismal credit history, bankruptcies, evictions, federal tax liens, the fraudulent civil lawsuit against Budget, other civil judgments against him and statements from two former employers that Hart had stolen their property. Schilling saw the report as the smoking gun he needed, an exposé of Ray Hart's true character. Bill Warren's insistence on bringing Carter into the case had been a stroke of genius; when the truth came out in court, Schilling felt he'd surely be acquitted.

For a while, Schilling hoped that there might not even be a trial. Not long after Carter's report, the court granted Warren's motion to dismiss Schilling's prosecution, sending it back to another grand jury for a new determination of probable cause. Maybe, Schilling thought, the second grand jury would refuse to return an indictment, ending the case once and for all. But it turned out to be a hollow victory. At the prosecutor's request, the grand jury not only re-indicted Schilling, but also added an additional aggravated assault charge, based on medical records showing that Hart had two separate broken bones. Although the drug trafficking allegation was reduced to a charge of simple possession, the bottom line was that Schilling now had to defend against five charges, not the original four. Warren's strategy of remanding the case to the grand jury didn't pay off in the end, merely delaying the trial for another six months.

A short while after this, Schilling and Warren had a falling out when the lawyer asked for more money. The motion to dismiss the case had exhausted the initial retainer and Warren told Schilling that he needed an additional fee for the remainder of the pre-trial proceedings, plus a daily fee for trial, estimating that the trial would probably take at least two weeks to complete. Schilling had assumed that the $7,500 he had previously paid to Warren would cover the entire representation, including the trial, but Warren insisted that he had made it clear at the outset that the first payment was merely an initial retainer.

There was no way Schilling could afford the fee. He had already sold his truck, motorcycle and other personal possessions, as well as much of the inventory from his business. By now he had little else of value. Warren suggested that he should withdraw from the case and Schilling would be given a public defender to represent him until the eve of trial. If Schilling's family was able to pay his trial fee, he could resume the representation at that time, reasoning that Carter had already completed his investigation and most of the remaining pre-trial court appearances would be mere continuances. Dejected, Schilling parted company with the lawyer, very sure that neither he nor his family would be able to afford the trial fee.

Robert Aron, a lawyer in the Legal Defender's Office, the smaller of the county's two indigent defense agencies, was appointed to take over Schilling's case. Schilling liked Aron, who told him stories of prior trial successes and seemed excited by Ted Carter's report. But Schilling was sure that he'd never get the same quality of representation from a public defender that Warren could have provided, forgetting that the motion to return the case to the grand jury on which Schilling had pinned so much hope and on which his lawyer had allocated a good deal of the fee, had failed.

Nothing else was going well for Schilling either. His girlfriend, Brenda Chase, was threatening to leave him, claiming that she was no longer able to cope with Schilling's emotional outbursts. The state bar had assigned his complaint against Frank Mahoney to an arbitrator. Bill Warren had promised to testify on his behalf at the arbitration hearing, but when he tried to speak to Warren, one of his assistants did not put the lawyer on the line, saying that Schilling still owed Warren money. In the end, it would be Schilling's word against Mahoney's. Then on the day of the hearing, he saw Mahoney and the arbitrator, another lawyer, chatting amicably. Schilling figured they probably were friends, so he was not surprised when the arbitrator ruled that Mahoney was entitled to the entire fee.

Still, Schilling was optimistic that he would win the case when the jury learned of Hart's record. Robert Aron and Thornton's lawyer had jointly filed a motion with the judge to allow the defendants to introduce evidence about Hart's troubled past and drug addiction. They had not yet disclosed Carter's report to the prosecution, but their motion referred to several of the facts that Carter had uncovered. Aron expected the judge to rule on the motion at the hearing, along with a prosecution motion to consolidate Schilling's case with Thornton's, so that there would be only one trial instead of two.

However, on the morning the motion was to be presented, Thornton appeared in court an hour late, not taking the case seriously enough, in Schilling's view. Once there, Thornton acted cocky, as if he would beat the charges, since the only evidence the state had against him was the testimony of Hart, who had not identified him until a year after the incident. Thornton seemed annoyed with his public defender, Dale Harris, who kept urging him to accept the prosecutor's plea bargain. Schilling also was annoyed because the state had made a far more attractive offer to Thornton than to him. Primarily, this was because the evidence against Schilling was stronger and the prosecutor had labeled Schilling as the ringleader.

When the judge took the bench, he ascertained that the defense lawyers had no objection to the prosecution's motion to consolidate the trial of the two defendants, then granted the motion. However, he frustrated Schilling by deferring his ruling on the defense's motion until the eve of trial. Aron was not sure at this juncture how much evidence the defense would be allowed to introduce to sully Hart's credibility with the jury. Winning appeared a lot less certain.

Later, Betty Koto, an evidence technician at the Phoenix crime laboratory, prepared her report on the fingerprint comparisons she had completed. Detective Reynolds had now requested the lab to compare the prints of the victim and two defendants with the latent fingerprint impressions lifted from the crime scene two years earlier. Koto's report was to be good news for both the prosecutor and Steve Schilling, but a disaster for James Thornton. None of Schilling's fingerprints were found at the scene, even though it was his own house. However, Thornton's thumbprint was found on the gearshift of the car that had been backed into Schilling's garage on the night of the incident. Even worse for Thornton, his palm print was on the lid of the trunk that had been slammed over Ray Hart.

The investigation was meandering into its third year by September of 1997.

Left to right: Paul Ahler, Gary Lowenthal, and County Attorney Rick Romley as Lowenthal begins his tenure at the County Attorney's Office of Maricopa County.

The author on the steps of the Maricopa County Courthouse.

Photograph of Ray Hart's injuries, taken at the hospital.

Steve Schilling's home, the scene of the assault and kidnapping of Ray Hart. Note Hart's car in garage and Schilling's prized Harley-Davidson in the driveway.

Schilling's computer, with a bag of methamphetamine hidden inside.

The trunk of Ray Hart's car, still parked in Schilling's garage, in which Hart was locked, bound and gagged and expecting to be dumped in the desert.

Above, the author addresses a judge in a sidebar conference. Below, he addresses members of a jury in a reenactment of a courtroom scene.

Chapter 17

Justice Delayed

I found myself constantly busy trying to stay on top of my cases, envying other prosecutors who seemed much more adept at handling routine matters quickly. The agency wanted us to document every minor occurrence in every case, a largely unnecessary and—for me—hugely time-consuming requirement. It also took hours and hours to draft thoughtful sentencing recommendations and reasonably thorough responses to defense motions, which I considered my professional responsibility. Almost every day, I arrived early and remained late, frequently taking files home to read late into the night. Most of the other prosecutors left at 5:00 and the office was almost empty an hour later, as well as on the weekends. I could not understand how my colleagues avoided falling hopelessly behind in their responsibilities. I would later learn that some of them didn't. Tasks that could easily affect the outcome of cases often remained undone.

Some of the other Gang/ROP prosecutors continued to offer me files, knowing I wanted to gain more experience taking cases before juries. These were generally two-day trials of defendants in the repeat offender program. Typically, the defendants were caught at the scene of their crimes and confessed. In most cases, the defendants declined to testify, to keep the jury from learning of their prior convictions. The only reason the cases went to trial was the prosecution's rigid plea bargaining policy for the repeat offender program. While I was happy to get these courtroom experiences, I yearned for a big case. Before I returned to academe, I wanted full exposure to the real circumstances and consequences of today's criminal justice system.

One soon came my way. Gerry Baylor, my Gang/ROP colleague, asked me if I would be interested in trying an intriguing kidnapping case with two defendants. It was scheduled for jury trial a little over two weeks later. "The date is certain," he assured me, "because the judge has refused to grant any further postponements." Baylor regretted that he would be unable to try it himself, but he had an unalterable conflict in his schedule. If I was willing, the case was "ready to go." Of course, he quickly added, there were a few pre-trial motions still pending, but all of the state's witnesses had been subpoenaed, both for the hearing and the jury trial, which was likely to consume two full weeks.

Baylor invited me into his office and pointed to a large stack of color photographs. I gasped at the first picture I picked up. It depicted a mangled man on a blood-soaked hospital bed, his eyes swollen shut. "He was repeatedly assaulted over a six hour period," Baylor said, shaking his head, "and locked in a car trunk." He believed the dispute arose over stolen property or drugs. Both the defendants and the victim were involved in the methamphetamine culture. Handing me four bulging file folders, Baylor suggested, "Why don't you read them over the weekend and let me know your decision."

I nodded. "I'll tell you on Monday if I will take the case." I glanced at the top folder. The name on it was Stephen Christopher Schilling.

That Friday night, I spread out the numerous court files on my living room sofa and coffee table; then I flipped on the television and joined about two-and-a-half billion other people that were morbidly fascinated by the funeral procession and burial of England's jewel, Princess Diana, who had been killed in a car crash a few days earlier. As the evening progressed, I danced dizzily between Ray Hart's harrowing escape from Steve Schilling's garage and the replaying of the papparazzi's insane, high speed pursuit of the Princess through the streets of Paris. The intimate details of Diana's relationship with Dodi Al Fayed grabbed for my attention, but surprisingly, the bizarre arrest of James Thornton proved to be even more captivating. Eventually, with a flick of the remote control, the funeral was gone and the story of Hart, Schilling and Thornton engulfed me.

I was a bit disconcerted by this point, as the two defense lawyers had been assembling their evidence for more than a year, while I would have only seventeen days to prepare for trial. In addition, the battles were to begin in seventy-two hours, with a hearing on a defense motion to suppress all evidence resulting from the arresting officer's entry into Schilling's garage without a search warrant. Baylor had mentioned in passing I would have to argue several other pre-trial motions before we selected a jury. But things were quite a bit more unsettled than he'd indicated. In a recent development, Thornton's lawyer claimed that she had not received all the evidence the state was required to disclose. Moreover, the state's case was not as ready for trial as I would have liked; neither the police nor the prosecution had interviewed a key defense witness, Brenda Chase, and the laboratory reports seemed—to my untrained eye—to be incomplete. I worried that I might be getting in over my head.

Despite Gerry Baylor's optimism, it seemed to me that the defense lawyers might have a viable chance of creating reasonable doubt. Schilling's girlfriend would probably testify that Hart had initiated the struggle with Schilling by reaching for the gun that lay on Schilling's desk, thus supporting a claim of self defense in connection with the events that occurred early in the evening of July 3. James Thornton's testimony was more difficult to predict, because the police had not interrogated him when he was arrested. I assumed that he would corroborate Schilling's version of the events after Chase had left the house, telling the jury that one of the two men who had never been arrested, the one named Pat, inflicted Hart's injuries and that neither Thornton nor Schilling could control Pat. Schilling himself had insisted to the police that he was not even present when most of Hart's injuries occurred. Proving the state's case might turn on Hart's credibility. The defense lawyers planned to introduce evidence of his two prior felony convictions, his numerous schemes, thefts and alleged burglary of Schilling's home. No doubt they would contend this led to the violent incident on July 3.

A depressing thought crossed my mind: this would probably be my one chance at a major trial and, despite the defendants' guilt, *I might lose the case.* If I wanted, I could avoid this risk by simply returning the files to Baylor, explaining that this case would need more of my time than I could devote. A daunting "To Do" list relating to more than thirty other cases lay on my desk at the prosecutor's office and I had yet to prepare in earnest for a jury trial in a burglary prosecution that was scheduled to begin the following week.

But the Schilling case intrigued me. Unable to tear myself away through the night, I read and re-read the files while taking extensive notes, determined to learn every nuance of the case. I knew by morning that this was the case I had been seeking all along.

While the conflicting accounts of what occurred the night of the crime held my attention, the most striking aspect of the story was the extraordinary fact that it had taken more than three years for the case to get to trial. Arizona's procedural rules were similar to those in most states, prescribing that criminal prosecutions were to be tried within one hundred eighty days after the defendant's first court appearance, and the state's supreme court had placed trial courts under a mandate to meet this deadline in ninety-nine percent of all cases. However, if each party agreed to postpone a case and the trial judge was willing, the procedural rules could be circumvented. It was not at all unusual for a case to exceed the one-hundred-eighty-day time frame; delay was an epidemic, not just in Arizona, but in criminal courts throughout the country.

Nevertheless, the time table of the Schilling case was extreme. It had taken more than six times the maximum allowed under the rules, having been scheduled for trial on twenty-two separate occasions. Fourteen of these were what the local courts called "non-firm" trial dates, meaning that no one really expected the trial to go forward. At these times when the case was announced in open court, the judge merely asked the lawyers how they were progressing in their pre-trial preparations, urged them to move the proceedings along expeditiously and set a new trial date a month or two down the road. Sometimes the assigned prosecutor or defense lawyers did not even appear in person, instead relying on a substitute "warm body" to stand in for them. Typically, the warm body was not sufficiently familiar with the case to be able to say whether it would be ready for trial in the next thirty or sixty days.

However, eight of Schilling's twenty-two trial dates had been designated as "firm." This meant that the court expected on every one of these occasions for each party to be ready to pick a jury and present its evidence. In these instances, the jury commissioner sent notices to approximately fifty prospective jurors to come to the courthouse and, even if the prosecutor believed that the court would probably postpone the trial again, it was still necessary to subpoena all of the state's witnesses. Several of those witnesses were police officers who routinely expected to go to court as part of their work. But others, including the neighbors of Steve Schilling who witnessed Ray Hart's escape and the emergency room physician who treated Hart, had to rearrange their schedules to be present in court for each of those eight trial dates, not knowing until the last moment whether the trial would be continued.

The many postponements of the case affected four people more than all others: Ray Hart, James Thornton, Steve Schilling and Brenda Chase. Like the other prosecution witnesses, Hart received a subpoena whenever the case was set for trial. Gerry Baylor instructed him to call the prosecutor's office each time, on the day before he was to testify, to ascertain if the trial was going to proceed as scheduled. Sometimes the secretary who answered his calls did not know if he would be needed in court. When this happened, he had to call back several times to get definite answers. Other times, she simply told him that the case had been postponed, with no explanation. His family could not understand why Schilling and Thornton were still walking around, getting away with what they had done to him. The hospital and doctors who had treated him were constantly demanding that he pay them. His wife was frightened that Schilling would suddenly appear one day to harm him, as Schilling had apparently tried to do a few months after the crime when he and several of his buddies had driven their motorcycles past Hart's home, displaying guns. Each postponement increased the fear and frustration. Both Hart and his wife desperately wanted closure, but it seemed that it would never occur.

James Thornton had also struggled through the delays. Schilling repeatedly told Thornton that they would prevail at trial because of all the evidence they had against Hart, but each time Thornton went to court, his public defender tried to persuade him to accept the prosecution's plea bargain. The first public defender assigned to his case told him that he would surely lose at trial, because his fingerprints had been found on the lid of Hart's car trunk and a guilty verdict assured a lengthy prison sentence. His second defender, Ellen Tate, seemed much more willing to fight for him in court, but she too urged him to accept the plea agreement. Thornton looked agitated whenever he went to court, with Schilling whispering in one ear and his lawyer in the other. With all the conflicting advice and his own dubious prospects, he worried about the future. Each time the judge postponed the trial it simply meant that he had more time to agonize over his decision and another unpleasant confrontation to look forward to the next time he was in court.

Thornton acquired the custody of his seven-year-old son a few months after his arrest, when his ex-girlfriend was sentenced to prison. Thereafter, every time he went to court, he worried that he too would be taken into custody, not knowing what arrangements he should make for the boy. He also had no idea what would happen to his house and all his belongings if he failed to return. Strangely enough, his former girlfriend served her entire prison sentence before Thornton's case finally ended, relieving at least one of his anxieties. Still, he hated going to court.

Unlike the jittery Thornton, a more egotistical and self-assured Steve Schilling arrived in court promptly and calmly for each of his twenty-two trial dates, in addition to his fifteen other court appearances for arraignments, pre-trial hearings and settlement conferences, sometimes waiting for hours before his case was called, only to have it postponed to a later date. Nevertheless, the many postponements were bringing him financial ruin. His family provided almost no help in paying his legal bills, roughly $23,000 for private lawyers and an investigator. He sold all of his assets to defend himself, eventually having to accept an attorney from the Office of the Legal Defender.

As the case dragged on and on, Schilling could no longer afford to make his mortgage payments or pay his utility bills and he resorted to a variety of tactics to fend off disaster. He mailed unsigned checks to pay his bills, hoping that his creditors would believe that he was merely careless, all the while trying to buy a little more time. When bill collectors called him on the telephone, he complained that he had not received overdue notices in the mail. A compulsive gambler, he went as often as he could to the casinos on local Indian reservations, looking for the stroke of luck that would get him back on track. It never occurred.

In addition, Ray Hart had sued Schilling for $300,000 for Hart's medical bills, lost employment and pain and suffering. Unable to afford a lawyer to defend the civil action, Schilling stalled, hoping the criminal case would be resolved first in his favor. When Hart's lawyer sought a default judgment against him, Schilling filed a hand-written pleading, denying Hart's allegations and counter-claiming for the damage Hart had caused to Schilling's house. Shortly thereafter, Schilling filed for bankruptcy, but he tried to delay this proceeding too, failing to appear in court for an examination by the lawyers representing his creditors. Finally, he could no longer hold off the inevitable and lost his house. Now everything was gone but his freedom.

The trial delays affected Brenda Chase, Schilling's girlfriend, as deeply as Hart, Thornton or Schilling himself. As Shilling's troubles mounted, so did his inner rage. He became increasingly abusive toward her, both verbally and physically. He accused her of seeing other men behind his back, he followed her when they were not together and placed anonymous calls to her apartment to see if she was home. Once, he appeared at a home where she was working as a pediatric nurse, falsely accusing her of having an affair with someone who lived there. Several times he threatened to kill her. Finally, she went to court to obtain an order of protection, directing him to stay away from her. Despite the order, when she tried to move from her apartment, he nevertheless showed up to stop her, getting into a fist fight with a friend of hers who was helping move her furniture and belongings.

Trying to escape her problems with Schilling by using methamphetamine, Brenda lost a great deal of weight. Frequently she became anxious and tearful, sometimes expressing paranoid beliefs that government agents were secretly following her. Her drug dependency led to the suspension of her nursing license. Finally she snapped and had to be hospitalized for amphetamine psychosis, paranoia and depression. Emotionally distraught, Brenda moved to another state to live with her mother. If either side wanted her as a witness when the case went to trial, they would have to go and get her.

Meanwhile, the trial postponements went on and on. There were many explanations and excuses. One factor was the number of times the lawyers changed. Three different law firms or agencies handled Schilling's case. Although the Maricopa County Public Defender's Office always represented Thornton, his case was reassigned to different attorneys within the agency three times, for one reason or another. I was the fourth prosecutor in the case. It had been more than three years since Ray Hart's escape from the car trunk and the scheduled trial date had been postponed many, many times. Each time a new defense lawyer or prosecutor entered the case (before me), the attorney requested and received at least two continuances to review the evidence, interview witnesses, file appropriate motions and prepare for trial.

Even when the lawyers were fully prepared, other circumstances necessitated postponing the trial several times. Bill Warren's motion to dismiss Schilling's case, requiring a new indictment and arraignment, delayed the proceedings for several months. The state also dismissed Thornton's case, sending it back to the grand jury on a technical ground. Once both defendants were properly indicted, another two months went by when the prosecution sought to consolidate their cases. All three parties filed numerous other pre-trial motions, some important and others trivial, further delaying the proceedings. Key witnesses were unavailable on some of the trial dates. On others, one of the lawyers would be in trial in another court or would have a scheduling conflict with a case that was about to be tried. If the defendant in the other case was in custody, unlike Schilling and Thornton, that case would have priority for proceeding to trial.

At this point in time, the lawyers played predominant roles in determining when their cases would go to trial, sometimes after multiple postponements. With heavy caseloads, both prosecutors and defense attorneys almost always felt that they were not as prepared for trial as they would like. If the lawyer on one side sought a continuance to complete preparations or to try a case in another court, the attorney on the other side normally accommodated the request, recognizing that the shoe could easily be on the other foot. When defendants were in custody pending trial, there were both constitutional and practical limits on the number of continuances granted. But when defendants were not incarcerated, there was little constraint on the postponements. Trial judges could prevent unnecessary delay only if they took a tough stance against the lawyers. While a few judges did, most others sympathized with counsel.

However, when the number of trial postponements grows, so also does the size of case backlogs, the length of judicial calendars and the amount of public expenditure necessary for court personnel. Faced with increasing budgetary concerns, court administrators have begun to prod individual judges to deny trial postponements and, in some cases, this pressure has been heavy-handed. One Arizona judge, fearing the repercussions that might occur if he granted a continuance, told the lawyers arguing before him, "We have all been told at a criminal judges' meeting that if we are not going to follow the policy [limiting postponements] then we can be transferred to another division of the court immediately. I don't intend, nor do I want to pick up and move on a moment's notice. ...I'm afraid you guys are stuck on this."

Chapter 18

Liberty and Legitimacy

My first opportunity to observe Steve Schilling and James Thornton occurred two days after I took the case. The occasion was a routine two-hour hearing on a motion filed by Schilling's court-appointed lawyer, Robert Aron, to suppress evidence obtained from an allegedly illegal search and seizure. It was not an especially difficult motion, because the case law supported the state's position.

Schilling was much smaller than I had envisioned. Throughout the morning, he appeared to be tense, never smiling, even when one of the lawyers in the case preceding ours made several funny comments. I sensed that he was studying me the entire time, watching me with lasers during my examination of the witnesses, not hostile, but listening carefully to everything I said. On the other hand, Thornton arrived thirty minutes late and chose to sit in the back row of the courtroom, seeming as bored as Schilling was intense. His hair was long and shaggy, his clothing disheveled. I learned later that he had no idea who I was.

At the conclusion of the hearing, the judge took the matter under advisement, promising a ruling in a few days. No one, including Aron, expected the judge to grant the motion.

The next day, Thornton's lawyer, Ellen Tate, filed a motion to postpone the trial, stating in her supporting memorandum that she was transferring to the juvenile division of the public defender's office and that Thornton's new public defender would need time to prepare his case for trial. I was delighted, since I too wanted more time. However, Robert Aron looked visibly upset, complaining that he had spent months persuading Brenda Chase to testify at the trial and it had been difficult for him to arrange a date that was agreeable to both her and the court. He had purchased her round-trip ticket from the state in which she now lived and did not relish making new arrangements with the airline, the court and especially Brenda. All parties agreed that we needed an immediate ruling on the motion, so the judge's judicial assistant arranged for the lawyers to meet in his chambers the following Monday.

Benjamin Harris was the fifth judge to preside over Schilling's prosecution, receiving the assignment the previous year when the case was consolidated with Thornton's. A crusty sort on even the best of days, Harris had become increasingly short tempered with the lawyers at each of the recent postponements. He had set a strict deadline for the completion of pre-trial witness interviews, declaring in July that he would countenance no excuses for further delays in the case. To no one's surprise, he was in a foul mood when we met in his office to discuss Tate's motion.

Both defense lawyers immediately pounced on me, insisting that I was the logical one to break the impasse. If I would offer a plea agreement that removed the mandatory sentencing restrictions on Judge Harris, giving him the discretion to sentence the defendants to probation if he believed it appropriate, they would accept the deal and there would be no need for Thornton's continuance or Brenda Chase's testimony. Moreover, they argued, the state would no longer incur the considerable expense of a long jury trial.

But the county attorney's deadly weapon policy did not permit such an agreement. Instead, it required a prison sentence, at least for Schilling, because the evidence indicated that he had pointed a gun at Hart without legal justification. Schilling's prior counsel had twice before requested a deviation from this policy and had been turned down, with nothing changing in the case since those decisions were made. I was free to extend an offer to Thornton that rendered him eligible for probation, but the essential decision in the disposition of Schilling's case was the county attorney's, not mine or the judge's.

Harris stated testily to Tate that he would not postpone the trial to allow another lawyer to get up to speed. The Public Defender's Office would have to arrange for her to try the case, he declared, regardless of her transfer to juvenile court. However, Tate stunned everyone in the room when she asked the judge to sever the trials of the two defendants. If Schilling's trial proceeded as scheduled, she argued, Thornton's could follow it, giving his new lawyer two additional weeks to prepare. Additionally, Aron would be able to call Chase as a witness, as he had planned.

It was a good move for Thornton. His public defenders had urged him all along to accept the deal offered by the state, pleading guilty to aggravated assault with the sentence to be left to the discretion of the judge. Thornton had never been able to make up his mind, afraid that Harris would sentence him to prison even under the plea agreement and hopeful for an acquittal if the case went to trial. Severing his case from Schilling's not only would give his new lawyer more time to prepare, it would also provide him with an opportunity to see how Schilling's trial turned out. If Schilling was found guilty, Thornton would know that it was not worth the gamble to go to trial. But if Schilling was acquitted, the prosecution would probably offer Thornton a better plea bargain, one that would guarantee him probation.

However, the severance motion proved potentially disastrous for Schilling. Aron had expected Thornton to testify at a joint trial, telling the jury that Schilling had not harmed Hart after Brenda Chase left Schilling's house. But if the two defendants' trials were severed and Schilling's proceeded first, Thornton's lawyer would almost certainly not permit him to testify for Schilling while Thornton's own prosecution was pending. Thus, if Harris granted Tate's motion, Schilling would lose a potentially important defense witness at his trial.

Moreover, both Hart and Schilling had prior felony convictions and opposing counsel would be permitted to bring this to the jury's attention when cross-examining them. If Schilling and Thornton were tried together, Aron hoped that it might not be necessary to call Schilling as a witness, since the jury would learn his version of the events from Thornton's testimony. The jury would then learn about Hart's felonious background, but not Schilling's. This was especially important to Aron, because Schilling's defense was premised on portraying Hart as the villain in the case, a lying crook who had broken into Schilling's home and stolen his valuable property. However, if Schilling went to trial without Thornton, he would probably have no choice but to testify.

I decided to support Tate's motion for the same tactical reasons that caused Aron to oppose it. If the jurors were going to learn that Hart had an unsavory background, I wanted them to know that Schilling had been in trouble too. Additionally, the thought of cross-examining Schilling made my adrenaline flow. I believed he was lying about the incident and I wanted a crack at him, face to face.

Harris granted Tate's severance motion, ordering that Schilling's case would proceed to trial before Thornton's. It appeared that my desire to cross-examine Schilling would be granted.

When I returned to my office after the hearing, a surprise waited on my desk. The state police had submitted a new case for prosecution, requesting auto theft and drug possession charges against a suspect who had been arrested and released a few weeks earlier. I was to make the charging decision, because the suspect was already on my active caseload. This was not unusual. I charged new cases each week, sometimes relating to defendants already in the system, and the charges requested in this case were routine. Nevertheless, I was astonished when I read the suspect's name: Stephen Christopher Schilling.

Greg Rollins, the officer who had filed the report, was a member of a police task force assigned to catch car thieves. Rollins patrolled the parking lots of the budget motels alongside the freeway approaching Phoenix from the north. The task force had recovered over one-hundred-fifty stolen vehicles from these parking lots during the previous eight months and when Rollins cruised slowly under a gaudy "$59 per night" sign flashing at freeway drivers on a Tuesday morning, he found another: an almost new GMC pick-up truck with an extended cab, custom wheels and a Harley-Davidson motorcycle frame in its bed. The truck had been backed into a bush at the rear of the parking lot, far from the motel rooms, even though the lot was otherwise empty. The shrubbery obscured the truck's license plate, scratching the paint on the tailgate. Someone had gone to great lengths to conceal the plate.

Rollins checked the license number on the computer in his patrol car, learning that the plate had been stolen from a parked car two months earlier. A second computer check, on the vehicle identification number from the truck's dashboard, disclosed that the pick-up itself was stolen. The registration book at the front desk of the motel indicated that

Schilling had checked into one of the rooms the previous evening, identifying his vehicle as a "GMC PU." A surveillance team waited two hours for Schilling to emerge from the room, then watched him walk to the truck, unlock the door with a key and sit in the driver's seat.

The police immediately arrested Schilling and searched the truck. They found a magazine on the front passenger seat with three zip-lock bags jammed between the pages. Inside the plastic bags, the officers discovered an off-white crystal substance later determined to be methamphetamine and underneath the passenger seat was a glass pipe with burned residue that also looked like meth. Someone had also obliterated the identification number from the motorcycle frame in the bed of the pick-up. When Rollins read Schilling his Miranda rights, he invoked them, asking to speak with his lawyer.

As I read on, I realized that Rollins's request for a new prosecution against Schilling could have a profound impact on the kidnapping and assault case. The addition of a new case would give me far greater leverage in plea negotiations, possibly obviating the necessity for a trial. Even if Schilling still refused to enter into a deal, he would not be eligible for pre-trial release on Rollins's theft and drug possession charges, because he allegedly committed the crimes while he was on pre-trial release in connection with his existing case. Thus, Schilling would be in custody when he went to trial, making it much more difficult for him to present a strong defense.

On the other hand, the County Attorney's office policies prohibited me from filing charges against a suspect if I did not believe there was a "reasonable likelihood of conviction" on those charges. In this case, it was a close call.

The evidence indicated persuasively that Schilling possessed the stolen truck, stolen license plate, three bags of methamphetamine and meth pipe. He wrote on the motel registration form that he had a GMC pick-up truck; he entered the truck the following morning with a key; and he sat in the driver's seat, in full control of the vehicle. However, I also had to prove that he *knew* the truck was stolen and that the methamphetamine was hidden in its passenger compartment. On these questions, the evidence was mixed. The manner in which the truck was parked certainly indicated that the person who parked it wanted to hide its license plate. But the crime lab did not find Schilling's fingerprints on the stolen license plate, the zip-lock bags or the meth pipe. There were many possible innocent explanations for Schilling's possession of a pick-up truck and its ignition key and he was likely to come up with one in his testimony at trial. Conviction was anything but a sure bet.

There was a chance of conviction, perhaps even a good chance, but I asked myself was there a reasonable likelihood? When I asked other prosecutors, they seemed evenly divided. Some urged me to go ahead, largely for the tactical advantage I would gain over Schilling. Others disagreed, saying that I should not charge one case merely to enhance another. To this second group, the correct question was whether I would charge the new case in the absence of the existing one.

Clearly, the reasonable likelihood of conviction standard was subjective. What was its purpose? I knew that the county attorney did not want to squander valuable public resources without a high probability of success. I could actually save the county's money by filing the new charges and trying to force Schilling to accept a plea bargain. However, there was an ethical element too. I would be seeking to take away Schilling's liberty and the legitimacy of the prosecution depended on the degree to which I was certain of his guilt. *Was I totally certain of his guilt in this new case?* I asked myself this question over and over without a definite answer.

I decided against filing the theft and drug possession charges. Ten days later, when the long awaited trial date finally arrived, Schilling would not be in custody.

Chapter 19

Preparing for War

During these last days, I wanted to spend every waking moment readying myself for Schilling's trial, shutting out the world around me. With close to fifty other active cases, however, I could ill afford this luxury. Almost every day, I had to attend court hearings, negotiate plea bargains, prepare motions and interview witnesses. I had to take a routine burglary case to trial a week before Schilling's was scheduled to begin, cutting three full days from my preparation time. There was simply no way to avoid such demands and to concentrate solely on the Schilling matter.

The prosecutor of a major felony can usually count on a police investigator to assist in such tasks as bringing the physical evidence to court, preparing exhibits and making sure that witnesses appear when scheduled. The principal investigator, called the "case agent" in Arizona, also usually sits with the prosecutor during trial, to attend to inevitable last-minute problems. I needed all the help I could get from Detective Reynolds, my case agent in *Schilling*, who had been with the Phoenix police for close to three decades. *Schilling* had been Reynolds' case for over three years, since the day after the offense.

However, Reynolds did not call me back when I telephoned him for an appointment to see the physical evidence at the police warehouse. Frustrated, I sought the advice of Gerry Baylor, who maintained a keen interest in Schilling's prosecution, even though he was trying another case. Baylor rolled his eyes sympathetically and sighed. He had not told me about his problems with the detective.

Reynolds had not followed up on the night detectives' requests for laboratory analyses of the physical evidence found at the crime scene and Baylor had to call him several times a year later. The detective had testified before the grand jury giving his own interpretation of Schilling's statements, with the result the case had to be remanded for a new indictment. He had volunteered the information, both to the grand jury and to Schilling's lawyer, that Hart had admitted stealing Schilling's property, even though none of the police reports made reference to the admission and Hart consistently denied that he had ever made such a statement. Reynolds also had told the grand jury that Schilling possessed the methamphetamine found in his computer for the purpose of sale, despite what the prosecutor felt was a lack of evidence to support this claim.

In the three years since the offense, the detective hadn't located Pat and Cliff, the two other men who came to Schilling's aid in the altercation with Hart. Cliff, at least, should not have been difficult to find, since he lived in Schilling's neighborhood, across the street, only four or five houses away. The police hadn't arrested James Thornton until a year after the crime, even though Hart had repeatedly prodded them to act. Although Reynolds interviewed Brenda Chase, a key eyewitness in the case, there was no record of their conversation. According to Schilling, the detective had called him on the telephone, trying to convince him to turn in his friends. Not only was this unlikely to succeed, but Schilling had already been charged and was represented by counsel, who had not been consulted.

Baylor offered no explanation for what had happened between the prosecutor's office and the police detective and advised me not to use Reynolds as my trial investigator, not even to call him as a witness. Instead, he suggested that I contact Rob Nicholson, one of the night detectives who had conducted the initial crime scene investigation. Nicholson still called Baylor for periodic updates on the case, even though his formal role had ended three years earlier.

I followed Baylor's counsel. Fortunately, Nicholson readily agreed to help me out, beginning with a meeting at the police property room a few days later to sort through the evidence. He later brought it to court and managed to find the time to sit with me at the prosecutor's table during the testimony of key witnesses.

　　In planning my strategy, I felt strongly that I needed to get the jury's attention and to give them a clear and compelling story. To do this, I needed to begin with a witness who could paint a vivid picture, then make sure that the problems in my case were sandwiched between powerful pieces of evidence and in the end, appear before them for one last time to make my final impression. It would help if I could keep my witnesses and exhibits to a minimum, to avoid over-trying the case. Baylor had sent subpoenas to nineteen witnesses before handing the case off to me and I had subpoenaed three of my own. There were several dozen items of physical evidence in police lockers, as well as a stack of medical records and more than a hundred photographs of Hart's injuries and the crime scene. Now I would have to make difficult choices about what was most important to present.

　　It was also important to anticipate the defense's case when planning my own. Schilling's lawyer had filed notice that he intended to call nine defense witnesses, including Brenda Chase, who observed much of the incident, but was now living in another state. Although Reynolds had spoken briefly with Chase shortly after the offense, neither the police nor the prosecutor's office had taken a detailed statement from her and I would not have an opportunity to interview her until she arrived in Phoenix a few hours before she was to take the stand. I expected that her testimony would contradict Hart's, but I was not sure what she would say, making the preparation of my own case that much more challenging. Additionally, Schilling's lawyer had not tipped his hand on whether Schilling himself would testify.

　　I assumed that he would. In the end, I believed, the trial would boil down to a credibility contest between Hart and Schilling. Each had a felony record, which the jury would learn about when he testified. Each had also made pre-trial statements that seemed inconsistent with certain aspects of his testimony. However, Hart had been interviewed by the police several more times than Schilling, thus giving Schilling's lawyer more ammunition to work with than I had. Hart also had two prior felony convictions to Schilling's one. Since I needed to persuade the jury that Hart's allegations were true beyond a reasonable doubt, it was important to spend as much time as possible preparing him for his testimony.

Hart seemed aloof when I called him and he appeared disappointed that Baylor was no longer handling the prosecution. He sounded discouraged and certain that the upcoming trial would be postponed, just as it had been countless times before. He struck me as unenthusiastic when I tried to make an appointment to go over his testimony. Nevertheless, he reluctantly agreed to come to the County Attorney's Office ten days before trial, "for all the good it will do," he said disgustedly. I sent him a copy of each police report that included one of his statements, highlighting those portions that were inconsistent with other statements he had made, urging him to be ready to talk about the inconsistencies when we met. I didn't feel encouraged by his attitude.

However, Hart was nothing like the person I expected. He arrived promptly for our meeting, dressed neatly in khakis and a blue sport shirt, his clean-shaven face showing no traces of the battering it had taken three years earlier. To me, he looked more like a suburban burglary victim than a man with a felony record. I looked closely for signs of current drug use, but could detect none. Although he spoke slowly, it quickly became apparent that this was his normal manner. Under one arm, he carried the police reports in a manila folder, along with notes he had made regarding his statements. I had misconstrued his manner on the telephone as one of disinterest; indeed, Hart felt very strongly about the case and wanted to cooperate.

We spent twenty minutes discussing his current circumstances. He had just come from a meeting with a marriage counselor and was resigned to the fact that he and his wife were heading toward a divorce. He was terribly saddened, he said, by the realization that he would be separated from his daughter. Yet he was pleased that his three years of probation were coming to a conclusion, apparently successfully. He had paid restitution, participated in the drug rehabilitation program his probation officer recommended and passed all his random urinalyses. Although someone had left an anonymous message on his probation officer's answering machine a few months earlier, saying that he was using methamphetamine again, Hart denied the allegation and when the probation officer had come to his house to administer a drug test, it was negative. Hart assumed that the caller had been one of Schilling's friends. His probation officer informed him, just a week before our meeting, that she would petition the court to reduce the convictions to misdemeanors.

Hart was looking forward to finally gaining justice in his torturous episode with Schilling. He had driven his car by Schilling's house on many occasions, thinking about how much he wanted Schilling to pay for what he had done, and the trial, he hoped, would provide that opportunity. The need for retribution had apparently been his strongest motivation for kicking his methamphetamine addiction. He laughed at the irony: "Schilling is responsible for my sobriety."

He had pored over the police reports in the manila folder, obviously taking the task of trial preparation very seriously, explaining to me that he had recently been through a jury trial in his products liability law suit against Budget Stores and it had gone very poorly. "My lawyer did very little to prepare me for testifying in court and the attorney for Budget cut me to ribbons on cross-examination, causing me to confuse important facts, then lose my temper," he said, obviously embarrassed. "I'm determined not to let that happen again with the lawyer representing Schilling."

We discussed the wording and accuracy of each prior statement he had made in connection with the case against Schilling. I reminded him that minutes after his escape from the car trunk in Schilling's garage, a patrol officer had questioned him at a neighbor's house. He talked to a second officer on his way to the hospital, then to a detective in his hospital room. Seven months later, he gave yet another statement to a police detective and he also testified about the kidnapping and assault incident during his deposition in the civil law suit against Budget. We discussed how each statement might be construed as being inconsistent with one or more of the others or with the testimony of other witnesses at the upcoming trial. "If Schilling's lawyer dwells on these inconsistencies during cross-examination, I want you to be able to explain them."

Although most of the inconsistencies were inconsequential, one was troubling. Six months after the theft of his coin collection, Schilling finally filed a report with the Phoenix police and a detective, Harry Davis, interviewed Hart in regard to Schilling's accusations. Hart denied committing the burglary, just as he had in each of his prior police interviews. However, he told Davis he believed that the July 3 violence had nothing to do with Schilling accusing him of theft. He insisted that Schilling pulled a gun on him because he had threatened to tell the police that Schilling was fencing stolen property. This story was glaringly different from Hart's earlier accounts, as well as Schilling's statements and what I expected Brenda Chase's testimony to be.

Hart grudgingly admitted that his statement to Davis was inaccurate, but his explanation, that he "must have been confused" by Davis's questions, did not seem plausible to me. It appeared much more likely that, furious about Schilling's almost killing him, he had lied to Davis to put Schilling in a bad light. "And if it looks that way to me, it will look that way to a jury," I told him.

I was also concerned about other evidence that might impeach Hart's credibility. The defense's witness list included two people who, like Schilling, had employed Hart to do construction work at their homes. Both witnesses claimed that Hart had stolen their property and then lied about the theft when confronted. One of the witnesses had even gotten into a scuffle with Hart. Schilling's lawyer believed that the testimony of these witnesses would establish a pattern of conduct that undermined Hart's version of the events at Schilling's house on July 3. His motion to introduce this evidence had been filed months before trial, but the court had not yet ruled on its admissibility.

Hart disavowed both of these thefts, echoing his denial of Schilling's burglary, claiming that one of the defense witnesses held a grudge against him, while the other was mistaken. I suggested diplomatically that it might be in his interest to admit the crimes on cross-examination, if in fact he had committed them, since it was extremely unlikely that he would be prosecuted for relatively minor events occurring over three years earlier, and the prior thefts could not justify the aggravated assault and kidnapping he had endured. He remained adamant, however, despite the potentially devastating effect of this evidence.

We spent the remainder of the afternoon in a mock cross-examination, moving from topic to topic, covering Hart's felony record, the inconsistencies in his statements, his drug addiction, the thefts he allegedly committed and his possible motives for lying about the crimes charged against Schilling. If his answers sounded self-serving or evasive, we stopped to discuss them. I showed him how to be more precise and forthcoming and we tried it again.

I asked, "Weren't you granted probation in your own case in return for testifying against Mr. Schilling?"

"I wasn't guilty in my case," he responded excitedly. "I only accepted a deal because my lawyer talked me into it."

"How will that sound to a jury?" I asked. "The question isn't whether you were guilty in your case, but whether you are lying about Schilling to keep yourself out of jail. If that's not true, you should tell the jury very clearly."

I continued, "You were given probation in exchange for your testimony against Mr. Schilling, isn't that right?"

"No. I'm testifying because it's what happened."

During the intense hours we spent in that small conference room in the county attorney's office Hart improved his way of handling the thrusts and parries sure to be given by the defense in order to undermine his testimony. He showed he would hold up under a full grilling and not lose his composure. He offered reasonable explanations for the inconsistencies in his pre-trial statements—aside from his misrepresentation to Detective Davis—and he forthrightly admitted his long-term drug addiction and two felony convictions. Although he adamantly denied the prior thefts, I felt he would be a strong witness despite his past and that he was ready to go to trial.

Nevertheless, several occurrences unnerved me during the week before trial. Schilling's neighbor who took Hart into his home after his escape from the trunk of the car, called to say that he was going on vacation for two weeks and would not be available to testify at trial. Then the emergency room doctor who had treated Hart complained that he too would be unavailable on the day he was subpoenaed to appear in court. With a good deal of cajolery, I was able to persuade each witness, though they were both unhappy, to rearrange his schedule. However, Hart's subpoena was returned to me, unserved, the evening before the trial was to begin. The notation from the process server indicated that Hart was no longer living at the address listed on the subpoena and his telephone had been disconnected.

I panicked. Hart had seemed both cooperative and eager when we met at the County Attorney's office nine days earlier. Why would he bolt at the last minute? Without him, my case was in shambles, since his testimony was needed to prove each charge, and I doubted that Judge Harris would grant me a continuance of the trial. Schilling's lawyer would probably not agree to a plea bargain unless the charges were reduced significantly, but the county attorney's plea bargaining policy prohibited me from any further reductions. If the court dismissed the case, it would be unrealistic to start all over, filing new charges against Schilling three and a half years after the alleged crimes, with such an unreliable victim.

I sent an urgent request to the investigative staff of the prosecutor's office, pleading that they find Hart. The trial was to begin the following afternoon, but we probably would not need him for a couple of days, since there were pre-trial motions to argue and it would likely take a full afternoon to pick the jury. This gave us a small window to locate Hart and persuade him to testify.

As the time grew shorter, I wondered why anyone would ever choose this work. However, the next morning, the investigator sent to locate Hart did just that. My main witness had not fled after all; he had simply moved to his mother's house after separating from his wife. He was, in fact, still looking forward to his day in court.

Chapter 20

The Eleventh Hour

Upon arriving in court that Thursday afternoon, I learned that Judge Harris was already in trial on a murder case that would last for another three weeks. Since Harris had previously decreed that there would be no further continuances of our trial, the superior court's administrative office placed the Schilling trial in a "case transfer." This meant that *Schilling* would be re-assigned to the first court that became available to handle a long trial. We could be delayed for a few hours, or days, or perhaps even weeks. I would get almost no advance warning of when and where the trial was to begin. I bit my lip pensively. Calling my witnesses again, especially Schilling's neighbor and the emergency room physician and telling them about this new development, would not be pleasant.

A day later, however, to my surprise the court administration assigned the Schilling trial to Judge Roger T. Paxton, to begin the following Monday, September 29, at 1:30 P.M. Although the short duration of the delay minimized the disruption of witnesses' schedules, Judge Paxton's courtroom was in Mesa, at the opposite side of the Phoenix metropolitan area from the neighborhoods in which Schilling, Hart and the other witnesses resided. My own office was in the county attorney's suite in downtown Phoenix. I was going to be separated throughout the trial from my mentors and support staff in the prosecutor's office, on whom I relied so heavily. I was not particularly familiar with any of the prosecutors in the Mesa office and knew none of the secretaries, investigators or court personnel.

I sought to learn whatever I could about Judge Paxton, but my colleagues rarely handled cases in Mesa and most were unfamiliar with him. A couple of veteran prosecutors believed that I had been given a good break. Paxton had a reputation for imposing tough sentences and generally siding with the state in his legal rulings. This was welcome news, especially the part about the legal rulings, since there were several difficult motions pending in Schilling's case, motions that would have to be decided before the trial began. One concerned the admissibility of evidence relating to Hart's thefts from prior employers. Paxton's ruling on this issue could determine the outcome of the case.

Meanwhile, Steve Schilling had been having his own problems accepting the long delay and didn't know as yet that his case had been reassigned and a final trial date had been set. He had to confront his bad fortune. If the case had gone to trial during the first two years after his arrest, he would have been represented by a lawyer of his own choosing. However, when he ran out of money, he had to accept publicly funded counsel, Robert Aron from the Office of the Legal Defender. Schilling thought Aron was a nice man who appeared to love his work, but to Schilling the lawyer always seemed to be preparing for other trials, never having sufficient time for Schilling's case. Even worse, Aron had told him that Aron's wife was scheduled to have a baby during the second week of trial, just when the defense would present its case. For the first time, Schilling wanted a postponement, but Aron told him it was too late.

When he learned of his case's reassignment, Schilling viewed the commute to Mesa as a hardship, both for his family and for himself. He had long since sold his motorcycle and pick-up truck and was now driving an ancient, unreliable jalopy. Concerned about the car's dependability, he set off at noon, ninety minutes before the first day of the trial was to begin, just to be safe. As he had feared, the car broke down as he exited the freeway in Mesa, a half-mile from the courthouse. The recorded temperature that afternoon was 101 degrees, but it was much hotter in the direct mid-day sun as Schilling pushed the car to the courthouse parking lot, wearing a white shirt and tie. He finally arrived at 1:29 P.M., drenched in sweat, just in time to join the lawyers in Judge Paxton's chambers for preliminary discussions.

Distinguished-looking and graying, Judge Paxton was all business when we introduced ourselves, instructing us on the protocol of his courtroom and declaring firmly that the trial would proceed as expeditiously as possible. His procedural rules reflected this, limiting the scope of witness examination, discouraging conferences outside the presence of the jury and prohibiting speeches by the lawyers when making objections. He emphasized the importance of punctuality in his courtroom, warning us not to file last-minute motions. Both lawyers had assumed that we would spend most of the first afternoon presenting oral argument on the admissibility of evidence relating to Hart's checkered history, but Paxton wanted to select a jury first. He set aside an hour the following morning for argument on all of the pending pre-trial motions and instructed us to be ready for opening statements. Looking at me, he declared, "Be ready to call your first witness promptly thereafter." After three-and-a-half meandering years, the case was now on a lightning fast track.

Thirty minutes later, forty-five prospective jurors packed into Paxton's small, windowless courtroom. Although only twelve would ultimately determine Schilling's fate, our goal that afternoon was to winnow the panel to fourteen members. We agreed to select two extra jurors in case it became necessary to excuse anyone during the trial. If all fourteen remained when the jury's deliberations were to begin, the court clerk would randomly select two of the jurors to serve as alternates.

Aron and Schilling conversed quietly at the defense table as everyone waited for the judge to enter the courtroom to preside over the jury selection. Aron wore a handsomely tailored navy blue double-breasted suit, seemingly more expensive than one would expect to be worn by a public defender. Schilling appeared nervous to me, but he also looked highly presentable in a white shirt, tie and jacket, nothing like the drug addict and foul-mouthed biker I wanted the jurors to see. I sat alone at the other counsel table, hoping that the two-against-one scenario might neutralize the assumption of some jurors that the state had greater resources at its disposal than the defense. Aron looked as equally intent on the jury's first impressions of the participants, especially his client. He huddled with Schilling, conveying the image of a close-knit unit.

The purpose of jury selection, known to the legal profession as "voir dire," is to assure, as much as possible, that fair and impartial fact-finders determine the parties' fates. The formal rules relating to voir dire vary considerably from locale to locale and informal practices sometimes differ from one courtroom to the next or from year to year. In some, the questioning of individual jurors can be conducted either by the judge or by counsel. When I was a criminal defense attorney in California, most courts gave the lawyers wide latitude in examining the jury panel, on the assumption that the attorneys had far greater familiarity than the judge with the factual nuances of the case and the witnesses who would be called to testify, and thus were in a better position to ferret out the potential biases or prejudices that could infect the jury's deliberations.

At the time of the Schilling trial, this practice had changed in most states, as the principal responsibility for questioning prospective jurors shifted to the judge. Too many lawyers had abused voir dire, asking manipulative questions designed less to uncover biases than to sway jurors to their view of the case. Many courts felt that voir dire conducted by attorneys unduly prolonged the time needed to select a panel, adding to the backlog of cases on judicial calendars. At the time of Schilling's trial, procedural rules permitted trial lawyers to question individual jurors, but only on a showing of good cause. Although some judges continued to give attorneys a fair amount of leeway in voir dire, others placed stricter limits on counsel's role.

Judge Paxton definitely fell in the latter category, informing us beforehand that he would conduct virtually all of the examination himself, covering those subjects he deemed relevant. If either of us wanted to ask specific questions after he was finished, we had to clear them with him first, on a question-by-question basis. Paxton would permit us to ask only those questions that he considered "appropriate."

When the proceedings began, it quickly became apparent that Paxton would direct most of his inquiries to the entire group of forty-five. His questions addressed such issues as whether the jurors knew any of the parties or witnesses in the case, whether any jurors or their family members were employed in law enforcement and whether any had ever been charged with kidnapping or aggravated assault or had been a victim of a similar offense. If a juror had relevant information in answer to a question, the juror was to raise his or her hand. Paxton then asked a few brief follow-up questions of the juror, followed by two queries.

"Is there anything about that experience that would cause you to be biased or prejudiced against either party in this case?"

"Do you think you can be fair to both sides?"

The scripting was not inappropriate, since most of the factors that might bias a juror are not case-specific and judges typically employ similar practices. However, Paxton next explained to the panel that "we have to speed it up to the extent we can because of the time involved." I was concerned, because most of his questions did not encourage jurors to share doubts about their impartiality, but instead served to shore up their willingness to serve. The jurors only had a short time to raise questions or the information went undisclosed. Additionally, I felt Paxton's limited questioning did not cover any of the potentially volatile issues that swirled around Schilling and Hart. We learned absolutely nothing about the prospective jurors' attitudes relating to guns, unlawful drug use, self defense, home burglary or the use of force to defend property. By discouraging us from asking our own questions and forcing us to clear each of them with him in advance, it was extremely difficult to discover potential biases on these issues.

The only issue fully aired during voir dire was the hardship jurors might experience if selected. When Paxton announced that the trial was expected to last for at least two weeks, fifteen prospective jurors raised their hands, eager to tell of the many misfortunes that would befall them if they were forced to serve. Some of their claims were extremely compelling: a nurse employed at a local hospital explained that she was needed to operate a lung machine for open heart surgery; an elementary school teacher worried that her substitute, an inexperienced student teacher, would be unable to handle the children with special needs in her classroom; the sole proprietor of a small retail business pleaded that he was in the middle of his annual inventory, requiring him to work fifteen hour days. Others on the panel had already scheduled trips to far-away places. But some simply did not want to be trapped in a courtroom for a long trial.

I silently hoped that every juror claiming hardship would be excused, regardless of the validity of the explanation. Most of the witnesses in the case were mine and I could be blamed if the trial dragged on. The juror I wanted least was one who resented being there. Fortunately, one consequence of Judge Paxton's focused questioning on jury biases was that only four jurors were excused because of their inability to be impartial. Each of them was allowed to go. Even if the judge

granted all fifteen of the hardship requests, we would still have a sufficient number of prospective jurors remaining.

The court rules allotted six peremptory juror challenges to each
party. Lawyers usually play their hunches when exercising these challenges,
relying on seat-of-the-pants logic and mine were probably typical. I
wanted to remove anyone who might secretly feel that Hart got what he
deserved, anyone who might harbor a grudge against the police or anyone
who might believe that violence was an acceptable way to address wrongs.
When questioned, none of the prospective jurors expressed anything close
to these views. But then again, I wondered about the opinions they didn't
express.

Nevertheless, I was pleased with the fourteen jurors who
remained after those with hardships had been excused and the parties
had used their peremptory challenges. It was a well-educated, middle-
class jury, consisting of eight women and six men, including three
housewives, four in management positions, an engineer, a nurse, two
government employees and three office workers. Almost all of the jurors
were older than Steve Schilling and several were either middle-aged or
retired. Each of the three jurors younger than Schilling had children at
home. None of the fourteen had a criminal record or any relatives with
records. Only two had prior jury experience in a criminal case. In both
instances the jury had convicted the defendant. It appeared, I felt, to be
a jury that would not feel sympathetic toward a person who solved his
problems violently, taking the law into his own hands. Most importantly, none of the fourteen jurors had any reservation about sitting
through what promised to be a long trial.

The next morning I arrived at 7:45 to assist Judge Paxton's court
clerk in organizing and numbering the seventy-two exhibits I would later
show to the jury. The clerk had lectured me at the completion of jury selection on the importance of getting my physical evidence to court before the
trial began. As the person responsible for preparing the minutes of each
day's proceedings and drafting the language of the judge's rulings, the clerk
could make life miserable for a lawyer who failed to show proper respect. I
wanted to make her job easier.

Spending the morning in Paxton's courtroom also gave me an
opportunity to talk to his bailiff and administrative assistant, who turned

out to be eager to share their initial impressions of the jury, Steve Schilling and Robert Aron, and to warn me of the judge's pet peeves. I observed Paxton's interactions with the lawyers appearing before him, to get a feel for how he ran his courtroom. The morning calendar included several contested proceedings, causing Paxton to be about forty-five minutes behind schedule, making him more than a little testy.

When Paxton finally turned his attention to the pre-trial motions in the Schilling case, he brusquely informed Aron and me that we had only thirty minutes to make our oral arguments, since he had to leave the courthouse immediately at noon for an important appointment. He was also determined not to force the jurors to wait in their assembly room when they arrived at 1:30 P.M. If we wanted the motions decided before the trial began, we would have to sail through them as quickly as possible.

Altogether, there were six motions to be argued, three filed by each side. The defense wanted to inform the jury during Ray Hart's cross-examination that he had two prior felony convictions and sought permission to explore the underlying facts in the two cases. Aron also wanted to introduce testimony pertaining to prior thefts committed by Hart, lies he had told and the specifics of his drug addiction. My predecessor, Gerry Baylor, had filed a motion to preclude the defense's evidence of Hart's prior bad conduct, as well as a motion to inform the jury of Steve Schilling's prior felony conviction and another to permit testimony relating to an assault he had allegedly committed on one of Brenda Chase's friends. Each motion required the court to weigh the relevance of the evidence in question against its potential for poisoning the jury or unnecessarily prolonging the trial. We had to pack a great deal into thirty minutes, a challenge made even more difficult because Paxton was new to the case and unfamiliar with its facts.

The most critical motion, by far, was the defense's attempt to introduce testimony to show that Hart had stolen from two former employers, then had lied about the thefts to cover them up. Baylor had seen this evidence as mud slinging, intended to divert the jury's attention from the facts of what happened to Hart. Nevertheless, it troubled me deeply; the two witnesses were credible and Hart would look bad when he denied committing the thefts. Not only would it hurt his credibility, but it also might lead the jury to believe that he got what he deserved from Schilling and his friends. The other motions paled in importance.

The oral argument took place in the judge's chambers, with only the attorneys, the defendant, the judge and a court reporter present. Paxton's thirty-minute limitation may have rattled Aron, who presented his side of the argument first. He began by discussing Hart's prior convictions, then rambled in his presentation, jumping from issue to issue, confusing the judge by going into minutiae of the prior incidents, failing to show their relevance to the trial. Paxton interrupted him several times, insisting that he get to the point, and this seemed to unsettle Aron even more. When it was my turn, I sensed that Paxton might not appreciate what was important and what was not. I hinted that my motion relating to Schilling's prior assault was not essential to my case, without explicitly saying so, hoping that the judge would even-handedly deny each side's attempt to besmirch the character of the other's key witness. My allotted time ended quickly. The judge seemed impatient, pushing us out the door, promising to announce his rulings later in the day.

After the many postponements of his case, Ray Hart was surprised by the call from the prosecutor's office informing him that the trial was finally going ahead and that he would testify the following Tuesday afternoon. All weekend he felt as if he was in the middle of a dream, unsure of whether it was a nightmare. Had the time for justice finally arrived or would he be humiliated again? The trial was to be held in Mesa, in an unfamiliar setting. Was this a bad omen? He worried that some of Schilling's friends would be waiting for him in the parking lot outside the courthouse. To elude them, he decided to arrive at noon, ninety minutes early.

Hart found me in the empty corridor outside Judge Paxton's courtroom, but I declined to join him for lunch, explaining, "I am anxious to finish preparing my opening statement to the jury." His mother and sister were not going to arrive until 1:30, so he decided to get a light lunch on his own at the cafeteria on the ground floor of the courthouse. After choosing a sandwich, he took his place at the end of a long line waiting to pay the cashier, not yet recognizing the person who stood directly in front of him.

The realization felt like touching a power line. Hart and Schilling had not seen one another for over three years, not even from a distance. Now they were inches apart.

A wide-eyed Hart watched intently as Schilling turned around. Hart was certain that the pounding in his chest could be heard by everyone in the cafeteria.

Each man stared at the other for several seconds.

"You asshole!" Schilling finally bellowed.

"You will pay for what you did now," Hart said quietly but firmly.

"You're a lowlife."

Hart turned away, his knees trembling.

Schilling sauntered away, ending the brief confrontation, not wanting Hart to see how shaken he was. A few minutes later, Hart threw up in the bathroom outside the cafeteria.

I too was experiencing stomach problems, nervous about my opening statement. I was an experienced public speaker, routinely lecturing to classes of over one hundred students; however, as a prosecutor I was concerned about connecting to the jury on a personal level. I had felt awkward the previous day when Paxton permitted me to ask a few questions during the voir dire, adding to my self consciousness. This was supposed to be my stage, with everyone watching, an opportunity to set the tone for the entire trial, surely a moment to savor. Somehow, however, I felt insecure stepping onto it.

The purpose of an opening statement is to give the jury a preview of the evidence. Trial advocacy textbooks advise lawyers to keep the opening statement short, using simple language, while court rules admonish counsel to state the facts in a non-argumentative fashion, avoiding the rhetorical flash of closing argument. However, the line between fact and argument often is blurry, allowing creative advocates to use their opening statements to entice juries with colorful language.

In this case, I told myself, brevity was essential, since some of the evidence was open to interpretation. I faced substantial risk. The scope of the testimony to be presented by both the defense and the prosecution was still unclear because the judge had not yet ruled on the pre-trial motions. Though I'd been impressed with his demeanor at our meeting, I still was not confident that all of Hart's testimony would be fully consistent with the version of the facts I hoped to present. Most of all, I felt I needed to stress the broad themes of my theory of the case and why I felt Schilling was guilty.

When I returned to the courtroom, the gallery was far emptier than it had been the previous afternoon. Thirty-one of the forty-five prospective jurors had now departed, never to be seen again. The other fourteen sat in their assigned places in the jury box. Only five persons watched from the gallery. Steve Schilling's mother and sister sat in the first row directly behind Aron and Schilling, while Ray Hart's mother and sister sat with him across the aisle, in the first row behind the prosecution table. Thereafter, two to four members of each family would attend each session of the trial, always seated in the same location, like the bride and groom's respective families at a wedding. But unlike guests at a wedding, the enmity between the two sides was evident to everyone in the room.

Schilling sat quietly at the defense table, slightly pale, wearing the same shirt as the previous day, with a different tie. I was unaware of his lunch hour confrontation with Ray Hart, but I noticed that Schilling appeared more agitated and his eyes blinked rapidly, a possible indication that he had taken drugs since the morning session.

Everyone rose when the judge entered the room. When they were seated, it was time for Paxton to give the jury their preliminary instructions.

Judge Paxton's deep sonorous voice offered these instructions:

"I want to tell you the rules you should follow to decide this case. Understand that it is your duty as jurors to follow these instructions.

"It is also your duty to determine the facts. And from the *facts,* I mean what actually happened. You should determine the facts only from the evidence produced in court. You should not guess about any fact. You must not be influenced either by sympathy or by prejudice. You must not be concerned with any opinion that you may feel that I have about this case. You are the sole judges of what happened." His gaze was pinned on the jurors, as he went on.

"You must consider all of these instructions. Do not pick out one instruction or part of one instruction and disregard the others. However, after you have determined the facts, you may find some instructions no longer apply.

"You must then consider the instructions that do apply together with the facts as you have determined them to be. Decide this case by applying these instructions to the facts which you find."

I watched the jurors scrutinize the judge and wondered what they were thinking.

"In the opening statements and closing arguments, the lawyers will talk to you about both the law and the evidence. What the lawyers say to you is not evidence, but it might help you understand the law and the evidence.

"You must find the facts from the evidence presented in court. The evidence which you are to consider consists of any exhibits that are admitted into evidence and the testimony of the witnesses.

"For the benefit of those of you that do not have any prior jury experience, if an objection to a lawyer's question is sustained, you should disregard that question and any answer given.

"Any testimony stricken from the court record should not be considered by you." Judge Paxton paused, looking from one to the other of the men and women before him.

"And in deciding whether the defendant is guilty or not guilty, do not consider the possible punishment. Punishment is decided by the judge and not by the jury. The State must prove all of its case against the defendant with its own evidence. The defendant is not required to testify. The decision on whether to testify is left to the defendant acting with the advice of his attorney. You must not conclude the defendant is likely to be guilty because the defendant does not testify. You must not let this choice affect your deliberations in any way.

"You must decide the believability of witnesses. In doing so, take into account such things as their ability and opportunity to observe, their memory and manner while testifying, any motive or prejudice that they might have and any inconsistent statements. Consider each witness's testimony in light of all of the other evidence in the case.

"Now, the State has charged the defendant with the crimes of kidnapping, three counts of aggravated assault and possession of methamphetamine. These charges are not evidence against the defendant and you must not think the defendant is guilty just because of these charges. The defendant has entered pleas of not guilty. These pleas of not guilty mean the State must prove every part of these charges beyond a reasonable doubt.

"Evidence can be divided into what we call direct evidence and circumstantial evidence. Direct evidence is the testimony of a witness that saw an event. Circumstantial evidence is the proof of a fact from which the existence of another fact may be inferred. You must determine the weight to be given to all of the evidence without regard to whether it is direct or circumstantial." The judge tilted his head slightly, saw a juror nod in understanding, then went on.

"With respect to the burden of proof, the State has the burden of proving the defendant guilty beyond a reasonable doubt. In civil cases, it is only necessary to prove that a fact is more likely true than not or that its truth is highly probable. In criminal cases such as this, the State's proof must be more powerful than that. It must be beyond a reasonable doubt.

"Proof beyond a reasonable doubt is proof that leaves you firmly convinced of the defendant's guilt. There are very few things in this world that we know with absolute certainty and in criminal cases the law does not require proof that overcomes every doubt. If, based on your consideration of the evidence, you are firmly convinced that the defendant is guilty of the crime charged, you must find him guilty. If, on the other hand, you think there is a real possibility that he is not guilty, you must give him the benefit of the doubt and find him not guilty.

"In deciding whether or not the State has proven the defendant guilty beyond a reasonable doubt, you must start with the presumption that the defendant is innocent. The State must then prove the defendant guilty beyond a reasonable doubt. This means the State must prove each element of the charge beyond a reasonable doubt. If you conclude the State has not met its burden of proof beyond a reasonable doubt, then you must find the defendant not guilty of the charge."

I tried to pay attention as the judge droned on, but I could think of nothing except my own turn, which was coming soon. My opening statement revolved in my mind as I tried not to let my nervousness get out of hand.

"By fairly recent rule amendment, jurors are now permitted, in criminal cases, to ask questions during the course of trial, either of the witness on the witness stand or of the Court. I suggest to you: Please do not make yourself advocates in doing so, however. The purpose of the rule is simply to permit you to have a point clarified or to go into something that perhaps has not been covered or covered adequately by counsel." The judge eyed the clock on the wall and quickened his pace.

"This is the procedure that I would like for us to use if you do have a question during the course of this trial. We would request that you write it out on a piece of paper. Do not sign it. Get the attention of Dan, my bailiff, and I'll get that question and go over it with counsel. If we feel that the question is appropriate, it will be asked. If it is not appropriate, it will not be asked," the judge said firmly.

"Please understand that any questions you might ask during the course of trial will be subject to the same scrutiny that the questions of counsel are subjected to.

"Now, we do request that if you have a question, to use a little timing, if you would, please. If it is of a witness and the witness is about ready to leave the witness stand, make sure your question is submitted prior to that time. Once the witness has left the courtroom, it's a little bit difficult for us to assist you in that regard, so use some timing if you would, please.

"I'll now ask my clerk to read the formal charges against Mr. Schilling, please."

The young clerk began in a sing-song voice: "In the Superior Court of the State of Arizona in and for the County of Maricopa, State of Arizona, plaintiff, versus Stephen C. Schilling, defendant.

"Count one, kidnapping, a dangerous offense.

"Count two, aggravated assault, a dangerous offense.

"Count three, aggravated assault.

"Count four, aggravated assault.

"Count five, possession of dangerous drugs.

"The grand jurors of Maricopa County, Arizona accuse Stephen Christopher Schilling, charging that in Maricopa County, Arizona, count one, Stephen Christopher Schilling, on or between the third day of July 1994 and the fourth day of July 1994, knowingly restrained Raymond Hart with the intent to inflict death, physical injury or a sexual offense on him, in violation of Arizona law."

"Count two, Stephen Christopher Schilling on or between the third day of July 1994 and the fourth day of July 1994, using a gun, a deadly weapon or dangerous instrument, intentionally placed Raymond Hart in reasonable apprehension of imminent physical injury, in violation of Arizona law.

"Count three, Stephen Christopher Schilling, on or between the third day of July 1994 and the fourth day of July 1994, intentionally, knowingly or recklessly caused injury to Raymond Hart by any means of force which caused a fracture of any body part, nose, to Raymond Hart, in violation of Arizona law.

"Count four, Stephen Christopher Schilling, on or between the third day of July 1994 and the fourth day of July 1994, intentionally, knowingly, or recklessly caused injury to Raymond Hart by any means of force which caused a fracture of any body part, hand, to Raymond Hart, in violation of Arizona law." My stomach clenched. The clerk was moving to the end of her recitation.

"Count five, on July fourth, 1994, knowingly possessed or used methamphetamine, a dangerous drug, in violation of Arizona law.

"A true bill.

"Richard M. Romley, Maricopa County Attorney. Gerry Baylor, Deputy County Attorney. Martin J. Tullo, foreman of the grand jury." She paused, then went on.

"To which the defendant enters pleas of not guilty."

The judge nodded at his clerk.

"Thank you."

"Now, folks, the charges that have just been read to you are not evidence in this case. You must not think the defendant is guilty simply because he has been charged with these crimes. He has entered pleas of not guilty. That means the State must prove him guilty beyond a reasonable doubt.

"We'll begin now with the opening statements."

He looked toward me. I hoped that my nervousness didn't show. "Mr. Lowenthal, you may proceed, sir."

I took a deep breath: at last the Schilling trial was beginning.

Chapter 21

The Prosecution Strikes

Rising to my feet, I told myself that I had instructed two generations of law students to maintain eye contact with individual jurors and forced myself to do so, but as I looked in the general direction of the jury, I saw only a blur. My tension was palpable; I felt a jolt of jitters. Paxton cocked an eye at me.

"Your Honor," I said falteringly, "may I use the podium?"

"You may."

"I'll try not to kill myself here," I remarked after tripping on an easel stand.

"All right," the judge nodded.

The tension broke with the jury's laughter. The judge put up a hand for quiet.

"Thank you, Your Honor. May it please the Court, Mr. Aron, ladies and gentlemen of the jury, as His Honor Judge Paxton has indicated to you, this is an opportunity at the beginning of the trial for the lawyers to make their opening statements to you.

"I'm going to be presenting the case for the State of Arizona and Mr. Aron will be presenting the case for the defendant.

"As Judge Paxton has just told you, my words and Mr. Aron's words are not evidence, and so I want to emphasize, if anything I say in my opening statement or in my closing argument at the end of the trial is in conflict with the evidence that you hear from the witnesses who testify on the witness stand or the physical evidence that you see in evidence, disregard what I say and go with the evidence.

"However, I am given this opportunity to make an opening statement. The purpose is to give you a road map to make it easier for you to follow the evidence as it comes in during the trial, so you'll have a sense of where all the pieces of the puzzle fit together.

"With that in mind, I'm going to tell you now what the State's case will be and what the evidence will show. The evidence will show that this is a case about an angry man who took the law into his own hands. The angry man believed that another man, Raymond Hart—he's sitting in the front row of the courtroom today—the angry man believed that Raymond Hart had stolen some property from him about a week before July third and fourth of 1994.

"The angry man went into a violent rage. In this violent rage, he took Raymond Hart as his hostage. The angry man held Raymond Hart as a hostage with a cocked pistol, pointing it at the victim, threatening to kill him. The pointing of the pistol, which caused fear in Raymond Hart, fear for his life, that's the basis for one of the aggravated assault counts."

"This angry man then called upon three of his friends, three henchmen, to help him take the law further into his own hands. With the help of his three accomplices, the angry man viciously beat Ray Hart so badly that Hart had bruises all over his body, that he needed stitches on several places on his head, and that he had a broken nose. Recklessly causing injury, the broken nose, is a second-degree aggravated assault count. The broken hand is the basis for the third of the aggravated assault counts."

Though my words may have been dramatic, my nervousness hadn't abated. Several times I relied on the podium to support me, which unnecessarily separated me from the jury. As I went on, I began to relax a little and even though the butterflies fluttered in my stomach, I was able to articulate my theme: "the angry man who took the law into his hands."

"This angry man, with his buddies, also tied up Mr. Hart. They tied him with rope, with electrical cord, with duct tape, and with a towel. They tied his hands and his feet behind his back so he couldn't move. And they gagged him. And they blindfolded him. And they beat him some more. And they beat him with a metal rod and with an aluminum baseball bat and with the butt of one or maybe two guns while he was tied up and unable to defend himself. And that's the basis of the kidnapping charge.

"They restrained him with the intent to inflict bodily injury. After blindfolding him and gagging him and tying him up, they then dumped him into the trunk of a car. Fortunately, he was able to escape before anything further happened to him."

Once again I took up my theme:

"Ladies and gentlemen, the angry man who did all of those things is the defendant, Stephen Schilling. It all occurred on the evening of July third, all the way through the early morning hours of July fourth.

"Raymond Hart, the victim in this case, had been remodeling the defendant's home. He had completed work on the defendant's garage and was then remodeling the defendant's kitchen. About a week before the violent assault/kidnapping occurred, the defendant, Mr. Schilling, came to believe that someone had stolen some of his property from his home. He chose not to call the police. Instead, he accused more than one person of committing this offense. But after a few days, his suspicions began to focus on Raymond Hart, the victim." I ran my tongue across my lips.

"Mr. Hart, during that week, was working on another project in Cottonwood, Arizona, another work project. The defendant went looking for Mr. Hart, found him in Cottonwood, told him he thought he'd stolen some items from him and demanded to search Mr. Hart's car and his brother's home where he was staying at the time. The defendant didn't find any stolen property and went home.

"A few days later, Mr. Hart came back to Phoenix to complete the work on the defendant's house and showed up at the defendant's home the early evening of July third. The defendant was waiting. When he arrived there, when Mr. Hart arrived there, Mr. Schilling was there with his girlfriend, a woman named Brenda Chase. Even though a week had gone by since the alleged theft had occurred, the defendant had not yet called the police."

For me, time had frozen as I retraced the traumatic day of the crime. I hoped the jury felt the impact similarly.

"When Mr. Hart arrived at the house, he was confronted in

several ways. You'll hear about that from Ms. Chase how the defendant accused him of stealing the defendant's property. Mr. Hart denied it. They tried to lure the victim, Mr. Hart, into the living room of the defendant's home by telling him that other people might be harmed because of this theft and to protect other people, if he knew what had happened, he better tell about it. Mr. Hart said, 'I didn't do it.' Ms. Chase left. She came back a few minutes later with a black pack in her hand, a small fanny pack, and said: 'Aha, look what I found in Mr. Hart's car.'

"She dumped out onto a desk some items, Rolex watches or fake Rolex watches, and the defendant said, 'That's mine,' and she said, 'I found this in his car.' Mr. Hart denied that it was in his car. 'I don't know where it came from,' he said.

I heard my own voice take on a razor edge and fastened my eyes on Schilling.

"The defendant, at this point, went berserk. He grabbed the gun. He pointed it at Mr. Hart. He threatened to kill him. He screamed and he yelled, demanding that Mr. Hart admit that he stole property from him. Mr. Hart denied it. The defendant asked Ms. Chase to get him his cordless phone. And while he had Mr. Hart seated and had the gun in his other hand, he used the phone to call other people and ask them to come over. He called over his three buddies, and then over the next several hours they proceeded to beat him with," I felt my passion rising as I said, "with a baseball bat, with a metal rod, with the butt of a gun, with their fists, with their boots, to kick, to pound and beat, to tie him up and pound and beat some more.

"Finally, after several hours and several threats on his life, Mr. Hart said, 'I know where your property is,' and told the defendant where the property, supposedly, was. They dumped Mr. Hart into the trunk of an automobile that was backed into the defendant's garage. That automobile was Mr. Hart's automobile that he had parked in front of the house several hours earlier. They put Mr. Hart in the trunk of that car, tied up, still bound and gagged, closed the trunk, closed the garage door, and they left, presumably to get the property."

I paused to explain that Hart later was able to force the trunk lid open. "He stumbled out of the car, found a pair of pliers, and cut the duct tape on his feet. Even though the rest of his body was still bound, he managed to get out of that garage alive. He ran to the house next door, knocked on the door. It's 12:30 in the morning now. The next-door neighbor, who was in bed at the time, heard someone pounding on his door, crying, 'Let me in. Help, help. I've been beaten.' He looked through the peep hole, saw a man bloody and bound. He was afraid to let him in the house, so he called 911, the first person to call the police, one week after the property was, allegedly, stolen from the defendant."

I tried to convey the intense fear Hart must have felt.

"Mr. Hart could not get into a second neighbor's house. He was afraid the people were going to come back and afraid what the people would do to him, because he lied about the property being where it was. When no one answered there, Hart went to a third house, pounded on the door and begged, 'Please let me in.' This neighbor let him in and also called 911 and the police arrived moments later." I paused for a moment and took a breath.

Knowing that much of my case would rely on the testimony of Ray Hart, I concluded my summary. "We'll hear from both neighbors and we'll hear from all the police officers who conducted investigations in this case, and there were several. And the physical evidence that the police officers collected and the statements and the testimony of these two neighbors will corroborate everything that Ray Hart tells you about everything that happened to him that night."

I could feel Schilling's eyes shooting daggers at me. I took a step forward. The courtroom seemed stunned, almost eerily silent, as I made my final remarks.

"And after you hear all of the evidence, you will be convinced beyond a reasonable doubt that the defendant, a very angry man," I said, pausing, waiting for the jury to absorb these words, "committed the crimes of kidnapping, three counts of aggravated assault, and possession of dangerous drugs."

Chapter 22

The Defense Answers

Blond, good-looking and wearing another suit clearly more upscale than my own, Robert Aron argued against the portrait of Schilling that I had drawn and presented a competing theme in his opening statement, depicting the case as a story of "one person's trust and another's betrayal."

"May it please the Court, Mr. Lowenthal, ladies and gentlemen of the jury, this is not a case about an angry man. This is a case about trust and betrayal. This is a case about the trust that Mr. Schilling put in Mr. Hart and the betrayal that Mr. Hart gave to Mr. Schilling.

"The evidence is going to show that on June twenty-fourth, twenty-fifth, 1994, Mr. Hart burglarized Mr. Schilling's home. How on July third, Mr. Hart had been caught red-handed with items that were taken out of Mr. Schilling's home. They were found by Brenda Chase, who found them in his car.

"You see, Mr. Hart and Mr. Schilling were friends. They had known each other for several years. They kind of had a business relationship. Mr. Hart had a business called Total Remodeling, remodeled houses, worked on homes. Mr. Schilling had a business where he bought and sold secondhand items. The two kind of complimented each other, as you'll find. Mr. Hart would need items for remodeling.

Mr. Schilling had those kind of items. It was kind of a hand-in-glove relationship.

"But Mr. Hart began to run into some problems about that period of time. And since they were friends, Mr. Schilling hired Mr. Hart to do some remodeling for him. Mr. Hart had remodeled for him before. But on June twenty-fourth of that year, Mr. Hart was left in Mr. Schilling's house to do some remodeling. Mr. Schilling left that evening and came back the next day. And when he came back, he found out something unusual had occurred in his house, that a number of items he had found had come up missing. Old coin collections that he had that were of sentimental value from his father. Other items. A gun. Other valuable items. Some cash. Items he thought he had secured were all missing, items that totaled at least seven thousand dollars if you had to sell it right on the street, but actually, probably worth more than that."

Aron's manner was low-key and, unlike me, he looked relaxed. I wondered if he just covered his feelings better than a novice like me.

"And Mr. Schilling became concerned that his friend had committed a burglary or had stolen items out of his house. Mr. Schilling found out that Mr. Hart had gone out of town to do some remodeling there. He went to him to talk to him about it. He denied it. So Mr. Schilling came back home.

"But when Mr. Hart came back to Phoenix on July the third, he paged Mr. Schilling, who was at his girlfriend's house, and Mr. Hart said, 'I need to come over and talk about the remodeling. It's not finished.' So he did. He came over to Mr. Schilling house. And while he was there, Mr. Schilling engaged Mr. Hart in a conversation in his house.

"In that period of time, Brenda Chase went into Mr. Hart's car and found a black fanny pack that she had purchased for him and other items she recognized had been taken from Mr. Schilling's house. She came back in and exclaimed, 'Look what I found here.' And at that point, Mr. Hart reached, lunged towards a handgun sitting on the desk. This occurred in the office of Mr. Schilling's home. And a struggle ensued. They were fighting over the gun and Mr. Schilling prevailed and told Mr. Hart to sit down."

Aron was trying to refute or discredit the version that Hart or other witnesses would testify to. I could only hope that the jury could distinguish between style and substance.

"And they were looking through the bag, the black fanny pack. They found the watches, found the other items, also found a pack of methamphetamine that was in there. Mr. Hart wanted the methamphetamine, but they secured it away from him. That was placed inside the computer. Also, they found some telephone numbers in there that Mr. Schilling started dialing. One of those was Mr. Hart's brother, but as they spoke, other friends had called Mr. Schilling, because he had call waiting. And some of those people came over at that time.

"One, you'll hear, was a friend of his, that being James Thornton, and he came over with his girlfriend. They saw Mr. Hart was sitting there. No injuries had taken place at that point in time. Two other gentlemen came over. You'll hear about them. And then Ms. Chase leaves. She goes to work. But shortly after she leaves to go to work or in that immediate time frame, Mr. Hart continues begging them not to call the police. He didn't want them brought in on this matter."

I looked over to Schilling, his pale eyes were hooded, but his head nodded.

"So after Ms. Chase leaves, Mr. Hart attacks these gentlemen, tries to make a break for the door in order to escape from being blamed for the burglary. And when he does so, he begins to fight with these gentlemen, and he hits them, and, yes, some blows are exchanged.

"Mr. Hart attacks Mr. Schilling and his friends trying to escape. At that point in time, a general melee results, with Mr. Hart kicking into walls, knocking over furniture, creating general havoc throughout the house. You'll be shown pictures that document that. They're restraining him to hold him down. He demands that the police not be called in this regard.

"Now, he says 'I'll tell you where the stolen property is. Just don't call the police.'

"'Tell us where the property is. Tell us where it is.'

"'Well, I have it in a trailer. It's over in a trailer.'

"And Mr. Schilling says, 'I know where that is.' He gets on his motorbike and he leaves.

"At that point in time, there's still two other gentlemen, plus

James Thornton, still left inside the house. When Mr. Schilling returns, everybody is gone. Mr. Thornton is gone. Two other gentlemen are gone. And Mr. Hart is gone. Nobody placed Mr. Hart inside the trunk. Nobody sat there beating him, torturing him to exchange any type of information that he had."

His voice had a good mix of dignity and insistence. What was missing, I thought, was the ring of truth.

"We submit that any injuries that were suffered by Mr. Hart came as a result of the injuries sustained when Mr. Hart attacked these gentlemen."

According to Aron's story of the events, Schilling had placed his faith in Hart by offering him work when he was down on his luck, and Hart had repaid him by burglarizing his home. Schilling had not reported the burglary because he hoped his friend would come to his senses and set things right. When he confronted Hart with evidence that confirmed his guilt, Hart reached for a gun, initiating a "general melee," with Hart himself throwing punches, kicking a hole in the living room wall, knocking over furniture and creating havoc throughout the house. Schilling had struck Hart, but only in self defense. Later, when Hart (trying to find a way to escape), told Schilling a lie, claiming that he had hidden the stolen property in a trailer across town so that Schilling would try to find the stuff, Schilling left the house to retrieve it. Hart was left behind with Schilling's friends still untied and relatively uninjured.

Aron ended with a statement that had been resounding in my mind.

"Credibility is going to be paramount in this case. You, as jurors, have been chosen because of your ability to sit and weigh the facts in evidence and judge accordingly. So you'll see when people get up on the stand. You are the ones who are to determine where credibility lies and judge whether or not you think that they're believable. And we want to make sure that you'll listen to all the evidence before you decide the facts of this case, before you render judgment. Keep an open mind throughout the entire proceedings. I think that when you get through weighing the evidence and judging the credibility of each of the witnesses, you will decide that Mr. Schilling is not guilty of the accusations against him. Thank you."

Judge Paxton nodded. "Thank you, Mr. Aron."

He looked over at me solemnly. I knew what he was thinking and it unsettled me.

"Mr. Lowenthal, you may call your first witness."

I sprang to my feet. "Your Honor, we'll call Raymond Hart as the State's first witness."

Chapter 23

The Victim Speaks

Raymond Hart appeared surprisingly relaxed when he walked forward toward the witness box, wearing a knit shirt and dark trousers, fully aware that everyone in the room, especially the jury, was scrutinizing his demeanor. When he settled into the chair, he was no more than five feet from the nearest juror, a young woman with a three-year-old son at home. Hart's eyes met Schilling's for a moment before he allowed himself to look at the jury for the first time. Schilling continued to stare at him, still blinking, squirming a bit in his chair. Schilling seemed less sure of himself than he had the previous day during jury selection.

I began by having Hart introduce himself to the jury. Answering my questions, he identified the members of his family and briefly described his current employment, which consisted of supplying building materials to large commercial developments, including the new baseball park under construction for the Arizona Diamondbacks. Although none of this was relevant to the issues in the case, I wanted Hart to feel comfortable speaking to the jury before we turned to the more emotional issues of the case. The jury, in turn, seemed to have a natural curiosity to learn about him. However, I quickly moved to another topic when I sensed that Judge Paxton was becoming impatient.

Hart explained how he and Steve Schilling had met, then described the arrangements he had made with Schilling to build his garage and remodel his kitchen. Next, he told the jury of his week-long trip to a small town ninety minutes north of Phoenix, where he helped his brother on a construction job. He described Schilling's visit there, in which Schilling told him that someone had broken into his house to steal his coin collection. Hart said that Schilling explained to him that he was investigating every possible suspect, including Hart. After Schilling had thoroughly searched his car and living quarters, Hart assumed that he was no longer under suspicion and he remained at the construction site long enough to finish the job.

This brought Hart to the day of the crime. We had gotten into a smooth rhythm of question and answer and everyone in the courtroom, including Schilling's family, watched intently and seemed to listen to every word he said.

Hart told how he went to Schilling's house between 5:30 and 6:00 in the evening to discuss the completion of the remodeling work, unaware of the danger that lurked inside. At my suggestion, he rose from the witness chair and stepped to an easel a few feet away to label each room on a large diagram of the house that had been prepared before trial. He also looked through a group of photographs taken by the police, identifying the front of the residence, the living room, kitchen, Schilling's office, the other two bedrooms and the garage. I noticed two of the jurors leaning forward, seemingly ready to enter the house and witness the unfolding events.

Hart described how Schilling and his girlfriend, Brenda Chase, met him at the front door and ushered him into the living room. Then, soon after Hart seated himself on the sofa, Schilling disappeared into one of the back rooms. Chase seemed unusually friendly, directing their conversation to the burglary, urging Hart to confide in her if he knew anything about it, since she was worried that Schilling was becoming unstable and might hurt innocent people. This appeared to be a ruse, a clumsy attempt to get him to implicate himself. Uncomfortable, he denied any knowledge of the theft.

Schilling quickly reappeared, suggesting to Hart that they move to his office in the rear bedroom to discuss the remainder of the remodeling. Now Chase disappeared.

Hart sensed that there would be trouble when Schilling sat

behind his desk, motioning him to sit a few feet away. His heart beat rapidly the next moment, as he watched Schilling pull out a large, black semi-automatic handgun, which he placed on the desk. Schilling told Hart he wanted to talk about the burglary, not the remodeling. For Hart, that was the moment the room began to spin.

A couple of minutes later, Chase burst into the office, excitedly waving a black leather fanny pack, claiming that she had found it in Hart's car. She dumped the pack on Schilling's desk and some broken jewelry spilled out. Hart was stunned. He had never seen the pack or the jewelry, before that moment.

Schilling flew into a rage. Grabbing the weapon, he shouted at Hart that he was going to kill him. Pointing the gun directly at Hart's face, he pulled back the hammer.

Hart told how he froze, terrified.

Chase screamed, begging Schilling not to shoot.

An eternity seemed to pass before Schilling gained control of his senses. He ordered Hart to return to the living room, pushed him down on the sofa and demanded to know what he had done with his property, carefully blocking Hart's path to the front door with the gun in one hand and a cordless telephone in the other. Hart started to rise to his feet, protesting that he had nothing to do with the burglary, but Schilling stepped forward and kicked him in the face with the tip of his cowboy boot, knocking him back onto the sofa.

At some point in the blur of events that followed, Chase left the house to go to work. Continuing to point the gun at Hart, Schilling called his neighbor, Cliff, on the phone, asking him to come over to help. He made a similar call to a friend named James Thornton, who arrived shortly after Cliff. James brought another man with him. He called the giant with long hair, tattoos and a gun in his belt Pat.

I phrased my next questions to prompt Hart to tell of his ordeal in his own words.

"Did James have anything in his possession when he came into the house?"

"A metal baseball bat," he said softly.

"What happened next?"

"He walked right up to me, with a full swing, hit me across the chest and shoulders and knocked me down with it."

"When you say hit with a full swing, was he using an object?"

"The baseball bat."

"Had you gotten up from the sofa or were you still sitting on the sofa?"

"I think I was sitting on it. The blow just knocked me backwards. Then he went around the sofa and started hitting me in the head with the baseball bat."

I motioned him to speak louder. I wanted to emphasize his terror for the jury.

"Where?"

"On my head, my shoulders."

"Was he saying anything during this time?"

"Just that he figured it was me."

"Where was the defendant during this?" I looked directly at Schilling, who was showing signs of discomfort.

"He was standing right in front of me with the gun on me." Hart's voice conveyed anxiety and anger.

"Did the defendant say anything during this point in time when James was hitting you?"

"I think he kicked me a couple times. I don't remember him saying anything to me though."

"Did James remain in the room that entire evening?"

"For most of the evening. He left one time, I think, to go get the guy he called Pat."

"About how long was it after he came that—How long after the first time that James arrived did he leave to get this man?"

"I really don't know. Maybe an hour. Maybe shorter. I really can't remember."

" How long was he gone?"

"It didn't seem like he was gone very long at all."

"Could you estimate in time?"

"Maybe ten, fifteen minutes."

"Had you seen Pat before?"

"I had seen him one time prior to this time."

"Do you know his name?"

He nodded. "Pat Richards."

"Could you describe Pat, to the best of your recollection?"

"He's about six foot tall, skinny, real long hair, tattoos, dressed like a biker, carried a gun everywhere he went on his side."

"Did he have a gun that night?"

"Yes," Hart said reflectively.

"What happened when Pat and James arrived?"

"Well, then Pat came up to me."

"And what, if anything, did he do or say?"

"He started punching me, telling me I better fess up, tell him where the stuff is and, basically, just started beating on me for awhile."

"Where on your body was he punching you?"

"He was punching me in the face."

"Did this cause any bleeding?"

"Oh, yeah."

"Where?"

"Blood was coming down all over my face. I was hit on the head with a bat earlier, while Steve was kicking me. My whole face was blood— my whole head was bloody."

The scene he described was so horrifying, I looked over and saw one of the jurors flinch.

"So the defendant was present while Pat was punching you?"

He nodded, "Oh, yeah."

"Did the defendant ask him to stop?"

"No," he said firmly.

"Were you still on the couch, on the sofa, during this period of time when Pat was punching you, James had returned?"

"Yes. I was on the couch."

"Did you do anything to try to deflect these blows?"

"I put my hands up over my head. I was trying to, just, basically, covering my face."

"Could you illustrate to us how you were trying to protect your face?"

"I put my hands up over my head."

"Could you put them up there again so I can describe it?"

I turned toward the court stenographer. "Let the record reflect that the witness has his hands—"

Hart went on. "They were out"

I tried to explain more fully, "—out in front of his head and his elbows pointed in front of him and his hands roughly about the level of his head." Then I added, "I'm not sure if that's completely accurate."

Paxton cut in. "I would prefer to let the jury make the determination, rather than me affirming. Let the jury make the determination."

I nodded and said, "Okay." I turned back to Hart. "Were they saying anything to you about the stolen property during this time?"

"They were trying to get me to admit that I had taken it. I kept telling them I didn't know anything about it, but they just continued to beat the crap out of me."

"How long, altogether, did you remain on that couch?"

"Seemed like forever, but probably an hour, thirty minutes to an hour."

"Could you explain how or why you got off the couch?"

His voice dropped. "I figured it was my only chance. They were going to kill me." The courtroom was pin-drop quiet as he continued. "They were all telling me that. I made a run for the door and just—I managed to get to the door, get it open while they was all on top of me beating me with their guns, bats. I was screaming out the door for help, but they managed to fight me back in, throw me on the ground."

I let him go on for a few moments, then I followed up. "Now, where was this struggle that you've just been describing in relationship to the door?"

"It was right at the door."

"Inside the house; outside the house?"

"Inside. My head was outside for a moment. They got me back in. They was beating me on the head with guns, pipes. They beat me down on the ground."

"Was the defendant participating in this struggle?"

"Oh, yeah."

"What was he doing?"

"He was hitting me with his gun."

"What about—With the gun that you identified as being similar to the gun we saw in the courtroom?"

"Yes."

"What was Pat doing?"

"He was beating me, too, with his gun."

"What about James?"

"He had the baseball bat and was hitting me in the lower back and anywhere that he could get a hit."

"What about Cliff?"

Hart mulled the question over. "I don't know if he was just trying to just help them fight me down or just standing there. I'm not sure where he was."

I prodded him. "You only recall the other three?"

"Yes."

"What was your purpose when you rushed to the door?"

He paused, and said ruefully, "To get out of there."

"Did you intend to attack anyone when you rushed toward the front door?"

"Basically, if they got in my way. I mean I was running to the door to get out. I wasn't aiming for a person. I was aiming for the door."

"What did you think, at the time, was going to happen to you if you didn't get out?"

"They were going to kill me, because they had been telling me that all night."

"How did this struggle at the front door end?"

"With me on the ground."

"Where?"

"Right in front of the door, inside the house."

A few questions followed about Hart's general impressions.

"What, if anything, happened to you when you ended up on the floor?"

"Once I was on the floor, they all started kicking me, hitting me some more, and then they tied me up."

"With what objects did they tie you up?"

"I'm not sure. At first I thought it was an extension cord or a belt. I think they tied the extension cord around my hands and then a belt around my feet, wrapped a belt around my hands so my feet and hands were tied together behind my back."

"Where were you when this occurred?"

"I was laying on the floor, inside, by the front door."

"Did anyone hit you, kick you after you were tied up?"

"They all did."

"When you say 'they all did,' did that include the defendant?"

"Yes."

"Did any of them use any objects?"

"Not right then. They were just kicking me, kicking me in the face, stomach."

"Do you know if you were bleeding when they kicked you on the carpet?"

"Quite a bit by then, yes."

"Did they do anything about that?"

"They kept bringing newspapers in to put underneath me. Every time I'd roll off of them, they'd kick me in the head to stay on the newspaper so I didn't get blood all over the carpet."

"Was this beating continual or did it stop during periods of time?"

"It stopped for periods of time. They would stop for a little bit and go, I'm assuming, back there to the back office."

"Do you know from either your observations or what you heard, what they were doing in the back office?"

"What I think they were doing?"

"From either—not what you think, from your observations. Of what you heard, do you know what they were doing?"

"No."

"Did any of them come back into the living room from the office?"

"I believe it was James and Steve came back in."

"What, if anything, were you doing when they came back into the living room?"

He looked at me as if it was self explanatory and said, "I was trying to get loose."

"Explain that."

"I was trying to get free from the ropes and stuff and I was getting pretty close to getting loose when they came back in."

"What happened?"

"They both started beating me again and then they blindfolded me, so I couldn't see when they were there, and then they wrapped duct tape around me real tight, wrapped duct tape on my hands, head, feet, turned on the radio, which I was laying right next to, kind of not blaring, but enough to where I couldn't hear if they were around me."

I paused. A crucial moment had arrived. "Your Honor, may counsel approach the bench?"

I asked for a recess and fortunately the judge agreed. Because of the horror of what he had gone through, Hart was grabbing the jury's attention and not letting go. But I knew for me it would be far more challenging to prepare the jury for the questions that would follow. Rarely did a prosecution witness have so many vulnerabilities. Aron's cross-examination could point to the numerous inconsistencies in Hart's pre trial statements; his prior convictions; his well-documented animosity toward Schilling; his drug addiction and the plea bargain he had entered while Schilling's case was pending, implying that he was cooperating with the state to save his own skin. The only way to mute the blare of Aron's trumpet would be to bring up as much of the impeaching evidence as possible in my own questioning, in a matter-of-fact fashion, both to deflate its value and to show that we had nothing to hide.

However, when I had begun Hart's direct-examination, Judge Paxton had not yet ruled on the defense's pre-trial motions relating to Hart's prior bad acts. Aron badly wanted the jury to know of them. In addition, he wanted to cross-examine Hart on his extensive history of methamphetamine addiction, both to show how desperate he was on July 3, 1994 and to suggest that the drugs the police found were his, not Schilling's.

This presented me with a dilemma. If I failed to ask Hart about these matters on direct-examination and the judge subsequently allowed Aron to explore them in detail, he might be able to destroy Hart's credibility. On the other hand, it was still possible that the judge would deny Aron's pre-trial motions. In this case, I would be snatching defeat from the jaws of victory by unnecessarily exposing Hart's problems myself.

Paxton saved me—during this mid-afternoon recess—just when I was reaching a critical juncture in Hart's direct-examination. As the jury was leaving the room, he announced that he wanted to see the lawyers in chambers, along with the court reporter. Surprisingly, Schilling chose not to join us, instead electing to talk with his family in the hallway, probably unaware of the import of the moment.

When Paxton announced his decisions on the pre-trial motions they could not have been worse for Aron. First, he sanitized Hart's prior convictions, ruling that Aron could inform the jury on cross-examination only that Hart had two convictions on his record, without delving into the nature of the underlying crimes. Additionally, if Hart admitted in his testimony that he was an addict, Paxton would not permit Aron to question him on the extent of his addiction or on specific instances of drug use. Finally, he said he would not allow either party to introduce evidence on prior bad acts committed by either the victim or the defendant. Although I could not present testimony to show that Schilling had assaulted another man on a previous occasion, the ruling was far more harmful to the defense.

We returned to the courtroom and I continued my direct examination. "What happened next?"

"That's when they kicked and beat me for awhile, and then used duct tape and duct tape my hands and feet up, wrapped duct tape on my eyes, mouth, eyes, face, all around my head."

"Was this tighter or looser than you had been tied in the evening?"

"My hands and feet were real tight."

"What were the position of your hands and feet when you were tied this second time?"

"They were behind my back and tied to my feet, just like this, and then tied to my ankles."

"Were your hands and feet secured separately or were they tied together?"

"They were tied together."

"After this, did all four of the individuals remain in the house?"

"That was right after I tried to get away and stuff?"

I wanted to be sure that they jury got the full picture. "Let me rephrase the question. Did all four of the individuals remain in the house throughout the entire episode in which you were beaten?"

"No."

"At what point did someone leave?"

"Steve had Cliff leave, gave him a cellular phone and a police scanner, to go down to the corner in case any police officer came so he could warn Steve ahead of time."

"Did anyone else besides the defendant point a gun at you?"

"Pat did. He stuck it in my mouth a couple times and pulled back the hammer."

"While these events were occurring, did Pat say anything to you?"

"He said they were going to kill me and he was talking about giving me a shot of something so I wouldn't keep trying to get loose."

"Did Pat say what would happen to you if and when you were killed?"

"He was talking about—he and Steve were talking about just taking me out in the desert in the trunk of my car, killing me, leaving me out there, but James Thornton was trying to talk them into—he said he knew a guy that worked with the coroner's office, then they could get, you know, if they could get a hold of them, they could have me cremated and then no one would find me."

At this point, I started to bury the damaging evidence in the middle of Hart's terrifying account. "Mr. Hart, you, yourself, have been convicted on August twelfth, 1994, criminal action CR94-01576. You were convicted of an undesignated offense that was later reduced to a— were you convicted of an undesignated offense that was later reduced to a misdemeanor?"

"Yes."

"Were you blindfolded at all during this evening?"

"Most of the evening until the blood was so thick on my head the tape wouldn't stick no more." The jurors were now staring at him with astonishment.

"Do you know what objects were used to hit you while you were blindfolded?"

"I'm not sure, because I couldn't see it, but it felt like a pipe and boots, mainly, but I'm not sure because I couldn't see it."

Along the way, we covered his methamphetamine addiction and his other prior conviction. I hoped to hide the damaging reflections that Hart's past left on the matter of his believability in the testimony of his brutal beating. I asked my questions in simple yes-and-no phraseology, and always quickly returned to the events that transpired in Schilling's home that terrible evening.

"At what point in time do you finally leave the living room?"

"Later on that night when they picked me up and put me in the trunk of the car."

"Were you blindfolded at that time?"

"I believe so."

"How many people, to your knowledge, picked you up and took you into the car?"

"Three. I remember two, one on each side and one holding my feet."

"Did you walk to the trunk?"

"No. They carried me with my arms and feet behind me. They grabbed onto my arms and feet and lifted me up."

"At the time they put you in the trunk, did you know whose trunk it was?"

"No."

"Did you later find out whose trunk it was?"

"Yeah."

"Whose was it?"

"It was mine."

"What happened when you were placed in the trunk of the car?"

"I begged them to loosen the tape because I couldn't even feel my hands anymore. They were just totally numb, and I was trying to get them to get me some water or something. And when I opened my mouth, they dumped Kool-Aid in my mouth, and I opened it again, and they shot that, whatever was in that syringe, shot it in my mouth."

The jurors were sitting up ramrod straight now. All had their eyes on him, no one looking away or showing any gestures of inattention.

I went on.

"Let's talk a minute about the syringe. When was the first time that night you were made aware of a syringe?"

"When Steve and James were talking to Pat about going and getting something that would knock me out."

"What, if anything, was said about a syringe?"

"That Pat could go get one and bring it back and give me a shot of it so that I wouldn't resist and try to get away no more."

"Did he in fact, bring a syringe?"

"Yes, he did."

"Did you see the syringe?"

"Yes."

"When you saw the syringe, did you say anything?"

"Yeah. I begged him not to, and I was fighting, trying to not let him stick it in me and then I started telling him, at that time, that I would tell him where the stuff was."

"Did you, in fact, tell them where the property was?"

"Yes."

"What did you say?"

"I told them it was in a trailer on Forty-fourth Street, the parking lot of an apartment building."

"Was the property there?"

He shook his head. "No."

"Why did you tell them that?"

Hart was silent for a moment. He looked as if he was wincing inwardly. "It was my last hope of getting away. I was hoping they would leave me to go check and I—it would give me a chance to get away."

I glanced in their direction and I could see the jury was moved. "How long after that did they put you in the trunk?"

"Right afterwards."

"When they put you in the trunk, did they close the lid?"

"Yes."

"Then what happened?"

"After they left, I heard a truck leave. And as soon as I heard Steve's bike start off, I started fighting, trying to get out and the trunk popped open." I nailed down a few particulars. Then I asked.

"What happened when the trunk lid popped open?"

"I tried to get out. Finally, I rolled out of the car and fell on the ground."

"Then what happened."

"I scooted over to where the tool box was and managed with my hands behind my back to get a pair of pliers out and I cut my feet loose so I could stand up. Then when I stood up, I could hardly walk from whatever they gave me. I managed to get to the garage door and open it up just enough for me to get out."

"What did you do after that?"

"I ran to the house next door."

"What happened when you went to the house next door?"

"I pounded on the door, kicked it, was screaming, yelling for somebody to help me and somebody came to the door, but they wouldn't open it. And I begged them just to, at least, untie my hands so I could get away, because I knew they were going to be coming back. I told them if they come back and I'm out here, they're going to definitely kill me."

"Do you recall what the next-door neighbor said to you?"

"I took off before—I don't remember. I just knew they weren't going to open the door. I took off and ran to the next house."

"What happened when you went to the next house?"

"Nobody came to the door."

"What did you do then?

"I went to the house next to that one."

"What happened there?"

"A guy came to the door and he had a gun, because he didn't know what he was facing. But he opened the door and let me in. Shortly after I got in the house, he was trying to get the stuff off my hands, from around my neck, but he couldn't do it. Then the paramedics came and they all started cutting it off."

"Did the police also arrive?"

"Yes."

"Did you tell the police officers at the scene what had happened to you that night?"

"Yes."

"Did you receive any treatment from the paramedics at the scene?"

He nodded, "Yes, quite a bit."

"Did you remain there very long?"

"No. They took me out, because they was worried about head injury, because blood was coming out of my ears."

Schilling had eagerly awaited his day in court for over three years. He had turned down the prosecution's pre-trial plea bargain, because he believed that he was the true victim, not Hart. He felt that everyone would understand who was the good guy and who was bad when all the evidence came out in court. He had found some of the defense's witnesses himself, bringing them to his lawyers' attention. Each of the attorneys, first Frank Mahoney, then Bill Warren and finally Robert Aron—had said that the truth would come out in the end.

During the afternoon recess, before my direct examination had concluded, Schilling was conversing quietly with his mother in the corridor outside Judge Paxton's courtroom when Aron approached, saying that he wished to speak with Schilling privately. Schilling assumed that Aron wanted to consult with him on Hart's cross-examination and was irritated that Aron sought his advice so much. The lawyer, not the client, was supposed to be the expert on trial strategy. Schilling liked Bill Warren's aggressive style much more; Aron seemed to him too preppy.

Aron ushered him into a small, windowless room where witnesses were supposed to wait before they were called into court to testify. Aron took a deep breath, then began with "I know you're not going to like this." Seconds later, the brick hit Schilling squarely between the eyes. He had not anticipated the judge's ruling disallowing all of the evidence relating to Hart's unsavory past.

Schilling began by threatening to fire Aron and take over his own defense; surely he could do a better job with the case. Aron argued against this course of action, pointing out that Schilling could preserve a possible post-conviction claim of constitutionally inadequate defense counsel if he allowed Aron to continue representing him. One could not overturn a conviction on this ground if he represented himself at trial. Next, Schilling asked if they could still accept the plea agreement offered before trial, but Aron doubted that the prosecution would bargain at this late stage. Aron reminded him that they still had Brenda Chase as a witness and Schilling himself would be able to set the jury straight on what really happened on the night of the incident. But the trial was going to be about that night alone.

When I completed Hart's direct examination I reflected that he had come across far better than I expected. His concession that he had a prior felony record had come at an opportune moment during his chilling account of the escape from Schilling's garage and the treatment he received at the hospital. I had watched the jury from the corner of my eye while he testified on this touchy issue. No one seemed fazed by his admissions.

Aron obviously had counted on emphasizing the very issues in his cross-examination the judge ruled out-of-bounds and no longer could do so. He scored points by eliciting from Hart that he had sued Schilling for monetary damages, thus giving him a motive for lying about his injuries. He also got Hart to testify that he was still in pain four months after the beating at Schilling's house, then countered by reminding him of his pre-trial statement in which he said that he had fully recovered by this time. However, instead of settling for whatever value he could wring from these points, he quibbled with Hart for close to thirty minutes on the extent of his injuries, trying to suggest, as Schilling wanted, that Hart was grossly exaggerating. This line of questioning made no sense to me, because the emergency room physician and Detective Nicholson would later corroborate that Hart's injuries were substantial.

Aron suggested forcefully that Hart's inaccurate statement to Detective Davis was dishonest, but this had little bite, since I had already covered this issue on direct examination. Aron spent twenty minutes asking Hart about the various blows he had taken to his head. Instead of bolstering the defense, this backfired and reinforced the direct examination.

Hart walked briskly from the courtroom at the end of the afternoon, unscathed. It was the low point in the trial for Schilling.

Chapter 24

Counterpunches
in the Middle Rounds

I was giddy on the drive home after that first day of trial, greatly relieved that my worst fears were now safely behind me. Hart's testimony had focused entirely on the incident of July 3. He had been much stronger than I had expected on the witness stand and would not be needed to testify again. Although I had learned many years earlier not to trust a jury's non-verbal reactions to a witness, I nonetheless found myself succumbing to this temptation, deriving considerable confidence from the jurors' intense attention during Hart's testimony, hoping this indicated that they found him credible.

I turned my attention to the next several days and felt good that a progression of solid citizens would take the stand to corroborate as much of Hart's story as possible.

The first witnesses were going to be Schilling's neighbors. Merle Shuler, the middle-aged auto mechanic who lived next door, would describe the shrill terror in Hart's voice when he begged to be allowed into Shuler's home, pounding his head against the front door, a blood-soaked towel wrapped around his head. Next would be Mike Connor, the telecommunication technician a few houses away who had helped Hart. Hart had trembled when Connor attempted to untie the electrical cord that bound his hands behind his back. These were the jury's peers.

Next, I planned to call a series of public servants. Ted Rice, the first police officer to arrive at the scene, would testify that Hart appeared to be in great pain when the paramedics attended to his wounds in Connor's kitchen. Another officer, Carl Tate, was going to recount the circumstances of Schilling's arrest. Then the emergency room physician who treated Hart at John C. Lincoln Hospital would explain his injuries to the jury. In the days to follow, I expected to call several technicians from the police crime laboratory and two night squad detectives.

In a case with two competing versions of "what happened," I had a tremendous advantage, because the prosecution told its story first. Even though Judge Paxton had given the standard preliminary instruction that warned the jury not to make up its mind until all the evidence was in, countless studies have demonstrated that first impressions are almost always lasting. As a practical matter, the jurors would form opinions as they processed each bit of information and once those opinions were formed, it would be a challenge for the defense to dispel them, despite the legal requirement that the burden of proof never shifted from the prosecution.

I not only had an opportunity to bolster Hart's story, but also to undermine the defense's case even before it began. Aron had informed the jury in his opening statement that Schilling would rely on a claim of self defense, contending that Hart initiated the violence and that most of Hart's injuries were inflicted by others, after Schilling had left the house. To cast doubt on this defense, I planned to ask Officer Tate to testify about a statement Schilling made when he was arrested, admitting that he had struck Ray Hart "a couple of times" that night. According to Tate's report, Schilling did not mention anything about self defense. Similarly, one of his neighbors could testify about a conversation he had with Schilling in mid-July, two weeks after the incident with Hart. Schilling told the neighbor that he had caught someone stealing from him and had hit him, but said nothing about defending himself.

I told myself this was going to be the easiest part of my case.

But it wasn't.

First, much of my evidence had little probative weight. No matter how many witnesses I called to corroborate Hart's story, they touched only the periphery of his account, describing his injuries, but not how they occurred or who inflicted them. On these crucial questions, the case still turned on whether Hart was telling the truth. No one, other than Hart himself, testified that Schilling had pulled a gun on him without provocation. The only person to witness the initiation of conflict between Hart and Schilling was Brenda Chase, who had been summoned by the defense and she would not arrive from her new home in another state until the following Monday, after most of my witnesses had already testified. Chase was almost certainly going to side with Schilling on the important issue of self defense, making it two witnesses against one. There was also no evidence to corroborate Hart's assertion that Schilling himself participated in the beatings that occurred after Chase had left the house. The jury might find Schilling's version more believable than Hart's, when even a tie in the credibility contest would go to the defense. There was ample room for reasonable doubt.

Meanwhile, Robert Aron found a second wind. I had to admire his skill when questioning the remaining prosecution witnesses, eliciting chunks of information that weakened the state's case.

He was especially effective in cross-examining the police officers who responded to the 911 call before the night squad detectives arrived at the scene. Testifying more than three years after the incident, the two officers had little or no recollection of specific details, apart from those they had recorded in their respective police reports. When Aron zeroed in on matters not explicitly covered in the reports, they tried to fill the gaps by testifying to what they assumed the facts to be, based on vague memories. But they contradicted one another on small but possibly significant points. For example, they disagreed on how certain items of physical evidence were collected and placed in the trunk of one officer's patrol car. This later became important when the serology evidence was questioned.

Aron pressed Officer Tate on the circumstances of his conversation with Schilling at the time of the arrest. Aron stated facts, then asked questions such as "Would you agree?" or "Is that correct?" This forced the officer to either confirm or deny Aron's assertions.

"Your purpose there at that time was not to conduct a full interview of Mr. Schilling. Is that correct?" Aron prodded.

"That's correct."

"You just wanted to gather some basic facts or gain a basic understanding of what occurred. Is that right?"

"Yes."

"Your conversation wasn't very long, was it?"

"No. Not very long."

Aron paused, allowing the jury to ponder whether Schilling had a sufficient opportunity to volunteer anything about self defense.

"When you have a conversation with someone, you don't write down every particular thing that person may or may not be saying. Is that not right?"

"That's correct."

"So your entire conversation with Mr. Schilling was not recorded, I take it?"

"No, it wasn't."

The implication was clear: if Schilling said something about defending himself, it might not have found its way into the officer's report.

Paxton took a mid-afternoon recess after Tate left the stand.

Looking around, I noticed that Ray Hart was absent, even though, as the victim, he had the right to remain in the courtroom throughout the trial, while other witnesses were prohibited. He had been present when the first of Schilling's neighbors testified and I assumed— still unaware of his encounter with Schilling in the cafeteria—that he wanted to follow the proceedings closely. Later his sister came over to explain that her brother found reliving the ordeal and listening to witnesses distressing. He did not want to hear the doctor describe his injuries. He also did not want to be around when Schilling and Brenda Chase testified. I urged Hart's sister to remain, since Schilling's family was well represented on the other side of the room.

As a legal matter, I needed the testimony of the attending physician, Fred McBride, to establish a necessary element of two of the assault charges, an allegation that two of Hart's bones had been fractured. The doctor provided this evidence by reading and explaining Hart's x-rays. He also testified that Hart seemed to be in considerable pain, with bruises on his torso and multiple lacerations on his face and scalp. However, like the patrol officers who preceded him, the doctor had no specific recollection of the case, relying exclusively on his contemporaneous notes and the hospital's records. He could not identify pictures of Hart lying on a hospital bed.

On cross-examination, McBride gave the defense two little points and one big one. The CT scan of Hart's skull showed no brain injury consistent with being beaten repeatedly with an iron pipe and aluminum bat. Additionally, the notation on Hart's chart that he was "alert and oriented times four" meant that he was able to think with perfect clarity when he was interviewed by Detective Nicholson in the hospital, allowing him to choose what he would say carefully. More important, one of his two broken bones was a fracture of the fifth metacarpal, a knuckle on his right hand. The physician testified that this injury was commonly known as a "boxer's fracture." Although it was consistent with receiving a blow from a blunt object, it occurred most frequently when a person made his hand into a fist and threw a punch at another person.

Deflated by McBride's testimony, I hoped to make up ground the next day, beginning with Bill Telgarden, the detective who obtained the warrant to search Schilling's home. Telgarden was a veteran, bound to make a good impression on the jury. I planned for him to testify for at least ninety minutes, since I needed him to identify each item of physical evidence found at the house, laying a foundation under the rules of evidence to show the exhibits to the jury. Telgarden would be followed by three witnesses from the Phoenix Police Department's crime laboratory, who would tell the jury about the tests they had performed on the evidence.

However, my plans went awry when Telgarden's car broke down on the way to court, delaying him for more than an hour. Judge Paxton was highly displeased, not wanting the jury to have to wait idly. He urged me to put someone else on the stand, anyone, if only to fill the time.

My only available witness was Detective Nicholson, my star, whom I had hoped to save until last, after all my other witnesses had testified. He was familiar with every aspect of the case, would be able to tie up loose ends, and could authenticate the color photographs of Hart's wounds taken at the hospital. Powerfully graphic, the photos offered me a perfect opportunity to end the state's case with a flourish. Calling Nicholson out of order would ruin these plans, but Paxton had a different agenda, leaving me no choice. I'd have to play my best card now.

My anxiety rose precipitously. I wanted to draft my direct-examination questions in advance, to make sure that each witness's testimony flowed smoothly, with nothing overlooked. Caught off guard, I had not yet prepared Nicholson's direct. I also had no idea how to operate the Elmo, a device that scanned three-by-five photographs and displayed them on a thirty-inch television screen set before the jury. To calm my anxiety, I told myself that Nicholson was an experienced witness who knew exactly where we were going, that he was already familiar with the photos I had selected, and that I could use the questions I'd planned for Telgarden, since Nicholson would have to stand in for him, identifying the physical evidence seized from Schilling's house. Nevertheless, I longed for my usual crutch of intense advance planning.

But I had forgotten just how stunning the pictures of Hart's injuries were. Three feet from the nearest juror, he lay on a hospital bed, a circle of blood on the pillow beneath his head. The bearded face on the screen looked nothing like the man who had testified two days earlier. A nasty laceration ran across his left cheek, leading to his eye, which was purple and swollen shut, with congealed blood in his hair, ears and disfigured nose. He had a deep gash on the right side of his forehead, ligature marks on his wrists and ankles, and ugly bruises on his neck, chest, back and hips.

Before trial, I had been concerned that the gory picture show might inflame the jury, especially the images of Hart's head and torso. Although relevant to the assault and kidnapping charges against Schilling, the photographs added little to the testimony of the four prosecution witnesses, including the emergency room physician, who had already described Hart's physical condition to the jury before Nicholson took the stand. But I changed my mind when Aron made the terrible mistake of suggesting during Hart's cross-examination that he had exaggerated the extent of his injuries. The gashes, lacerations, black eyes and broken bones were very real. I wanted the jury to appreciate what Schilling and his friends had done. In any event, the visceral effect was muted by my inability to master the zoom control on the

Elmo, denying the jury a close-up view of Hart's wounds and much of the physical evidence in Schilling's house.

The images of Schilling's house were equally revolting, with blood everywhere. Most noticeable was the ugly reddish-brown stain that dominated the living room carpet, but the pool that had soaked through the newspapers in the trunk of Hart's car, parked in the garage, was almost as large. One thing was clear: it had been mayhem.

To supplement the photos, I offered into evidence certain items taken from the crime scene, including Schilling's gun, the metal pipe found on the living room sofa, a section of carpet, pliers and duct tape found on the floor of the garage, and the plastic bag containing methamphetamine that had been removed from a compartment in Schilling's computer. Several of these items were enclosed in sealed plastic bags with a legend in bold, capital letters, "**BIOHAZARDOUS!**" The bags went unopened. At the judge's suggestion, I also did not move into evidence the large garbage bag from Schilling's kitchen, with blood-soaked newspaper, clothing, belts and duct tape inside.

Nicholson testified that one of the exhibits in evidence, a blue nylon backpack, belonged to Hart. The detectives had found Hart's things in one of its compartments and two coin magazines in another. During the next recess, I idly looked through the backpack, feeling a small object in one of the many pockets inside. Curious, I unzipped the pocket, reached in and pulled out a glass pipe that the police had apparently missed three years earlier. I was reasonably certain it was Hart's, but he was not present to verify this. A few minutes later, I showed the pipe to Aron, who showed it to Schilling before returning it.

Nicholson's cross-examination was a turning point in the trial.

Aron started slowly, with questions about Nicholson's interview of Hart in the hospital emergency room, asking the detective to affirm one fact at a time, just as Aron had done with Tate, McBride and the other prosecution witnesses. He established that Nicholson had been thorough in questioning Hart, taking extensive notes, recording everything of substance Hart said during the hour-long interview. Additionally, Nicholson agreed, Hart had understood his questions and was coherent in his responses.

Then the stingers began. Hart failed to mention to Nicholson several of the details that he included in the story he later told to the jury. Other facts in his testimony were inconsistent with his statement to the detective. This was good ammunition for Aron's closing argument, when he would contend that Hart was lying.

Moving on to the crime scene investigation, Aron focused his initial questions on the stains in Schilling's house. He established that Nicholson was highly experienced in identifying patterns in blood splatter, including those that would occur when an object with fresh blood on it—such as a metal pipe or a baseball bat—was swung forcefully. None of the spots on the walls or furniture in Schilling's house were consistent with such patterns. Apart from the large soaked-in splotch on the carpet that appeared to have been made by a bloody object resting against it, Nicholson was unable to say with certainty how the stains had occurred.

Aron then settled on a frequently used strategy when defense lawyers cross-examine cops, asking about everything that *wasn't* done, to imply that the investigation was careless and sloppy. In this case, it was an effective ploy.

On direct, Nicholson had characterized the smudges and spots in various locations throughout Schilling's house as "blood" stains. Aron challenged this, displaying several of the prosecution's photos on the television screen, where the jury could see reddish blemishes on walls, floor and furniture, in Hart's car trunk, and on such items as newspapers, duct tape, the metal pipe and articles of clothing. Nicholson acknowledged that many of the stained surfaces and items had not been impounded during the search or preserved for testing. Of the items that were seized, most had not been analyzed by the crime laboratory. There was no way of knowing that the stains were Hart's blood. In fact, Nicholson admitted, he could not be certain that the stains were even blood.

Two of the items that Nicholson had submitted to the crime laboratory for blood testing were Schilling's boots and trousers. After Officer Tate had seized these items from Schilling, he placed them together inside a plastic bag. Nicholson acknowledged that the pants and boots should have been preserved separately, then had to admit that he could not be sure that the blood on one of these items had not been transferred from the other.

Aron directed Nicholson's attention to a photograph of the desk in Schilling's office, which he displayed to the jury on the television screen. The black fanny pack lay on one side of the desk top, just where Brenda Chase had apparently dumped it. A watch and other items of jewelry were strewn about, near the fanny pack. Nicholson acknowledged that these items had not been seized in the police search. Thus, there was no way of knowing if Hart's fingerprints were on the fanny pack or the jewelry.

Aron hoped the jury would infer that the police had been interested in only one side of the story. He asked Nicholson if he had questioned Hart about the events that led to the July 3 incident at Schilling's house. Nicholson had not.

Aron ended the forceful cross examination by showing the blue nylon backpack to the detective, who identified it as Hart's. He knew this because Hart had told him so. At Aron's request, Nicholson searched through each of its compartments, at last pulling out the glass pipe. A few of the jurors looked puzzled, at least until Nicholson explained: it was the type of pipe commonly used for smoking methamphetamine.

Arizona adopted a unique procedural rule in the mid-1990s, allowing jurors to submit questions to be asked of witnesses. The questions had to be written and unsigned, then reviewed by the judge and lawyers outside the jury's presence, to determine if they were permissible under the rules of evidence. If a question was ruled to be appropriate, either the judge or one of the lawyers would then pose it to the witness.

In other courts in the United States, juries are confined to listening to the evidence introduced by counsel, then deciding the facts by applying the rules imposed by the court. But this was not always so. Before the sixteenth century, English juries played an active role in investigating the facts at trial. However, as trial lawyers became prevalent and rules of evidence came into existence, the jury's role became increasingly passive. Critics of the American justice system have occasionally suggested giving jurors the right to question witnesses, but these suggestions have been resisted by attorneys, who do not want to relinquish control over their cases. Hence, the Arizona approach is exceptional.

The *Schilling* jury now had questions for Detective Nicholson, but they were not ones that I welcomed. One of the unsigned notes asked if all of the blood found at the scene of the crime was Ray Hart's blood. Another juror asked if the police found fingerprints on the bag of drugs, and if so, whose they were.

Clearly, members of this jury had a sense of ownership, paying careful attention to the evidence elicited by the lawyers, not fully satisfied, wanting clarification. This is precisely what the state supreme court had sought in adopting the reform. As a law professor, I welcomed the change, but the questions asked by the *Schilling* jury did not bode well for my case. Nicholson could not answer those questions, but, I regretted, my next witnesses could.

The first of these witnesses was Joyce Carter, a police chemist who had testified at least forty times before, mostly in murder prosecutions. In July 1995, a year after the incident at Steve Schilling's house, Carter had attempted to compare a sample of Ray Hart's blood with dried blood scraped from four items of physical evidence: the butt of Schilling's gun, a swatch of fabric from his sofa, his blue jeans and the tip of one of his cowboy boots. The blood from the gun was definitely human blood, but it had deteriorated so much in the year since the incident that a comparison with Hart's blood was impossible without DNA testing, which Carter was not authorized to do. The blood from the other three items was consistent with Hart's blood, meaning that he could not be excluded as the source of these blood stains.

The only inference from Carter's testimony favorable to the prosecution was that Hart's blood may have found its way onto Schilling's sofa, pants and boot. Of course, the blood on the sofa and jeans could have come from four percent of the general population, or more than 100,000 persons living in the Phoenix area. Almost a half million of the county's residents could have been the source of the blood on Schilling's boot. And, since neither the police nor the prosecution had sought to obtain a sample of Schilling's own blood, Carter could not rule him out.

Rob Nicholson was furious. He had submitted twenty-six items of evidence to the crime laboratory for blood testing on July 4, 1994. A reasonably prompt comparison with samples of Schilling's and Hart's blood would have provided the answers the jury wanted. However, Nicholson had no connection with the case between July 1994 and October 1997 and neither the police investigator nor the prosecutor had seemed to care enough to get the lab work completed. When Ben Reynolds had finally requested a comparison with Hart's blood in 1995, only a handful of items were submitted. Gerry Baylor, the prosecutor assigned to the case for almost three years, had not requested a sample from Schilling. I also contributed to the problem by not seeking a court order for Schilling's blood in September 1997, when I took over the case. I failed to discover the inadequacy of the blood tests until my last minute preparations and by then we were already beginning the trial.

Nicholson had also requested fingerprint analyses of numerous items seized in the search of Schilling's house, including the bag of methamphetamine, the duct tape and belts used to bind Hart, the magazine in Schilling's gun and the metal bar found in his living room. None of these analyses were performed. The only fingerprint evidence introduced at Schilling's trial was the report of Betty Koto, another crime laboratory technician. In 1996, two years after the offense, Koto compared Schilling's, Hart's and James Thornton's prints with fingerprint impressions lifted from Hart's car when it was found in Schilling's garage. None of Schilling's fingerprints matched those from the car. However, Thornton's prints were on the driver's door handle, the gear shift lever and the lid of the trunk.

The physical evidence had demonstrated that Thornton had participated in Hart's kidnapping, but there was no physical proof Schilling had. The momentum in the trial had clearly shifted and neither Brenda Chase nor Steve Schilling had yet testified. I rested my case, knowing that I still had much work to do in cross examining Aron's witnesses.

Chapter 25

Throwing Zingers in Court

Coffee in hand, I arrived early the following Monday morning at the front desk of the Legal Defender's Office. As the receptionist called Robert Aron to inform him of my arrival, I noticed a woman sitting alone in a conference room across the lobby, staring intently at me. I tried not to be too obvious, but I looked back. Slender and attractive, perhaps thirty-something, she had long auburn hair and was wearing a modest but flattering suit. I reddened as our eyes locked. The woman was accustomed to being noticed.

Moments later, Aron ushered me into the conference room and introduced me to Brenda Chase. The purpose of the meeting was to give me an opportunity to conduct a tape recorded interview before she testified as the first defense witness that afternoon. I had spent a good deal of the weekend preparing her cross-examination and this interview would enable me to decide which questions to ask and which to avoid.

Aron left us alone in the conference room for about five minutes while he tracked down a tape recorder. Chase was reticent to engage in small talk, but I nevertheless learned that she had arrived the previous evening, spending the night with friends. Now married and employed as a registered nurse in another state, she had done well in the previous two years. There was something genuine about her that I instinctively liked, fully aware that the jury would too.

I pondered her motivation for testifying. Before her departure from Arizona, she had told a defense investigator that she was running away from Steve Schilling's abuse. She clearly did not enjoy this re-visit to the world of methamphetamine and her life with Schilling, but she also seemed singularly loyal to him. Even though she was under sub-poena, the defense could not have gotten her to fly to Phoenix with-out full cooperation. When Aron returned, I learned that he and Chase had grown up in neighboring towns and they had talked fre-quently on the telephone during the past year. She trusted him.

It was a difficult interview. Chase paused for several seconds after each question. She also stopped frequently in the middle of her answers, either collecting her thoughts or simply wary of me. Uneasy, with my anxiety rising, I sometimes failed to wait for her complete responses, ask-ing follow-up questions just when she was ready to continue, with the result that we spoke simultaneously. But when I managed to be patient, she gave a full preview of the evidence she would offer for the defense that afternoon.

Her story was riveting, but I still had unanswered questions.

According to Chase, she had been at Schilling's house one Friday evening in late June, ten days before Schilling's July 3 confrontation with Hart. She remembered seeing Hart there and Schilling telling Hart that he was going to gamble that night at one of the casinos near Phoenix. Hart knew, just as she did, what this meant: Schilling would be away from the house all night. It was then that Hart told Schilling that he was going to northern Arizona to work on a project with his brother.

The next day, Schilling called her and said he'd been robbed. He was especially upset about the coins, which he said were missing and worth over ten thousand dollars. All he wanted was to get his property back and he thought he had a better chance if he found the burglar him-self, rather than reporting the crime to the police. They discussed who might be responsible. Hart was the prime suspect. He had access to the house and knew where everything was hidden. Schilling felt Hart was also capable of stealing from his friends.

Brenda and Steve talked about ways to get the property back. Chase said to him that she was aware that Hart was attracted to her and suggested that she might be able to induce him to say something about the burglary. Schilling thought this was an excellent idea. The plan was for Chase to spend time alone with Hart when he returned. All they needed was the right opportunity. It came on July 3.

Hart called Schilling to arrange a meeting at Schilling's home that evening to discuss the remodeling. When Hart arrived, Schilling retired to the back of the house, leaving Chase alone with Hart in the living room for about ten minutes. Sitting next to Hart on the sofa, she asked what he had been doing during the week he was away. Leery, Hart mentioned his new work and a gambling junket he'd taken, but said nothing about the burglary of Schilling's house. She brought up the subject. She told him that Schilling was planning to canvas coin shops in northern Arizona. He insisted he hadn't stolen the coins.

When Schilling rejoined them, he invited Hart to his office to discuss the remodeling. Chase said she looked outside and noticed Hart's car parked at the curb with its windows down. Curious, she scribbled a note and handed it to Schilling in his office, commenting casually for Hart's benefit that it was a telephone number Schilling had asked her to find.

The note said: "Keep him busy. I'm going to search his car."

According to Chase, she noticed a familiar leather strap on the floorboard under the seat. Excited, she opened the door, reached down and pulled out a black fanny pack, recognizing it immediately as one she had purchased for Schilling a few years earlier. Her heart skipped a beat when she looked inside, finding Schilling's imitation Rolex watch in one of the pockets.

Schilling and Hart were seated about three feet apart, behind and to the side of the desk, when Chase re-entered the office.

Pulling the watch out of the fanny pack, she said, "Look what I found in Ray's car!" Both men looked stunned.

Chase flipped the pack upside down onto the desk. Some of its contents appeared to be Hart's, including his wallet and a plastic bag filled with a suspicious white powder. Other items lay in the pile, including watch bands, cigarette lighters, gold chains and a lady's broach. These had been in the bottom drawer of Schilling's file cabinet.

Simultaneously, the two men became animated, one swearing he was innocent, the other enraged.

"I can't believe you did this!" Schilling shouted. "Where's the rest of my stuff?"

Hart claimed that he had found the bag at a thrift shop a block away from Schilling's house, then changed his story, saying he had retrieved it from inside a dumpster behind the store. He denied knowing where the remainder of the property was located.

Chase described how Hart then sprang from his seat, lunging for Schilling's gun, which lay on top of the desk. Schilling reacted instantaneously, reaching the weapon just as Hart did.

Chase was terrified the next few seconds as she watched the struggle for the gun, aware that the weapon usually was loaded.

Schilling gained control, shoved Hart back into his chair and abruptly slammed the gun on the desk, still screaming. He took Hart's drugs from the pile in front of him and placed them inside his computer, where his cat could not get them.

Hart dashed from the office, trying to get out the front door, but Schilling caught him from behind and threw him onto the living room sofa. Hart continued to deny his guilt.

Schilling's frustration mounted. Standing by the front door with a cordless telephone, he tried calling a telephone number written on a piece of paper he'd found in the fanny pack. He reached Hart's brother, who provided no leads on the stolen property. Just about then, Schilling received a call from a friend who lived in his neighborhood, a man named Cliff. Chase heard Schilling tell Cliff that he had caught the person who'd stolen his coins.

A few minutes later, Cliff joined them in the living room. Then, just before Chase departed for work, around 9:30 P.M., James Thornton came to the front door. Thornton invited Schilling to go on a Fourth of July outing the next day, then left.

According to Chase, when she drove off, Hart was still unharmed.

As I expected, Chase presented herself well to the jury that afternoon. Her attractive courtroom demeanor had to have given a tremendous boost to Schilling's claim that he acted in self defense, at least during the initial stage of the incident. Cross-examining her would be treacherous. Although I had many angles to work with, I could not afford to be heavy-handed with such a likeable witness, a tenet of cross examination I had learned painfully when questioning an elderly woman in my first DUI prosecution.

Nevertheless, certain details in Chase's courtroom testimony were inconsistent with earlier statements she had made and I wanted to revisit them.

I queried her about the plans she had made with Schilling. "Before Ray came over on the evening of July third to Mr. Schilling's house, you had a conversation with Mr. Schilling about what you would do before Ray came over, didn't you?"

"I don't recall."

"You suggested to Mr. Schilling, did you not, that you could talk the property out of Mr. Hart didn't you? Yes or no?"

"No."

"Did you tell Mr. Schilling that you thought Mr. Hart would confess to you and, therefore, you should be alone with him while Mr. Schilling waited in the back room?"

"No."

I looked searchingly at her, wondering what had really happened and why she now was so unsure, when earlier she had made definitive statements on these matters. "Do you remember having a conversation on May thirty-first, 1995, with an investigator working with Mr. Schilling in the Moon Café in Phoenix?"

"Yes."

"You had that conversation?"

"Yes."

"That investigator was a man named Ted Carter?"

"Yes."

"Did you tell Mr. Carter that you believed Mr. Hart had a crush on you and you suggested to Mr. Schilling that you be allowed to talk the property out of him? Did you say that to Mr. Carter?"

"It wasn't worded like that, no. No, I don't recall saying that." I saw the blood drain out of her face.

"You're saying you didn't say that?"

"I don't recall saying that he had a crush on me."

"You didn't say that to Mr. Carter, words to that effect?"

"Steve might have told him, maybe. I don't recall."

"I'm not asking about Steve. I'm asking you about you talking with Steve's investigator on May of 1995 and your saying to him that you believed that Mr. Hart had a crush on you. You didn't say that?" I feigned geniality. "I'm sorry. You're shaking your head. But for the record—"

"I don't recall saying that, no."

"Are you saying you didn't say words to that effect?"

"I'm saying I don't recall saying those words."

"Did you tell Mr. Carter that you suggested to Mr. Schilling that you thought Mr. Hart would confess to you if you could be alone with him?"

"I don't recall saying that, no."

"In fact—you didn't do that. Did you, in fact, suggest to Mr. Schilling that Mr. Hart—"

"I don't recall."

"—get him alone with you?"

"No. I don't recall."

"You didn't say that to Mr. Schilling?"

"I don't—no."

"You didn't say it?"

"I don't—no. I can't believe I would say that."

"Did you tell Mr. Carter that, together, you and Mr. Schilling planned to create some time for you and Mr. Hart to be alone?"

"No."

"You didn't say that?"

"No."

"When Ray came over, you were alone with Mr. Hart for ten, fifteen minutes in the front room, weren't you?"

She nodded, "Yes, sir."

"Mr. Schilling was in the back, right?"

"Yes, sir."

"During that time, it was your purpose to try to get Mr. Hart to say something about the burglary, wasn't it?"

She shook her head. "No, sir. It was not planned."

Another inconsistency. I pushed on. "Was your purpose to get

Mr. Hart to say something about the burglary?"

"It was an opportunity. And I just asked him where he'd been the last week." She was speaking very quietly now. I looked at her pensively.

"Did you say something to him, anything to the effect that Mr. Schilling suspected someone else of committing the burglary and he might seriously harm or kill that other person, and if Mr. Hart would confess to it, some innocent person would be saved?"

She stared up at me. "No, sir."

"You didn't say that?"

"No, sir."

I went on to ask her about the altercation she had said she witnessed between Schilling and Hart after she found Schilling's Rolex watch in a bag in Hart's car. One day after the incident, she told a police officer that it had been only a verbal argument. She had failed to mention the struggle for the gun, the centerpiece of her courtroom testimony.

She also told the officer, Jim Rosner, that she had left the house at 8:00 P.M. to begin a night shift on a nursing assignment. Apprised of the officer's report, she admitted on cross-examination that her earlier testimony, that she'd departed at 9:30, might have been inaccurate and that her statement to Rosner, made over three years earlier, was more likely to be correct. This ninety minute difference would become significant during Schilling's testimony.

Seven months after the July 3 incident, she spoke on the telephone with another officer, a detective investigating the burglary at Schilling's house. She gave this officer a detailed itemization of the things she found in the black fanny pack, but did not include the bag of methamphetamine that the police later removed from Schilling's computer. She could not offer an explanation for the oversight.

She also acknowledged certain other facts on cross-examination that supported Hart's version of the events, while undermining Schilling's. Among them:

How Schilling angrily pointed the gun at Hart after he had already gained the upper hand in the altercation and was no longer defending himself.

How she tried to get Schilling to call the police, but he declined to do so.

How Schilling kicked Hart while Hart was seated on the living room sofa.

How when she picked Schilling up at the jail on the afternoon of July 4, he had no injuries.

How Schilling "usually" stored his drugs in the computer in his office.

She also admitted that, like Hart, she had been a methamphetamine addict in 1994.

The defense's case was unraveling.

Robert Aron asked for a recess after Brenda Chase's testimony to discuss its import with his client, whom he planned to call to the stand next, since his other witnesses were not subpoenaed to appear until the following day. However, Judge Paxton, ever vigilant to push ahead with the trial, told Aron that he would not take the afternoon break until a half hour later. Reluctantly, Aron announced Schilling as his next witness.

Schilling's edginess was palpable. Talking rapidly with his eyes blinking, he became confused when Aron asked him how old he was, going back and forth between twenty and thirty-two, his correct age. Then he stumbled when trying to explain where he lived. He seemed unsure if he should say he resided with his sister or disclose that he lived with his current girlfriend. I thought to myself that if I listened carefully I might hear his nerves jangling, twenty-five feet away. Aron apparently had similar thoughts, for he asked Schilling if it would be difficult to remember the incident with Hart.

This seemed to snap Schilling into focus. He replied that he remembered the events vividly. "Like it was yesterday almost," he said with a red-faced scowl.

Schilling's eyes flashed with anger as he told how he felt violated when he discovered the burglary. The stolen property had included out-of-circulation currency dating back to the early 1800s and commemorative coins from the 1940s, his only inheritance from his father, who'd died when he was a year old. What wounded him most, however, was the realization that the thief had to have been someone he knew well, someone he had trusted.

Almost immediately, he knew who had done it. The distinct foot prints outside his rear door could only have been made by Hart's flip-flops.

Aron asked why he hadn't called the police at that point.

"I thought he was my friend," Schilling responded. "I was wrong, obviously."

He agreed with almost all of Brenda Chase's testimony relating to the events she witnessed on July 3. Hart had arrived close to 8:00 in the evening, not between 5:30 and 6:00, as Hart claimed. Schilling admitted that he was angry when Chase found the fanny pack in Hart's car, but Hart was yelling just as loudly as he was and Hart definitely went for the gun first.

Schilling insisted that he had not pointed the gun at Hart purposely after gaining its control. He explained Chase's contrary testimony by acknowledging that he waved the weapon around briefly after the struggle, then added: "I didn't do like Ray said, put it to his head. He would have pointed it at me if he took it, I'm sure."

According to Schilling, not long after Chase left, James Thornton returned in his pick-up truck, accompanied by his friend Pat, who looked "intimidating." When Schilling opened the front door to let them in, Hart jumped from the living room sofa, grabbed the coffee table in front of him, hurled it forward and rushed toward the door. The coffee table almost knocked James into the television set.

Then, Schilling related, he turned and caught a glimpse of Hart charging at him, then on top of him, pushing him toward the still open door. Suddenly, they were throwing punches at one another.

It would have been a fair fight, just Hart and Schilling, Schilling said, but Hart began to kick wildly, with such force that he punctured the wall next to the television set. When Schilling stumbled, James just stood there, bewildered, but Pat jumped on the pile, pulling Hart off Schilling. Hart was still out of control, thrashing and kicking, so Pat and James tied his feet together with a belt.

Schilling said he had been injured in the melee. His nose had been bloodied and one of his fingers throbbed for days, apparently jammed in the scuffle. He saw a few spots of blood on his newly purchased carpet and tried to clean them off with a stain remover. They could easily have been his own, not Hart's.

He was going to call the police, but Hart begged him not to, shouting, "Don't call the cops! Don't call the cops! I'll tell you where your stuff is."

Schilling said he left the house around 10:30 to look for the stolen property in a trailer parked behind Hart's wife's apartment complex, several miles away. Hart, Pat and James were seated in the living room when he departed, with Hart still uninjured. Pat and James had wanted to rough him up, but Schilling would not let them. In Schilling's version, there had been some fisticuffs, but no one had hit Hart with hard objects, such as a baseball bat or a metal bar. While there may have been a little blood on the floor, it was nothing like the huge splotches depicted in the prosecution's photographs.

When Aron finished his questioning, Schilling looked in my direction, eager to fight it out, mano-a-mano, doing whatever it took to keep his freedom.

We parried over Schilling's statements to Carl Tate, the police officer who arrested him. According to Tate's report, Schilling said that he had been away from the house for "twenty to twenty-five minutes." This implied that he had left around 12:30 A.M., since Tate saw Schilling drive up on his motorcycle a few minutes before 1:00. Schilling insisted that Tate had it all wrong; he had departed to look for the stolen property at 10:30 P.M. and was away for more than two hours.

When I asked if Tate's testimony was inaccurate, Schilling exclaimed, "You tell me. You've got the police report in front of you."

He desperately wanted the jury to believe that he and Hart had been together for barely over two hours, with Brenda Chase present for more than half this time. His frustration grew when I pointed out that Chase had testified that she'd probably left around 8:00. She was wrong, he insisted.

She was also mistaken, he asserted, when she testified that he had kicked Hart when he was sitting on the sofa. Instead, he had kicked Hart in self defense when Hart jumped up abruptly and started to rush at him, adding that he had only kicked him in the shin.

I asked if he had testified incorrectly. He had kicked Hart in the head, not the leg, hadn't he?

No, he asserted again, it was the shin.

Had he told a detective that he'd kicked Hart in the head?

"No, that's a lie," he retorted, his face dark with venom, "I can't kick over my waist, let alone over someone's head."

We revisited Schilling's encounter with Officer Tate. I commented that he'd told Tate that the burglary had occurred four or five days before the July 3 incident, not nine days.

"So I can't count. *Sorry*," he said tartly.

I asked if a photograph of his living room accurately depicted its appearance on the night of July 3, 1994.

"Tell me when the pictures were taken and I'll tell you."

I was annoyed and snapped back. "I'm asking the questions, Mr. Schilling."

Immediately, I worried that I had stepped over the line, badgering him. If Judge Paxton dressed me down in front of the jury, it would hurt the State's case.

But Paxton said nothing. Yet.

Keeping a tight rein over the courtroom, Paxton had instructed both Aron and me not to delve into either Schilling's or Hart's criminal record, apart from the narrow fact that each had previously been convicted of a felony. He also instructed us to inform our witnesses of this restriction.

I asked Schilling if it was correct that he refused to call the police after Chase found the fanny pack. His reply echoed his direct-examination, asserting that Hart had pleaded with him not to make the call. Then he volunteered, "I guess he was on probation for something."

Paxton went ballistic. I wasn't sure if he was angry at Schilling or me when he abruptly excused the jury, his faced flushed.

Once the jury left the room, he addressed Aron while pointing toward his client.

"This guy has been throwing zingers—I call them zingers—throughout his testimony. He slips something in, with every opportunity. If he does it again, I'm going to impose sanctions."

The judge then glanced toward the door at the side of the courtroom, the door leading to the lock-up area. The threat in his eyes was clear.

The jury returned and I pushed ahead with my questioning, relieved that Paxton's wrath was not directed at me, but still concerned that the situation could quickly change. My plan had called for pushing Schilling on point after point, trying to get him riled, and I decided to stick to my agenda. Schilling, in turn, refused to back down.

Soon enough, he succumbed to temptation, forgetting Paxton's admonition, volunteering self-serving comments that went beyond my questions, shooting his own questions back at me and peppering his answers with caustic remarks about Hart.

We returned, yet again, to his exchange with Officer Tate. I pointed out that he had said nothing to Tate about self defense.

Schilling snapped. Rising from his chair, his voice exploded in fury: "The hell I didn't!"

I had to step back. It looked as if he was about to come after me.

Again, Paxton stopped the proceedings, demanding to see the lawyers in chambers.

"I'm getting close to having it with this witness and his snippy attitude and continued inability to listen. If he thinks he can start cussing in the courtroom, I intend to do something about it," he warned.

Paxton held back on his earlier threat to remand Schilling into custody. However, with Schilling's temper exploding, it looked to be just a matter of days.

The next day, there were no sparks in the courtroom because Aron's wife had a baby and we got twenty-four hours off. Grateful for the time away, I spent most of it preparing the closing argument I would deliver at the end of the week.

After Schilling, the defense called only one other significant witness, Harry Davis, the detective who had been assigned to investigate Schilling's burglary complaint. Aron wanted Davis to testify about the telephone interview he conducted with Ray Hart early in 1995, in which Hart told him that his altercation with Schilling stemmed from his accusing Schilling of fencing stolen property, not from Brenda Chase's discovery of the fanny pack. However, Judge Paxton sustained my objection to this evidence, since Hart had admitted that he had made the statement to Davis and that it was false. There was nothing else of substance Aron could ask the witness, but I was free to go into other matters on cross-examination.

I questioned Davis about his initial conversation with Schilling, six months after the burglary. Although Davis was not investigating the assault and kidnapping incident, it was integrally related to the burglary in Schilling's mind and he described the confrontation with Hart after Brenda Chase's discovery of the fanny pack.

I asked if Schilling had said anything about a struggle for a gun.

"No," he replied, "not a struggle."

"Did he say what he did with the gun?"

"He said that he put the gun toward Mr. Hart's head…Mr. Schilling told me that he had held Ray, Ray Hart at gunpoint and directed Ray into the living room."

I inquired if Schilling had mentioned anything occurring while Hart was on the couch.

"He kicked him."

"Did he say where he kicked him?"

"He kicked him in the head."

"Were those Mr. Schilling's words?"

"Yes."

I called only one minor rebuttal witness, but he added little to the case, since the jury had already heard from the victim, the defendant and all others who could corroborate or dispute their stories. The case, at least as presented by Aron and me, boiled down to Hart's and Schilling's credibility.

The courtroom became tense as everyone's attention now turned to the jury. Although Ray Hart had been absent from court for several days, on this one he sat alongside his mother and sister. His wife never appeared, nor did the defendant's older brother and mentor. As usual, the two families refused to acknowledge one another.

Each party had submitted proposed jury instructions earlier in the week. After the jury was excused on the day Schilling testified, we'd met for an additional hour in Paxton's chambers to wrangle over which instructions the judge would actually give to the jurors. Aron wanted the judge to inform the jury that a citizen had the right to make an arrest, if there was a reasonable basis to believe the arrested person had committed a felony. He also sought an instruction on the right to use force to prevent the imminent commission of a crime. I asked Paxton to instruct the jury that one could possess a drug even if it was only temporarily in his control, as well as a broad instruction on accomplice liability, to the effect that a person could be held accountable for a confederate's criminal acts that were committed when he was not present.

Paxton did not go along with Aron or me. He decided to give none of the instructions we had requested. Instead, he informed us that when he instructed the jury after our closing arguments he would use a set of jury instructions that had previously been approved by the state's supreme court. Apparently, he did not want to risk that an appeals court would later find that the language in one of the requested instructions was legally incorrect, requiring a reversal of his judgment. Still, his basic instructions on reasonable doubt and self defense would give both lawyers much to discuss when we addressed the jury.

It was now time for Robert Aron and I to give our closing arguments.

Chapter 26

Closing Arguments

Judge Paxton's face was firmly set. "The record may reflect the presence of the jury, counsel and Mr. Schilling. We'll begin now, folks, with the closing arguments of counsel."

I rose and walked forward. "Thank you, Your Honor. May it please the Court, Mr. Aron." I paused and looked over at the jury.

"In my opening statement to you, I told you that this is a case about an angry man who took the law into his own hands and that's exactly what it was. The State has proved beyond a reasonable doubt that on the night of July third and July fourth, 1994, the defendant committed five separate crimes.

"After counsel and I have given our closing arguments, Judge Paxton will give you the instructions on the law. And he will tell you what it is the State must prove in order to prove the defendant guilty beyond a reasonable doubt on each of the five charges.

"My talking to you now is my opportunity to go over the judge's instructions and go over each of the elements of the crimes and to explain to you why the State's evidence has met our burden of proof.

"Let's go over the elements of the five crimes, as Judge Paxton will instruct you, in the next few minutes. The first count is kidnapping. What it is, we must prove—to prove the defendant is guilty of kidnapping, his Honor will tell you in order to find the defendant guilty beyond a reasonable doubt, the State must prove three separate things. The first of those

things is that the defendant knowingly restricted another person's movements. So that's knowingly restricted movement.

"The second element is really an expansion of what we mean
by restriction. And the Court will tell you that the State must prove
certain things in order to have a restriction. We must show that the
defendant used physical force or intimidation, that the defendant substantially interfered with the other person's, Raymond Hart's, movement.

"And the third, that that substantial interference was either by
moving him from place to place or by confining him. I'm going to
summarize those three as either physical force or intimidation, substantial interference and either moving him or confining him.

"The third thing we must prove beyond a reasonable doubt in
order for you to find the defendant guilty of kidnapping is that the defendant's intent in restraining or restricting Mr. Hart was the intent to either
inflict death or physical injury.

"Let's review the evidence and determine whether we've met our
burden of proof." I hoped I was not being too academic as in the next
few minutes I attempted to show how Schilling knowingly restricted
Hart's movements and confined Hart or moved him forcefully as part of
that substantial interference. Then I went on, "Of course, you have Raymond Hart's own testimony on those issues, but on every important
respect, his testimony was corroborated and corroborated with powerful
evidence in this case.

"First, the defendant ordered Raymond Hart at gunpoint to
move from the office to the living room. How do we know that? We don't
have to rely on Raymond Hart's testimony. We have Steve Schilling's own
pretrial statement to Detective Davis, a statement that he came into this
court and denied making on Tuesday. And then Detective Davis, called
by the defense as a witness, impeached Schilling's testimony and said,
'Yes, that's what he told me.'

"These are the elements of knowingly restricting, substantially
interfering and moving a person from one place to another. He also
directed Hart at gunpoint to sit on the sofa in the living room. Again, an
admission to Detective Davis. He held Raymond Hart at bay on that sofa

until his friends came over.

"What did Brenda Chase tell you about that? The defendant held his gun while he was standing between Raymond Hart on the sofa and the front door. That also is substantially restricting and interfering with a person's ability to come and go. By the defendant's own admission, his own words as a witness on two separate occasions, he prevented, with physical force, prevented Raymond Hart from leaving that house. That also constitutes those elements of kidnapping." I took a deep breath and paused to look at the jury. The jury waited. I went on and my words were no longer catching in my throat.

"He also admitted to at least some of the tying up of Raymond Hart, that he participated in it. That also meets the elements of kidnapping. And remember how Raymond Hart was tied up. He was tied up with electrical cord. He was tied up with rope. He was tied up with belts. And most effectively, he was tied up with duct tape. That is knowingly restricting a person's movement. That is substantial interference with an individual's ability to move. That is confining a person.

"Also, ladies and gentlemen, carrying, participating with two other people and carrying someone and dumping him, hog-tied, into the trunk of his car, that also qualifies. Any one of those parts of the events that occurred that night meets the elements of kidnapping." I was beginning to relax a little, and glanced over at Schilling. He was sitting upright and he wasn't smiling.

"There are two separate questions left. Was physical force or intimidation used to accomplish this kidnapping? And also: Was there the intent to inflict death or physical injury?

"Was there physical force or intimidation to accomplish this kidnapping? Take a look at the ligature marks that Detective Nicholson talked about. One of the jurors asked a question, 'Can we look at each individual photograph?' Yes, you can. If you request them, you can take them into the jury room and look at them. Take a look at the ligature marks. Is that evidence of the use of force to make that restraint happen? You bet it is.

"Is pointing a gun at someone intimidation? Yes. Is kicking someone on the head while you're restraining them on a sofa, is that use of force? Yes.

"Is telling someone who's tied up with duct tape that you're going to have him cremated intimidation? Yes, again.

"Finally, was this kidnapping with intent to commit death or physical injury? Raymond Hart certainly thought they were going to try to kill him." I turned next to the defendant's intent. And then I moved on to the State's need to prove the defendant guilty beyond a reasonable doubt of the second charge, which was aggravated assault.

"The gun is a deadly weapon regardless of whether it's loaded. He intentionally pointed that gun at Raymond Hart. And when he did, Raymond Hart was afraid for his life. That's count two."

After I reviewed the evidence on intention, I turned to Raymond Hart's state of mind.

"Was Raymond Hart actually afraid?" I paused and let a moment of silence fill the room. "Of course he was. He told you he thought they were going to kill him. In addition to his testimony, we have the really poignant testimony of the two neighbors who told you that at 12:30 in the morning, Raymond Hart pounded on their doors, a blood-soaked Raymond Hart pounded on their doors, pleading with them to let him in their house. 'Help me, help me. They're trying to kill me.' Was he afraid of imminent physical injury? Of course he was. And was that a reasonable fear? Use your common sense."

I turned to another important point, one that might impact heavily on Schilling's sentence, if he was convicted.

"There are special considerations to count one that the judge will tell you about, that I need to comment on. That's the question of dangerousness. If you find the defendant guilty of kidnapping in count one and aggravated assault in count two, you must make a further determination. You must decide whether or not each of these crimes is one the law calls a dangerous crime. And the only issue on dangerousness is: Was the crime involved, of either kidnapping or aggravated assault, committed with the use of a deadly weapon or the threatened exhibition of a deadly weapon?

"In other words, did the defendant, in committing that crime, use or exhibit a deadly weapon? And so by count two, by every definition of count two, if you find him guilty of count two, it should be an easy question on the additional issue of dangerousness. Count one, in restraining him, did he use a deadly weapon? Did he threaten him with a deadly weapon? That should be an easy question too."

I dealt with the other counts one by one. Then I asked a crucial question. I looked around. Several jurors were watching with great interest.

"Was the defendant's belief that Raymond Hart stole his property a valid reason for a brutal beating? And we don't contest he believed that Hart stole his property. Is that a valid reason for a brutal beating? Does he answer that question? If the defendant, by his own testimony, was not aware of the gun on his desk until Raymond Hart jumped him from behind, as he told you, why was it a loaded gun? Interesting question. If the defendant and his friends didn't assault Mr. Hart, what explains the broken nose and the broken hand? That's another question. If the defendant really was away from his home for close to two hours as he testified, why did he tell Officer Tate that he had been gone for only twenty, twenty-five minutes? That's a good question too. If the defendant and his friends did not knowingly restrain Raymond Hart with duct tape, electrical cord and belts, were the neighbors and police simply having hallucinations?" I could not help the barest wisp of a smile as I went on.

"Here's an important one. If the defendant didn't participate in all that tying up of Mr. Hart and the beating of Mr. Hart when he was tied up, how come the defendant's own bloody T-shirt was in the same garbage bag? You'll see a few pictures of this garbage bag with blood-soaked newspapers and belts that were used to tie up Mr. Hart. If he left one small amount of blood on the rug, how did that happen? If the defendant didn't knowingly exercise control over the methamphetamine, why did he put it in a secret compartment in his computer?

"Another question: why did the defendant's own next-door neighbor testify that the defendant told him that he beat up Raymond Hart, if what he did was an act in self-defense? There's also this question: How did the defendant know the car was Raymond Hart's in his garage? I asked the defendant that and you can judge his credibility by his answer. But I think there's an even more interesting question from that conversation. Why wasn't he surprised to see Raymond Hart's car in his garage—why didn't he say, 'Hey, what's that car doing in my garage?' if he had nothing to do with it? See if that question is answered. The answer to every one of those questions is the same. It's the same answer. And that answer is: Because he's guilty. That's the answer to every one of those questions. Thank you."

Judge Paxton looked over at me. "Thank you, Mr. Lowenthal. Mr. Aron."

"May it please the Court, Mr. Lowenthal, ladies and gentlemen of the jury." Aron looked tired. Nevertheless, he returned to the theme of "trust and betrayal" in his closing argument, then moved in another direction, drawing the jury's attention to the prosecution's burden of proof.

"Ladies and gentlemen, I said at the outset of this case that this is really a case about trust and betrayal. And that's really what has happened here and the evidence you've seen over the past several days shows that. Mr. Schilling trusted Mr. Hart and Mr. Hart betrayed that trust and stole from him. It was not just a belief. The evidence proved that, the evidence that you've seen over the past several days. But what is the evidence? What is evidence?

"The evidence comes from the stand. The evidence comes from the physical evidence that you have and, also, your own common sense, the life experiences each and every one of you carry here into this jury service. That's why we have a jury, so that you all can compile and pool your knowledge together. Use your common sense. Nobody said you had to check it in at the door when you came in here. But also, when you're applying the facts, when you're examining the evidence, remember that there's a burden of proof, and, under our system of justice, the State has the burden of proof. What does that mean?

"In a burden of proof situation, the standard is this, ladies and gentlemen: Beyond a reasonable doubt. The judge will instruct you and you'll have an instruction on what that means. Well, does that mean beyond any doubt, beyond all doubt? No, it doesn't. It's something that has to leave you firmly convinced. Does it mean like in a civil case if you're suing somebody for money, that, well, maybe more likely than not he did this? No, that's not what the State has to prove and that's not the burden of proof you should hold him to. That is the burden of proof, ladies and gentlemen, that you have to apply.

"That is the standard of our system of justice that our forefathers said way back in 1776."

Aron next discussed everything the police failed to do, hoping to raise a reasonable doubt in the jury's mind. "Why didn't the state fingerprint the gun? Because it might show Mr. Hart's fingerprints? Why didn't they fingerprint the bar? Why didn't they fingerprint the meth pipe? Why didn't the police fingerprint the baggie of methamphetamine? They submitted it for prints. You heard the detective say that. But why didn't they show that? Why didn't they want to show that it wasn't Ray Hart's fingerprints? Also remember that the State didn't take samples of all the blood stains inside the living room. Mr. Schilling described that, yes, he was bleeding…these are questions you need to be asking yourselves."

As the prosecutor, I could get in the last word with a rebuttal argument. I was a bit miffed at Judge Paxton for limiting me to half the time it took Aron to present his argument, but, in truth, the restriction was reasonable. In fact, it probably helped the State's case, forcing me to dispense with a great deal of minutia. With little time remaining, I asked the jury to look around the courtroom. I swallowed hard. From out of the corner of my eye, I could see the jury watching me. The room was quiet. As I moved purposefully to the end, I felt everything move into place.

"When I look around the courtroom, when you look around the courtroom, what do we see? There's Mr. Aron, Mr. Schilling's defense lawyer, who, throughout this trial and again today in his closing argument, has repeatedly demonstrated a terrific capability to be an advocate for his client. And when you look around this courtroom, look at each other, because Mr. Schilling has, in the American criminal justice system, what people in many other places don't have: a right to trial by a jury of his peers. You're that jury.

"Raymond Hart came into this courtroom, Mr. Schilling's courtroom, last week to testify. And he's come in today as a visitor. Raymond Hart, in 1994, was accused of a serous crime. Raymond Hart did not have a learned judge when he had his trial on July third, July fourth,

1994. Raymond Hart certainly did not have a presumption of innocence. Raymond Hart did not have a defense lawyer zealously protecting his rights. And most of all, Raymond Hart did not have a jury of his peers to determine his guilt, unless you consider James, Cliff, Pat and the defendant to be a jury of one's peers. The defendant is guilty of all the charges against him."

The bailiff gave each member of the panel a typed copy of the judge's instructions, and some of the jurors read along while Paxton recited the words aloud, while others simply listened. I doubted that they paid attention to the legalese in such terms as "reasonable apprehension," "imminent physical injury," "lesser included charge," "substantial and unjustifiable risk," "dominion and control," "constructive possession" and "dangerous instrument." A judge's precision in using such words when instructing a jury is the stuff of the legal profession, sometimes making the difference between a defendant's freedom and a life behind bars or, perhaps, even death. But these were not the words of the office workers and housewives on our jury. One woman in the back row watched Schilling during much of Paxton's recitation, more interested in his demeanor than the legal definitions.

After the judge gave his final instructions to the jury, Steve Schilling stood stiffly, watching the jury file out of the courtroom at 3:00 P.M. Robert Aron had told him to remain close by, just in case they returned with a verdict that afternoon. The longer they were out, the better his chances for an acquittal, at least in Aron's view. Schilling decided to join his family in the cafeteria, but was too nervous to eat, though his sister and step-father were optimistic about the outcome.

Judge Paxton had said that he'd send the jury home for the night if it did not have a verdict by 5:00 P.M. Schilling looked like he was having difficulty sitting still, unable to follow the conversation at the table. Instead he kept anxiously watching the clock, which seemed to get stuck at 4:35 before it inched toward the top of the hour. At 4:55, Robert Aron appeared, saying that Paxton wanted to meet with Schilling and the lawyers in his chambers. The jury had sent a note with a question to the judge, but Aron did not know its contents.

We soon found out.

"We are deadlocked on three and four," the note read, referring to two of the three aggravated assault charges. "Can counts three and four be combined with count two?"

Although the meaning of the note was ambiguous, Aron and I agreed that the jury had to consider each count separately. Paxton instructed his bailiff to inform the panel of this. Schilling was smiling, trying to appear confident, but only succeeded in looking devious.

A second note from the jury came moments later, asking "May we have ten more minutes please? What if we are deadlocked on a charge?"

Aron wanted the jury to deliberate further, while I agreed to settle for verdicts on four of the five counts. We agreed to reconvene in court with the jury present so that Paxton could inquire if it had reached an impasse, if further deliberations would help and if there was anything the judge or lawyers could do to assist the deliberations.

The foreperson, a young blond woman in the front row, spoke in a soft voice, barely audible, when she addressed the court, saying, "I'm not sure time will resolve this issue, sir." The jury had reached a verdict on three counts, had already signed the necessary forms, and wanted to call it quits on the other two. The deadlock related to counts three and four, the allegations that Schilling had broken Hart's bones. We agreed to acquiesce to the jury's request.

Schilling stood up as the clerk read the three verdicts. Guilty of kidnapping, designated as a dangerous offense. Guilty of aggravated assault, designated as a dangerous offense. Guilty of possessing methamphetamine. At Aron's request, the judge polled the jury to make sure that each verdict was unanimous. He then set a date for sentencing, ordered the sheriff's office to take Schilling into custody immediately and thanked the jury for its service.

Schilling looked stunned. Totally unprepared for this, he steadied himself with his shaking hand on the table as guards came to take him back to the Madison Street Jail.

A euphoric Ray Hart embraced his sister.

Chapter 27

Going Separate Ways

Anxious to catch the jurors before they went home, Aron and I rushed to their deliberation room the moment Judge Paxton left the bench. As it turned out, ten of the twelve were waiting for us, eager to discuss their verdict and interested in whatever we could tell them about Schilling and Hart. Aron wasted no time, detailing the defense evidence that had been ruled inadmissible at trial, asking if it would have made a difference in the outcome of the case. The jurors seemed confused by the question, unsure of what to say. One mentioned that they were comfortable with the verdict they had reached. Then, after a brief but awkward silence, I asked about the course of their deliberations. I was especially interested in why they had been unable to agree on two of the charges.

There had been no dissent, the jurors told us, on the three charges for which they returned a verdict, although individual members of the panel were curious to know whether Hart had actually stolen Schilling's property. It had not mattered in their deliberations, since all concurred that Schilling should not have taken the law into his own hands, regardless of Hart's guilt. One commented that the evidence on the first two counts had been cut-and-dried. Schilling had pointed his gun at Hart, threatening his life and preventing him from leaving the house; these facts alone established both the kidnapping and aggravated assault charges, as well as the allegation that they were dangerous crimes. The jurors had also spent little time discussing the drug charge, primarily because Hart, Schilling and Brenda Chase had agreed in their testimony that Schilling secreted the bag of methamphetamine in his computer.

They had hung by a count of 11-1 on the other two counts of the indictment, the charges that Schilling was responsible for fracturing Hart's nose and hand. One of the five men on the jury had steadfastly maintained that these injuries could easily have occurred after Schilling left the house. The juror paid little heed to the arguments of the other eleven that Schilling was guilty as an accomplice even if he did not strike the blows that broke Hart's bones. After debating this question for an hour, they simply decided to quit, hoping that a verdict on the other charges would be sufficient to bring the case to a conclusion.

It was. The first two counts in the indictment, which charged Schilling with kidnapping and aggravated assault, were by far the most important, largely because the jury had found these crimes to be dangerous. This meant that Schilling was ineligible for probation and the absolute minimum prison term the judge could impose under the state's mandatory sentencing law was seven years, with no opportunity for early release until six of those years were served. In contrast, Schilling would have been eligible for probation on the two counts for which there was no verdict. Even if Paxton sentenced him to prison on those counts, the sentence would likely be concurrent with the other prison terms he was required to serve. Hence, the jury's intuition was prescient; the two counts were promptly dismissed, never to be recharged.

Ray Hart's euphoria over the verdict proved to be short-lived. Paxton's staff departed from the courtroom not long after Aron and I had left to seek out the jury, leaving several members of Schilling's family alone with Hart, his sister and niece. Hart waited for Schilling's relatives to leave, but they were not going to make it easy for him. One hissed angrily that Hart had destroyed Schilling's life. Another cursed him. Hart looked away and said nothing until they finally exited through the rear door.

A deputy sheriff finally came and escorted Ray Hart, his sister and niece to their car.

A week later James Thornton arrived at Judge Harris' court for his scheduled trial date. He had been shocked to learn that Steve Schilling was again in jail. Thornton could not understand what had gone wrong. Schilling's jury must have been insane. Moreover, the thought that his own case might now go to trial disturbed him. It had been a month since he had seen or heard from Bob Williams, his new public defender, and he felt totally unprepared.

When Williams appeared in court thirty minutes later, he asked Thornton to meet with him in the hallway outside Harris' courtroom. Williams explained that he had spoken with Schilling's lawyer and me and that we had both confirmed that Schilling faced a mandatory prison sentence, possibly as long as twenty-one years. Thornton's own chances did not look good, Williams said, since his fingerprints had been found on the lid of Hart's trunk. Williams added that he had persuaded me to stick with the deal that previously had been offered: if Thornton pled guilty to attempted kidnapping, he would be eligible for probation. Even if the judge decided to send him to prison, I had agreed that the maximum term would be only three years.

Thornton accepted the plea bargain, but a problem quickly developed when we tried to put it on the record.

Before accepting a plea agreement, the judge must determine if the defendant is entering it voluntarily and if there is a factual basis to support the conviction. In Arizona, as in most other states, judges usually accomplish this by asking the defendant to state the facts, or at least to agree to a rendition set forth by the prosecutor or defense lawyer. In this case, however, Thornton refused to acknowledge that he had participated in Hart's beating or that he had anything to do with tying Hart up and throwing him into his car trunk, instead telling Harris that his recollection of the incident at Schilling's house was fuzzy, because he had been heavily medicated with prescription drugs at the time it occurred.

Williams proposed a "no contest" plea, one in which Thornton would not admit his guilt, but instead avow on the record that the prosecution had sufficient evidence to convict him at trial, without having to take a position on the accuracy of the state's case. As a practical matter, such a plea had the same legal effect as a guilty plea, supporting a conviction and giving the judge the authority to impose a sentence. However, both the court's rules and the county attorney's policies permitted no contest pleas "only after due consideration of . . . the interest of the public in the effective administration of justice."

  This presented me with a dilemma. I strongly suspected that Thornton was not truthful in his claim that his mind had been clouded by medication. Two years earlier, he appeared to have had a clear recollection of the events when he gave a statement to Schilling's investigator. A good case could be made that the "interest of the public" required me to withdraw from the proposed agreement and insist that we go to trial. However, to me, Thornton was probably the least culpable of the three men who had beaten and terrorized Hart. And after talking it over with my office, it was concluded that the "effective administration of justice" called for conserving judicial resources. I entered the deal.

  Judge Harris scheduled the sentencing hearing for mid-November, then directed Thornton to report as soon as possible to the probation department's central office, a few hundred yards from Harris' courtroom. This set the stage for Thornton's interview with the probation officer, who would prepare a pre-sentence report to the court, recommending either prison or probation. Unlike Schilling, Thornton had a genuine opportunity to walk away from his criminal case as a free man.

  Most out-of-custody defendants who pled guilty reported to the probation department immediately after leaving court. In many cases, the defense lawyer accompanied the client, spending the available time preparing him for the crucial pre-sentence interview. For unknown reasons, however, Thornton and Williams did not go to the probation department that morning, with the result that the probation officer assigned to Thornton's case scheduled an interview in late October. When Thornton failed to appear for the interview, the probation officer arranged another appointment five days later. Thornton missed this one too, after calling to confirm the date and time. The probation officer left him a phone message to schedule yet another appointment, but Thornton never returned the call.

A high school drop-out, Thornton lacked basic organizational skill and instead relied on others to help him manage his affairs. His father, who owned a tire store, provided him with an apartment and a weekly allowance in return for repairing tires at the shop. Steve Schilling made a point of reminding him of his court dates, urging him to dress appropriately and show up on time. But when no one was around to keep him on track, Thornton neglected to follow through in his commitments, hurting himself in the process. Eighteen months earlier, in his first felony case (based on a drug possession arrest), he had blown his one opportunity for a dismissal by forgetting to enroll in a pre-trial diversion program. Now, he screwed up again, failing to meet with his probation officer.

Although Thornton reported to court only a few minutes late on the morning he was to be sentenced, Judge Harris refused to proceed, displeased that the pre-sentence report lacked input from the defendant. Thornton tried to explain that the probation department office was a long drive from his home, that he had been confused over the scheduling of one of his interviews and that another of the appointments conflicted with his work hours. Unimpressed, Harris remanded him into custody, scheduling a new sentencing hearing on December 12, the day after Schilling was to be sentenced in Judge Paxton' court. Thornton's interview with the probation officer would take place in jail.

Steve Schilling's pre-sentence report was far more thorough than most others in non-capital cases. The probation officer who prepared it gathered a lot of information, obtaining Schilling's criminal history records from the state's data base and a set of police reports from the County Attorney's Office, along with my sentencing recommendation. He also interviewed an unusual number of interested parties, including Ray Hart, a victim-witness advocate assigned to verify Hart's medical expenses, Rob Nicholson, Robert Aron, Schilling's mother and his brother. The probation officer met with Schilling for two-and-a-half hours at the Madison Street Jail, asking the defendant for his version of the offense, as well as an account of his upbringing, education, family relations, employment history, prior criminal cases and experience with alcohol and drugs. Although the report included what I felt were a few inaccuracies, it provided Judge Paxton with a reasonably complete picture of the defendant.

Schilling had a great deal at stake. The state legislature had set a presumptive prison sentence of ten and a half years for kidnapping, the most serious of the three charges, when it was designated as a dangerous offense. But Paxton could also deviate from the presumptive term, with his alternatives ranging between seven and twenty-one years. Similarly, he could sentence Schilling to anywhere between five and fifteen years on the aggravated assault charge, and between one and just under four years on the drug possession count. It was likely that the judge would allow the three prison terms to be served concurrently because the crimes were part of a single episode. However, if Paxton wanted to be punitive, he could "stack" the sentences, putting Schilling away for close to forty years.

Aron requested and obtained a one-hour mitigation hearing, to take place on the morning that Paxton was to determine Schilling's fate, allowing the defense to present evidence on why leniency was appropriate. Schilling wanted Paxton to sentence him to only seven years, the minimum permitted for the kidnapping charge under the state's mandatory sentencing laws, with the prison terms on the other two crimes to run concurrently. While I did not oppose concurrent sentences, I had recommended eighteen years in my memo to the probation officer, with Detective Nicholson's concurrence.

Sixteen persons addressed letters to Paxton on Schilling's behalf. Each member of his immediate family wrote a personal plea for leniency. The most impressive came from his sister, who described him as "not just my brother but my best friend." Other letters came from his fiancée, childhood friends who had moved from Arizona, a business associate, a former employer and several persons he had helped over the years. Most were thoughtful, specific and well-crafted efforts to shed light on his character. Several writers commented that he was remorseful, while others noted his devotion to family. A few wrote that his loss of control in the Hart episode was inconsistent with his general character, which was variously described as compassionate, non-violent, generous, hard working and honest. One woman described how Schilling had talked her husband out of a suicide attempt. Another told the judge that Schilling had been a mentor for her two sons, rewarding them for good report cards and taking them to sporting events.

When the day of Schilling's sentencing arrived, his supporters filled the gallery in Paxton's courtroom, many prepared to speak on his behalf. Aron chose only eleven to address the court, cautious to avoid unnecessary repetition by asking each person to share unique information about the defendant. We agreed that it would not be necessary for the witnesses to testify under oath and I passed on the opportunity to cross-examine them.

One woman, who had known Schilling for ten years, told Paxton that Schilling had graciously helped her family on many occasions, both financially and emotionally. As an example, she cited the period in her life when she was incapable of spending time with her terminally ill father. Schilling visited him twice each week, easing her burden.

Schilling's brother-in-law spoke on behalf of several members of Schilling's family, telling Paxton of the love they felt for the defendant, their profound sense of sorrow and the tremendous pain Schilling had endured during the three years since the offense.

The next speaker, a woman, told Paxton that Schilling was her daughter's godfather. When the woman's own parents were in a car wreck, Schilling offered to pay her airfare to Florida.

The mother of Schilling's fiancée told Paxton that Schilling went to church with her daughter and grandson.

One of the Schilling's male friends told Paxton of his admiration for Schilling's Harley-Davidson. When Schilling was forced to part with the bike to pay for his defense, he sold it to the friend, even though he could have received more for it elsewhere.

A young woman described the difficulty of her first Christmas as a single parent, unable to afford presents for her two-year-old son. Unexpectedly, she said, Schilling appeared at her front door with a bag full of toys. Her son, now six years old, had not forgotten this gesture. In a note to Santa Claus, he had written: "Please don't put Steve in jail, Love Bret."

Schilling's sister also spoke about his generosity, telling Paxton that Schilling had donated toys to a local children's hospital on several occasions and had delivered boxes of yarn to nursing homes.

The last witness, Schilling's mother, talked about his childhood, remembering the time he had collected money for the Jerry Lewis telethon, begging her to take it immediately to the television station to make sure that it found its way to the beneficiaries.

I had trouble believing some of these statements. I remembered Schilling's felony record, the savage crime against Hart and his brutal treatment of Brenda Chase. However, these were sincere, law-abiding members of the community whose concern for Schilling appeared both genuine and profound, suggesting there was more to his nature than had previously been revealed.

The defendant's older brother was visibly angry. The prosecutor's office had overcharged the case, he argued, just to get plea bargaining leverage against his brother. "Let the punishment fit the crime," he urged, and in this case he felt that his brother had merely made a "mistake," using bad judgment when trying to get his property back from a thief. His decision not to turn Hart over to the police had been made in kindness, not vengeance.

This was not a wise argument. Paxton had heard the medical testimony, seen the bloody duct tape and been shocked by the photos of Hart's injuries. Downplaying the seriousness of Schilling's misconduct was not likely to nudge the judge toward leniency.

The defendant himself was more effective when it was his turn to address the court. He began by apologizing to both Paxton and me for his behavior during the trial, admitting that he had been too emotional, too "worked up" over his three-and-a-half year nightmare. Then he apologized to Hart, adding: "I only hope the best for him. And I hope he's not, I'm glad he's not hurt from the events or the wounds he suffered on July third." After thanking his family and friends for the support they had shown, Schilling asked Paxton for mercy, expressing a desire to return to his family and get his life back on track.

At the end of the hearing, all eyes turned to the judge, who shifted some papers before gazing at Schilling. The three sentences would be served concurrently, Paxton said, because the kidnapping and assault charges were based on closely related acts and all three crimes arose from the same set of circumstances. This meant, as a practical matter, that the only important sentence was the one for kidnapping, the most serious of the three offenses. Though expected, the ruling was a relief to Schilling. Nevertheless, his paramount concern was the amount of time he would be locked up on the kidnapping charge. The presumptive term was ten-and-a-half years, but Paxton could easily deviate from this.

"I think you are fortunate," Paxton commented, "that you have so many people come forward and speak on your behalf. That speaks well of you." The judge then stated that he counted this as a mitigating circumstance, along with Schilling's expression of remorse. But, he added, these factors had to be weighed against the elements that aggravated the crime, including the presence of accomplices and multiple weapons, Schilling's prior conviction and, most importantly, the extent of Hart's injury and emotional trauma: "It was absolutely terrifying for him." The aggravation significantly outweighed the mitigation, Paxton said, as he sentenced Schilling to thirteen years in prison.

Thornton's sentencing hearing was much shorter than Schilling's. The defendant's mother, father and stepmother made brief pleas for leniency, asking Judge Harris to place Thornton on probation, allowing him to help support his two sons and assist in the care of his gravely ill stepfather. His lawyer had little to add and Thornton himself said almost nothing. When interviewed by the probation officer, he had minimized his role in the incident, claiming he had left Schilling's house before Hart was thrown into the trunk of his car. I was tempted to point out that Thornton's account was inconsistent with a prior statement he had given to Schilling's investigator, but I knew Harris was already aware of Thornton's thumb print on the gear shift lever and palm print on the lid of the trunk.

Despite Thornton's denial of responsibility, I asked Harris to follow the plea agreement, which placed a three year cap on any prison sentence to be imposed, a short term for one who had actively partici-pated in such a serious crime. I noted that Thornton had been the least culpable of the three assailants and had only a minor prior record. Harris followed this recommendation, imposing a three-year prison term.

Chapter 28

After the Trial

Steve Schilling continued to fight his case from his prison cell. His only success came in his initial appeal, when the court subtracted thirty-seven days from his thirteen-year sentence, crediting him for a period of pre-trial incarceration that Judge Paxton had overlooked. But his conviction itself was affirmed, both on appeal and in subsequent proceedings, despite his repeated claims that Robert Aron had provided constitutionally inadequate representation. He squabbled with his latest court-appointed lawyer, Barry Taylor, who spent several months searching the record for viable issues, then filed a pleading that conceded he could find none. Schilling sent Taylor an angry letter, accusing the lawyer of handling his case in a sloppy manner with an "unwillingness to communicate." In the end, he represented himself in a post-conviction petition, which was turned down by both the trial judge and the appellate court.

Schilling's falling-out with Taylor reflected his experience with every other attorney who had represented him. Ten years earlier, after his conviction for drug trafficking, he filed a petition claiming that his lawyer had lied to him to induce him to plead guilty. He fired Frank Mahoney, his first lawyer in the kidnapping case, then filed a grievance against Mahoney with the state bar, seeking a refund of Mahoney's fee, alleging that Mahoney had neglected his defense. He became angry when his next attorney refused to testify against Mahoney at an arbitration hearing. Finally, his principal argument in his post-conviction petition was a claim that Robert Aron had advised him to reject a plea bargain, erroneously predicting that they would win at trial. Schilling did not part company with any of his lawyers happily.

I visited Schilling at a prison in Tucson. Although his hair was noticibly gray and thinner, he looked fit, apparently making good use of the little recreation time he was permitted, three days each week, at seven in the morning. He had worked in the prison primarily as a porter. His disciplinary record had been uneven, with minor citations for fighting, disobeying orders and refusing to work, and major write-ups for theft and drug possession. However, if he maintained reasonably good behavior in the years to come, he would be released in December, 2008, with his full sentence expiring two years later.

Apart from his lingering anger towards his defense lawyers, Schilling expressed few ill thoughts about his treatment. He felt that the police who arrested and interrogated him had been polite, although he was also sure they had not waited for the warrant to arrive before searching his house. The jury's verdict had also been reasonable, based on "what they heard." He did not like Judge Paxton's accusation that he had been throwing zingers, but Paxton had generally been fair during the trial. As for me, Schilling said he felt that I had merely been doing my job, even when my cross-examination was aggressive. He had not intended to offend the judge with his answers, but he said, "I was fighting for my life, shooting my answers out as fast as you were asking them, not trying to be disrespectful."

Nevertheless, Schilling felt profoundly bitter. His incarceration was unjust, he believed, because he, not Hart, had been the true victim, and he could not understand why everyone, including his own lawyers, failed to see this. Everywhere he turned, he remarked, "I was the bad guy. No one seemed to care that this guy had robbed me." The only exception was his family, who had stood behind him from the night he was arrested to the day of his sentencing and continued to sustain him in prison, sending him money on a regular basis. He continued to revere his brother, and his sisters had brought him the two objects in his cell that he most valued, a television set and a guitar.

James Thornton spent two-and-a-half years in the Arizona prison system, either serving meals, working in kitchens or shoveling dirt, earning ten cents an hour at each job, with thirty percent set aside for Ray Hart's restitution. For most of his term, Thornton was housed in a facility near Winslow, Arizona, five hours from his two sons, whom he never saw. He was later transferred to Perryville, a prison closer to home, but he felt that the physical conditions there were much worse than at Winslow. According to Thornton, his mattress was older than the prison itself and he found himself rolling up old clothes to serve as a pillow. The food, at least, was tolerable. When he had been incarcerated in the Maricopa County Jail, he had been required to pay a dollar a day for the privilege of eating green baloney.

When asked in prison to reflect upon his experience, Thornton offered a two-sided view. Almost every month for two full years, he had sat in the back row of Judge Harris' courtroom observing the proceedings in other cases, sometimes for hours at a time while he waited for his own case to be called. He was highly impressed with Harris, who always treated defendants fairly, regardless of their means. He said that his respect for the judge made his own sentence more tolerable.

Most of Thornton's comments focused on the lawyers he encountered. He felt no hostility towards the prosecutors who had handled his case. Garry Baylor, the principal attorney, had seemed very young, in his opinion, not fully in control, wanting to please the defense lawyers but always doing what the higher-ups in the County Attorney's Office instructed him to do. On the other hand, Thornton felt bitter towards Schilling's lawyers and the attorney representing Budget Stores, who he felt had each given him a false sense of security, telling him that he would not get into trouble by coming forward. But he saved his sharpest criticism for his first public defender, who had represented him at most of his court appearances. He called him a man who "treated me like a number, like they do here in prison." While Schilling's lawyers talked about going to trial, Thornton's public defender had told him he was guilty, according to Thornton, and only wanted to discuss a plea bargain, anxious to move to his next case.

Released from prison in June, 2000, Thornton managed to do well for a period, taking responsibility for the care of his younger son, completing a mandatory drug program and working again for his father. However, after a while, he began to associate with friends from his prior world, had a falling out with his father and eventually resumed old habits. When his father and step-mother would no longer have anything to do with him, he began to drift, sometimes staying with a girlfriend, sometimes disappearing for weeks at a time. Remarkably, he avoided arrest, but, according to one member of his family, this was only because he had "not been caught."

Ray Hart maintained contact with me after Schilling's trial, usually by telephone, with an occasional visit to my office at the university. Hart and his wife had separated by the time of the trial, and divorced a year later, leaving him the non-custodial parent of his eight-year-old daughter. Nevertheless, he had managed to stay away from methamphetamine since that fateful summer in 1994, an extraordinary achievement, considering the turmoil in his home life and the always-present memory of drug-induced euphoria. He was rewarded when the superior court reduced his two felony convictions to misdemeanors, acknowledging his successful completion of probation. He continued to work in the Phoenix area, building houses and boats with Styrofoam insulation. In 2000, he married a third wife, and when he visited me in 2002, he had graduated from construction work to management, with a comfortable salary, employed by a large company that supplied drywall products to contractors and developers. His daughter, now twelve, divided her time between his home and her mother's. He was well-tanned, with a gold stud in one ear and a touch of gray in his closely cropped beard, a far different man than the one who had testified five years earlier. As in previous visits, he brought me up to date on his personal life, enjoying my continued interest.

I asked him how he felt about the handling of his case. Hart had mixed feelings. The police, he said, had been sympathetic and helpful on the night of the offense, both in Schilling's neighbor's house and at the hospital, but this soon changed. He felt the detective in charge of the investigation for the next three years treated him "like dirt, acting as if he did not care about apprehending Pat and Cliff." With regard to the court proceedings, he believed that James Thornton's sentence was far too light. Moreover, while the court had ordered Thornton and Schilling to pay him almost six thousand dollars in restitution, he had received only a miniscule amount from Thornton and nothing from Schilling.

Despite these sentiments, Hart said, he no longer dwelled on the case. While the desire to bring Schilling to justice had dominated his thoughts before the trial, he learned to put both Schilling and the crime out of his mind. "When I do think about it, I feel lucky, believing that I narrowly missed being killed by Schilling and his friends," he said. He also appreciated that July 3, 1994 had been the nadir of his life. Kicked out by his wife, hopelessly addicted to methamphetamine and about to be sentenced for two felonies, he undoubtedly would have continued his downward spiral, eventually dying, if the brutal incident at Schilling's house had not occurred.

Somehow, it had transformed him. Ray Hart liked the man he became.

Afterword

July 2003

When I left the County Attorney's Office early in 1998, I began to reflect on the meaning of my experience. Initially, my thoughts focused on a dream I had during my last weeks as a prosecutor. The setting for the dream was a strange courtroom. Alone at the prosecutor's table, I watched a steady line of persons address the judge, offering outrageous reasons for lowering the bail for a nondescript defendant sitting at the next table. A woman with a small child at her side told the court that she just couldn't manage without the defendant's help. An employer claimed that he'd have to close his business and lay off his other workers if the defendant missed just one more day. A priest described the defendant's angelic nature. Each remark was more astounding than the last. Worse, the judge seemed to be lapping it up. Was I the only one in the courtroom who saw through the defendant? He was dangerous, a *rapist*. Why didn't they get it?

Suddenly, I awoke, finding myself in bed, drenched in sweat, my dream ending just before the rapist was to go free. I lay awake for another half hour, trying unsuccessfully to make sense of the bizarre courtroom scene, hoping it would not reappear when I drifted back to sleep.

I have considered the dream on many occasions, finding additional nuances each time. At one level, I have come to appreciate, as never before, the uniquely important role prosecutors play in America's justice system. Who else can we rely upon to hold defendants fully accountable for the harms they have caused? The judge in my dream listened carefully to everyone in the packed courtroom who stepped forward to speak on behalf of the accused. Even the most dispassionate jurist would have found it extremely difficult not to succumb to such pressure by lowering the defendant's bail, at least without the presence of a prosecutor to remind the court of the defendant's dangerousness. Prosecutors frequently find themselves in such courtroom situations. It takes courage to be the sole person insisting upon accountability, with the defendant's mother weeping in the front row.

But the dream has also triggered disquieting thoughts.

First, it has reminded me of how many prosecutors see the world divided between "us and everyone else." They believe that no one outside their office, even judges, can be trusted. At times during my experience, I may have crossed this dangerous line, but I have come to understand many of the factors that bring it about, factors that continue to isolate lawyers employed as prosecutors from the other participants in the criminal courts. Prosecutors are often feared by defendants and despised by their families; harangued by victims and their families alike; scorned by defense lawyers; resented by both police and judges; and often stripped of power by those who run the prosecution agency. This unfriendly work environment brings about an unhealthy sense of alienation, distancing prosecutors from everyone around them, a circumstance that probably contributed to the high turnover I observed in the County Attorney's Office.

However, prosecutors were not the only persons I encountered who felt alienated and isolated from the other participants in the criminal courts. Many defense lawyers, devoted to their clients' interests, perceived that no one else in the justice system appreciated that defendants were human beings who deserved to be treated with respect. Judges felt powerlessness and marginalized when prosecutors dictated the terms of plea bargains that set in stone the sentences defendants would receive. Some of the crime victims I met believed that no one cared about their needs. And many police officers I came to know felt cut off from their cases once charges were filed in court.

Along with this pervasive insularity, I found bitterness and animosity everywhere I looked. Many defense attorneys were angered by the harsh sentences meted out to their clients, primarily blaming prosecutors, but also unhappy that judges would do nothing to correct what they viewed as manifest injustice. A large segment of the prosecutor's office believed that defense lawyers, with a few exceptions, were dishonest at heart and did not follow the same high ethical standards expected of prosecutors. This rankled many of the younger lawyers in the County Attorney's Office, affecting how they dealt with both defense attorneys and their clients. Both prosecutors and defense counsel regularly belittled the courts for pushing them to trial when they were unprepared. Many police officers loathed defense lawyers for twisting the words in their police reports and resented prosecutors for refusing to file charges in many of their cases, while agreeing to lenient plea bargains in others.

Many prosecutors and public defenders I met took pride in their valuable public service, performed their work diligently and scrupulously, and followed high ethical standards, even when the standards might hurt their cause. The same lawyers typically treated adversaries, judges, victims and defendants with courtesy, regardless of ill feelings they may have silently harbored. Their dedication and graciousness exemplified what is best about the legal profession and since my return to law teaching, I have asked some of these lawyers to participate in my classes, encouraging my students to follow their examples.

However, I was surprised during my tenure as a prosecutor to find a disturbing level of ineptitude, laziness and discourtesy on both sides of the adversary process. As an educator of lawyers, I was, at times, embarrassed by the quality of practice in the criminal courts.

The manner in which police and prosecutors associated with the Schilling case failed to complete investigations and prepare adequately for trial was by no means exceptional. Some of the detectives I encountered during my nine months as a prosecutor wanted little or nothing to do with ongoing investigations, once the County Attorney's Office filed charges in their cases. At the same time, many prosecutors counted on cases being resolved by plea bargains, obviating the need for full pre-trial preparation. When defendants occasionally rejected their plea agreements, these prosecutors found themselves going to trial without laboratory analyses of potentially important physical evidence or pre-trial interviews of eyewitnesses. Inexperience and insufficient training accounted for some of these shortcomings, but these were not the only contributing factors. Some of the law enforcement officers and prosecutors I met were simply unwilling to put forth the effort necessary to prepare the cases competently.

While many of the defense lawyers who crossed my path were diligent and courteous, others were habitually tardy for court hearings and occasionally very late, without alerting the courts in advance or apologizing afterward. I observed some defense counsel ignoring their clients and their families when they appeared in court before their cases were called. Some of my fellow prosecutors were no better, failing to keep victims and police informed of developments in cases. Frequently, prosecutors or defense lawyers, standing in for colleagues, would participate in important proceedings such as sentencing hearings with no preparation or familiarity with the case. Attorneys on both sides could be rude or insensitive to opposing counsel, judges and non-lawyers alike.

Not long after I left the County Attorney's Office, the Arizona Supreme Court instituted a three-hour course on professionalism and required all members of the state bar to enroll in the course once, within the first few years it was offered. The course has focused largely on the types of deficiencies I observed in the criminal courts, emphasizing the importance of decorum, civility toward adversaries and responsible relations with clients and other non-lawyers. Similarly, the administration at my law school has begun to include a discussion of issues relating to professionalism in the orientation program it conducts for new students and the dean has encouraged faculty to continue this dialogue in our law classes. Some professors have done so.

These are well-conceived ideas, but still woefully inadequate to address what I see as a pervasive problem in the legal community, at least with respect to those lawyers practicing in the criminal courts. The legal profession must do much more to merit the title of "profession." In our law schools, we should expose our students to transcripts and video footage of lawyers at their best and worst, develop a regular, ongoing dialogue with lawyers and judges about professional conduct, set high standards for students and faculty alike and hold all members of the law school community accountable when they fail to meet those norms. The bar and the courts should require lawyers to participate in

interactive programs on professional behavior every year and should
subject them to meaningful discipline for such matters as lack of preparation, sub-standard client representation and rudeness. Lack of dedication and boorish behavior should never be tolerated.

I have continued to feel that *State v. Schilling* was my most significant experience as a prosecutor. Like the jury, I assumed that Hart had
stolen Schilling's property, but nevertheless I believed and still believe that
Schilling was guilty of aggravated assault and kidnapping. Regardless of
the legitimacy of Schilling's grievance against Hart, I feel strongly that it
is simply wrong for a victim to take the law into his or her own hands.
Schilling's thirteen-year sentence was a stiff penalty, but not inappropriate in view of the seriousness of Hart's injuries, the terror he experienced
and Schilling's prior felony record.

Still, I am troubled by the disparity between Schilling's punishment and Thornton's three year prison term. I feel it was appropriate for
Schilling to receive a lengthier sentence than Thornton, because Schilling
initiated the violence, solicited the aid of his fellow assailants and had a
marginally more serious prior record than Thornton. On the other hand,
Schilling had no history of violence and unquestionably was emotionally
distraught at the time of the incident, believing that Hart had broken
into his home, stolen valuable property and lied about it when confronted. This likely clouded Schilling's judgment. To his credit, a substantial number of persons addressed the court at his sentencing hearing to
attest to his otherwise good character. Thornton, however, had almost
nothing to offer to mitigate his punishment. Hart had not wronged him
personally and there was no evidence that he was confused or distracted
when he battered Hart's head with a metal baseball bat, hog-tied him,
backed his car into Schilling's garage and slammed the trunk lid over
Hart. While a legitimate basis existed for punishing Schilling more
harshly than Thornton, requiring Schilling to serve a prison term more
than four times greater than Thornton's was disproportionate.

The disparity can only be explained by the fact that Schilling
exercised his constitutional right to trial in a case in which he believed,
again with cause, that he had a fair chance for an acquittal. If he had
accepted the plea bargain offered to him before trial, he would have
received a sentence of three and a half years, which would have been pro-

portionate to Thornton's sentence, although lenient in relation to the harm caused to Hart. The lack of severity in Thornton's sentence bothers me much less than the price Schilling paid, not for the crime, but for turning down his plea bargain. The framers included in the sixth amendment a right to a jury trial, as well as a right to confront and cross-examine one's accusers in court. A person should not be punished for nine-and-a-half years, almost quadrupling his sentence, for taking advantage of the rights extended to him by his government.

The disparity between Schilling's and Thornton's sentences has impressed upon me, in ways that I had not previously appreciated, the untoward effects of mandatory sentencing laws. The jury's finding that Schilling's kidnap and aggravated assault crimes were "dangerous" precluded Judge Paxton from imposing a sentence that would have been proportionate to Thornton's punishment. The dangerousness designation not only prohibited Judge Paxton from granting probation, but also substantially increased the range of Schilling's possible prison sentences, with a presumptive term of eleven years, a maximum term of over thirty-nine years and a minimum of seven. The prosecution had been able to offer Schilling a three and a half year sentence as part of its pre-trial plea bargain by promising to dismiss the dangerousness designation, thereby permitting punishment of less than seven years.

In 1978, the Arizona legislature passed the law requiring severe punishment for crimes designated as dangerous, in effect taking away trial judges' discretion to impose moderate sentences in all cases in which the prosecution chose to pursue the dangerousness label. It was not an unusual law. Every legislature in the United States has enacted similar mandatory sentencing statutes over the past three decades. In recent years, may experienced jurists and lawyers have complained about this tendency to strip trial judges of discretion. Recently, for example, Anthony Kennedy, one of the more conservative justices of the United States Supreme Court, eloquently criticized the nation's mandatory sentencing laws.

Before I became a prosecutor, I had been aware of the harshness and frequent unfairness of mandatory sentencing laws, but had not appreciated the disparities they could bring about. Steve Schilling was an unusual defendant only because he listened to his brother and refused to accept the prosecutor's sentence, instead gambling on a trial. The great majority of defendants I encountered as a prosecutor were more risk adverse, accepting the substantial discounts in punishment I offered in my plea bargains, even when they and their counsel believed that there were legitimate reasonable doubt issues in their cases. Schilling was sentenced more harshly than almost all similarly situated defendants only because he exercised his constitutional rights.

The problem is national, not local, in scope. In many states, at least ninety-five percent of criminal prosecutions result in plea bargains, with the terms of those bargains routinely set by the prosecution. With regard to cases prosecuted in the federal courts, Congress passed a law in 1984 that not only authorized the establishment of sentencing guidelines, but also severely restricted the discretion federal judges traditionally possessed to impose especially lenient or severe sentences, based on the circumstances of an individual case. Then, in 2003, Congress further tightened its restrictions on judicial sentencing discretion, virtually eliminating a judge's ability to sentence a defendant compassionately when unusual or compelling mitigating circumstances exist. Two months after President Bush signed the 2003 law, a federal judge in New York abruptly quit, complaining in a press interview that: "Congress is mandating things simply because they want to show how tough they are on crime with no sense of whether this makes sense…"

Whatever can be said of this state of affairs, it is not what I always understood as justice. Judges, not politicians, should determine punishment.

The reallocation of sentencing power from judges to prosecutors is particularly egregious in the courts where I prosecuted cases, because the state of Arizona uses a merit selection process for judicial appointments to the superior court in its urban counties. A commission consisting of both lawyers and non-lawyers thoroughly screens applicants for judicial vacancies, then sends the names of anywhere from three to five highly qualified and experienced candidates to the governor, who selects a judge from the commission's list. Most of the judges I observed during my time as a prosecutor were courteous and hard working, exercising good judgment in their rulings, an indication that the merit selection process generally works well.

However, these judges make meaningful sentencing decisions only in those cases in which prosecutors cede them the power by including explicit terms in plea agreements that leave sentencing to the court's discretion. When there is a high turnover of prosecutors, as there was in the Maricopa County Attorney's Office, this means that felony sentencing decisions are routinely made by relatively inexperienced and inadequately trained prosecutors who frequently lack depth in their judgment.

To achieve consistency in the decisions made by individual deputy prosecutors, Rick Romley, the Maricopa County Attorney, has implemented a detailed set of office policies relating to charging and plea bargaining in certain types of cases. But it is in my opinion a false consistency, which like mandatory sentencing laws, gives undue weight to a narrow range of factors that contribute to the seriousness of an offense and the need for stern punishment, while ignoring all the other factual nuances of a case that relate to the crime, the victim and the offender.

In *State v. Schilling*, the existing office policy differentiated between Schilling and Thornton, because Schilling pointed a gun at Hart. The relevant policy required a substantial prison sentence whenever a defendant used a gun in the commission of a crime. The mandatory prison policy did not apply to Thornton, because he did not brandish a gun during the incident, even though he repeatedly struck Hart in the head with a metal bat and easily could have killed him or have caused permanent brain damage. Applying the policy, the prosecutor who handled the case before me offered Thornton a deal that gave the judge discretion to place him on probation and set a maximum sentence of three years in prison. The same prosecutor offered Schilling a plea bargain that required a three and a half year prison sentence, virtually the minimum term permissible under the gun policy. When Schilling turned down the offer and lost at trial, the mandatory sentencing law guaranteed a much longer sentence.

To me, Schilling's pointing a gun at Hart after discovering that Hart had burglarized his home and stolen his coins should not have been among the principal reasons for punishing Schilling sternly. While wrong, it paled in comparison to Schilling's solicitation of accomplices to assist him in battering Hart for several hours, tying the victim up, throwing him in a car trunk and torturing Hart with the threat that they would dump his body in a remote area of the desert in 110-degree heat, where he would slowly die. Yet the sole fact that mattered significantly under the prosecutor's policy was the pointing of Schilling's gun.

Perhaps Schilling would have insisted on going to trial even if he had been offered the same plea bargain as Thornton, but I doubt it. As much as the mandatory sentencing laws, the plea bargaining policy, which singled out one circumstance from the many that contributed to the seriousness of the crime, resulted in the gross disparity between the sentencing of the two defendants in the beating of Ray Hart.

The other problem that has troubled me most is the question of delay. Today several state and local courts, including those in Arizona, have adopted strict measures to try to speed up cases and reduce backlog. In Maricopa County, for example, individual trial judges can no longer grant postponements of longer than five days in the cases before them. When prosecutors or defense lawyers want a longer continuance, they must justify it before a special judge hand-picked by the court administration to serve on a "continuance panel." Known locally as the Star Chamber, the six judges on the panel are extremely reluctant to grant postponements, and when they do, they normally limit them to twenty days or less. Both defense lawyers and prosecutors, including Rick Romley, have complained bitterly that the court's rush to judgment has resulted in the denial of legitimate postponements for essential preparation. If not done carefully, fixing one problem can easily lead to others; tragic injustices may occur when one side or the other is forced to trial when not ready. Guilty defendants sometimes go free, while innocent persons are convicted.

I am left with the underpinning philosophy that if *State v. Schilling* resulted in justice, it was, in the words of my mentor, down and dirty. The system is seriously flawed. We can, we must, do better.